THE COBRA

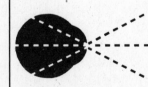

THE COBRA

FREDERICK FORSYTH

THORNDIKE PRESS
A part of Gale, Cengage Learning

GALE
CENGAGE Learning

Detroit • New York • San Francisco • New Haven, Conn • Waterville, Maine • London

GALE
CENGAGE Learning

Thorndike Press® Large Print Core.
The text of this Large Print edition is unabridged.
Other aspects of the book may vary from the original edition.
Set in 16 pt. Plantin.

LIBRARY OF CONGRESS CATALOGING-IN-PUBLICATION DATA

Forsyth, Frederick, 1938–
  The cobra / by Frederick Forsythe.
    p. cm. — (Thorndike Press large print core)
  ISBN-13: 978-1-4104-2915-5
  ISBN-10: 1-4104-2915-6
  1. United States. Drug Enforcement Administration—Fiction.
2. Special operations (Military science)—Fiction. 3. Drug
traffic—Colombia—Fiction. 4. Cocaine industry—Colombia—
Fiction. 5. Drug control—Fiction. 6. Large type books. I. Title.
PR6056.O699C63 2010b
823'.914—dc22   2010020416

Published in 2010 by arrangement with G. P. Putnam's Sons, a member of Penguin Group (USA) Inc.

For Justin and all the young agents, British and American, who, at great risk, are deep undercover in the struggle against narcotic drugs.

CHARACTERS

BERRIGAN, Bob Deputy Director, DEA

MANHIRE, Tim Ex–Customs Officer, Commander MAOC

DEVEREAUX, Paul The Cobra

SILVER, Jonathan Chief of Staff, the White House

DEXTER, Calvin Executive Officer, Project Cobra

URIBE, Álvaro President, Colombia

CALDERON, Felipe Chief of Colombian Anti-Drug Police

DOS SANTOS, Colonel Chief of Intelligence, Colombian Anti-Drug Police

ESTEBAN, Don Diego Head of Cocaine Cartel

SÁNCHEZ, Emilio Head of Production, the Cartel

PÉREZ, Rodrigo Former FARC Terrorist, the Cartel

LUZ, Julio Lawyer, Board Member of the Cartel

9

LARGO, José-María Head of Merchandising, the Cartel

CÁRDENAS, Roberto Board Member of the Cartel

SUÁREZ, Alfredo Head of Transportation, the Cartel

VALDEZ, Paco Enforcer, the Cartel

BISHOP, Jeremy Computer Expert

RUIZ, Fr. Carlos Jesuit Priest, Bogotá

KEMP, Walter UNODC

ORTEGA, Francisco Inspector, Madrid Anti-Drug Police

McGREGOR, Duncan Ship Converter

ARENAL, Letizia Madrid-based student

PONS, Francisco Cocaine pilot

ROMERO, Ignacio Representative of Cartel, Guinea-Bissau

DIALLO, Jalo Head of State, Guinea-Bissau

ISIDRO, Fr. Priest, Cartagena

CORTEZ, Juan Welder

MENDOZA, João Ex-Major, Brazilian Air Force

DIXON, Casey Commander, SEAL Team 2

EUSEBIO, Fr. Village Priest, Colombia

MILCH, Eberhardt Customs Inspector, Hamburg

ZIEGLER, Joachim Customs/Criminal Division, Berlin

VAN DER MERWE Inspector, Customs/ Crime Investigation, Rotterdam

CHADWICK, Bull Commander,
  SEAL Team 3

ACRONYMS AND
ABBREVIATIONS

AFB Air Force Base
BAMS Broad Aspect Maritime Surveillance
BKA German Federal Criminal Police
CIA Central Intelligence Agency
CRRC Combat Rubber Raiding Craft (U.S.)
DEA Drug Enforcement Administration
FARC Colombian Revolutionary/Marxist Organization
FBI Federal Bureau of Investigation
FLO Forces of Law and Order
HMRC Her Majesty's Revenue & Customs
ICE Immigration and Customs Enforcement
MAOC-N Maritime Analysis Operations Centre for Narcotics
MI5 Security Service (UK)
NSA National Security Agency
PEO Presidential Executive Order
RATO Rocket-Assisted Take-Off
RFA Royal Fleet Auxiliary
RHIB Rigid Hull Inflatable Boat (U.S.)
RIB Rigid Inflatable Boat (UK)

SAS Special Air Service Regiment
SBS Special Boat Service
SEALs U.S. Navy Special Forces
SOCA Serious and Organised Crime Agency
UAV Unmanned Aerial Vehicle
UDYCO Anti-Drug Unit, Madrid
UNDOC United Nations Office of Drugs and Crime
ZKA German Federal Customs Police

PART ONE
COIL

CHAPTER 1

The teenage boy was dying alone. No one knew and only one would have cared. He lay, skeletal from a life ruined by drugs, on a stinking palliasse in the corner of a filthy room in an abandoned block. The slum was in one of the failed housing schemes called a "project" in Anacostia, a part of Washington, D.C., of which the city is not proud and which tourists never visit.

If the boy had known his death was going to start a war, he would neither have understood nor cared. That is what drug abuse does to a young mind. It destroys it.

The late-summer dinner at the White House was small by the standards of presidential hospitality. Just twenty diners in ten couples sat down after drinks in an antechamber, and eighteen were most impressed to be there.

Nine of these were major volunteers working for the Veterans of Foreign Wars, that nationwide body that concerns itself with the welfare of those who have worn the uniform of any of the Armed Forces.

The nine years to 2010 had produced a huge number of men and some women returning from Iraq or Afghanistan, injured or traumatized. As commander in chief, the President was offering his thanks for what his nine guests from the VFW had been able to do. So they and their spouses were invited to dine where the legendary Abraham Lincoln once ate. They had had the private tour of the apartments, guided by the First Lady herself, and were seated beneath the attentive gaze of the majordomo to await the pouring of the soup. So it was slightly embarrassing when the elderly waitress began to cry.

She made no sound but the tureen in her hands began to tremble. The table was circular, and the First Lady was on the far side. She glanced up from the guest being served and saw the tears running quietly down the cheeks of the waitress.

The majordomo, who missed nothing that could disoblige his President, followed her gaze and began to move silently but fast around the table. He nodded urgently to a nearby waiter to take the tureen before there was a disaster, and eased the elderly woman away from the table toward the swing door to the pantry and kitchen. As the pair disappeared from view, the First Lady dabbed her mouth, murmured an apology to the retired general on her left, rose and followed.

In the pantry, the waitress was by now sitting, her shoulders shaking, murmuring, "I'm sorry, I'm so sorry." The expression on the face of the majordomo indicated he was not in a forgiving mood. One does not break down in front of the Chief Executive.

The First Lady gestured to him that he should return to the soup serving. Then she stooped over the weeping woman, who was dabbing her eyes on the edge of her apron and still apologizing.

In response to a couple of gentle questions, waitress Maybelle explained her extraordinary lapse. The police had found the body of her only grandson, the boy she had raised since his father died among the rubble of the Trade Center nine years earlier when the child was six.

They had explained to her the cause of death as declared by the medical examiner and informed her that the cadaver was in the city morgue awaiting collection.

And so in the corner of a pantry, the First

Lady of the USA and an elderly waitress, both descended from slaves, comforted each other, while a few feet away the leading lights of the VFW exchanged stilted conversation over soup and croutons.

Nothing more was said through the meal, and it was only when the President was removing his tuxedo in the private apartments two hours later that he asked the obvious question.

Five hours after that, in the near darkness of the bedroom, with only a sliver of light from the permanent glare over the city of Washington seeping through the bulletproof glass and past the curtain, the First Lady became aware that the man beside her was not asleep.

The President had been in large part raised by his grandmother. The relationship between a boy and his grandma was both known to him and deeply important. So although it was his habit to rise early and put himself through rigorous calisthenics to stay in shape, he could not sleep. He lay in the darkness and thought.

He had already decided the fifteen-year-old, whoever he was, would not go to a pauper's grave but to a decent burial in a proper churchyard. But he was intrigued by the cause of death in one so young and hailing from a poor but devotedly respectable household.

Just after three, he swung his long, thin legs out of bed and reached for a robe. There was a sleepy "Where are you going?" from beside him. "I won't be long," he replied, knotted the belt and padded through to the dressing room.

When he lifted the handset, the reply took two seconds. If the duty operator was sleepy at that hour of the night when the human spirit is at its lowest, she did not show it. Her inquiry was bright and eager.

"Yes, Mr. President."

The light on her console told her exactly who was calling. For his part, the man from Chicago still had to remind himself that he could have anything he liked anytime of the day or night simply by asking for it.

"Would you raise the director of the DEA, in his home or wherever he is?" he asked. There was no surprise from the operator. When you are That Man, if you want to exchange pleasantries with the President of Mongolia, it will be arranged.

"I'll have him momentarily," said the young woman far below in the comms room. She tapped fast at a computer keyboard. Minuscule circuits did their job, and a name flashed up. A query as to private

21

phone number produced ten digits on the screen. They referred to a handsome town house out in Georgetown. She made the connection and waited. At the tenth ring, a bleary voice answered.

"I have the President for you, sir," she told him. The middle-aged public servant became unbleary very quickly. Then the operator transferred the boss of the federal agency known formally as the Drug Enforcement Administration on the line to the room upstairs. She did not listen in. A light would tell her when the men were done and she could disconnect.

"Sorry to trouble you at this hour," said the President. He was immediately assured it was no trouble at all. "I need some information, maybe advice. Could you meet with me this morning, nine o'clock, in the West Wing?"

Only courtesy made it into a question. Presidents issue instructions. He was assured the director of the DEA would be in the Oval Office at nine a.m. The President hung up and went back to bed. At last he slept.

In an elegant redbrick house in Georgetown, the lights were on in the bedroom as the director asked an uncomprehending lady in curlers what the hell that was about.

Senior civil servants, roused personally by their supreme authority at three a.m., have no choice but to think something has gone wrong. Perhaps badly so. The director did not return to sleep but went down to the kitchen to fix juice and coffee and do some serious worrying.

Across the Atlantic, it was dawn. On a bleak gray and rain-slashed sea off the north German port of Cuxhaven, the MV *San Cristobal* took on her pilot. The skipper, Captain José-María Vargas, had the helm, and the pilot beside him gave murmured instructions. They spoke in English, the common language of the air and the sea. The *San Cristobal* turned her nose and entered the outer roads of the estuary of the Elbe. Sixty miles later she would be guided into Hamburg, Europe's biggest river port.

At 30,000 tons, the *San Cristobal* was a general freighter flying the flag of Panama. Forward of the bridge, as the two men stared into the murk to pick up the buoys marking the deep channel, was row upon row of steel sea containers.

There were eight levels of them below-decks and four above. Lengthwise, there were fourteen rows from the prow to the bridge, and the vessel was wide enough to take eight from side to side.

Her papers would say, quite rightly, that she had begun her voyage in Maracaibo, Venezuela; then proceeded east to complete her cargo with a further eighty containers of bananas at Paramaribo, capital and sole port of Suriname. What the papers would not say was that one of those last sea containers was very special because it contained bananas and one other consignment.

The second cargo had flown in a tired old Transall cargo plane, bought very second-hand from South Africa, out of a remote hacienda in upstate Colombia, over Venezuela and Guyana, to land at an equally remote banana plantation in Suriname.

What the old cargo plane had brought had then been stacked, brick by brick, at the far back end of a steel sea container. The bricks were jammed from wall to wall and from floor to roof. When they were seven layers deep, a false rear wall had been welded into place, then sanded and painted, along with the whole of the rest of the interior. Only then were the hard green, unripe bananas hung on their racks to remain, chilled but not frozen, all the way to Europe.

Flatbed trucks had growled and snorted through the jungle to bring the export order to the coast, and there the *San Cristobal* had

24

taken them aboard to become her deck cargo and complete her capacity. Then she cast off and headed for Europe.

Captain Vargas, a scrupulously honest mariner who did not know about the extra cargo he carried, had been to Hamburg before and never ceased to marvel at its size and efficiency. The old Hanseatic port is like not one but two cities. There is the city where people live around the Outer and Inner Alster waterways, and there is the sprawling port city containing the continent's biggest sea container facility.

With 13,000 port calls a year, 140 million tons of freight moves in and out, docking at any of the 320 berths. The container port alone has four terminals, and the *San Cristobal* was allocated to Altenwerder.

As the freighter eased herself at five knots past Hamburg, coming awake on the western bank, the two men at the helm were served strong Colombian coffee, and the German sniffed the aroma with appreciation. The rain had ceased, the sun was struggling through and the crew were looking forward to their shore time.

It was close to midday when the *San Cristobal* slid into her allotted berth, and almost at once one of the Altenwerder's fifteen gantries moved into position and began to heft the containers off the freighter and onto the quay.

Captain Vargas had said good-bye to the pilot who, shift over, had departed for his home in Altona. With engines closed down and standby power running the needed facilities, and with the crew, passports in hand, going ashore for the bars of the Reeperbahn, the *San Cristobal* seemed at peace, the way Captain Vargas, whose career and home she was, liked her.

He could not know that four containers up from his bridge, two layers down and three rows from the starboard side, there was a container with a small and unusual logo on its side. One would have to look hard to find it, for sea containers have all sorts of scratches, daubs, identity codes and owners' names painted on them. This particular logo was in the form of two concentric circles, and in the smaller, inner one, a Maltese cross. It was the secret identity code of the *Hermandad,* or Brotherhood, the gang behind ninety percent of Colombian cocaine. And down on the quay there was just one pair of eyes that would recognize that sign.

The gantry was lifting the containers from the deck to a moving army of computer-driven wheeled drones called Automatic

Guided Vehicles, or AGVs. These, controlled from a tower high above the quay, removed the steel crates from quay to storage area. That was when an official, moving unnoticed between the AGVs, saw the design with the two circles. He used his cell phone to make one call, then hurried back to his office. Miles away, a flatbed truck began to roll toward Hamburg.

At that hour, the director of the DEA was shown into the Oval Office. He had been there several times before, but the huge antique working desk, the draped flags and the seal of the Republic still impressed him. He appreciated power, and this place was pure power.

The President was in an affable mood, exercised, showered, breakfasted and casually dressed. He bade his visitor sit on one of the sofas and joined him on the other.

"Cocaine," he said. "I want to know about cocaine. You have a huge amount of material about it."

"A shedload, Mr. President. Files several feet thick if you put them in a column."

"Too much," said the President. "I need about ten thousand words. Not page after page of stats. Just the facts. A synthesis. Just what it is, where it comes from — as if I didn't know — who makes it, who ships it,

27

who buys it, who uses it, what it costs, where the profits go, who benefits, who loses, what are we doing about it!"

"Just cocaine, Mr. President? Not the others? Heroine, PCP, angel dust, methamphetamine, the ubiquitous cannabis?"

"Just cocaine. Just for me. 'Eyes only.' I need to know the basic facts."

"I will order up a new report, sir. Ten thousand words. Plain language. Top secret. Six days, Mr. President?"

The commander in chief rose, smiling, hand outstretched. The meeting was over. The door was already open.

"I knew I could count on you, Director. Three days."

The director's Crown Victoria was waiting in the car parking lot. On command, the driver brought it swerving to the door of the West Wing. In forty minutes, the director was back across the Potomac in Arlington, ensconced in his top-floor suite at 700 Army Navy Drive.

He gave the job to his head of operations, Bob Berrigan. The younger man, who had made his bones out in the field rather than behind a desk, nodded glumly, and muttered, "Three days?" The director nodded.

"Don't eat, don't sleep. Live on coffee. And, Bob, don't stint. Make it as bad as it is. There may be a budget hike in here down the line."

The ex–field operative headed down the corridor to tell his PA to cancel all meetings, interviews and engagements for three days. Desk jockeys, he thought. Delegate, ask the impossible, go out for dinner and look for the money.

By sundown, the *San Cristobal*'s cargo was onshore, but it was still inside the port perimeter. Flatbed trucks were choking the three bridges they had to cross to pick up their imports. Stuck in a tailback along the Niederfelde Brücke was one from Darmstadt with a swarthy man at the wheel. His papers would show he was a German citizen of Turkish extraction, a member of one of Germany's largest minorities. They would not reveal that he was a member of the Turkish mafia.

Inside the perimeter there would be no tailback. Customs clearance for a certain steel container from Suriname would be problem-free.

So vast is the quantity of freight entering Europe via Hamburg that a rigorous examination of every container is quite simply impossible. German customs, the ZKA, does what it can. Around five percent of

29

incoming cargoes secure close examination. Some of these are random, but most derive from a tip-off, something odd about the description of the cargo and its port of departure (bananas do not come from Mauritania) or just inadequate paperwork.

The checks may involve opening the sea container by breaking the seals, measuring containers for secret compartments, chemical tests in the on-site laboratory, the use of sniffer dogs or just X-ray inspection of the collector truck. Around 240 trucks in a single day are X-rayed. But one banana container would have no such problems.

This container had not been taken to the HHLA Fruit and Refrigeration Centre because it was tagged to depart the docks too quickly to make that worthwhile. Clearance at Hamburg is achieved largely by the IT-based ATLAS system. Someone had entered the twenty-one-digit registration number of the consignment into the ZKA computer and cleared it for release before the *San Cristobal* had come around the last curve in the river Elbe.

When the Turkish driver had finally inched his way to the head of the queue by the dock gate, his steel container was cleared for collection. He presented his papers, the ZKA man in his booth by the gate tapped them into his computer, noted the clearance for a small import of bananas for a modest little fruit company in Darmstadt and nodded the go-ahead. In thirty minutes, the Turkish driver was back over the bridge, gaining access to the sprawling network of Germany's autobahns.

Behind him rode one metric ton of pure Colombian cocaine. Before sale to the final inhalers, it would be "cut" or "bashed" to six or seven times its original volume with the addition of other chemicals like benzocaine, creatine, ephedrine or even the horse tranquilizer ketamine. These simply convince the user he is getting a bigger thrill than could be acquired from the amount of cocaine actually going up the nose. Further bulk can be achieved with simple but harmless white powders like baking soda and icing sugar.

With every kilo of a thousand grams converted into seven thousand, and the buyers paying up to $10 U.S. per gram, each kilo of pure would finally sell out at $70,000. The driver had a thousand such kilos behind him, a street value of $70,000,000. Based on the *pasta* bought from the Colombian jungle peasants for $1,000 a kilo, there was enough to cover the cargo plane to Suriname, a fee for the banana plantation, the tiny freight charge on the *San Cristobal* and $50,000 slipped into the Grand Cayman account of the corrupt official in Hamburg.

The European gangsters would bear the cost of blenderizing the hard bricks into talc-like fine powder, cutting to multiply the bulk and merchandising to the users. But if the overheads from jungle to Hamburg dock gate were five percent and the European overheads another five, there was still ninety percent profit to split between the cartel and the mafias and gangs across Europe and the USA.

The American President would learn all this from the Berrigan Report, which hit his desk three days later as promised.

While he read the report after dinner, another two tons of Colombian pure in a pickup truck sneaked across the Texan border near a small town called Nuevo Laredo and vanished into the American heartland.

Dear Mr. President,
I have the honor to present the report on the narcotic cocaine as requested by you.

ORIGINS: Cocaine derives solely from

the coca plant, a weedy undistinguished shrub that has grown since time immemorial in the hills and jungles of the northwestern arc of South America.

Over that same period it has been chewed by local natives who found that its effect was to mute their permanent hunger and stimulate their mood. It rarely produces flowers or fruit; its stem and twigs are woody and without application; only the leaves contain the drug.

Even then the drug constitutes well under one percent of the leaf by weight. It takes 375 kilograms of harvested leaf — enough to fill a pickup truck — to create 2.5 kg of coca paste — the intermediate form — which in turn will provide one kilo of pure cocaine in the familiar white powder form.

GEOGRAPHY: Of the global supply today, approximately 10% comes from Bolivia, 29% from Peru and 61% from Colombia.

However, Colombian gangs take over the product of the two smaller contributors at the coca paste stage, complete the refining and merchandise virtually 100% of the drug.

CHEMISTRY: There are only two chemical processes needed to turn the harvested leaf into finished product and both are extremely cheap. That is why, given the desperate poverty of the jungle farmers who grow what is virtually only a very tough and hardy weed, eradication at source has proved so far impossible.

The raw leaves are steeped in an old oil drum in acid — cheap battery acid will do — which soaks out the cocaine. The sodden leaves are then scooped out and thrown away, leaving a sort of brown soup. This is shaken up with alcohol or even gasoline, which leaches out the alkaloids.

These are skimmed off and treated with a strong alkali such as sodium bicarbonate. This mixture delivers a scummy off-white sludge which is the basic paste, or "pasta." This is the standard unit of the cocaine trade in South America. This is what the gangsters buy off the peasants. About 150 kg of leaves have become 1 kg of pasta. The chemicals are easily obtained and the product is easily transportable from jungle to refinery.

FINISHING: In secret refineries, also usually hidden by the cover of the jungle, the pasta is converted into snow-white cocaine hydrochloride powder (the full name) by adding more chemicals such as hydrochloric acid, potassium permanganate, acetone, ether, ammonia, calcium carbonate, sodium carbonate, sulfuric acid and more gasoline. This concoction is then "reduced," the residue dried, and what is left is the powder. All the ingredient chemicals are cheap and, being involved in many legitimate industries, easy to acquire.

THE COSTS: A coca-growing peasant, or "cocalero," may work like a dog all year harvesting up to six crops from his jungle patch, each crop netting him 125 kgs of coca leaf. His total production of 750 kgs of leaf will yield five kilos of pasta. After his own overheads, he may earn just $5,000 a year. Even after refining to powder, one kilogram can be priced at about $4,000.

THE PROFITS: These are the highest for any product in the world. That single kilogram of Colombian "pure" rises from $4,000 to $60,000 to $70,000 just by traveling three thousand miles from the coast of Colombia to the USA or five thousand miles to Europe. Even that is not the end. The kilogram will, at the buyer's end, be "cut" (adulterated) to six times its weight and volume without loss of price per gram. The users will finally pay the last dealer in the chain about $70,000 for that sugar-bag-sized kilogram that left the coast of Colombia valued at just $4,000.

RESULTS: These profit margins guarantee that the big operators can afford the finest technology, equipment, weaponry and expertise. They can employ world-class minds, bribe officialdom — in some cases up to the national presidential level — and are almost embarrassed by the number of volunteers clamoring to help in the transportation and merchandising of their product in exchange for a cut. No matter how many low-level "mules" are caught and sent to prison, there are always thousands of the destitute and/or stupid prepared to volunteer to take the risks.

STRUCTURES: After the killing of Pablo Escobar of the Medellín cartel and the retirement of the Ochoa brothers of Cali, the gangsters in Colombia split into up to a hundred mini-cartels. But over the past three years, a new and gigantic cartel has emerged that has unified them all under its domination.

Two independents who tried to hold out were found dead after spectacular suffering, and resistance to the new unifiers ceased. The mega-cartel calls itself the Hermandad, or "Brotherhood," and operates like a major industrial corporation with, in back, a private army to guard its property and a psychotic punishment squad to enforce its discipline.

The Brotherhood does not manufacture cocaine. It buys the entire product of every mini-cartel as the finished white powder product. It offers a "fair" (its own definition) price not on a take-it-or-leave-it basis, but on a take-it-or-die basis. After that, the Hermandad merchandises to the world.

QUANTITIES: Total product is about 600 tons per year, and this divides into about 300 tons for two destinations: the USA and Europe, almost the only two continents that use the drug. Given the profit margins listed above, the total profits are not calculated in hundreds of millions of dollars but in tens of billions.

DIFFICULTIES: Because of the vast profits, it may be there are twenty traders between the cartel and the end user. These traders may be transporters, passers on or final sellers. That is why it is extremely hard for the FLO (Forces of Law and Order) in any country to touch the big players. They are massively protected, use extreme violence as a deterrent and never even touch the product personally. The smaller fry are constantly caught, tried and jailed, but they seldom "squeal" and are immediately replaced.

INTERCEPTIONS: American and European FLO are in a constant state of war with the cocaine industry, and interceptions of cargo in transit or captures of depots are ongoing. But the FLO of both continents achieve only around 10 to 15% of the cocaine market, and, given the staggering margins, this is not enough. It would be necessary to raise the "intercept" and "confiscate" levels to 80% or more to cripple the industry. If they lost 90%, the cartels would implode and the cocaine industry would at last be destroyed.

CONSEQUENCES: Only thirty years ago cocaine was popularly regarded as mere "nose candy" for socialites, bond traders and entertainers. Today it has grown to a massive national scourge causing disastrous societal damage. On two continents, the FLO estimate that around 70% of acquisitive street-level crime (car theft, burglary, mugging, etc.) is carried out to get the funds to support a habit. If the "perp" is high on the particularly vicious by-product of cocaine called "crack," insensate violence may accompany robbery.

Beyond that, the profits of cocaine, once laundered, are used to fund other crime forms, especially trafficking weapons (also used for crime and terrorism) and people, most particularly illegal immigrants and abducted girls for the sex-slave trade.

SUMMATION: Our country was quite properly devastated by the destruction in the fall of 2001 of the World Trade Center and the attack on the Pentagon, which cost almost 3,000 lives. Since then no American inside the homeland has died from foreign-generated terrorism, but the war on terrorism goes on and must go on. Yet in that decade, a conservative estimate must put the figure of destroyed lives through narcotic drugs at ten times that 9/11 casualty cost, and half of these by the chemical called cocaine.

I have the honor to remain,
Mr. President,
ROBERT BERRIGAN
Deputy Director (Special Operations)
Drugs Enforcement Administration

Around the time the Berrigan Report was being delivered by messenger to the White House, a British ex–customs officer sat in a nondescript dockside office in Lisbon staring in extreme frustration at a picture of a battered old trawler.

Tim Manhire had spent his whole adult life as an excise man, not always the most popular of professions but one he believed to be profoundly necessary. If revenue-gathering for a greedy government from a hapless tourist does not quicken the blood, his job in the dusty back streets of Lisbon's dockland was a fulfillment of a sort, and would have been more so but for the frustrations of that old enemy: inadequate resources.

The small agency he headed was MAOC-N, yet another acronym in the world of law and order. It stood for Maritime Analysis Operations Center for Narcotics and drew together experts from seven countries. The six partners of the UK were Portugal, Spain, Ireland, France, Italy and the Netherlands. Portugal was the host, and the director was a Britisher, transferred from HMRC (Her Majesty's Revenue & Customs) to SOCA (Serious and Organised Crime Agency) to take the job.

What MAOC did was to try to coordinate the efforts of the European FLO and naval forces to counter the smuggling of cocaine from the Caribbean Basin across the Atlantic to the twin coasts of Western Europe and West Africa.

The reason for Tim Manhire's frustration that sunny morning was that he could see another fish with a big and valuable cargo about to slip the net.

The photo had been taken from the air, but beyond taking pretty pictures the patrol aircraft had been helpless to do anything. It had simply passed the image within seconds to MAOC many miles away.

The photo showed a shabby beam trawler on whose bow was the name *Esmeralda-G.* She had been found by a stroke of luck just on the cusp of darkness and dawn in the eastern Atlantic, and the absence of a wake indicated she'd just hove to after cruising unseen through the night. The definition was good enough for Manhire, peering through the magnifying frame above the picture, to see that the crew was about to drape her from stem to stern with a blue tarpaulin. This was the standard practice for cocaine smugglers at sea to avoid detection if they could.

They cruised at night, then spent the day bobbing silently beneath a tarpaulin that blended with the surrounding sea, extremely hard to spot from above. At sundown the crew peeled back the tarpaulin, stowed it and cruised on. It took time, but it was also safer. To be caught at dawn about to drape the tarpaulin was a giveaway. This was no fish catcher. Her cargo was already in the hold, up to a ton of white powder, multi-wrapped and baled to prevent salt and water damage, where it had been since loading at a rotten timber jetty in a creek of Venezuela.

The *Esmeralda-G* was clearly heading for West Africa, probably the narco-state of Guinea-Bissau. If only, Manhire groaned, she had been farther north, passing the Spanish Canary Islands, or Portugal's Madeira or Azores. Either country could have put a Coast Guard cutter to sea to intercept the trafficker.

But she was way down south, a hundred miles north of the Cape Verde Islands — but they could not help anyway. No equipment. And it was no good asking the line of failed states running in a curve around from Senegal to Liberia. They were part of the problem, not the solution.

So Tim Manhire had appealed to six European navies and the USA, but they had no frigate, destroyer or cruiser in the neighborhood. The *Esmeralda-G,* having seen the aircraft that photographed them, would have realized they were spotted and would have abandoned the tarpaulin trick to cruise hard for landfall. They had only two hundred nautical miles to go, and even at a plodding ten knots would be safe among the mangrove swamps off the Guinea coast before the morrow.

Even after an interception at sea, the frustrations did not end. After a recent stroke of luck, a French frigate had responded to his plea and found, with MAOC's directions, a coke-carrying freighter four hundred miles out. But the

French were obsessed with legal niceties. Under their rules, the captured smugglers had to be towed to the nearest "friendly" port. That happened to be another failed state — Guinea-Conakry.

Then a French magistrate had to be flown from Paris to the captured ship for *"les formalités."* Something about the rights of man — *les droits de l'homme.*

"Droits de mon cul," murmured Jean-Louis, Manhire's colleague on the French contingent. This even the Britisher managed to recognize as "rights of my arse."

So the freighter was impounded, the crew arraigned and the cocaine confiscated. Within a week the ship had slipped her moorings and sailed. She was crewed by her own team, who had easily secured bail from a magistrate who had graduated from a dusty Peugeot to a new Mercedes, and the impounded bales had, sort of, vaporized.

So the director of MAOC sighed and filed the name and image of the *Esmeralda-G.* If she was ever seen again . . . But she would not be. Forewarned, she would be rerigged as a tuna fisher and renamed before entering the Atlantic again. And even if she did, would there be another lucky aircraft belonging to a European navy that just happened to be flying past when the tarpaulin was flapping in the breeze? It was a thousand to one.

That, thought Manhire, was most of the problem. Tiny resources and no retribution for the smugglers. Even if they were caught.

A week later, the U.S. President sat alone with his director of Homeland Security, the super-agency that collated and overlorded the thirteen primary intelligence-gathering agencies of the USA. He stared at his commander in chief in astonishment.

"Are you serious, Mr. President?"

"Yes, I believe I am. What do you advise?"

"Well, if you are going to try to destroy the cocaine industry, you will be taking on some of the most vicious, violent and ruthless men in the world."

"Then I guess we are going to need someone even better."

"I think, sir, you mean even worse."

"Do we have such a man?"

"Well, there is a name, or rather a reputation, that comes to mind. He was for years head of counterintelligence at the CIA. Helped trap and destroy Aldrich Ames when he was finally allowed to. Then he headed Special Ops for the Company. Almost trapped and assassinated Osama bin Laden, and that was before 9/11. Released

45

two years ago."

"Released?"

"Fired."

"Why?"

"Too ruthless."

"Against colleagues?"

"No, sir. I believe against our enemies."

"There's no such thing. I want him back. What was his name?"

"I forget, sir. Out at Langley, they just referred to him by his nickname. They called him the Cobra."

CHAPTER 2

The man the President sought was named Paul Devereaux, and when he was finally traced, he was at prayer. He regarded prayer as profoundly important.

Devereaux was the scion of a long line of those families who come as near to being aristocracy as the Commonwealth of Massachusetts has had since 1776. From his young manhood, he had always had private means, but what marked him out in those early days was his intellect.

He attended Boston College High School, the main feeder unit for one of the leading Jesuit universities in the USA. There he was tagged as a very high flier indeed. He was as devout as he was scholarly and seriously thought of entering the priesthood as a Jesuit. Instead he accepted an invitation to join another exclusive community, the CIA.

To the twenty-year-old who had swept through every exam his tutors could throw at him and was mastering foreign languages on a yearly basis, it was a question of serving his God and his country by fighting communism and atheism. He just chose the secular rather than the clerical road.

Inside the Company, he rose fast because he was unstoppable, and if his detached intellectualism did not make him Langley's most popular, he cared not a fig. He served in the three main divisions: Operations (Ops), Intelligence (Analysis) and Counterintelligence (Internal Security). He saw out the Cold War in 1991 with the collapse of the USSR, a goal to which he had devoted twenty hard years, and remained *en poste* until 1998, when Al Qaeda blew up two U.S. embassies, in Nairobi and Dar es Salaam.

Devereaux had already become a skilled Arabist, holding that the Soviet division was too crowded and too obvious. Mastering Arabic in several different dialects, he was the right man for the job when the Company formed a Special Ops unit to concentrate on the new threat — Islamic fundamentalism and the global terrorism it would spawn.

His departure into retirement in 2008 fell squarely into the category of the old puzzle: did he jump or was he pushed? He, naturally, would maintain the former. A charitable observer would call it mutual. Devereaux was old school. He could recite the Koran better than most Islamic scholars and had absorbed at least a thousand of the leading Commentaries. But he was surrounded by bright young things whose ears appeared seam-welded to their BlackBerrys, a device he despised.

He loathed political correctness, preferring courtly good manners, which he practiced to all, save those who were clearly the enemies of the one true God and/or the United States. These he destroyed without qualm. His final departure from Langley was occasioned when the new director of Central Intelligence indicated most firmly that, in the modern world, qualms were a must-have.

So he took his leave with a quiet and insincere cocktail party — another convention he could not stand — and retired to his exquisite town house in the historic town of Alexandria. There he could immerse himself in his formidable library and collection of rare Islamic artworks.

He was neither gay nor married, a speculation that had once occupied much chatter around the watercoolers along the corridors of the Old Building at Langley — he had flatly refused to move into the new building. Eventually, the chatterers were forced to concede what was obvious. The Jesuit-trained intellectual and ascetic Boston Brahmin was not interested. That was when some clever fast-track boy had remarked that he had all the charm of a cobra. And the name stuck.

The young staffer from the White House went first to the residence at the junction of South Lee and South Fairfax streets. The housekeeper, the beaming Maisie, told the lad her employer was at church and gave him directions. When the young man returned to the car by the curb, he looked around and thought he might have regressed two centuries.

And well he might. Alexandria was founded by English merchants in 1749. It was "antebellum" not just in the sense of existing before the Civil War; it preceded the War of Independence. Once a river port on the Potomac, it had prospered from sugar and slaves. The sugar ships, creeping upriver from Chesapeake Bay and the wild Atlantic beyond, used old English building bricks for ballast, and it was of these the merchants built their fine houses. The effect was still more Old Europe than New World.

The man from the White House climbed back beside the driver and gave directions for South Royal Street and to look for St. Mary's Catholic Church. He eased open the door and left the hum of the streets for the silent calm of the nave, looked around and perceived a single figure kneeling up by the altar.

His feet made no sound as he crept the length of the nave past the eight stained-glass windows that were the only illumination. A Baptist, he caught the faint odor of incense and the wax of the burning votive candles as he approached the kneeling silver-haired figure praying before the white-clothed altar surmounted by a simple gold cross.

He thought he was quiet, but the figure raised a single hand to admonish him not to break the silence. When the praying man had finished his orisons, he rose, inclined his head, crossed himself and turned. The man from Pennsylvania Avenue tried to speak, but another hand was raised, and they proceeded calmly back down the nave to the vestibule by the door to the street. Only then did the older man turn and smile. He opened the main door and spotted the limo across the street.

"I have come from the White House, sir," said the staffer.

"Many things change, my young friend,

51

but not the haircuts or the cars," said Devereaux. If the staffer thought "White House," which he adored using, would have the usual effect, he was wrong.

"And what does the White House wish to say to a retired old man?"

The staffer was perplexed. In a society paranoid about youth, no one called themselves old, even at seventy. He did not know that in the Arabic world, age is revered.

"Sir, the President of the United States wishes to see you."

Devereaux remained silent, as though thinking it over.

"Now, sir."

"Then I think a dark suit and a tie is in order, if we can pause by my house. And as I do not drive, I have no car. I trust you can bring me there and home again?"

"Yes, sir. Of course."

"Then let us go. Your driver knows where I live. You must have been there to see Maisie."

At the West Wing, the meeting was brief and took place in the office of the chief of staff, a hard-nosed Illinois congressman who had been with the President for years.

The President shook hands and introduced his most trusted ally in all Washington.

"I have a proposition to put to you, Mr. Devereaux," said the Chief Executive. "In a way, a request. No, in every way a request. Right now I have a meeting I cannot butt out of. But no matter. Jonathan Silver will explain everything. I would be grateful for your reply when you feel able to give it."

And with a smile and another handshake, he was gone. Mr. Silver did not smile. It was not a habit of his except rarely, and then only when he heard an opponent of the President was in deep trouble. He took a file off his desk and proffered it.

"The President would be grateful if you would first read this. Here. Now." He gestured to one of the leather armchairs at the back of the room. Paul Devereaux took the file, sat, crossed his elegantly suited legs and read the Berrigan Report. When he was done, ten minutes later, he looked up.

Jonathan Silver had been working on papers. He caught the old secret agent's gaze and put down his pen.

"What do you think?"

"Interesting, but hardly innovative. What do you want of me?"

"The President wishes to know this. Would it be possible, with all our technology and Special Forces, to destroy the cocaine industry?"

Devereaux gazed at the ceiling.

"A five-second answer would be valueless. We both know that. I will need time to conduct what the French call a *projet d'étude*."

"I don't give jackshit what the French call it" was the reply. Jonathan Silver rarely left the USA except for his beloved Israel, and when he was away, he loathed every minute of it, especially Europe, and even more especially France.

"You need study time, right? How long?"

"Two weeks, minimum. And I will need a letter of empowerment requiring every authority in the state to answer my questions frankly and truthfully. Otherwise the answer will still be valueless. I presume neither you nor the President wish to waste time and money on a project doomed to failure?"

The chief of staff stared back for several seconds, then rose and strode from the room. He returned five minutes later with a letter. Devereaux glanced at it. He nodded slowly. What he held was enough to overcome any bureaucratic barrier in the country. The chief of staff also held out a card.

"My private numbers. Home, office and cell. All encrypted. Totally secure. Call me anytime, but only for a serious reason. From now on, the President is out of this. Do you need to keep the Berrigan Report?"

"No," said Devereaux mildly. "I have memorized it. Ditto your three numbers."

He handed the card back. Privately, he mocked the "totally secure" boast. A few years earlier, a British computer geek with mild autism had gone through all the firewalls of NASA and the Pentagon databases like a hot knife through marshmallow. And that was from a cheap gizmo in his bedroom in North London. The Cobra knew about real secrecy; that you can keep a secret between three men only if two are dead; that the only trick is to be in and out before the bad guys have woken up.

A week after the Devereaux-Silver conference, the President was in London. It was not a state visit but the next level down, an official one. Still, he and the First Lady were welcomed by the Queen at Windsor Castle, and an earlier and genuine friendship was refreshed.

That apart, there were several working discussions with a stress on the ongoing problems of Afghanistan, two economies, the EU, global warming/climate change and trade. On the weekend, the President and his wife had agreed to spend two relaxing days with the new British Prime Minister at the official country retreat, a magnificent Tudor mansion called simply Chequers. Saturday evening found the two couples taking coffee after dinner in the Long Gallery. As there was a chill in the air, a roaring log fire sent the light of its flames flickering off the walls of hand-tooled, morocco-bound antique books.

Whether two heads of government will ever get on as people, or develop the empathy of true friendship, is completely unforeseeable. Some do, others do not. History records that Franklin D. Roosevelt and Winston Churchill, while never entirely without their differences, liked each other. Ronald Reagan and Margaret Thatcher were genuine friends despite the gulf between the Englishwoman's steely convictions and the Californian's folksy humor.

Between the British and the Europeans at that level, there has rarely if ever been more than formal courtesy, and often not even that. On one occasion the German Chancellor, Helmut Schmidt, brought over a wife so formidable that Harold Wilson, descending for dinner, gave vent to one of his rare barbs of humor, remarking to the assembled staff, "Well, wife-swapping's out."

Harold Macmillan could not abide

Charles de Gaulle (mutual) while having affection for the much younger John F. Kennedy. It may have to do with the common language, but not necessarily.

Considering the gulf between the backgrounds of the two men sharing the warmth of the log fire that autumn evening, as the shadows deepened and the Secret Service patrolled with the British SAS outside, it was perhaps surprising that in three meetings — one in Washington, one at the UN and now at Chequers — they had developed a friendship on a personal level.

The American had the disadvantaged background: Kenyan father, Kansas-born mother, Hawaii and Indonesia raising, the early struggles against bigotry. The Englishman came from a stockbroker married to a county magistrate, a nanny as a baby, private education at two of the most expensive and prestigious junior and senior schools in the country. That kind of background can endow with the sort of easy charm that may or may not mask inner steel. With some it does, with others it does not.

At a more superficial level, there was much more in common. Both men were still under fifty, married to beautiful women, fathers of two children still school-aged, both men with top college degrees and an adult lifetime spent in politics. And both with the same almost obsessional concerns for climate change, Third World poverty, national security and the plight, even at home, of those whom Frantz Fanon called "the wretched of the earth."

While the Prime Minister's wife showed the First Lady some of the earliest books in the collection, the President murmured to his British opposite:

"Did you have time to glance at that report I gave you?"

"Certainly. Impressive . . . and worrying. We have a massive problem over here. This country is the biggest user of cocaine in Europe. I had a briefing two months ago from SOCA, our own Serious Crime people, about the spin-off crime that derives from it. Why?"

The President stared into the fire and chose his words.

"I have a man at the moment looking into the sheer feasibility of an idea. Would it be possible, with all our technology and the skill of our Special Forces, to destroy that industry?"

The Prime Minister was taken aback. He stared at the American.

"Your man, has he reported yet?"

"Nope. I expect his verdict momentarily."

"And his advice. Will you take it?"

"I guess I will."

"And if he advises it is feasible?"

"Then I think the USA may go with that."

"We both spend huge amounts of treasure trying to combat narcotic drugs. All my experts say complete destruction cannot be done. We intercept cargoes, we catch the smugglers and the gangsters, we send them to jail, long-term. Nothing changes. The drugs keep flooding in. New volunteers replace the jailbirds. The public appetite continues to increase."

"But if my man says it can be done — would Great Britain come in with us?"

No politician likes to be hit way below the belt, even by a friend. Even by the President of the USA. He played for time.

"There would have to be a real plan. It would have to be funded."

"If we go ahead, there will be a plan. And funds. What I would like are your Special Forces. Your anti-crime agencies. Your secret intelligence skills."

"I would have to consult my people," said the Prime Minister.

"You do that," said the President. "I'll let you know when my man says what he says, and whether we are going ahead."

The four prepared for bed. In the morning they would attend matins at the local Norman church. Through the night the guards would patrol, watch, check, survey and check again. They would be armed and armored, with night-vision goggles, infrared scanners, movement sensors and body-heat detectors. It would be extremely unwise to be a patrolling fox. Even the specially imported U.S. limousines would be under guard all night so that they could not be approached.

The American couple, as always with heads of state, had the Lee Room, named after the philanthropist who had donated Chequers to the nation after total restoration in 1917. The room still contained its huge four-poster bed, dating, perhaps not very diplomatically, from the time of George III. During the Second World War, the Soviet Foreign Minister, Molotov, had slept in that bed with a pistol under his pillow. That night in the fall of 2010, there was no pistol.

Twenty miles down the coast south of the Colombian port and city of Cartagena is the Gulf of Urabá, a shore of impenetrable and malarial mangrove swamps. As Air Force One was lining up for its final approach bringing the presidential couple back from London, two strange crafts slipped out of an invisible creek and turned southwest.

They were of aluminum, pencil-slim, up to sixty feet long, like needles in the water, but at the stern of each were four Yamaha 200 outboard engines side by side. The cocaine community called them "go-fasts," and both their shape and power were designed to enable them to outstrip anything else on water.

Despite their length, there was little room on board. Huge extra fuel tanks took up most of the space. Each also carried 600 kilograms of cocaine in ten large white plastic drums, which were themselves hermetically sealed against damage by seawater. To enable them to be handled, each drum was encased in nets of blue polyethylene cord.

Between the drums and the fuel tanks, the crew of four crouched uncomfortably. But they were not there to be comfortable. One was the helmsman, a highly skilled operator who could handle the go-fast easily at its forty-knot cruise speed and take her up to sixty knots, sea permitting, if she was pursued. The other three were muscle, and all were going to be paid a fortune by their standards for seventy-two hours of discomfort and risk. In fact, their combined rewards were a tiny fraction of one percent of the value in those twenty drums.

Clearing the shallows, the captains opened up to forty knots over a flat sea to begin their long cruise. Their target was a point on the ocean seventy nautical miles off Colón, Republic of Panama. There they would make sea rendezvous with the freighter *Virgen de Valme,* who would be coming west out of the Caribbean heading for the Panama Canal.

The go-fasts had three hundred nautical miles to make rendezvous, and even at forty knots they could not make it by sunrise. So they would spend the next day hove to, bobbing in the sweltering heat under a blue tarpaulin, until darkness enabled them to continue. Then they could accomplish the transshipment of cargo at midnight. That was their deadline.

The freighter was there as the go-fasts approached, showing the right sequence of lights in the right pattern. Identification was confirmed with preagreed but meaningless sentences shouted across the darkness. The go-fasts came alongside. Willing hands hauled the twenty drums upward onto the decks. These were followed by empty fuel tanks which were soon lowered back down, brimful. With a few Spanish salutations, the *Virgen de Valme* proceeded toward Colón, and the go-fasts turned for home. After another day bobbing invisibly on the ocean, they would be back in their mangrove swamps before dawn of the third day, sixty hours after they left them.

The $5,000 each crewman received — $10,000 for the skippers — regarded as a king's ransom. What they had carried would sell from dealer to user in the USA for around $84 million.

By the time the *Virgen de Valme* entered the Panama Canal, she was just another freighter waiting her turn, unless someone had ventured down to the bilges below the floor of the lowest hold. But no one did. A man would need breathing equipment to survive down there, and the crew passed off their equipment as firefighting gear.

Clearing Panama on the Pacific side, the freighter turned north. She slid past Central America, Mexico and California. Finally, off Oregon, the twenty drums were brought to deck level, prepared and hidden under canvas covers. On a moonless night, the *Virgen de Valme* turned at Cape Flattery and headed down the Juan de Fuca Strait, bringing her cargo of Brazilian coffee to Seattle for the discriminating palates of America's coffee capital.

Before she turned, the crew heaved twenty drums overboard, suitably weighted with chains, enough to cause each drum to sink gently to the bottom in a hundred feet of water. Then the captain made a single cell phone call. Even if the monitors of the National Security Agency at Fort Meade, Maryland, were listening (which they were), the words spoken were aimless and harmless. Something about a lonely seaman seeing his girlfriend in a few hours.

The twenty drums were marked by small but brightly colored buoys that bobbed on the gray water at dawn. That was where the four men in the crab boat found them, looking exactly like markers for lobster pots. No one saw them haul the drums out of the deep. Had their radar showed them any patrol boats within miles, they would not have gone near. But the GPS position of the cocaine was accurate to a few square yards, so they could pick their moment.

From the Fuca Strait, the smugglers headed back into the patchwork of islands north of Seattle and made landfall at a point on the mainland where a fisherman's track led down to the water. A large beer truck awaited. After transfer, the drums would head inland to become part of the three hundred tons brought into the USA each year. Everyone involved would be paid later in agreed accounts. The crabmen would never know the name of the ship nor the owner of the beer truck. They did not need to know.

With the landing on U.S. soil, the ownership of the drug had changed. Until then it belonged to the cartel, and all involved would be paid by the cartel. From the beer truck, it belonged to the U.S. importer, and he now owed the cartel a staggering amount of money that would have to be paid.

A price for 1.2 metric tons of pure had already been negotiated. Small fry had to pay a hundred percent on placement of the order. Big players paid fifty percent, with the balance on delivery. The importer would sell his cocaine with impressive markups between the beer truck and the human nostril in Spokane or Milwaukee.

He would "settle" with the layers of middlemen and cutouts that kept him out of the grip of the FBI or the DEA. And it would all be in cash. But even when the cartel had been paid its outstanding fifty percent of purchase price, the American gangster would still have a vast ocean of dollars to launder. These would filter outward from himself into a hundred other illegal enterprises.

And across America, more lives would be ruined by the white powder.

Paul Devereaux found he needed four weeks to complete his study. Jonathan Silver called him twice, but he would not be hurried. When he was ready, he met the presidential chief of staff in the West Wing again. He bore a slim folder. Disdaining computers, which he regarded as thoroughly insecure, he memorized almost everything, and, if he had to deal with a lesser brain, wrote succinct reports in elegant if old-fashioned English.

"Well?" demanded Silver, who prided himself on what he called his no-nonsense approach and hardball attitude but which others referred to as sheer rudeness. "You have come to a view?"

"I have," said Devereaux. "Subject to certain conditions being rigorously fulfilled, the cocaine industry could be destroyed as a narcotic mass industry."

"How?"

"First, how not. At the point of source, the creators are beyond reach. Thousands of dirt-poor peasants, the *cocaleros*, growing their weed in thousands of patches of scrub under the canopy of the jungle, some patches no larger than an acre. So long as there is a cartel prepared to buy their wretched paste, they will produce it and bring it to the buyers in Colombia."

"So smacking the peasants is out?"

"Try as one may, and the present Colombian government really does try, unlike certain of its predecessors and most of its neighbors. But Vietnam ought to have taught us all some home truths about jungles and the people who live in them. Trying to wipe out ants with a rolled-up newspaper is not an option."

"So, the refining laboratories? The cartels?"

"Again, not an option. Like trying to take a moray with your bare hand inside its own hole. This is their territory, not ours. Inside Latin America, they are the masters, not we."

"Okay," said Silver, already running short of his severely limited patience. "Inside the U.S., after the shit has landed in our country? You have any idea how much treasure, how many tax dollars, we spend nationwide on law enforcement? Fifty states, plus the Feds? It's the national debt, goddammit."

"Exactly," said Devereaux, still unruffled despite Silver's rising irritation. "I believe

the federal government alone spends fourteen billion dollars a year on the narcotics
war. That does not even begin to touch the
holes in the budgets of the states, all fifty of
them. That is why suppression onshore will
not work either."

"So where is the key?"

"The Achilles' heel is water."

"Water? You want to put water in the
coke?"

"No, water under the coke. Seawater.
Apart from one single land route up from
Colombia to Mexico via the narrow spine
of Central America, which is so easily
controllable that the cartels do not use it,
every gram of cocaine heading for the USA
or Europe . . ."

"Forget Europe, they're not in," snapped
Silver.

". . . has got to travel over, across or under
the sea. Even from Colombia to Mexico, it
goes by sea. That is the cartel's carotid
artery. Cut that, the patient dies."

Silver grunted and stared across his desk
at the retired spy. The man stared calmly
back, seeming not to care a damn if his find-
ings were accepted or not.

"So, I can tell the President his project is
'go' and you are prepared to take it on?"

"Not entirely. There are conditions. I fear

68

they are not negotiable."

"That sounds like a threat. No one threatens the Oval Office. Back off, mister."

"It is not a threat, it is a warning. If the conditions are not met, the project would simply fail, expensively and embarrassingly. These are they."

Devereaux pushed his slim file across the desk. The chief of staff opened it. Just two sheets that looked as if they had been typed. Five paragraphs. Numbered. He read the first.

" '1. I will need total independence of action within the ambit of absolute secrecy. None but the tiniest group around the commander in chief need know what is happening or why, no matter how many feathers are ruffled or noses put out of joint. Everyone below the Oval Office need know only what they need to know; and that shall be the least to accomplish the task required of them.'

"The federal and military structure does not leak," snapped Silver.

"Yes, it does," said the imperturbable Devereaux. "I have spent half my life trying to prevent them or repairing the damage later."

" '2. I will require presidential authority giving me powers plenipotentiary to require and receive without demur complete co-operation from any other agency or military unit whose cooperation is vital. That must begin with automatic patch through of every scrap of information reaching any other agency in the anti-narcotics campaign to the HQ of what I wish to call "Project Cobra.' "

"They'll go crazy," growled Silver. He knew information was power, and no one willingly ceded even one smidgen of their power. That included the CIA, DEA, FBI, NSA or the Armed Forces.

"They all now come under Homeland Security and the Patriot Act," said Devereaux. "They will obey the President."

"Homeland Security is about the terrorism threat," snapped Silver. "Narc smuggling is crime."

"Read on," murmured the CIA veteran.

" '3. I will need to recruit my own staff. Not many, but the ones I need must be seconded to the project without query or refusal.' "

The chief of staff raised no objection until he came to number four.

" '4. I will need a budget of two billion dollars, to be disbursed without check or examination. I will then need nine months to prepare for the onslaught and a further nine months to destroy the cocaine industry."

There had been covert projects before and secret budgets, but this was huge. The chief of staff could see red lights flashing. Whose budget would be raided? FBI? CIA? DEA? Or would the Treasury be asked for fresh funds?

"There has to be supervision of expenditure," he said. "The money men won't bear the departure into a clear blue sky of two billion dollars because you want to go shopping."

"Then it won't work," Devereaux replied calmly. "The whole point is that when action is taken against the cocaine cartel and industry, they must not see it coming. Forewarned is still forearmed. The nature of the acquired equipment and personnel would betray the game plan, and that will assuredly leak to some investigative reporter or blogger the moment accountants or bookkeepers take over."

"They don't have to take over, just monitor."

"Same difference, Mr. Silver. Once they get involved, cover is blown. And once your cover is blown, you're dead. Trust me. I know."

It was an area the Illinois ex-congressman

knew he could not dispute. He passed to condition five.

" '5. It will be necessary to recategorize cocaine from a Class A drug whose importation is a crime in law to a national threat whose importation or intended importation is an act of terrorism.' "

Jonathan Silver came out of his chair.

"Are you crazy? This changes the law."

"No, that would need an act of Congress. This simply alters the category of a chemical substance. That needs only an Executive instrument."

"What chemical?"

"Cocaine hydrochloride is only a chemical. It happens to be a banned chemical, whose importation contravenes U.S. criminal law. Anthrax is also a chemical, as is VX nerve gas. But the first is classed as a 'bacteriological weapon of mass destruction' and VX as a 'chemical weapon.' We invaded Iraq because what passes for our intelligence service since I left was persuaded that it possessed them."

"That was different."

"No, it was exactly the same. Reclassify cocaine hydrochloride as a threat to the nation, and all the dominoes topple in sequence. Throwing a thousand tons a year at us isn't a crime anymore: it's a terror threat.

Then, we can lawfully respond in kind. All the law is already in place."

"Everything we have in the locker?"

"The lot. But deployed outside our territorial waters and airspace. And invisibly."

"Treat the cartel as we would Al Qaeda?"

"Crudely but effectively put," said Devereaux.

"So what I have to do . . ."

The silver-haired Bostonian rose.

"What you have to do, Mr. Chief of Staff, is decide how squeamish you are, and, more important, how squeamish the man down the hall is. When you have decided that, there is not much more to say. I believe the job can be done, but these are the conditions without whose fulfillment it cannot be done. At least not by me."

Without being bidden to leave, he paused in the doorway.

"Please let me know the response of the commander in chief in due course. I shall be at home."

Jonathan Silver was not accustomed to being left gazing at a closed door.

In the USA, the highest administrative decree that can be issued is the Presidential Executive Order. They are habitually made public, for they can hardly be obeyed if they are not, but a PEO can be completely secret, known simply as a "finding."

Although the old mandarin from Alexandria could not know it, he had convinced the abrasive chief of staff who in turn convinced the President. After consultation with a much surprised professor of constitutional law, cocaine was quietly recategorized as a toxin and a national threat. As such, it came within the ambit of the war against threats to the safety of the nation.

Well west of the Portuguese coast and almost abreast of the Spanish frontier, the MV *Balthazar* ploughed her way north with a declared general cargo for the Euro port of Rotterdam. She was not large, a mere 6,000 tons, with a captain and a crew of eight, and they were all smugglers. So lucrative was the criminal side of their labors that the captain was going to retire a wealthy man to his Venezuelan homeland within two years.

He listened to the weather forecast for Cape Finisterre, which lay only fifty nautical miles ahead. It was for a wind at strength four and a choppy sea, but he knew the Spanish fishermen with whom he had a sea rendezvous were hardy mariners and could work in a lot more than a brisk chop.

Portuguese Oporto was well behind him and Spanish Vigo lay unseen to his east when he ordered his men to bring the four large bales up from the third hold where they had lain since being taken aboard from a shrimper a hundred miles off Caracas.

Captain Gonçalves was careful. He refused either to enter or leave port carrying contraband, least of all this one. He would take aboard only far out at sea and off-load in the same manner. Short of being denounced by an informant, his caution made it unlikely he would be caught. Six successful Atlantic crossings had given him a fine house, raised two daughters and put Enrique through college.

Just after Vigo, the two Spanish fishing boats appeared. He insisted on the harmless-sounding but crucial exchange of greetings as the trawlers bucked in the chop beside him. It was always possible Spanish customs men had penetrated the gang and were now masquerading as fishermen. Realistically, if that had happened, they would be storming aboard by now, but the men half a cable away from his bridge were the men he had come to meet.

Contact made, identities confirmed, the trawlers slipped away into his wake. Minutes later, the four bales tumbled over the taff-

75

rail into the sea. Unlike those dropped off Seattle, these were designed to float. They bobbed on the water as the *Balthazar* headed north. The trawler men hauled them on board, two each, and bundled them into the fish holds. Ten tons of mackerel were poured over them, and the fishing boats headed for home.

They came from the small fishing town of Muros on the Gallaecian coast, and when they cruised in the dusk past the mole into the inner harbor, they were "clean" again. Outside the harbor, other men had hauled the bales out of the sea to the beach where a tractor and trailer waited. No other wheeled vehicle could manage the wet sand. From the tractor trailer, the four bales went into a panel van advertising "Atlantic Scampi" that set off for Madrid.

A man from the Madrid-based importing gang paid them all off in cash, then went to the harbor to settle with the fishermen. Another ton of Colombian pure had entered Europe.

It was a phone call from the chief of staff that brought the news and a messenger who brought the paperwork. The letters of authority gave Paul Devereaux more power than anyone beneath the Oval Office had

had in decades. The money transfers would come later, when he decided where he wanted his $2 billion lodged.

Among the first things he did was look up a telephone number he had kept for years but had never used. He used it now. It rang in a small bungalow in a side street of a modest town called Pennington, New Jersey. He was in luck. It answered at the third ring.

"Mr. Dexter?"

"Who wishes to know?"

"A voice from the past. My name is Paul Devereaux. I think you will remember it."

There was a long pause, as by one who has just been hit in the solar plexus.

"Are you there, Mr. Dexter?"

"Yes. I'm here. And I well recall the name. How did you get this number?"

"Not important. Discreet information used to be my stock-in-trade, as you will also recall."

The man in New Jersey recalled extremely well. Ten years earlier he had been the most successful bounty hunter the U.S. ever produced. Unwittingly, he had crossed the Boston Brahmin working out of CIA HQ in Langley, Virginia, and Devereaux had tried to have him killed.

The two men were as unalike as chalk and cheese. Cal Dexter, the wiry, sandy-haired, friendly, smiling, small-town attorney of Pennington, had been born in 1950 in a roach-infested Newark slum. His father had been a construction worker fully employed through World War II and Korea creating new factories, dockyards and government offices along the Jersey Shore.

But with the ending of the Korean War, work had dried up. Cal was five when his mother walked out of the loveless union and left the boy to be raised by his father. The latter was a hard man, quick with his fists, the only law on many blue-collar jobs. But he was not a bad man and tried to live by the straight and narrow, and to raise his toddler son to love Old Glory, the Constitution and Joe DiMaggio.

Within two years, Dexter Senior had acquired a trailer home so that he could move where the work was available. And that was how the boy was raised, moving from construction site to site, attending whichever school would take him, and then moving on. It was the age of Elvis Presley, Del Shannon, Roy Orbison and the Beatles, over from a country Cal had never heard of. It was also the age of Kennedy, the Cold War and Vietnam.

His formal education was fractured to the point of near nonexistence, but he became wise in other ways: streetwise, fightwise. Like his departed mother, he did not grow tall, topping out at five feet eight inches. Nor was he heavy and muscular like his father, but his lean frame packed fearsome stamina and his fists a killer punch.

By seventeen, it looked as if his life would follow that of his father, shoveling dirt or driving a dump truck on building sites. Unless . . . In January 1968 he turned eighteen, and the Vietcong launched the Tết Offensive. He was watching TV in a bar in Camden. There was a documentary telling him about recruitment. It mentioned that if you shaped up, the Army would give you an education. The next day, he walked into the U.S. Army office in Camden and signed on.

The master sergeant was bored. He spent his life listening to youths doing everything in their power to get out of going to Vietnam.

"I want to volunteer," said the youth in front of him.

The master sergeant drew a form toward him, keeping eye contact like a ferret that does not want the rabbit to get away. Trying to be kindly, he suggested the boy sign for three years, as opposed to two.

"Good chance of better postings," he said. "Better career choices. With three years you could even avoid going to Vietnam."

"But I want to go to Vietnam," said the kid in the soiled denims.

He got his wish. After boot camp, and with his noted skill driving earthmoving equipment, he was sent to the Engineer Battalion of the Big Red One, the First Infantry Division, based right up in the Iron Triangle. That was where he volunteered to become a Tunnel Rat and enter the fearsome network of scary, black and often lethal tunnels dug by the Vietcong under Cu Chi.

In two tours of nearly suicidal missions in those hellholes, he came back to the States with a hatful of medals, and Uncle Sam kept his promise. He was able to study at college. He chose law, and got his degree at Fordham, in New York.

He had neither the backing, the polish nor the money for the big Wall Street firms. He joined the Legal Aid Society, speaking up for those destined to occupy the very lowest reaches of the legal system. So many of his clients were Hispanic that he learned fluent and rapid Spanish. He also married and had a daughter, on whom he doted.

He might have spent all his working life among the unrepresented destitute, but when he was just over forty, his teenage daughter was abducted, forced into prostitution and sadistically murdered by her gangster pimp. He had to identify her battered body on a marble slab at Virginia Beach. The experience brought back the Tunnel Rat, the one-on-one man killer.

Using his old skills, he tracked down the two pimps behind his daughter's death and gunned them down, with their bodyguards, on a pavement in Panama City. When he returned to New York, his wife had taken her own life.

Cal Dexter abandoned the courts and appeared to retire to become a civil attorney in the small New Jersey town of Pennington. In fact, he took up his third career. He became a bounty hunter, but, unlike the great majority of his trade, he operated almost exclusively abroad. He specialized in tracking down, snatching and bringing back for due process in the USA those who had committed evil crimes and thought they had got away with it by seeking sanctuary in a non-extradition country. He advertised extremely discreetly under the pseudonym "Avenger."

In 2001, he had been commissioned by a Canadian billionaire to find the sadistic Serbian mercenary who had murdered the old man's aid-worker grandson somewhere in

Bosnia. What Dexter did not know was that a certain Paul Devereaux was using the killer Zoran Zilic, now a freelance arms trader, as bait to lure Osama bin Laden to a rendezvous where a cruise missile could wipe him out.

But Dexter got there first. He found Zilic holed up in a filthy South American dictatorship, slipped in and hijacked the killer at gunpoint, flying him back to Key West, Florida, in his own jet. Devereaux, who had tried to have the interfering bounty hunter eliminated, found his two years of planning in ruins. It soon became irrelevant; a few days later, 9/11 would ensure that Bin Laden was not going to attend any unsafe meetings outside his caves.

Dexter vanished back into the persona of the harmless little lawyer from Pennington. Devereaux later retired. Then he had the time, and he used it to trace the bounty hunter called simply the Avenger.

Now they were both retired: the ex–Tunnel Rat who came up from the ranks and the dandified aristo from Boston. Dexter looked down at the handset and spoke.

"What do you want, Mr. Devereaux?"

"I have been summoned out of retirement, Mr. Dexter. By the commander in chief himself. There is a task he wishes performed. It affects our country quite grievously. He has asked me to accomplish it. I will need a first deputy, an executive officer. I would be most grateful if you would consider taking the post."

Dexter noted the language. Not "I want you to . . ." or "I am offering . . ." but "I would be most grateful . . ."

"I would need to know more. A lot more."

"Of course. If you could drive over to Washington to visit with me, I would be happy to explain almost everything."

Dexter, standing in the front window of his modest house in Pennington, looking out at the fallen leaves, thought it over. He was now in his sixty-first year. He kept himself in shape, and, despite several very clear offers, had declined to marry for a second time. All in all, his life was comfortable, stress-free, placid, small-town bourgeois. And boring.

"I'll come over and listen, Mr. Devereaux. Just listen. Then decide."

"Very wise, Mr. Dexter. Here is my address in Alexandria. May I expect you tomorrow?"

He dictated his address. Before he hung up, Cal Dexter had a question.

"Bearing in mind our mutual past, why did you pick me?"

"Very simple. You were the only man who ever outwitted me."

■ ■ ■ ■

PART TWO
HISS

■ ■ ■ ■

CHAPTER 3

For security reasons it was infrequent that the Hermandad, the controlling super-cartel of the whole cocaine industry, met in plenary session. Years earlier, it had been easier.

The arrival in the presidency of Colombia of fiercely anti-drug Álvaro Uribe had changed that. Under his rule, a clearing out of some elements of the national police force had witnessed the rise to the top of General Felipe Calderon and his formidable chief of intelligence in the anti-narcotics division, Colonel Dos Santos.

Both men had proved that, even on a policeman's salary, they were bribeproof. The cartel was not accustomed to this and made several mistakes, losing key executives, until the lesson was learned. After that, it was war to the knife. But Colombia is a big country with millions of hectares to hide in.

The unchallenged chief of the Brotherhood was Don Diego Esteban. Unlike a former cocaine lord, Pablo Escobar, Don Diego was no psychopathic thug drawn from the backstreet slums. He was of the old landed gentry: educated, courteous, mannerly, drawn from pure Spanish stock, scion of a long line of hidalgos. And he was always referred to simply as "the Don."

It was he who, in a world of killers, had, by force of personality, forged the disparate warlords of cocaine into a single syndicate, highly successful and run like a modern corporation. Two years earlier the last of those who had resisted the unification he demanded had departed in chains, extradited to the U.S., never to return. He was Diego Montoya, chief of the Cartel del Norte del Valle, who had prided himself on being the successor to the outfits of Cali and Medellín.

It was never discovered who had made the phone call to Colonel Dos Santos that led to the raid on Montoya, but after his media appearance, shackled hand and foot, there was no more opposition to the Don.

Colombia is slashed, northeast to southwest, by two cordilleras of high peaks, with the valley of the river Magdalena between them. All rivers to the west of the Cordillera Occidental flow to the Pacific or the Caribbean; all water east of the Cordillera Oriental flows away to join the Orinoco or the Amazon. This eastern land of fifty rivers is a vista of rolling open range studded with haciendas the size of counties. Don Diego owned at least five that could be traced and another ten that could not. Each had several airstrips.

The meeting of autumn 2010 was at the Rancho de la Cucaracha outside San José. The other seven members of the board had been summoned by personal emissary and had arrived by light aircraft after the dispatch of a score of decoys. Even though the one-time-use-and-throw cell phone was deemed extremely secure, the Don preferred to send his messages by handpicked courier. He was old-fashioned, but he had never been caught or eavesdropped upon.

That bright autumn morning, the Don personally welcomed his team to the manorial house in which he probably slept no more than ten times a year but which was maintained at permanent readiness.

The manor was of old Spanish architecture, tiled, and cool in the summer, with fountains tinkling in the courtyard and white-jacketed stewards circulating with trays of drinks under the awnings.

First to arrive from the airstrip was Emilio

Sánchez. Like all the other division heads, he had one single function to master: production. His task was to oversee every aspect from the tens of thousands of dirt-poor peasants, the *cocaleros,* growing their shrubs in Colombia, Bolivia and Peru. He brought in their *pasta,* checked the quality, paid them off and delivered tons of Colombian *puro,* packaged and baled, at the refinery door.

All this needed constant protection, not only against the forces of law and order but against bandits of every stripe, living in the jungles, ready to steal the product and try to sell it back. The private army came under Rodrigo Pérez, himself a former FARC terrorist. With his aid, most of the once-fearsome Marxist revolutionary group had been brought to heel and worked for the Brotherhood.

The profits of the cocaine industry were so astronomical that the sheer ocean of inflowing money became a problem that could be solved only by laundering from "tainted" dollars into "clean." Then they could be reinvested in thousands of legitimate companies worldwide; but only after deduction of overheads and contribution to the personal wealth of the Don, which ran to hundreds of millions.

The laundering was mainly accomplished by corrupt banks, many of whom presented themselves to the world as wholly respectable, using their criminal activities as an extra wealth generator.

The man charged with laundering, Julio Luz, was no more a thug than the Don himself. He was a lawyer specializing in financial and banking law. His Bogotá practice was prestigious, and if Colonel Dos Santos had his suspicions, he could never raise them above that level. Señor Luz was the third to arrive, and the Don greeted him warmly as the fourth SUV arrived from the airstrip.

José-María Largo was the *supremo* of merchandising. His arena was the world that consumed the cocaine and the hundreds of gangs and mafias that were the clients of the Hermandad for its white powder product. He was the one who concluded the deals with the gangs spread across Mexico, the USA and Europe. He alone assessed the creditworthiness of the long-established mafias and the constant stream of newcomers who replaced those caught and jailed abroad. It was he who had chosen to award a virtual European monopoly to the fearsome Ndrangheta, the Italian mafia native to Calabria, the toe of Italy, sandwiched between the camorra of Naples and the Cosa Nostra of Sicily.

He had shared an SUV, because their aircraft had arrived almost together, with Roberto Cárdenas, a tough, scarred old street fighter from Cartagena. The interceptions by customs and police at a hundred ports and airports across the U.S. and Europe would have been five times higher but for the "facilitating" functions of bribed officials. These were crucial, and he was in charge of them all, recruitment and payoff.

The last two were delayed by weather and distance. Lunch was about to be served when an apologetic Alfredo Suárez drove up. Late though he was, the Don's courtesy never failed, and he thanked his subordinate warmly for his effort as if a choice had been involved.

Suárez and his skills were vital. His specialty was transportation. To secure the safe and unintercepted transit of every gram from refinery door to handover point abroad was his task. Every courier, every mule, every freighter, liner or private yacht, every airplane, large or small, and every submarine came under him, along with their crews, stewards and pilots.

Argument had raged for years over which of the two philosophies was the better: to ship cocaine in tiny quantities but by thousands of single couriers or to send huge consignments but far fewer of them.

Some had it that the cartel should swamp the defense of the two target continents with thousands of expendable know-nothing mules carrying a few kilos in their suitcases or even just one, swallowed into their stomachs in pellet form. Some would be caught, of course, but many would get through. The sheer numbers would overwhelm the defenses. Or so ran the theory.

Suárez favored the alternate. With three hundred tons to supply to each continent, he favored about one hundred operations per year to the U.S. and the same to Europe. Cargoes should be from one to ten tons, justifying major investment and planning. If the receiving gangs, having taken delivery and paid up, wished to split the cargoes into penny packets, that was their business.

When it failed, it failed badly. Two years earlier, the British frigate *Iron Duke,* patrolling the Caribbean, had intercepted a freighter and confiscated five and a half tons of pure. It was valued at $400 million, and that was not street value because it had not yet been adulterated six-to-one.

Suárez was nervous. What they had been convened to discuss was another huge interception. The U.S. Coast Guard cutter *Dallas* had taken two tons from a fishing boat trying to slip past it into the creeks near Corpus Christi, Texas. He knew he would have to defend his philosophy with all the advocacy at his disposal.

The only one from whom the Don kept a chilly distance was his seventh guest, the near-dwarf Paco Valdez. If his appearance was ludicrous, no one laughed. Not here, not anywhere, not anytime. Valdez was the Enforcer.

He stood barely five feet three inches, even in his Cuban "lifts." But his head was inordinately large and, weirdly, had the features of a baby, with a slick of black hair on top and a pursed, rosebud mouth. Only the blank black eyes gave hint of the psychopathic sadist inside the little body.

The Don acknowledged him with a formal nod and thin smile. He declined to shake his hand. He knew the man the underworld had nicknamed "El Animal" had once plucked out the entrails of a living man to toss them on a brazier with that hand. The Don was not sure he had washed his hands afterward, and he was very fastidious. But if he were to murmur the name Suárez into one button ear, the Animal would do what had to be done.

The food was exquisite, the wines vintage and the discussion intense. Alfredo Suárez won his corner. His big-consignment philosophy made life easier for merchandising, the "facilitating" officials abroad and laundering. Those three votes swung it for him. He left the hacienda alive. The Enforcer was disappointed.

The British Prime Minister held his conference with "my people" that weekend, once again at Chequers. The Berrigan Report was passed around and read in silence. Then the shorter document prepared by the Cobra to define his demands. Finally, it was time for opinions.

Around the table in the elegant dining room, also used for conferences, was the cabinet secretary, controller of the Home Civil Service, from whom no major initiative could be kept anyway. Next to him sat the chief of the Secret Intelligence Service, known inaccurately by the media as MI6 and more commonly by its intimates and colleagues as the "Firm."

Since the retirement of Sir John Scarlett, a Kremlinologist, the simple title "Chief" (never "Director General") had gone to a second Arabist, fluent in Arabic and Pashtun, and with years in the Middle East and

Central Asia.

And there were three from the military. These were the chief of the Defence Staff, who would later, if need be, brief the chief of General Staff (Army), the chief of Air Staff and the First Sea Lord. The other two were the director of Military Operations and the director of Special Forces. All in the room knew that all three military men had spent time in Special Forces. The young Prime Minister, their superior in rank but junior in age, reckoned that if these three, plus the chief, could not cause a mischief to be performed on an unpleasant foreigner, no one could.

Domestic service at Chequers is always performed by the RAF. When the Air Force sergeant had served coffee and left, the discussion began. The cabinet secretary addressed the legal implications.

"If this man, the so-called Cobra, wishes to" — he paused and searched for the word — "enhance the campaign against the cocaine trade, which is already imbued with many powers, there is a danger he will have to ask us to break international law."

"I believe the Americans are going ahead with that," said the PM. "They are going to change the designation of cocaine from a Class A drug to national threat. It creates the category of terrorists for the cartel and all smugglers. Inside the territorial waters of the U.S. and Europe, they remain gangsters. Outside, they become terrorists. In that case, we have the powers to do what we do anyway, and have been since 9/11."

"Could we change, too?" asked the chief of the Defence Staff.

"We would have to," replied the cabinet secretary. "And the answer is yes. It would mean a statutory instrument, not a new law. Very quiet indeed. Unless the media got hold of it. Or the bunny huggers."

"That is why the need-to-know principle would have to keep those in the know to a very tiny group indeed," said the chief. "And even then any operation would need a damn good cover story."

"We mounted a hell of a lot of black ops against the IRA," said the director of Special Forces, "and since then against Al Qaeda. Only the tip of an iceberg ever got out."

"Prime Minister, what exactly do the cousins want from us?" asked the chief of the Defence Staff.

"So far as I can learn from the President, intel, input and covert-action know-how," said the PM.

The discussion ran its course, with many questions but few answers.

"And what do you want from us, Prime Minister?" This came from Defence Staff.

"Your advice, gentlemen. Can it be done and should we take part?"

The three military men were the first to nod. Then Secret Intelligence. Finally, the cabinet secretary. Personally, he loathed this sort of thing. If it ever blew up in their faces . . .

Later that day, after Washington had been told and the Prime Minister had offered his guests a roast beef lunch, a reply came from the White House. It said "Good to have you aboard" and asked that a U.S. emissary be received in London and offered some early help in the form of advice, nothing more at this stage. A photo came with the transmission. As the after-lunch port circulated, so did the photograph.

It bore the image of a onetime Tunnel Rat named Cal Dexter.

While men conversed in the wilds of Colombia and the orchards of Buckinghamshire, the man code-named the Cobra had been busy in Washington. Like the chief of the SAS across the Atlantic, he, too, was concerned with a plausible cover story.

He established a charity to bring succor to Third World refugees and in its name

98

took a long lease on a shabby and obscure warehouse in Anacostia, a few blocks from Fort McNair. This would house the offices on the top floor, and beneath that several floors of used clothing, fly sheets, tarpaulins, blankets and tents.

In reality, there would be little office work in the traditional sense. Paul Devereaux had spent years railing against the transformation of the CIA from a very hard-nosed spy agency into a vast bureaucracy. He loathed bureaucracy, but what he did want, and was determined to have, was a communications center to rival anyone else's.

After Cal Dexter, his first recruit was Jeremy Bishop, retired like himself, but one of the most brilliant communications and computer aces ever to serve at Fort Meade, Maryland, HQ of the National Security Agency, a vast complex of eavesdropping technology known as the "Puzzle Palace."

Bishop began to devise a comms center into which every scintilla of information about Colombia and cocaine acquired by thirteen intel-gathering agencies would be patched by presidential decree. For this, a second cover story was needed. The other agencies were told the Oval Office had ordered the preparation of a report to end all reports on the cocaine trade, and their cooperation was mandatory. The agencies grumbled but acquiesced. A new think tank. Another twenty-volume report that no one would ever read. What else was new?

And there was the money. Back in the CIA's SEE (Soviet/East Europe) division, Devereaux had come across Benedict Forbes, a former Wall Street banker who had been co-opted to the Company for a single operation, found it more exciting than trying to warn people about Bernie Madoff and stayed. That was in the Cold War. He, too, was now retired, but he had forgotten nothing.

His specialty had been covert bank accounts. Running secret agents is not cheap. There are expenses, salaries, bonuses, purchases, bribes. For these, monies must be deposited with facilities for withdrawal by both one's own agents and foreign "assets." These facilities will require covert identification codes. This was Forbes's genius. No one ever traced his little nest eggs and the KGB tried very hard indeed. The money trail can usually lead to the traitor.

Forbes began to draw down the allotted dollars from a bewildered Treasury and place them where they could be accessed as and when needed. In the computer age, this could be anywhere. Paper was for dodos. A few taps on a computer could release enough for a man to retire — so long as they were the right taps.

As his HQ was being established, Devereaux sent Cal Dexter on his first overseas assignment.

"I want you to go to London and buy two ships," he said. "It seems the Brits are coming in with us. Let us use them. They are rather good at this. A shell company is being set up. It will have funds. It will be the titular purchaser of the ships. Then it will disappear."

"What kind of ships?" asked Dexter. The Cobra produced a single sheet of paper, which he had typed himself.

"Memorize and burn. Then let the Brits advise you. The paper contains the name and private number of the man to contact. Commit nothing to paper, and certainly not to a computer or a cell phone. Keep it in your head. It's the only private place we have left."

Though Dexter could not know it, the number he would call would ring in a large green-and-sandstone block on the side of the Thames at a place called Vauxhall Cross. Those inside never called it that: only the "office." It was the HQ of Britain's Secret

Intelligence Service.

The name on the about-to-be-burned sheet was Medlicott. The man who would answer would be the deputy chief, and his name was not Medlicott. But the use of that word would tell "Medlicott" who was talking: the Yankee visitor who really was named Dexter.

And Medlicott would propose Dexter go to a gentlemen's club in St. James's Street to join a colleague named Cranford whose real name was not Cranford. They would be three at that lunch, and it was the third man who knew all about ships.

This byzantine routine had stemmed from the daily morning conference inside the office two days earlier. At the close of business, the chief had remarked:

"By the way, there is an American arriving in a couple of days. The PM has asked me to help him. He wants to buy ships. Covertly. Anyone know anything about ships?"

There was a pause for cogitation.

"I know a fellow who is the chairman of a major Lloyd's broker in the City," said the controller, Western Hemisphere.

"How well do you know him?"

"I broke his nose once."

"That's usually quite intimate. Had he upset you?"

"No. We were playing the wall game."

There was a slight chill. The phrase meant both men had gone to the ultra-exclusive school called Eton College, the only place where the bizarre and seemingly no-rules wall game was played.

"Well, take him to lunch with your shipping friend and see if the brokerage can help him buy ships on the quiet. It might make a tidy commission. Compensation for the broken nose."

The meeting broke up. Dexter's call duly came, from his room at the discreet Montcalm Hotel. "Medlicott" passed the American to his colleague "Cranford," who took the number and said he would call back. And he did, an hour later, to set up lunch the next day with Sir Abhay Varma at Brooks's Club.

"And I'm afraid suits and ties are required," said Cranford.

"No problem," said Dexter. "I think I can knot a tie."

Brooks's is quite a small club on the west side of St. James's Street. Like all the others, it has no nameplate for identification. The received wisdom is that if you are a member or invited, you know where it is, and if you are not it doesn't matter, but it is usually identified by the potted shrubs that flank the door. Like all St. James clubs, it has its character and patronage, and that of Brooks's tends to be senior civil servant and occasional spook.

Sir Abhay Varma turned out to be the chairman of Staplehurst & Company, a major brokerage specializing in shipping and situated in a medieval alleyway off Aldgate. Like Cranford, he was fifty-five, plump and jovial. Before he put on the weight during all those City Guild dinners, he had been an amateur champion-rated squash player.

As per custom, the men confined conversation at the lunch table to small talk — weather, crops, how was the flight — and adjourned to the library for coffee and port. Unheard by anyone else, they were able to relax under the gaze of the painted Dilettantes on the wall above them and talk business.

"I need to buy two ships. Very quietly, very discreetly, the purchase concluded by a shell company in a tax haven."

Sir Abhay was not in the slightest fazed. It happened all the time. For tax reasons, of course.

"What kinds of ships?" he asked. He never queried the American's bona fides. He was vouched for by Cranford, and that was good enough. After all, they had been at school together.

"I don't know," said Dexter.

"Ticklish," said Sir Abhay. "I mean, if you don't know. They come in all roles and sizes."

"Then let me level with you, sir. I want to take them off to a discreet shipyard and have them converted."

"Ah, a major refit. Not a problem. What are they supposed to end up as?"

"Is this between ourselves alone, Sir Abhay?"

The broker glanced at the spook as if to ask what kinds of chaps does this chap think we are?

"What is said in Brooks's, stays in Brooks's," murmured Cranford.

"Well, each is to become a floating base for U.S. Navy SEALs. Harmless to look at, not so harmless inside."

Sir Abhay Varma beamed.

"Aha, rough stuff, eh? Well, that clarifies things a bit. A total conversion. I'd advise against tankers of any kind. Wrong shape, an impossible cleaning job and too many pipes. Same with an ore carrier. Right shape but usually vast, bigger than you want. I'd go for a dry-bulk carrier, a grain ship, surplus to owner's requirements. Clean, dry, easy to convert, with deck covers that come off to let your chaps in and out fast."

"Can you help me buy two?"

"Not Staplehurst, we do insurance, but of course we know everyone in the market worldwide. I'm going to put you alongside my managing director, Paul Agate. Young, but smart as paint."

He rose and offered his card.

"Drop by the office tomorrow. Paul will see you right. Best advice in the City. On the house. Thanks for lunch, Barry. Give my regards to the chief."

And so they descended to the street and parted.

Juan Cortez finished work and emerged from the entrails of the 4,000-ton tramp steamer on which he had worked his magic. After the darkness of the lower hold, the autumn sun was brilliant. So bright he was tempted to reach for his black-fronted welder's helmet. Instead he pulled on dark glasses and let his pupils adjust to the light.

His grimy overalls clung to him, pasted by sweat onto his near-naked body. Beneath the fabric, he wore only undershorts. The heat down there had been ferocious.

There was no need to wait. The men who had commissioned the work would come in the morning. He would show them what he had done and how to work the secret access door. The cavity behind the plating of the inner hull was absolutely impossible to detect. He would be well paid. What contraband would be carried in the compartment he had created was none of his business, and if the stupid gringos chose to stuff white powder up their noses, that was none of his business either.

His business was to put clothes on the back of his faithful wife, Irina, food on the table and school books in the satchel of his boy, Pedro. He stowed his kit in the allocated locker and made his way to the modest Ford Pinto that was his automobile. In the neat bungalow, a real credit to a workingman, in the smart private estate beneath the hill called Cerro de La Popa, there would be a long, bracing shower, a kiss from Irina, a hug from Pedro, a filling meal and a few beers in front of the plasma-screen TV. And so, a happy man, the best welder in Cartagena drove home.

Cal Dexter knew London but not well, and that trading hub simply called the "City" or the "Square Mile" not at all. But a black cab, driven by a Cockney born and raised a mile east of Aldgate, had no trouble. He was dropped outside the door of the maritime insurance broker in a narrow backwater playing host to a monastery dating back to Shakespeare at five minutes before eleven o'clock. A smiling secretary showed him up to the second floor.

Paul Agate occupied a small office piled with files; framed prints of cargo ships adorned the walls. It was hard to imagine the millions of pounds' worth of insurance business that came and went out of this cubbyhole. Only the screen of a state-of-the-art computer proved that Charles Dickens had not just moved out.

Later, Dexter would realize how deceptive London's centuries-old money-market center was, where tens of billions in sales, purchases and commissions were generated each day. Agate was around forty, shirtsleeved, open-necked and friendly. He had been briefed by Sir Abhay Varma, but only just so far. The American, he was told, represented a new venture-capital company seeking to buy two dry-bulk carriers, probably surplus-to-requirement grain ships. What they would be used for he had not been told. Need-to-know. What Staplehurst would do was offer him advice, guidance and some contacts in the shipping world. The American was a friend of a friend of

Sir Abhay. There would be no invoice.

"Dry bulk?" said Agate. "Ex–grain ships. You're in the market at the right time. What, with the state of the world economy, there is quite a margin of surplus tonnage at the moment, some at sea, most laid up. But you will need a broker to avoid getting ripped off. Do you know anyone?"

"No," said Dexter. "Who can you recommend?"

"Well, it's a quite a tight world, we all know each other. Within half a mile, there's Clarkson, Braemar Seascope, Galbraith or Gibson's. They all do sales, purchases, charters. For a fee, of course."

"Of course." An encrypted message from Washington had told him of a new account opened in the British Channel island of Guernsey, a discreet tax haven that the European Union was trying to close down. He also had the name of the bank executive to contact and the code number required to release funds.

"On the other hand, a good broker will probably save a ship buyer more than the fee. I have a good friend at Parkside and Company. He would see you right. Shall I give him a call?"

"Please do."

Agate was on the phone for five minutes.

"Simon Linley's your man," he said, and wrote an address on a scrap of paper. "It's only five hundred yards. Out of here, turn left. At Aldgate, left again. Follow your nose for five minutes, and ask. Jupiter House. Anyone will tell you. Good luck."

Dexter finished his coffee, shook hands and left. The directions were perfect. He was there in fifteen minutes. Jupiter House was the opposite of the Staplehurst office: ultra-modern, steel and glass. Silent elevators. Parkside was on the eleventh floor, with picture windows that showed the dome of St. Paul's Cathedral on its hill two miles to the west. Linley met him at the elevator doors and took him to a small conference room. Coffee and gingersnaps appeared.

"You wish to buy two bulk-carrier ships, probably grain carriers?" asked Linley.

"My patrons do," corrected Dexter. "They are based in the Middle East. They wish for extreme discretion. Hence, a front company headed by me."

"Of course." Linley was not in the slightest fazed. Some Arab businessmen had skimmed the local sheikh and did not want to end up in a very unpleasant Gulf jail. It happened all the time.

"How big would your clients wish these ships to be?"

Dexter knew little of marine tonnages, but he knew a small helicopter would have to be stored, with rotors spread, in the main hold. He reeled off a list of dimensions.

"About twenty thousand tons gross, or twenty-eight thousand deadweight tons," said Linley. He began to tap into a computer keyboard. The large screen was at the end of the conference table where both men could see it. A range of options began to appear. Fremantle, Australia. St. Lawrence Seaway, Canada. Singapore. Chesapeake Bay, USA.

"The biggest repertoire would seem to be with COSCO. China Ocean Shipping Company, based in Shanghai, but we use the Hong Kong office."

"Communists?" asked Dexter, who had killed rather a lot of them in the Iron Triangle.

"Oh, we don't bother about that anymore," said Linley. "Nowadays they're the world's sharpest capitalists. But very meticulous. If they say they'll deliver, they deliver. And here we have Eagle Bulk in New York. Closer to home for you. Not that it matters. Or does it matter?"

"My clients want discretion only as to true ownership," said Dexter, "and both ships would be taken to a discreet yard for refit

111

and renovation."

Linley thought but did not say: A bunch of crooks who probably want to move some extremely dodgy cargoes, so they will want the ships reconfigured, renamed with new paperwork and put to sea unrecognizable. So what? The Far East is full of them; times are hard, and money is money.

What he did say: "Of course. There are some very skilled and highly discreet ship-yards in southern India. We have contacts there through our man in Mumbai. If we are to act for you, we shall have to have a memorandum of agreement, with an advance against commission. Once the ships are purchased, I suggest you put both on the books of a management company called Thame in Singapore. At that point, and with new names, they will disappear. Thame never talk to anyone about their clients. Where can I get hold of you, Mr. Dexter?"

The message from Devereaux had also included the address, phone number and e-mail of a newly acquired safe house in Fairfax, Virginia, which would act as mail drop and message taker. Being a Devereaux creation, it was untraceable and could close down in sixty seconds. Dexter gave it. Within forty-eight hours, the memorandum was signed and returned. Fairfax began their hunt. It would take two months, but before the end of the year two grain ships were handed over.

One came out of Chesapeake Bay, Maryland, the other had been at anchor in Singapore Harbor. Devereaux had no intention of keeping on the crew of either vessel. Both crews were generously paid off.

The American purchase was easy, being so close to home. A new crew of U.S. Navy men, masquerading as merchant sailors, took over, accustomed themselves to the vessel and eased her out into the Atlantic.

A crew of British Royal Navy men flew out to Singapore, also posing as merchant marines, took command and sailed out into the Malacca Strait. Theirs was the shorter sea journey. Both vessels headed for a small and reeking yard on the Indian coast south of Goa, a place mainly used for the slow breakup of graveyard vessels and possessed of a criminal disregard for health, safety and the danger of constantly leaching toxic chemicals. The place stank, which was why no one ever went there to examine what was going on.

When the Cobra's two ships entered the bay and dropped anchor, they virtually ceased to exist, but new names and new papers were discreetly logged with Lloyd's

International Shipping List. They were noted as "grain carriers" managed by Thame PLC of Singapore.

The ceremony took place, in deference to the wishes of the donating nation, in the U.S. Embassy in Abílio Macedo Street, Praia, Santiago Island, Republic of Cape Verde. Presiding with her usual charm was Ambassador Marianne Myles. Also present was the Verdean Natural Resources Minister and the Defence Minister.

To add gravitas, a full U.S. admiral had flown in to sign the agreement on behalf of the Pentagon. He, at least, had not the faintest idea what he was doing there, but the two gleaming white tropical uniforms of he and his ensign ADC were impressive, as they were supposed to be.

Ambassador Myles offered refreshments, and the necessary documents were spread on the conference table. The embassy's defense attaché was present and a civilian from the State Department whose identification was perfect and in the name of Calvin Dexter.

The Verdean ministers signed first, then the admiral and finally the ambassador. The seals of the Republic of Cape Verde and the United States were affixed to each copy, and the aid agreement was in place. Work could proceed on its implementation.

Duty done, flutes of sparking wine were decanted for the usual toasts, and the senior Verdean minister made in Portuguese the, for him, obligatory speech. To the weary admiral, it seemed to go on and on, and he understood not a word of it. So he just smiled his Navy smile and wondered why he had been hauled off a golf course outside Naples, Italy, and sent to a group of impoverished islands stuck three hundred miles into the Atlantic off the coast of West Africa.

The reason, his ADC had sought to explain to him on the flight down, was that the U.S., out of its habitual generosity to the Third World, was going to help the Republic of Cape Verde. The islands have absolutely no natural resources save one: the seas around them are teeming with fish. The republic has a one-cutter Navy but no Air Force worth the name.

With the worldwide growth of fishing piracy and the East's insatiable appetite for fresh fish, the Verdean seas, well inside the two-hundred-mile limit that was rightfully hers, were being gutted by poachers.

The U.S. was going to take over the airport on the remote island of Fogo, whose runway had just been extended by a donation from the European Union. There the U.S. Navy was going to build a pilot training facility, as a donation.

When it was done, a team of Brazilian (because of the Portuguese common language) Air Force instructors would move in with a dozen Tucano aircraft and create a Fisheries Air Guard, who were by training suitably selected, up-to-standard Verdean cadet pilots. With long-range-version Tucanos, they could then patrol the oceans, spot the malefactors and guide the Coast Guard cutter on to them.

So far, so marvelous, agreed the admiral, though it defeated him why he'd had to be dragged away from his golf just when he was getting on top of his putting problem.

Leaving the embassy in a flurry of handshakes, the admiral offered the man from State a lift back to the airport in the embassy limo.

"Can I offer you a ride back to Naples, Mr. Dexter?" he asked.

"Very kind, Admiral, but I am shipping back to Lisbon, London and Washington."

They parted at Santiago Airport. The admiral's Navy jet took off for Italy. Cal Dexter waited for the TAP schedule for Lisbon.

A month later, the first huge fleet auxiliary

brought the U.S. Navy engineers to the conical extinct volcano that is ninety percent of the island of Fogo, so called because that is the Portuguese for "fire." The auxiliary moored offshore where she would stay as a floating base for the engineers, a small piece of the U.S. with all the comforts of home.

The Navy Seabees pride themselves that they can build anything anywhere, but it is unwise to part them from their marbled Kansas steaks, potato fries and gallon jars of ketchup. Everything works better on the right fuel.

It would take them six months, but the existing airport could handle C-130 Hercules transports, so resupply and furlough was not a problem. That apart, smaller supply ships would bring girders, beams, cement and anything needed for the buildings, plus food, juices, sodas and even water.

The few Creole who lived on Fogo gathered, much impressed, to watch the ant army swarm ashore and take over their small airport. Once a day, the shuttle from Santiago came and went when the runway was clear of building kit.

When it was finished, the flight training facility would have, quite separate from the small cluster of civil-passenger sheds, an expanse of prefabricated dormitories for the cadets, cottages for the instructors, repair and maintenance workshops, aviation gas tanks for the turboprop Tucanos and a communications shack.

If anyone among the engineers noticed something odd, no mention was made of it. Also constructed to the approval of a civilian from the Pentagon named Dexter, who came and went by civil airliner, were a few other items. Gouged out of the rock face of the volcano was a cavernous extra hangar with steel doors. Plus a large reserve tank for JP-5 fuel, which Tucanos do not use, and an armory.

"Anyone would think," murmured Chief Petty Officer O'Connor after testing the steel doors of the secret hangar in the rock, "that someone was going to war."

CHAPTER 4

In the Plaza de Bolívar, named after the Great Liberator, stand some of the oldest buildings not only in Bogotá but in all South America. It is the center of Old Town.

The conquistadors were here, bringing with them, in their raging lust for God and gold, the first Catholic missionaries. Some of these, Jesuits all, founded in 1604 in one corner the school of San Bartolomé, and not far away the Church of St. Ignatius, in honor of their founder, Loyola. In another corner stood the original national Provincialate of the Society of Jesus.

It had been some years since the Provincialate officially moved to a modern building in the newer part of the city. But in the blazing heat, despite the favors of new air-conditioning technology, the Father Provincial, Carlos Ruiz, still preferred the cool stones and paving flags of the old buildings.

It was here, on a humid December morning that year, that he had chosen to meet the American visitor. As he sat at his oak desk, brought many years ago from Spain and almost black with age, Fr. Carlos toyed again with the letter of introduction requesting this meeting. It came from his Brother in Christ, the dean of Boston College; it was impossible to refuse, but curiosity is not a sin. What could the man want?

Paul Devereaux was shown in by a young novice. The provincial rose and crossed the room to greet him. The visitor was close to his own age, the biblical three score and ten: lean, fastidious in silk shirt, club tie and cream tropical suit. No jeans, or hair at the throat. Fr. Ruiz thought he had never met a Yankee spy before, but the Boston letter had been very frank.

"Father, I hesitate to ask at the outset but I must. May we regard everything said in this room as coming under the seal of the confessional?"

Fr. Ruiz inclined his head and gestured his guest to a Castilian chair, seated and backed in rawhide. He resumed his place behind his desk.

"How can I help you, my son?"

"I have been asked by my President, no less, to try to destroy the cocaine industry that is causing grievous damage to my country."

There was no further need to explain why he was in Colombia. The word "cocaine" explained it all.

"That has been tried many times before," said Fr. Ruiz. "Many times. But the appetite in your country is enormous. If there were not such a grievous appetite for the white powder, there would be no production."

"True," admitted the American, "a demand will always produce a supply. But the reverse is also true. A supply will always create a demand. Eventually. If the supply dies, the appetite will wither away."

"It did not work with Prohibition."

Devereaux was accustomed to the feint. Prohibition had been a disaster. It had simply created a huge underworld, which, after repeal, had moved into every other possible criminal activity. Over the years, the cost to the U.S. could be measured in trillions.

"We believe the comparison fails, Father. There are a thousand sources of a glass of wine or a dram of whisky."

He meant, But cocaine comes only from here. There was no need to say it.

"My son, we in the Society of Jesus try to be a force for good. But we have found by terrible experience that involvement in politics or matters of state is usually disastrous."

Devereaux had spent his life in the trade of espionage. He had long ago come to the view that the greatest intelligence-gathering agency in the world was the Roman Catholic Church. Through its omnipresence, it saw everything; through the confessional, it heard everything. And the idea that over a millennium and a half it had never supported or opposed emperors and princes was simply amusing.

"But where you see evil, you seek to fight it," he said.

The provincial was far too wily to fall for that one.

"What do you seek of the Society, my son?"

"In Colombia, you are everywhere, Father. Your pastoral work takes your young priests into every corner of every town and city . . ."

"And you wish them to become informers? For you? Far away in Washington. They, too, practice the seal of the confessional. What is told to them in that small place can never be revealed."

"And if a ship is sailing with a cargo of poison to destroy many young lives and leave a trail of misery in its wake, that knowledge, too, is sacred?"

"We both know the confessional is sacrosanct."

"But a ship cannot confess, Father. I give you my word no seaman will ever die. Interception and confiscation is absolutely the limit I have in mind."

He knew that he, too, would now have to confess to the sin of lying. But to another priest faraway. Not here. Not now.

"What you ask could be extremely risky; the men behind this trade, foul as it is, are utterly vicious and very violent."

For an answer, the American produced an item from his pocket. It was a small and very compact cell phone.

"Father, we were both raised long before these were invented. Now all the young have them, and most who are no longer young. To send a short message, there is no need to speak . . ."

"I know about texting, my son."

"Then you will know about encryption. These are encrypted far beyond the powers of the cartel ever to intercept. All I ask is the name of the ship with the poison onboard, heading for my homeland to destroy its young people. For profit. For money."

The Father Provincial permitted himself a thin smile.

"You are a good advocate, my son."

The Cobra had one last card to play.

"In the city of Cartagena is a statue to Saint Peter Claver of the Society of Jesus."

"Of course. We revere him."

"Hundreds of years ago, he fought against the evil of slavery. And the slave traders martyred him. Father, I beseech you. This trade in drugs is as evil as that in slaves. Both merchandise human misery. That which enslaves need not always be a man; it can be a narcotic. The slavers took the bodies of young people and abused them. Narcotics take the soul."

The Father Provincial stared for several minutes out of the window across the square of Simon Bolívar, a man who set people free.

"I wish to pray, my son. Can you return in two hours?"

Devereaux took a light lunch under the awning of a café in a street running off the square. When he returned, the leader of all Colombia's Jesuits had made his decision.

"I cannot order what you ask. But I can explain to my parish priests what you ask. So long as the seal of confession is never broken, they may decide for themselves. You may distribute your little machines."

124

■ ■ ■ ■

Of all his colleagues in the cartel, the one Alfredo Suárez had to work with most closely was José-María Largo, in charge of merchandising. It was a question of keeping track of every cargo, down to the last kilogram. Suárez could dispatch them, consignment by consignment, but it was vital to know how much arrived at the point of handover to the purchasing mafia and how much was intercepted by the forces of law and order.

Fortunately, every major intercept was immediately blazoned across the media by the FLO. They wanted the credit, kudos from their governments, always angling for larger budgets. Largo's rules were simple and ironclad. Big customers were allowed to pay fifty percent of the price of the cargo (and that was the cartel's price) on placement of an order. The balance would be owed after handover, which marked change of ownership. Smaller players had to provide one hundred percent as a single nonnegotiable deposit.

If the national gangs and mafias could charge astronomical fees at street level, that was their business. If they were careless or penetrated by police informants and lost their purchase, that, too, was their business. But confiscation of the cargo after delivery did not absolve them of the need to settle up.

It was when a foreign gang still owed the fifty percent balance, had lost their purchase to the police and refused to pay up, that enforcement was necessary. The Don was adamant about the value of terrible examples being set. And the cartel was truly paranoid about two things: theft of assets and informant betrayal. Neither was forgivable or forgettable, no matter what the cost of retribution. It had to be inflicted. That was the law of the Don . . . and it worked.

Only by conferring with his colleague Largo could Suárez know to the last kilo how much of what he shipped was intercepted before the point of handover.

Only this would show him what shipment methods had the highest chances of getting through and which the least.

Toward the end of 2010, he calculated that interception was running much as ever; between ten and fifteen percent. Given the telephone-number profits, this was quite acceptable. But he always lusted to bring the interception level down to single figures. If cocaine was intercepted while still in the possession of the cartel, the loss was wholly theirs. The Don did not like that.

Suárez's predecessor, now dismembered and decomposing under a new apartment block, had thrown his entire judgment, after the turn of the century a decade earlier, behind submarines. This ingenious idea involved the construction up hidden rivers of submersible hulls that, powered by a diesel engine, could take a crew of four, a cargo of up to ten tons, along with food and fuel, and then sink to periscope depth.

Even the best of them never went deep. They did not need to. All that showed above the water was a Perspex blister dome, with the captain's head peering out so that he could steer, and a tube to suck in fresh air for the engine and crew.

The idea was for these invisible submersibles to creep slowly but safely up the Pacific Coast from Colombia to northern Mexico and deliver huge quantities to the Mexican mafias, leaving them to smuggle it the rest of the way across the border into the USA. And they had worked . . . for a while. Then came the disaster.

The guiding genius behind their design and construction was Enrique Portocarrero, who masqueraded as a harmless shrimp fisherman out of Buenaventura down in the south on the Pacific Coast. Then Colonel Dos Santos had got him.

Whether he squealed under "pressure" or whether a search of his premises revealed traces, the main base of the submarine construction yards was discovered, and the Navy moved in. By the time Captain German Borrero had finished, sixty hulls in various stages of construction were smoking ruins. The loss to the cartel had been enormous.

The second mistake of Suárez's predecessor had been to send extremely high percentages of cargo to the U.S. and Europe by single mules, carrying one or two kilos each. It meant using thousands to carry just a couple of tons.

As Islamist fundamentalism caused the tightening of security in the Western world, more and more passenger suitcases were X-rayed and their illegal contents discovered. This led to a switch to belly cargoes. Idiots prepared to take the risk would numb their gullets with novocaine and then swallow up to a hundred pellets containing about ten grams each.

Some sustained an internal burst and ended their lives frothing on the airport concourse floor. Others were reported by sharp-eyed stewardesses as being unable to take food or drink on a long-haul flight. They were taken aside, given syrup of figs and given a lavatory with a filter screen at the bottom. American and European jails were filled to bursting with them. Still, over eighty percent got through by sheer volume of numbers and the West's obsession with civil rights. Then the predecessor to Suárez had his second stroke of bad luck.

It was pioneered in Manchester, England, and it worked. It was a new "virtual strip search" X-ray machine that would not only reveal the passenger as if naked but also reveal implants, insertions into the anus and the contents of the entrails. The machine was so silent that it could be installed below the guichet occupied by the passport control officer so that the presenter of the passport could be observed from thorax to calves by another officer in another room. As more and more Western airports and sea terminals installed them, the rate of intercept of the mules shot upward.

Finally, the Don had had enough. He ordered a change of chief executive of that division — permanently. Suárez had taken over.

He was a dedicated big-cargo man, and his figures showed clearly which were the best routes. For the U.S. it was by surface craft or aircraft up through the Caribbean to deliver to northern Mexico or the southern littoral of the U.S., with the cargoes carried mainly by merchant marine freighters for most of the way, and a final, at-sea transfer to private craft of the sort that teem along both coasts, from fishermen to speedboats to private yachts to leisure boats.

For Europe, he hugely favored the new routes; not direct from the Caribbean to Western and Northern Europe, where interceptions topped twenty percent, but due east to the ring of failed states that comprised the West African coast. With the cargoes changing hands there and the cartel paid off, it was up to the buyers to break the consignments down and filter them north over the deserts to the Mediterranean shore and then over to Southern Europe. And the destination he favored most was the small, ex-Portuguese, civil-war-ravaged failed state and narco-hellhole of Guinea-Bissau.

This was exactly the conclusion Cal Dexter was coming to as he sat in Vienna with the Canadian narco-hunter Walter Kemp of the United Nations Office on Drugs and Crime. The figures on UNODC tallied very closely with those of Tim Manhire down in Lisbon.

Starting only a few years earlier as the recipient of twenty percent of Colombian cocaine heading for Europe, West Africa was now taking over fifty. What neither man sharing a café table in the Prater Park sun could know was that Alfredo Suárez had increased that percentage to seventy.

There were seven coastal republics in West Africa that qualified for the police description "of interest": Senegal, the Gambia, Guinea-Bissau, Guinea-Conakry (ex-French), Sierra Leone, Liberia and Ghana.

After being flown or sailed across the Atlantic to West Africa, the cocaine filtered north by a hundred different routes and ruses. Some came by fishing boat, up the coast to Morocco, and then followed the old cannabis run. Other cargoes were flown across the Sahara to the North African coast and thence by small craft to the Spanish mafia across the Pillars of Hercules or to the Calabrian Ndrangheta waiting at the port of Gioia.

Some shipments went by exhausting land train right across the Sahara from south to north. Of extreme interest was the Libyan airline Afriqiyah, which links twelve major West African cities to Tripoli, just across the water from Europe.

"When it comes to freighting northward

to Europe," said Kemp, "they are all in it together. But when it comes to receiving from across the Atlantic, Guinea-Bissau is premier league."

"Perhaps I should go and have a look," mused Dexter.

"If you do go," said the Canadian, "be careful. Have a good cover story. And it might be wise to take some muscle. Of course, the best camouflage is to be black. Can you provide that?"

"No, not this side of the pond."

Kemp scribbled a name and number on a paper napkin.

"Try him in London. A friend of mine. He's with SOCA. And good luck. You'll need it."

Cal Dexter had not heard of the British Serious and Organised Crime Agency, but he was about to. He was back at the Montcalm Hotel by sundown.

Because of the former colonial connection, the Portuguese airline TAP is the only convenient carrier. Duly visaed, vaccinated and injected against everything the School of Tropical Medicine could think of and attested to by letter from BirdLife International as a foremost ornithologist specializing in the study of wading birds that

132

winter in West Africa, "Dr." Calvin Dexter was a week later flying out of Lisbon on the TAP night flight to Guinea-Bissau.

Sitting behind him were two corporals of the British Parachute Regiment. SOCA, he had learned, grouped just about every agency concerned with big crime and anti-terrorism under one banner. Within the network of contacts available to a friend of Walter Kemp's was a senior soldier who had spent most of his career with the regiment's Third Battalion, Three Para. It was he who had found Jerry and Bill based at the Colchester HQ. They had volunteered.

They were not Jerry and Bill anymore. They were Kwamé and Kofi. Their passports said they were firmly Ghanaian, and further paperwork swore they worked with BirdLife International in Accra. In fact, they were as British as Windsor Castle, but both had parents who hailed from Grenada. So long as no one interrogated them in fluent ga or ewe or Ashanti, they would do fine. They also spoke no Creole or Portuguese, but they were definitely African to look at.

It was after midnight and pitch-black when the TAP airliner touched down at Bissau Airport. Most passengers were going on to São Tomé and only a tiny trickle veered away from the transit lounge for passport control. Dexter led the way.

The passport officer scanned every page in the new Canadian passport, noted the Guinea visa, palmed the twenty-euro note and nodded him through. He gestured at his two companions.

"Avec moi," he said, adding, *"Con migo."*

French is not Portuguese, and neither is Spanish, but the meaning was clear. And he beamed good humor all around. Beaming usually works. A senior officer stepped forward.

"Qu'est-que vous faites en Guinée?" he asked.

Dexter feigned delight. He delved in his shoulder bag for a fistful of brochures featuring herons, spoonbills and others of the seven hundred thousand waterbirds that overwinter in Guinea-Bissau's vast swamps and wetlands. The officer's eyes glazed over with boredom. He waved them all through.

Outside there were no taxis. But there was a truck and a driver, and a fifty-euro note goes a long way down there.

"Hotel Malaika?" said Dexter hopefully. The driver nodded.

As they approached the city, Dexter noticed it was almost entirely black. Only a few points of light showed. Army curfew? No; there is no electricity. Only buildings with private generators have light after dark or power at any time. Happily, the Malaika Hotel was one. The three checked in and retired for what was left of the night. Just before dawn, someone shot the President.

It was Project Cobra's computer expert Jeremy Bishop who first spotted the name. Just as those obsessed by general-knowledge quizzes will prowl through dictionaries, encyclopedias and atlases vacuuming up facts they will never be asked, Bishop, who had no social life, spent his spare time prowling through cyberspace. Not surfing the Internet — that was far too simple. He had the habit of hacking effortlessly and invisibly into other people's databases to see what was there.

On a late Saturday evening when most of Washington was out enjoying the start of the festive season, he sat in front of a console and penetrated the arrivals and departures lists logged at Bogotá Airport. There was a name that cropped up repeatedly. Whoever he was, he flew from Bogotá to Madrid regularly, every fortnight.

His returns were less than three days later, giving him no more than fifty hours in the Spanish capital. Not enough for a vacation, too much for a stopover toward a further destination.

Bishop ran his name against the compendium of those known to be involved in any possible aspect of cocaine as supplied by the Colombian police to the DEA and copied to Cobra HQ. It was not there.

He broke into the database of Iberia Airlines, which the man used every time he traveled. The name came up under "frequent flier," with special privileges like priority status on overbooked flights. He always traveled first class and his return flight reservations were prebooked automatically unless canceled by him.

Bishop used his overriding clearance to contact the DEA people in Bogotá and even the British SOCA team in the same city. Neither knew him, but the DEA helpfully added that, from local reference books, he was a lawyer with an upscale practice that never did criminal-court work. Having run into the wall, but still curious, Bishop told Devereaux.

The Cobra absorbed the information, but did not think it merited the expenditure of much further effort. As a long shot, it was a mite too long. Still, a simple inquiry in Madrid would do no harm. Acting via the DEA team in Spain, Devereaux placed a request that on the man's next visit he be discreetly tailed. He, the Cobra, would appreciate knowing where he stayed, where he went, what he did and whom he met. With much rolling of eyeballs, the Americans in Madrid agreed to call in a favor from their Spanish colleagues.

The anti-drug unit in Madrid is the Unidad de Droga y Crimen Organizado, or UDYCO. The request was dumped on the desk of Inspector Francisco "Paco" Ortega.

Like all police, Ortega reckoned he was overworked, underequipped and definitely underpaid. Still, if the *Yanquis* wanted a Colombian tailed, he could hardly refuse. If the UK was the biggest single user of cocaine in Europe, Spain was the biggest arrival point and was equipped with a huge and vicious underworld. With their enormous resources, the Americans sometimes intercepted a piece of pure gold and shared it with UDYCO. A note was made that when, in ten days, the Colombian arrived again, he would be quietly tailed.

Neither Bishop, Devereaux nor Ortega could know that Julio Luz was the single member of the Hermandad who had never come to the attention of the Colombian police. Colonel Dos Santos knew exactly who all the others were, but not the lawyer and money launderer.

■ ■ ■ ■

By midday, after the arrival of Cal Dexter and his team in Bissau city, the affair of the dead President had been cleared up and the panic subsided. It was not another coup d'état after all.

The shooter had been the lover of the old tyrant's much younger wife. By midmorning both had disappeared into the bush far up-country, never to be seen again. Tribal solidarity would protect them as if they had never existed.

The President had been of the Papel tribe; his trophy wife was Balanta and so was her boyfriend. The Army was also mainly Balanta and had no intention of hunting down one of its own. The President had not been very popular. Another would eventually be chosen. It was the Army commander and chief of staff who held the real power.

Dexter rented a white SUV from Mavegro Trading, whose helpful Dutch proprietor put him in touch with a man with a small cabin cruiser to rent. It came with outboard engine and trailer. It would certainly be capable of cruising the creeks and inlets of the offshore Bijagós Archipelago looking for wading birds.

Finally, Dexter managed to rent a detached bungalow opposite the sports stadium recently erected by China, which was quietly recolonizing great tracts of Africa. He and his two helpers moved out of the Malaika and into their cottage.

On the drive from one to the other, they were caught up by a Jeep Wrangler which swerved across their path at an intersection. In just two days, Dexter had learned there were no traffic police and the lights rarely functioned.

As the SUV and the Jeep swerved within inches of each other, the front passenger in the Wrangler stared at Dexter from a few inches away but behind wraparound black shades. Like the driver, he was not African nor European. Swarthy, black-haired, with a pigtail and chains of gold "bling" around the neck. Colombian.

The Jeep had a chrome frame above the cab on which was mounted a rack of four powerful searchlights. Dexter knew the explanation. Many cocaine carriers came in by sea, never reaching the shabby little port of Bissau itself but transferring the bales out in the creeks among the mangrove islands.

Other carriers came by air, either to be dropped into the sea close to a waiting fishing boat or flown on into the hinterland. Guinea-Bissau's twenty-year guerrilla fight for independence from Portugal and fifteen-year civil war had bequeathed up to fifty airstrips cut out of the bush. Sometimes the coke planes landed there before flying back to the airport, empty and "clean," to refuel.

A night landing was safer, but as none of the bush strips had any laid-on power, they had no lights. But a receiving party of four or five pickups could use their roof-rack lighting to provide a brilliantly illuminated landing path for the few minutes needed. That was what Dexter could explain to his two paratroop escorts.

At the pestilential Kapoor shipyard south of Goa, the work on the two grain ships was in full flow. The man in charge was a Canadian-Scot named Duncan McGregor who had spent a lifetime in the shipyards of the tropics and had a skin like terminal jaundice with eyes to match. One day, if the swamp fever did not get him, the whisky would.

The Cobra liked retired experts as hirelings. They tended to have forty years on the job, no family ties and needed the money. McGregor knew what was wanted but not why. With the fee he was getting, he had no intention of speculating, and certainly not of asking.

His welders and cutters were local, his outfitter imported Singaporeans, whom he knew well. For their accommodation, he had leased and brought down a row of motor homes; they would certainly not tolerate the hovels of the local Goans.

The exteriors of both grain ships were to remain, he had been instructed. Only the interiors of the five enormous holds were to be converted. The farthest forward was to be a brig for prisoners, though he did not know that. It would have bunks, latrines, a galley for cooking, showers, and a wardroom with air-conditioning and even TV.

Next was another living area with the same but better. One day, either British Special Boat Service commandos or American Navy SEALs would live here.

The third hold needed to be smaller so that its neighbor could be large. The steel bulkhead between holds 3 and 4 had to be cut out and moved. This was being fitted out as an all-purpose workshop. The second-to-last hold, up against the sterncastle, was left bare. It would contain very fast inflatable RIB raiding craft powered by huge motors. This hold would have the only derrick above it.

141

The largest hold was taking the most work. On its floor, a steel plate was being made, which would be hoisted vertically by four hydraulic winches, one at each corner, until it was level with the deck above. Whatever would be strapped to that rising floor would then be out in the fresh air. In fact, it would be the unit's attack helicopter.

All through the winter under the still-blazing Karnatakan sun, the torches hissed, drills bored, metal clanged, hammers smashed and two harmless grain ships were turned into floating death traps. And far away, the names were changed as ownership passed to an invisible company managed by Thame of Singapore. Just before completion, those names would go on each stern, the crews would be flown back to take them over and they would steam away to whatever work awaited them on the other side of the world.

Cal Dexter spent a week acclimatizing before he took the boat into the heart of the Bijagós. He plastered the SUV with decals he had brought with him, advertising BirdLife International and the American Audubon Society. Lying prominently on the backseat for any passing observer to see were copies of the latest reports from the

Ghana Wildlife Society and the can't-do-without *Birds of Western Africa* by Borrow and Demey.

In fact, after the brush with the Wrangler at the intersection, two swarthy men were indeed sent to the bungalow to snoop. They returned to tell their masters the bird-watchers were harmless idiots. In the heart of enemy territory, "idiot" is the best cover there is.

Dexter's first chore was to find a place for his boat. He took his team west of Bissau city deep into the bush toward Quinhámel, the capital of the Papel tribe. Beyond Quinhámel, he found the Mansôa River leading down to the sea, and, on its bank, the hotel and restaurant Mar Azul. Here he slipped the cabin cruiser into the river and billeted Jerry in the hotel to look after it. Before he and Bill left, they had a sumptuous lobster lunch with Portuguese wine.

"Beats Colchester in winter," agreed the two paras. The spying on the offshore islands began the next day.

There are fourteen main Bijagós, but the entire archipelago comprises eighty-eight small blobs of land between twenty and thirty miles off the Guinea-Bissau coast. Anti-cocaine agencies had photographed them from space, but no one had ever penetrated them in a small boat.

Dexter discovered they were all swampy, hot, mangrove filled and feverish, but four or five, facing farthest out to sea, had been graced with luxurious snow-white villas on gleaming beaches, each with large dish aerials, state-of-the-art technology and radio masts to pick up signals from the faraway MTN service provider for mobile phones. Each villa had a dock and a speedboat. These were the exile residences of the Colombians.

For the rest, he counted twenty-three hamlets of fishermen, pigs and goats, leading a subsistence existence. But there were also fishing camps where foreigners came to rape the country's teeming fish reserves. There were twenty-meter canoes from Guinea-Conakry, Sierra Leone and Senegal with ice, food and fuel for fifteen days away from base.

These served South Korean and Chinese mother ships whose refrigerators could freeze the catch all the way back to the East. He watched up to forty canoes serving a single mother ship. But the cargo he really wanted to watch came on the sixth night.

He had berthed the cruiser up a narrow creek, crossed an island on foot and hidden himself in the mangroves by the shore. The

American and the two British paras lay covered in camouflage scrim with powerful binoculars as the sun went down ahead of them in the west. Out of the last red rays came a freighter that was most definitely not a fishing mother ship. She slipped between two islands, and the chain clattered as her anchor went down. Then the canoes appeared.

They were local, not foreign, and not rigged for fishing. Five of them, each with a crew of four natives, and an Hispanic in the stern of two of them.

On the side rail of the freighter, men appeared lugging bales bound with stout cord. The bales were heavy enough that it needed four men to lift just one over the side and lower it to a waiting canoe, which rocked and sagged as it took the weight.

There was no need for secrecy. The crew laughed and shouted in the high piping tones of the East. One of the Hispanics clambered aboard to converse with the captain. A suitcase of money changed hands, the fee for the Atlantic crossing, but a mere fraction of the eventual yield in Europe.

Guessing the weight of the bales and counting the number, Cal Dexter calculated two tons of Colombian pure had been unloaded as he watched through his binoculars. The darkness deepened. The freighter put on some of her lights. Lanterns appeared on the canoes. Finally, the transaction done, the canoes gunned up their outboards and chugged away. The freighter hauled up her anchor and swung on the ebb tide before turning for sea.

Dexter caught sight of the red/blue flag of South Korea and her name. The *Hae Shin*. He gave them all an hour to get clear, then motored back upriver to the Mar Azul.

"Ever seen a hundred million sterling, guys?"

"No, boss," said Bill, using the paratroop vernacular of a corporal to an officer.

"Well, you have now. That was the value of two tons of coke."

They looked glum.

"Lobster supper. Our last night."

That cheered them up. Twenty-four hours later, they had returned the cottage, boat and SUV and flown out, via Lisbon for London. The night they left, men in black balaclavas raided their villa, ransacked and then torched it. One of the Bijagós natives had seen a white man among the mangroves.

The report of Inspector Ortega was succinct and confined to the facts. It was therefore excellent. He referred to the Colombian lawyer Julio Luz only as "the target" throughout.

"The target arrived on the daily scheduled Iberia flight landing at 10:00. He was identified in the jetway from the first-class cabin door to the underground shuttle train running from Terminal 4 to the main concourse. One of my men in Iberia cabin-crew uniform tailed him all the way. Target took no notice of him nor took any precautions at being followed. He carried one attaché case and one grip. No main baggage.

"He checked through passport control and the Green Channel in customs and was not stopped. A limousine was waiting for him; a driver outside the customs hall with a notice saying 'Villa Real.' This is a major Madrid hotel. It sends limousines to the airport for privileged guests.

"A plainclothes colleague of mine was with him all the way and in the car that tailed the hotel limo. He met no one and spoke to no one until arrival at the Villa Real, Plaza de las Cortes 10.

"He checked in to a warm welcome and was heard to ask for his 'usual room,' which he was assured was ready for him. He retired to it, ordered a light salad lunch from room service at midday and appeared to sleep off the effects of the overnight flight. He took tea in the guests' café called East 47 and at one point was greeted by the hotel director Señor Felix Garcia.

"He retired to his room again, but was overheard to ask for a table for dinner in the gourmet restaurant on the first floor. One of my men, listening at his door, heard the sound of a football match, which he seemed to be watching on TV. As we were instructed under no circumstances to alert him, we were not able to check on phone calls in or out. (We could of course obtain these, but that would alert the staff.)

"At nine he descended for dinner. He was joined by a young woman, aged early twenties, student type. It was suspected she might be what you call a 'party girl,' but there was no hint of this between them. He produced a letter from his inside breast pocket. High-quality cream paper. She thanked him, lodged it in her purse and left. He returned to his room and spent the night alone.

"He took breakfast in the interior patio, also on the first floor, at eight, and was joined by the same young woman (see below). This time, she did not stay but handed over another letter, took one coffee and left.

"I had assigned an extra man, and he followed the young woman. She is a certain Letizia Arenal, aged twenty-three, studying fine arts at the Universidad Complutense. She has a modest studio flat in Moncloa, near the campus, lives alone on a modest allowance and seems to be completely respectable.

"The target left the hotel by cab at ten a.m. and was taken to the Banco Guzman on Calle Serrano. This is a small private bank serving high-end clients of which nothing bad is (or was) known. Target spent the morning inside and seemingly lunched with the directors. He left at three p.m., but at the door the bank staff helped him with two large hard-framed Samsonite suitcases. He could not carry them, but he did not need to.

"A black Mercedes arrived as if summoned and two men got out. They stowed both heavy cases in the trunk and drove off. Target did not accompany them but hailed a cab. My man did manage to photograph both men with his mobile phone. These have been identified. Both are known gangsters. We were not able to tail the Mercedes, because it was not expected and my man was on foot. His car was waiting around the corner. So he stayed with the target.

"Target returned to his hotel, took tea again, watched TV again, dined again (this time alone, attended only by the maître d'hotel Francisco Paton). He slept alone and left for the airport by hotel limousine at nine. He bought a liter of best-quality cognac in the duty-free, waited in the first-class lounge, boarded his flight and took off for Bogotá at 12:20 on schedule.

"In view of the appearance of two thugs from the Galicia gang, we would now like to take a keen interest in Señor Luz as and when he appears again. Clearly, the suitcases could contain enough five-hundred-euro notes to represent a settlement of accounts between Colombia and our own major importers. Please advise."

"What do you think, Calvin?" asked Devereaux, as he welcomed Dexter back from Africa.

"It's a slam dunk the lawyer is part of the cartel's money-laundering operation, but it would seem only for Spain. Or maybe other European gangs bring their dues to Serrano Street for debt settlement. But I would prefer the UDYCO to hold fire for one last trip next time."

"They could take the two gangsters, the bent lawyer, the money and corrupt bank in one swoop. Why not?"

"Loose ends. That letter, that girl. Why is he playing postman? And for whom?" Dexter mused.

"Someone's niece. A favor for a friend."

"No, Mr. Devereaux. There are mails, recorded delivery if you insist, or e-mails, faxes, texts, phone calls. This is personal, highly secretive. Next time friend Luz lands in Madrid, I'd like to be there. With a small team."

"So we ask our Spanish friends to hold off until you are ready? Why so cautious?"

"Never frighten shy game," said the former soldier. "Take the animal with one shot through the forehead. No mess. No misses. No half shots. No wounding. If we take Luz now, we will never know who is sending cream manila envelopes to whom and why. That would worry me for a long time."

Paul Devereaux regarded the former Tunnel Rat thoughtfully.

"I am beginning to understand why the Vietcong never got you in the Iron Triangle. You still think like a jungle creature."

CHAPTER 5

Guy Dawson lined up, braked gently, studied the flickering array of instruments once again, glanced at the tarmac glittering under the sun, made his request to the tower and waited for the "Clear for takeoff."

When it came, he eased the two throttles forward. Behind him, two Rolls-Royce Spey jet engines lifted their tone from a whine to a roaring howl, and the old Blackburn Buccaneer started to roll. It was a moment the veteran flier never ceased to savor.

At liftoff speed, the former naval light bomber became light to the touch, the wheel rumble ceased and she tilted up toward the wide blue African sky. Far behind, growing quickly smaller, Thunder City, the private-aviation enclave of Cape Town International, dropped away. Still climbing, Dawson set his first course for Windhoek, Namibia, the short and easy leg of the long haul north.

Dawson was only a year older than the veteran warplane he flew. He'd been born in 1961, when the Buccaneer was a prototype. It began its extraordinary career the following year when it entered operational squadron service with the British Fleet Air Arm. Originally designed to challenge the Soviet Sverdlov-class cruisers, it turned out to be so good at its job that it remained in service until 1994.

The Fleet Air Arm flew it off carriers until 1978. By 1969, the envious Royal Air Force had developed the shore-based version, which finally was eased out in 1994. In the meanwhile, South Africa had bought sixteen, which flew operationally for them until 1991. What even aircraft buffs seldom knew was that it was the vehicle that carried South Africa's atomic bombs until, by the eve of the "Rainbow Revolution," white South Africa had destroyed all six of them (apart from three gutted as museum pieces) and pensioned off the Buccaneer. What Guy Dawson flew that January morning 2011 was one of the last three flying in the world, rescued by warplane enthusiasts, maintained for tourist rides and kept at Thunder City.

Still climbing, Dawson turned away from the blue South Atlantic and headed almost due north toward the barren ocher sands of

Namaqualand and Namibia.

· His ex–Royal Air Force S.2 version would climb to 35,000 feet and fly at Mach .8, drinking eighty pounds of fuel every minute. But for this short leg, he would have plenty. With eight inboard tanks full, plus the bomb-bay-door tank and two more under-wing fuel tanks, his Bucc could carry her full load of 23,000 pounds, giving her a range at optimum power setting of 2,266 nautical miles. But Windhoek was well under 1,000.

Guy Dawson was a happy man. As a young pilot in the South African Air Force in 1985, he had been assigned to 24 Squadron, the cream of the cream despite the faster French Mirage fighters also in service. But the Buccs, already veterans of twenty years, were special.

One of its strange features was its totally enclosed bomb bay with its rotating door. On a light bomber that size, most ordnance was carried under the wings. Having the bombs inside left the exterior clean of drag and improved range and speed.

What the South Africans did was to enlarge the bomb bay even more and install their atom bombs, secretly prepared over years with Israeli help. A variation was to incorporate a huge extra fuel tank in that hidden bay and give the Bucc unmatchable range. It was the range and endurance, giving the Bucc hours of "loiter time" high in the sky, that had clinched it for the noncommittal, wiry American named Dexter who had visited Thunder City in October.

Dawson did not really want to lease his "baby" at all, but the global credit crunch had reduced his pension investments to a fraction of what he had expected for his retirement and the American's offer was too tempting. A one-year lease agreement was clinched for a sum that would get Guy Dawson out of his hole.

He had chosen to fly his own plane all the way to Britain. He knew there was a private group of Bucc enthusiasts based at the old RAF World War II field at Scampton, Lincolnshire. They, too, were restoring a couple of Buccaneers, but they were not ready yet. This he knew because the two groups of enthusiasts were always in touch, and the American knew it, too.

Dawson's trip would be long and arduous. The former navigator's cockpit behind him had been used for fee-paying tourists, but thanks to GPS technology he would fly alone from Windhoek far out over the South Atlantic to the tiny speck of Ascension Island, a British-owned outcrop in the midst of nowhere.

An overnight and a second refuel would see him heading north again to the airport at Sal in the Cape Verde Islands, then to Spanish Gran Canaria and finally to Scampton, UK.

Guy Dawson knew his American patron had set up lines of credit in each stopover to cover fuel and overnight expenses. He did not know why Dexter had chosen the veteran Navy attack plane. There were three reasons.

Dexter had searched high and low, and especially in his native America, where there was an entire culture of enthusiasm for old warplanes that were maintained in flying condition. He had finally settled on the South African Buccaneer because she was obscure. She would pass for an old out-of-commission museum piece being ferried from one place to another for display purposes.

She was simple to maintain and rugged to the point of being almost indestructible. And she could stay up there for hours on end.

What only he and the Cobra knew, as Guy Dawson brought his baby back to the land of her birth, was that this Buccaneer was not going to a museum at all. She was going back to war.

When Señor Julio Luz landed at Terminal 4, Barajas Airport, Madrid, in February 2011, the reception committee was somewhat larger.

Cal Dexter was already there idling in the concourse with Inspector Paco Ortega, quietly watching the stream of passengers emerging from the customs-hall doors. Both men were at the newsstand, Dexter with his back to the arriving target, Ortega riffling through a magazine.

Years earlier, after the Army, after the law degree, working as a Legal Aid counselor in New York, Cal Dexter had found he had so many Hispanic "clients" that it would be useful to master Spanish. So he had. Ortega was impressed. It was rare to find a *Yanqui* who spoke decent Castilian. It made it unnecessary for him to struggle in English. Without moving, he murmured:

"That's him."

Dexter had no problem with identification. His colleague Bishop had downloaded a membership portrait from the archives of the Bogotá Law Association.

The Colombian stuck to his normal procedure. He boarded the hotel limo, clung on to his attaché case, allowed the chauf-

157

feur to stow the grip in the trunk and relaxed on the drive to Plaza de la Cortés. The police unmarked vehicle overtook the limo, and Dexter, who had checked in earlier, was at the hotel first.

Dexter had brought to Madrid a team of three, all borrowed from the FBI. The Bureau had been curious, but all questions and objections were overridden by presidential authority. One of the team could go through any locking system. And fast. Dexter had insisted on speed. He had described the sort of problems they might meet, and the lockpicker had shrugged in dismissal. Was that all?

The second man could open envelopes, scan the contents in seconds and reseal the envelope invisibly. The third was just the sentinel. They were not billeted at the Villa Real but two hundred yards away, on permanent call by cell phone.

Dexter was in the lobby when the Colombian arrived. He knew the lawyer's room and had checked out the access. They were lucky. It was at the end of a long corridor from the elevator doors, lessening the chance of a sudden and unexpected interruption.

When it comes to watching a target, Dexter had long known the clichéd man in the trench coat pretending to read a newspaper in the corner or pointlessly standing in a doorway was as noticeable as a rhino on the vicarage lawn. He preferred to hide in plain sight.

He was in a loud shirt, hunched over his laptop, taking a cell phone call in too loud a voice from someone he called "honey bunny." Luz glanced at him for a second, summed him up and lost all interest.

The man was like a metronome. He checked in, took a light lunch in his room and remained there for a good siesta. At four he reappeared in the East 47 café, ordered a pot of Earl Grey and reserved his table for dinner. It seemed the fact that there were other superlative restaurants in Madrid — and that the October evening, though crisp, was fine — eluded him.

Minutes later, Dexter and his team were on his corridor. The sentinel remained by the elevator doors. Every time one came up and stopped with doors open, the men would indicate he was heading down. With polite smiles all around, the doors would close. When the elevator came down, the theater was in reverse. There was no pathetic tying and retying of shoelaces.

It took the locksmith eighteen seconds and a very clever piece of technology to penetrate the electronic door to the suite. Inside, the three worked fast. The grip had been neatly unpacked and its contents hung in the closet or laid carefully in drawers. The attaché case was on a chest.

It had locks protected by rollers with numbers 0 to 9. The locksmith attached a listening device with a stethoscope in his ears, rolled the drums carefully and listened. One by one, the numbers achieved their designated slot, and the brass catches flipped upward.

The contents were mainly paperwork. The material scanner went to work. Everything was copied onto a memory stick by hands in white silk gloves. There was no letter. Dexter, also in gloves, flipped through all the pockets in the lid. No letter. He nodded to the cabinets, of which there were half a dozen in the suite. The room safe was found in the cupboard beneath the plasma screen.

It was a good safe, but it was not designed to resist the technology, skill and experience of the man who trained and practiced at the Quantico break-in laboratory. The code turned out to be the first four figures of Julio Luz's membership number at the Bogotá Bar. The letter was inside; long, stiff, cream.

It was sealed by its own gum, but a strip

of clear adhesive tape was laid over the flap as well. The paperwork man studied it for several seconds, took a piece of technology from his own work case and appeared to iron the seal as one would press the collar of a shirt. When he was done, the envelope's flap lifted without resistance.

White gloves eased out the three folded sheets. With a magnifying glass, the copier checked for any strand of human hair or ultra-fine cotton that might be included as a trap-warning sign. There was none. The sender clearly relied on the lawyer to hand his epistle over intact to Señorita Letizia Arenal.

The letter was copied and replaced; the envelope resealed after the application of a clear and colorless liquid. The letter was placed back in the safe exactly as it had lain before disturbance; the safe closed and reset exactly as it had been. Then the three packed their kit and left.

At the elevator doors, the sentinel shook his head. No sign of target. At that moment, the elevator rose from below and stopped. The four men slipped quickly through the doors to the stairwell and went down on foot. Just as well; the doors opened to disgorge Señor Luz, heading back to his room for a scented bath and some TV before dinner.

Dexter and his team repaired to his own room, where the contents of the attaché case were downloaded. He would give Inspector Ortega everything in the case except the letter, which he now read for himself.

He did not attend dinner but stationed two of his team across the room from the Luz table. They reported that the girl arrived, dined, took the letter, thanked the messenger and left.

The next morning, Cal Dexter took the breakfast shift. He watched Luz take a table for two by the wall. The girl joined him, handing over her own letter, which Luz placed in his inside breast pocket. After a quick coffee, the girl smiled her gratitude and left.

Dexter waited until the Colombian departed, then, before the staff could reach the vacated table, he himself passed it and stumbled. He brought the Colombian's almost-empty coffeepot to the carpet. Cursing at his own clumsiness, he took a napkin from the table to dab the stain. A waiter rushed up to insist that that was his job. As the young man bent his head, Dexter slipped a napkin over the cup the girl had used, enveloped it and stuffed both into his trouser pocket.

After more apologies and assurances of *"De nada, señor,"* he walked out of the breakfast room.

"I wish," said Paco Ortega as they sat and watched Julio Luz disappear into the Banco Guzman, "that you would let us pick them all up."

"The day will come, Paco," said the American. "You will have your hour. Just not yet. This money laundering is big. Very big. There are other banks in other countries. We want them all. Let us coordinate and grab the lot."

Ortega grunted his assent. Like any detective, he had carried through stakeout operations that had lasted months before the final pounce. Patience was essential but hugely frustrating.

Dexter was lying. He knew of no other laundering operations like the Luz-Guzman linkage. But he could not divulge the whirlwind that Project Cobra was going to unleash when the cold-eyed man in Washington was ready.

And now he wanted to get home. He had read the letter in his room. It was long, tender, concerned for the young woman's safety and well-being and signed simply "Papá."

He doubted Julio Luz would now be

parted from the reply letter all day or night. Perhaps when he was in the first-class cabin back to Bogotá, he might fall asleep, but to do a "lift" of the attaché case above his head with the cabin crew looking on was out of the question.

What Dexter wanted to discover before any pounce was made was simply this: who was Letizia Arenal and who was Papá?

Winter was loosening its grip on Washington when Cal Dexter returned at the beginning of March. The forests cloaking those parts of Virginia and Maryland next to the capital were about to clothe themselves in a haze of green.

From the Kapoor yard south of Goa, a message had come from McGregor, who was still sweating it out among the stench of toxic chemicals and malarial heat. The two grain ships were close to their transformation. They would be ready for handover in their new role in May, he said.

He presumed their new role would be what he had been told. This was that a mega-wealthy American consortium wished to enter the treasure-hunting world with two ships equipped for deep-sea diving and wreck recovery. The accommodation would be for the divers and surface crew, the workshops for the servicing of their rigs and the large hold for a small spotter helicopter. It was all very plausible; it was just not true.

The final completion of the transformation from grain merchant to Q-ship would take place at sea. That was when heavily armed marine commandos would fill the berths, and the workshop/armories would contain some seriously dangerous kit. He was told he was doing a great job, and the two merchant marine crews would fly in at handover.

The paperwork was long since in place, should anyone search. The former ships had disappeared, and the two about to sail were the reconditioned MV *Chesapeake* and the MV *Balmoral.* They were owned by a company based in a law office in Aruba, flew the (convenience) flag of that tiny island and would be chartered to carry grain from the wheat-rich north to the hungry south. Their real ownership and purpose were invisible.

The laboratories of the FBI had produced a perfect DNA profile of the young woman in Madrid who had handled the coffee cup in the Villa Real. Cal Dexter had no doubt that she was Colombian, already confirmed by Inspector Ortega. But there were hundreds of Colombian youngsters studying in

Madrid. What Dexter craved was a matcher to that DNA.

In theory, at least fifty percent of the DNA should have derived from the father, and he was convinced "Papá" was in Colombia. And who was he who could ask a major player in the cocaine world, albeit a "technical," to play postman for him? And why could he not use the mails? It was a long shot, but he put the request to Colonel Dos Santos, intelligence chief of the anti-drug division of the Policía Judicial. While waiting for a response, he made two quick journeys.

Off the northeast shore of the coast of Brazil is an obscure archipelago of twenty-one small islands of which the main one gives its name to the group: Fernando de Noronha. It is only ten kilometers by three and a half, its total area twenty-six square kilometers. The only town is Vila dos Remédios.

It was once a prison island like France's Devil's Island, and the thick native forests were cut down to prevent the prisoners building rafts to escape. Shrub and scrub replaced the trees. Some wealthy Brazilians had away-from-it-all holiday villas there, but it was the airfield that interested Dexter. Built in 1942 by the U.S. Army Air Force

Transport Command, it would make a perfect site for a USAF unit operating Predator or Global Hawk drones, with their amazing capacity to loiter for hours aloft, looking down with cameras, radars and heat sensors. He flew in as a Canadian tourist resort developer, had a look, confirmed his suspicion and flew back out again. His second visit was to Colombia.

By 2009, President Uribe had effectively crushed the FARC terrorist movement which really specialized in kidnap and ransom demands. But his anti-cocaine efforts had been mainly offset by Don Diego Esteban and the mightily efficient cartel he had created.

In that year, he had offended his hard-left neighbors in both Venezuela and Bolivia by inviting American forces into Colombia to lend their superlative technology to help him. Facilities were offered at seven Colombian military bases. One of these was at Malambo, right on the northern coast by Barranquilla. Dexter went in as a serious defense writer with Pentagon approval.

Being in the country, he saw the chance to fly up to Bogotá and meet the formidable Colonel Dos Santos. The U.S. Army ran him up to Barranquilla Airport, and he caught the shuttle up to the capital. Between the still-warm tropical coast to the city in the mountains, the temperature dropped twenty degrees.

Neither the chief of the American DEA operation nor the leader of the British SOCA team in Bogotá knew who Dexter was or what the Cobra was preparing, but both had been advised, from their HQs on Army Navy Drive and the Albert Embankment, to cooperate. They all spoke fluent Spanish, and Dos Santos had perfect English. He was surprised when it was the stranger who mentioned a DNA sample that had been submitted a fortnight earlier.

"Strange that you should call at this moment," said the youthful and dynamic Colombian detective. "I got a match this morning."

His explanation of how the match was made was stranger than Dexter's arrival, which Dos Santos viewed as a mere coincidence. DNA technology had come late to Colombia due to the parsimony of governments prior to the presidency of Álvaro Uribe. He had increased the budgets.

But Dos Santos read feverishly every publication dealing with modern forensic technology. He had realized earlier than his colleagues that one day DNA would be an awesome weapon in identifying bodies, living and dead (and there were a lot of the latter). Even before his department's laboratories could cope, he had begun to collect samples as and when he could.

Five years earlier, a member of the Drug Squad's rogues' gallery had been in a car crash. The man had never been charged, never convicted, never imprisoned. Any New York civil rights lawyer would have had Dos Santos's badge for what he did.

He and his colleagues, long before the Don created the cartel, were convinced this man was a major career gangster. He had not been seen for years, and certainly had not even been heard of for two. If he was as big as they suspected he was, he would live constantly on the move, shifting from one disguise and safe house to another. He would communicate only by use-once-and-throw cell phones, of which he probably had fifty, constantly renewed after use.

What Dos Santos did was go to the hospital and steal the swabs that had been used on the crash victim's broken nose. When the technology caught up, the DNA was identified and filed. Fifty percent was in the sample sent from Washington with a request for help. He delved into a file and laid a photo on the desk.

The face was brutish, scarred, cruel. A

broken nose, pebble eyes, buzz-cut gray hair. It had been taken over ten years earlier but "aged" to show how the man ought to look today.

"We are now convinced he is part of the Don's inner circle, the one whose agents pay off the corrupt officials abroad who help the cartel bring its product through the ports and airports of America and Europe. The ones you call the 'Rats.' "

"Can we find him?" asked the man from SOCA.

"No, or I would have already. He comes from Cartagena, and he is an old dog now. Old dogs do not like to move far from their comfort zone. But he lives under deep cover, invisible."

He turned to Dexter, the source of the mysterious DNA sample of a very close relative.

"You will never find him, señor. And if you did, he would probably kill you. And even if you took him, he would never break. He is hard as flint and twice as sharp. He never travels; he sends agents to do his work. And we understand the Don trusts him totally. I fear your sample is interesting but takes us nowhere."

Cal Dexter looked down at the impenetrable face of Roberto Cárdenas, the man who controlled the Rat List. The loving papá of the girl in Madrid.

In the extreme northeast of Brazil is a vast land of hills and valleys, a few high mountains and much jungle. But also there are enormous ranches of up to half a million acres, grassland well watered by the myriad streams running down from the sierras. Because of their size and remoteness, their estate houses are realistically reached only by air. As a result, they each have one airstrip and sometimes several.

As Cal Dexter took the commercial flight back from Bogotá to Miami and Washington, an airplane was being refueled on one such strip. It was a Beech King Air, carrying two pilots, two pumpers and a metric ton of cocaine.

As the fuel-bowser team filled the main and supplementary tanks to the brim, the crew dozed in the shade of a palm-thatched lean-to. They had a long night ahead. An attaché case containing brick after brick of hundred-dollar bills had already been handed over to cover the fuel and the fee for the stopover.

If the Brazilian authorities had their suspicions about Rancho Boa Vista, two hundred miles inland from the port city of

Fortaleza, there was precious little they could do. The sheer remoteness of the estate meant the slightest hint of a stranger would be noticed. To stake out the complex of main buildings would be futile; using the GPS system, a drug plane could rendezvous with the fuel bowser miles away and never be seen.

For the owners, the fees paid for the fueling stops were rewards far beyond the returns from ranching. For the cartel, the stopovers were vital on the route to Africa.

The Beech C-12, more commonly the King Air, was originally designed and made by Beechcraft as a nineteen-seat, twin turboprop, general-purpose communications mini-airliner. It sold widely across the world. Later versions saw the seats ripped out for conversion to freight carrier and general-purpose hauler. But the version waiting in the afternoon sun at Boa Vista was even more special.

It was never designed to cross the Atlantic. With its all-up fuel load of 2,500 liters the two Pratt and Whitney Canada engines would take it 708 nautical miles. That was in still air, fully loaded, on long-range cruise setting with allowance for starting, taxi, climb and descent. To attempt to leave the coast of Brazil for Africa like that was a recipe for death in the center of the ocean.

In secret workshops belonging to the cartel, hidden beside jungle airstrips in Colombia, the "coke" planes had been modified. Clever artificers had installed extra fuel tanks not under the wings but inside the fuselage. There were usually two, one on each side of the freight hold, with a narrow passage giving access to the flight deck up front.

Technology is expensive, manpower cheap. Rather than have transfer of the extra fuel from the inboard tanks to the main tanks by electric power tapped off the engines, two "peons" were brought along. As the main tanks emptied far out in the dark sky, they began to pump manually.

The route was simple. The first leg was from a hidden airstrip in the Colombian jungle, constantly changed to evade the attentions of Colonel Dos Santos. The pilots would cover the 1,500 miles right across Brazil to Boa Vista on the first night. Flying at 5,000 feet in darkness above the canopy of the Mato Grosso rain forests, they were just about invisible.

At dawn the crew would tuck into a hearty breakfast and sleep through the heat. At dusk the King Air would be again tanked to the brim to face the 1,300 miles from the

New World to the Old at its narrowest point.

That evening, as the last light bled from the sky over Rancho Boa Vista, the pilot of the King Air turned into the light breeze, did his final checks and began to roll. His all-up weight was the manufacturer's maximum of 15,000 pounds. He would need 1,200 meters to get airborne, but he had over 1,500 of rolled-flat grassland. The evening star was twinkling when he lifted out of Boa Vista, and the tropical darkness descended like a theater curtain.

There is a saying that there are old pilots and there are bold pilots, but there are no old bold pilots. Francisco Pons was fifty and had spent years flying in and out of airstrips that would never feature in any official manual. And he had survived because he was careful.

His route was carefully plotted, no detail overlooked. He would refuse to fly in crazy weather, but that night the forecast was for a nice twenty-knot tailwind all the way. He knew there would be no modern airport at the other end but yet another strip hacked out of the bush and lit by the lights from six off-roads parked in a line.

He had memorized the dot-dot-dash signal that would be flashed at him as he approached, to confirm there were no ambushes waiting down there in the warm velvet of the African night. He would fly as usual between 5,000 and 10,000 feet, depending on the cloud layer, well below any need for oxygen. Of course he could fly through clouds all the way, if need be, but it was more agreeable to skim above the layer in moonlight.

With six hours airborne, even flying toward the east and the rising sun, even adding three hours of time change and two for another refuel from a bowser parked in the bush, he would be up and heading back over the African coast, one ton lighter with no cargo, before the African sunrise was more than a pink glow.

And there was the pay. The two pumpers in the back would be paid $5,000 each for three days and nights, for them a fortune. "Captain Pons," as he liked to be called, would collect ten times that and would soon retire a very wealthy man. But then, he was carrying a cargo with a street value in the great cities of Europe of up to a hundred million dollars. He did not think of himself as a bad man. He was just doing his job.

He saw the lights of Fortaleza under his right wing, then the blackness of the ocean replaced the dark of the jungle. An hour later, Fernando de Noronha slipped under the left wing, and he checked time and track. At 250 knots, his best cruise speed, he was on time and true heading. Then the clouds came. He climbed to 10,000 feet and flew on. The two peons started pumping.

He was heading for Cufar airstrip, in Guinea-Bissau, hacked out of the bush during the independence war fought by Amilcar Cabral against the Portuguese many years before. His watch said eleven p.m., Brazil time. One hour to go. The stars were brilliant above, the cloud layer thinning below. Perfect. The peons kept pumping.

He checked his position again. Thank the Lord for Global Positioning, the four-satellite navigator's aid, presented to the world by the Americans and free to use. It made finding a dark bush airstrip as easy as finding Las Vegas in the Nevada desert. He was still flying his course of 040°, as all the way from the Brazilian coast. Now he altered a few points starboard, dropped to 3,000 feet and caught the glitter of the moon on the river Mansôa.

To port he saw a few dim lights in the otherwise blacked-out country. The airport; they must be expecting the Lisbon flight or they would not waste the generator. He slowed to 150 knots and looked ahead for Cufar. In the darkness, fellow Colombians would be waiting, listening for the drone of the Pratt and Whitneys, a sound you could hear for miles over the croak of the frogs and the whining mosquitoes.

Up ahead, a single white bar of light flashed upward, a vertical pillar from a million-candlepower Maglite. Captain Pons was too close. He flashed his landing lights and turned away, then back in a sweeping curve. He knew the airstrip lay on a compass heading east to west. With no wind he could land either way, but by agreement the Jeeps would be at the western end. He needed to sweep in over their heads.

Wheels down, landing flaps, speed dropping, he turned onto final approach. Ahead of him, all the lights blazed alive. It was like noonday down there. He roared over the off-roads at 10 feet and a hundred knots. The King Air settled at her usual eighty-four knots. Before he could close engines and shut off the systems, there were Wranglers racing either side of him. In the back, the two peons were soaked in sweat and limp with tiredness. They had been pumping for over three hours, and the last fifty gallons sloshed in the inboard tanks.

Francisco Pons forbade any smoking on board his flights. Others permitted it, turning their craft, with the danger of petrol fumes, into flying fireballs in the event of a single spark. Safely on the ground, all four men lit up.

There were four Colombians, headed by the boss, Ignacio Romero, chief of all cartel operations in Guinea-Bissau. It was a big cargo, it merited his presence. Local natives hauled off the twenty bales that made up the ton of cocaine. They went into a pickup with tractor tires, and one of the Colombians took them away.

Also piled onto the bales were six Guineans, who were actually soldiers assigned by General Jalo Diallo. He was running the country in the absence of even a titular President. It was a job no one seemed to want. Tenancy tended to be short. The trick was, if possible, to steal a fast fortune and retire to the Portuguese Algarve coast with several young ladies. The "if possible" was the problem.

The bowser driver connected his pipes and began to pump. Romero offered Pons a cup of coffee from his personal flask. Pons sniffed it. Colombian, the best. He nodded his thanks. At ten to four, local time, they were done. Pedro and Pablo, smelling richly of sweat and black tobacco, climbed into the back. They had three more hours to rest as the main fuel tanks were used up. Then more pumping back to Brazil. Pons and his youthful copilot, who was still learning the ropes, bade Romero good-bye and went up to the flight deck.

The Wranglers had repositioned themselves so that when the searchlights came on, Captain Pons had only to turn around and take off toward the west. At five to four, he lifted off, a ton lighter now, and cleared the coast still in darkness.

Somewhere in the bush behind him, the ton of cocaine would be stored in a secret depot and carefully split into smaller consignments. Most would head north by any one of twenty different methods and fifty carriers. It was this diffusion into small packets that had convinced the Cobra the trade could not be stopped once the drug had made landfall.

But right across West Africa, the local help, up to President level, were not paid off in money but in cocaine. Converting this into wealth was their problem. They set up a secondary and parallel traffic, also heading north but in the hands of and under the control of black Africans exclusively. That was where the Nigerians came in. They dominated the in-Africa trade and merchandised their share almost exclusively through the hundreds of Nigerian communities spread over Europe.

Even by 2009 there had been a problem developing locally that would one day cause the Don to experience a red-haze rage. Some of the African allies did not want to remain mere commission takers. They wanted to graduate to being major players, buying direct from the source and turning their slim pickings into the white man's massive markup. But the Don had his European clients to service. He had refused to elevate the Africans' role from servant to equal partner. It was a sleeping feud that the Cobra intended to exploit.

Fr. Isidro had wrestled with his conscience and prayed for many hours. He would have turned to the Father Provincial, but that dignitary had already given his advice. The decision was a personal one, and each parish priest was a free agent. But Fr. Isidro did not feel a free agent. He felt trapped. He had a small encrypted cell phone. It would transmit to only one number. On that number would be a recorded voice; American accented but in fluent Spanish. Or he could text. Or he could stay silent. It was the teenager in the Cartagena Hospital who finally caused his decision.

He had baptized the boy and later confirmed him, one of the many youths of the priest's deeply poor and working-class dockside parish. When he was called to give the last rites, he sat by the bed and ran his beads through his hands and wept.

"Ego te absolvo ab omnibus peccatis tuis," he whispered. *"In nomine Patris, et Filii et Spiritus Sancti."* He made the sign of the cross in the air, and the youth died, shriven. The sister nearby quietly raised the white sheet to cover the dead face. Fourteen years old, and an overdose of cocaine had taken him away.

"But what sins had he committed?" he asked his silent God as he recalled the absolution while he walked home through the darkened dockyard streets. That night, he made the call.

He did not believe he was betraying the confidence of Señora Cortez. She was still one of his parishioners, born and raised in the slums, though now moved to a fine bungalow on a private housing estate in the shadow of Cerro de La Popa Mountain. Her husband, Juan, was a freethinker who did not attend Mass. But his wife came, and brought the child, a pleasant boy, high-spirited and mischievous as boys should be, but good-hearted and devout. What the señora had told him was not in the confes-

181

sional, and she had begged for his help. That was why he was not betraying the seal of confession. So he rang and left a short message.

Cal Dexter listened to the message twenty-four hours later. Then he saw Paul Devereaux.

"There is a man in Cartagena, a welder. Described as 'a craftsman of genius.' He works for the cartel. He creates hiding places inside steel hulls that are so skillfully made as to be virtually undetectable. I think I should visit this Juan Cortez."

"I agree," said the Cobra.

CHAPTER 6

It was a nice little house, neat and spruce, the sort that makes the statement that people who live there are proud of having risen from the working class to the level of skilled craftsman.

It was the local representative of the British SOCA who had traced the welder. The secret agent was in fact a New Zealander whose years in Central and South America had made him bilingual in Spanish. He had a good deep-cover job as a lecturer in mathematics at the Naval Cadet Academy. The post gave him access to all of officialdom in the city of Cartagena. It was a friend in City Hall who had traced the house from the land-tax records.

His reply to Cal Dexter's inquiry was commendably brief. Juan Cortez, self-employed dockyard artisan, and then the address. He added the assurance that there was no other such Juan Cortez anywhere near the private housing estates that clothe the slopes of Cerro de La Popa.

Cal Dexter was in the city three days later, a modestly monied tourist staying at a budget hotel. He rented a scooter, one of tens of thousands in the city. With a road map, he found the suburban street in the district of Las Flores, memorized the directions and cruised past.

The next morning he was down the street in the dark before dawn, crouching beside his stationary machine whose innards were on the pavement beside him as he worked. All around him, lights came on as people rose for the day. That included Number 17. Cartagena was a South Caribbean resort, and the weather is balmy all year round. Early on this March morning it was mild. Later it would be hot. The first commuters left for work. From where he crouched, Dexter could see the Ford Pinto parked on the hard pad in front of the target house and the lights through the blinds as the family took its breakfast. The welder opened his front door at ten minutes before seven.

Dexter did not move. In any case, he could not, his scooter was immobile. Besides, this was not the morning for following; simply for noting time of departure. He hoped Juan Cortez would be as regular the next day. He noted the Ford cruising past and the turn it took to head for the main road. He would be on that corner at half past six the next day, but helmeted, jacketed, straddling the scooter. The Ford turned the corner and disappeared. Dexter reassembled his machine and returned to his hotel.

He had seen the Colombian close enough to know him again. He knew the car and its number.

The next morning was like the first. The lights came on, the family breakfasted, kisses were exchanged. Dexter was on his corner at half past six, engine idling, pretending to call on his mobile phone to explain to the one or two pedestrians why he was stationary. No one took any notice. The Ford, with Juan Cortez at the wheel, cruised by at quarter to seven. He gave it a hundred yards and followed.

The welder passed through the La Quinta district and picked up the highway south, the coast road, the Carretera Troncal West. Of course, almost all the docks lay down there at the ocean's edge. The traffic thickened, but in case the man he followed was sharp-eyed Dexter twice swerved in behind a truck when red lights held them up.

Once he came out with his windbreaker reversed. It had been bright red before; now

185

it was sky blue. On another stop he switched to his white shirt. He was, in any case, one of a throng of scooterists on their way to work.

The road went on and on. The traffic thinned. Those left were heading for the docks on the Carretera de Mamonal. Dexter switched disguise again, stowing his crash helmet between his knees and donning a white woolen beanie. The man ahead of him seemed to take no notice, but with thinner traffic he had to drop back to a hundred yards. Finally, the welder turned off. He was fifteen miles south of town, past the tanker and petrochemical docks, to where the general-purpose freighters were serviced. Dexter noted the big promotional sign at the entrance to the lane leading down to the Sandoval shipyard. He would know it again.

The rest of the day he spent cruising back toward the city looking for a snatch site. He found it by noon, a lonely stretch where the road had only one lane each way and unpaved tracks leading down into thick mangrove. The road was straight for five hundred yards with a curve at each end.

That evening he waited at the junction where the lane to Sandoval shipyard came out to the highway. The Ford appeared just after six p.m., in deep, gathering dusk, with darkness only minutes away. The Ford was one of dozens of cars and scooters headed back into town.

On the third day, he motored into the shipyard. There seemed to be no security. He parked and strolled. A cheerful *"¡Hola!"* was exchanged with a group of ship workers strolling past. He found the employees' parking lot, and there was the Ford, waiting for its owner, as he toiled deep inside a drydocked ship with his oxyacetylene torch. The next morning, Cal Dexter flew back to Miami to recruit and plan. He was back a week later, but much less legally.

He flew into the Colombia Army base at Malambo where the U.S. forces had a joint Army/Navy/Air Force presence. He came by C-130 Hercules out of Eglin Air Force Base on the Florida panhandle. So many black ops have been run out of Eglin that it is simply known as "Spook Central."

The equipment he needed was in the Hercules, along with six Green Berets. Even though they came from Fort Lewis, Washington, they were men he had worked with before, and his wish had been granted. Fort Lewis is the home of the First Special Forces Group known as Operational Detachment (OD) Alpha 143. These were

187

mountain specialists, even though there are no mountains in Cartagena.

He was lucky to find them at base, home from Afghanistan, on their quite short threshold of boredom. When they were offered a short black op, they all volunteered, but he needed only six. Two of them, at his insistence, were Hispanic and fluent in Spanish. None knew what it was all about, and, outside of the immediate details, they had no need to know. But they all knew the rules. They would be told what they needed for the mission. No more.

Given the short time line, Dexter was pleased with what Project Cobra's supply team had achieved. The black panel van was U.S. built, but so were half the vehicles on the roads of Colombia. Its papers were in order and its registration plates normal for Cartagena. The decals pasted on each side read "Lavandería de Cartagena." Laundry vans seldom raise suspicion.

He checked out the three Cartagena police uniforms, the two wicker hampers, the freestanding red traffic lights and the frozen body, packed in dry ice in a refrigerated casket. That stayed on board the Hercules until needed.

The Colombian Army was being very hospitable, but there was no need to abuse their capacity for favors.

Cal Dexter checked the cadaver briefly. Right height, right build, approximate age. A poor John Doe, trying to live rough in the Washington forests, found dead of hypothermia, brought in to the morgue at Kelso by the Mount St. Helens wardens two days earlier.

Dexter gave his team two dry runs. They studied the five-hundred-yard stretch of narrow highway Dexter had chosen by day and by night. On the third night, they went operational. They all knew simplicity and speed were the essence. On the third afternoon, Dexter parked the van at the midsection of the long straight strip of highway. There was a track leading into the mangrove, and he put the van fifty yards down it.

He used the moped that came with his equipment to motor at four p.m. into the employees' parking lot at the Sandoval yard and, crouching low, let the air out of two of the Ford's tires; one at the back and the spare in the trunk. He was back with his team by four-fifteen.

In the Sandoval parking lot, Juan Cortez approached his car, saw the flat tire, cursed and went for the spare in the trunk. When he found this, too, was airless, he swore even more, went to the stores and borrowed a pump. When he was finally able to roll, the delay had cost him an hour, and it was pitch-dark. All his workmates were long gone.

Three miles from the yard, a man stood silently and invisible in the foliage by the road with a set of night-vision goggles. Because all Cortez's colleagues had left ahead of him, traffic was very light. The man in the undergrowth was American, spoke fluent Spanish and wore the uniform of a Cartagena traffic cop. He had memorized the Ford Pinto from the pictures provided by Dexter. It passed him at five minutes past seven. He took a torch and flashed up the road. Three short blips.

At the midsection, Dexter took his red warning light, walked to the center of the road and waved it from side to side toward the approaching headlights. Cortez, seeing the warning ahead of him, began to slow.

Behind him, the man who had waited in the bushes set a freestanding red light beside him, switched it on and, over the next two minutes, detained two other cars coming toward the city. One of the drivers leaned out and called, *"¿Que pasa?"* *"Dos momentos, nada más,"* replied the policeman. Two seconds, no more.

Five hundred yards up the strip toward the city, the second Green Beret in policeman's uniform had mounted his red light, and over two minutes flagged down three cars. At the center section, there would be no interruptions, and the possible eyewitnesses were just out of sight around curves.

Juan Cortez slowed and stopped. A police officer, smiling in a friendly manner, approached the driver's-side window. Due to the balmy night, it was already wound down.

"Could I ask you to step out of the car, señor?" Dexter asked, and opened the door. Cortez protested but stepped out. After that, it was all too fast. He recalled two men coming out of the darkness; strong arms; a pad of chloroform; the brief struggle; fading awareness; darkness.

The two snatchers had the limp body of the welder down the track and into their van in thirty seconds. Dexter took the wheel of the Ford and drove it out of sight down the same track. Then he jogged back to the road.

The fifth Green Beret was at the wheel of the van and the sixth came with him. At the roadside, Dexter muttered an instruction into his communicator, and the first two men heard it. They hauled their red lamps off the tarmac and waved the halted cars forward.

Two came at Dexter from the dockyard direction, three from the city side. Their curious drivers saw a police officer at the road edge standing next to a moped on its side and a man sitting dazed and holding his head beside it — the sixth soldier, in jeans, sneakers and bomber jacket. The policeman waved them impatiently on. It's only a spill; don't gawp.

When they were gone, normal traffic resumed, but the succeeding drivers saw nothing. All six men, two sets of red lights and a moped were down the track, being packed in the van. The unconscious Cortez went into a wicker basket. From the other came a form in a body bag, now limp and beginning to emit an odor.

Van and car changed places. Both backed up to the road. The limp Cortez had been relieved of his wallet, cell phone, signet ring, watch and the medallion of his patron saint from around his neck. The cadaver, out of its bag, was already in the gray cotton overalls of the exact type Cortez wore.

The body was "dressed" with all Cortez's personal identifying accessories. The wallet was placed under the rump when the corpse went into the driver's seat of the Ford. Four strong men, pushing from behind, rammed it hard into a tree just off the road.

The other two Green Berets took jerry-cans from the rear of their van and doused the Ford with several gallons. The car's own gas tank would explode and complete the fireball.

When they were ready, all six soldiers piled into the van. They would wait for Dexter two miles up the road. Two cars went past. After that, nothing. The black laundry van surged out of the entrance to the track and set off. Dexter waited beside his moped until the road was empty, took a petrol-soaked rag wrapped around a pebble from his pocket, lit it with a Zippo and, from ten yards, tossed it. There was a dull *whump,* and the Ford torched. Dexter rode away fast.

Two hours later, un-intercepted, the laundry van rolled through the gates of Malambo air base. It went straight to the open rear loading doors of the Hercules and up the ramp. The aircrew, alerted by a mobile phone call, had completed all the formalities and had their Allison engines ready to roll. As the rear doors closed, the engines increased power, taxied to takeoff point and lifted away, destination Florida.

Inside the fuselage, the tension evaporated in grins, handshakes and high fives. The groggy Juan Cortez was lifted out of the laundry basket, laid gently on a mattress, and one of the Green Berets, qualified as a corpsman, gave Cortez an injection. It was harmless, but would ensure several hours of dreamless sleep.

By ten, Señora Cortez was frantic. There was a recorded call on her answering machine from her husband while she was out. It was just before six. Juan said he had a flat tire and would be late, maybe up to an hour. Their son was long back from school, homework completed. He had played with his Game Boy for a while, then he, too, started to worry and tried to comfort his mother. She made repeated calls to her husband's cell phone, but there was no reply. Later, as the flames consumed it, the machine ceased to ring at all. At half past ten, she called the police.

It was at two in the morning when someone in Cartagena Police HQ connected a blazing car that had crashed and exploded on the highway to Mamonal and a woman in Las Flores frantic that her husband had not returned from his work in the docks. Mamonal, thought the young policeman on the graveyard shift, was where the docks were. He called the city mortuary.

There had been four fatalities that night:

a murder between two gangs in the red-light district, two bad car crashes and a heart attack in a cinema. The medical examiner was still cutting at three a.m.

He confirmed a badly burned body from one of the car wrecks, far beyond recognition facially, but some items had been recovered in still recognizable form. They would be bagged and sent to HQ in the morning.

At six a.m. the detritus of the night was examined at police HQ. Of the other three deaths, no one had been burned. One pile of residue still stank of petrol and fire. It included a melted cell phone, a signet ring, a saint's medallion, a watch whose bracelet strap still had fragments of tissue attached and a wallet. The last named must have been sheltered from the flames by the fact that the dead driver was sitting on it. Inside it were papers, some still readable. The driver's license was clearly that of one Juan Cortez. And the frantic lady calling in from Las Flores was Señora Cortez.

At ten a.m., a police officer and a sergeant came to her door. Both were grim-faced. The officer began:

"Señora Cortez, lo siento muchissimo . . ."
— I am deeply sorry. Señora Cortez then fainted clean away.

Formal identification was out of the question. The next day, escorted and sustained by two neighbors, Señora Irina Cortez attended the morgue. What had been her husband was but a charred, blackened husk of bone and melted flesh, lumps of carbon, insanely grinning teeth. The examiner, with the agreement of the silent policemen present, excused her even seeing what was left.

But she tearfully identified the watch, signet ring, medallion, melted cell phone and driver's license. The pathologist would sign an affidavit that these items had been removed from the corpse, and the traffic division would confirm that the body had indeed been the one retrieved from the gutted car that was provably the one owned by and being driven by Juan Cortez that evening. It was enough; bureaucracy was satisfied.

Three days later, the unknown American backwoodsman was buried in the Cartagena grave of Juan Cortez, welder, husband and father. Irina was inconsolable, Pedro sniffing quietly. Fr. Isidro officiated. He was going through his own private Calvary.

Had it been his phone call, he endlessly asked himself? Had the Americans let on? Betrayed the confidence? Had the cartel become aware? Presumed Cortez was going to betray them instead of himself being betrayed? How could the *Yanquis* have been so stupid?

Or was it just coincidence? A true, terrible coincidence. He knew what the cartel did to anyone they suspected, however feeble the evidence. But how could they have suspected Juan Cortez of not being their loyal craftsman, which in fact he had been to the end? So he conducted the service, saw the earth tumbling on top of the coffin, sought to comfort the widow and orphan by explaining the true love God had for them, even though it was hard to understand. Then he went back to his spartan lodgings to pray and pray and pray for forgiveness.

Letizia Arenal was walking on clouds. A dull April day in the city of Madrid could not touch her. She had never felt so happy or so warm. The only way she could be warmer was in his arms.

They had met at a café terrace two weeks earlier. She had seen him there before, always alone, always studying. The day the ice was broken, she was with a group of fellow students, laughing and joking, and he was just a table away. Being winter, the terrace was glassed in. The door had opened, and the street wind blew some of her papers onto the floor. He has stooped to pick them up. She bent down, too, and their eyes met. She wondered why she had not noticed before that he was drop-dead handsome.

"Goya," he said. She thought he was introducing himself. Then she noticed he was holding one of her sheets in his hand. It was a picture of an oil painting.

"Boys Picking Fruit," he said. "Goya. Are you studying art?"

She nodded. It seemed natural that he should walk her home, that they should discuss Zurbarán, Velázquez, Goya. It even seemed natural when he gently kiss her wind-chilled lips. Her latchkey almost fell from her hand.

"Domingo," he said. Now he really was giving her his name, not the day of the week. "Domingo de Vega."

"Letizia," she replied. "Letizia Arenal."

"Miss Arenal," he said quietly, "I think I am going to take you out for dinner. It is no use resisting. I know where you live. If you say no, I shall simply curl up on your doorstep and die here. Of the cold."

"I don't think you should do that, Señor Vega. So to prevent it, I shall dine with you."

He took her to an old restaurant that had

been serving food when the conquistadors came from their homes in the wild Estremadura to seek the favor of the King to send them to discover the New World. When he told her the story — complete nonsense, for the Sobrino de Botín in the Street of the Knife Grinders is old but not that old — she shivered and glanced around to see if the old adventurers were still dining there.

He told her he was from Puerto Rico, bilingual in English also, a young diplomat at the United Nations, intent one day to be an ambassador. But he had taken a three-month sabbatical, encouraged by his head of mission to study more of his true love, Spanish classical painting, at the Prado in Madrid.

And it seemed quite natural to get into his bed, where he made love as no man she had known, even though she had known only three.

Cal Dexter was a hard man, but he retained a conscience. He might have found it too cold-blooded to use a professional gigolo, but the Cobra had no such scruple. For him there was only to win or to lose, and the unforgivable option was to lose.

He still regarded with awe and admiration the ice-hearted spymaster Markus Wolf who had for years headed East Germany's spy network that ran rings around the counter-intelligence apparat of his West German enemies. Wolf had used honey traps extensively, but usually the opposite way from the norm.

The norm was to entrap gullible Western big shots with stunning call girls until they could be photographed and blackmailed into submission. Wolf used seductive young men; not for gay diplomats (although that was not beyond him at all) but for the overlooked, ignored-in-love spinster who so often toiled as the private secretaries of the high-and-mighty of West Germany.

The fact that when finally exposed as the dupes they had been, when it was clear to them the incalculable secrets they had taken from their masters' files, copied and passed to their Adonis, they finished up, drab and ruined, in the dock of a West German court or ended their lives in pretrial detention, it did not worry Markus Wolf. He was playing the Great Game to win and he won.

Even after the collapse of East Germany, a Western court had to acquit Wolf because he had not betrayed his own country. So while others were jailed, he enjoyed a genteel retirement until he died of natural causes. The day he read the news, Paul Devereaux mentally doffed his hat and said a prayer for the old atheist. And he had no hesitation in sending the beautiful alley cat Domingo de Vega to Madrid.

Juan Cortez drifted out of sleep by slow degrees, and for the first few seconds thought he might have gone to paradise. In truth, he was simply in a room such as he had never seen before. It was large, as was the double bed in which he lay, and pastel walled, with blinds drawn over windows beyond which the sun shone. In fact, he was in the VIP suite of the officers' club on Homestead Air Force Base in southern Florida.

As the mists cleared, he observed a terry-cloth robe over a chair near the bed. He swung his rubbery legs to the floor and, realizing he was naked, pulled it on. On the bedside table was a telephone. He lifted the handset and croaked *"¡Oiga!"* several times, but no one answered.

He walked to one of the large windows, eased back a corner of the blind and peeked out. He saw tended lawns and a flagpole from which fluttered the Stars and Stripes. He was not in paradise; for him, the reverse. He had been kidnapped, and the Americans had got him.

He had heard terrible tales of special

renditions in darkened planes to foreign lands, of torture in the Middle East and Central Asia, of years in the Cuban enclave called Guantánamo.

Although no one had answered the phone by the bed, it had been noted that he was awake. The door opened, and a white-jacketed steward came in with a tray. It contained food, good food, and Juan Cortez had not eaten since his packed lunch in the dockyard of Sandoval seventy-two hours earlier. He did not know it had been three days.

The steward put down the tray, smiled and beckoned him toward the bathroom door. He looked in. A marble bathroom for a Roman Emperor such as he had seen on TV. The steward gestured that it was all his — shower, lavatory, shaving kit, the lot. Then he withdrew.

The welder contemplated the ham and eggs, juice, toast, jam, coffee. The ham and coffee aromas filled his mouth with saliva. It was probably drugged, he reasoned, possibly poisoned. But so what? They could do with him what they wanted anyway.

He sat and ate, thinking back to his last memory; the policeman asking him to get out of his car, the steely arms around his torso, the stifling pad held up to his face, the sensation of falling. He had little doubt he knew the reason why. He worked for the cartel. But how could they possibly have discovered this?

When he had done, he tried the bathroom; used the lavatory, showered, shaved. There was a bottle of aftershave. He splashed it liberally. Let them pay for it. He had been raised in the fiction that all Americans were rich.

When he came back to the bedroom, there was a man standing there: mature, with gray hair, medium height, wiry build. He smiled a friendly grin, very American. And spoke Spanish.

"Hola, Juan. ¿Qué tal?" Hi, Juan. How are you? *"Me llamo Cal. Hablamos un ratito."* My name is Cal. Let's have a chat.

A trick, of course. The torture would come later. So they sat in two armchairs, and the American explained what had happened. He told of the snatch, the burning Ford, the body at the wheel. He told of the identification of the body on the basis of the wallet, watch, ring and medallion.

"And my wife and son?" asked Cortez.

"Ah, they are both devastated. They think they have been to your funeral. We want to bring them to join you."

"Join me? Here?"

"Juan, my friend, accept the reality. You cannot go back. The cartel would never believe a word you said. You know what they do to people they think have defected to us. And to all their family. In these things, they are animals."

Cortez started to shake. He knew only too well. He had never personally seen such things, but he had heard. Heard and trembled. The cutout tongues, the slow death, the wiping out of the entire family. He trembled for Irina and Pedro. The American leaned forward.

"Accept the reality. You are here now. Whether what we did was right or wrong, probably wrong, does not matter anymore. You are here and alive. But the cartel is convinced you are dead. They even sent an observer to the funeral."

Dexter took a DVD from his jacket pocket, switched on the big plasma screen, inserted the disc and pressed Play on the remote. The film had clearly been made by a cameraman on a high-rise roof half a kilometer from the cemetery, but the definition was excellent. And enlarged.

Juan Cortez watched his own funeral. The editors of the movie zeroed in on Irina weeping, supported by a neighbor. On his son Pedro. On Fr. Isidro. On the man at the back in black suit and tie and wraparound black glasses, he of the grim face, the watcher sent on the orders of the Don. The film cut.

"You see?" said the American, tossing the remote on the bed. "You cannot go back. But they will not come after you either. Not now, not ever. Juan Cortez died in that blazing car crash. Fact. Now you have to stay with us, here in the U.S. And we will look after you. We will not harm you. You have my word, and I do not break it. There will be a change of name, of course, and maybe some small changes in features. We have a thing called the 'Witness Protection Program.' You will be inside it.

"You will be a new man, Juan Cortez, with a new life in a new place; a new job, a new home, new friends. New everything."

"But I do not want new everything!" shouted Cortez in despair. "I want my old life back!"

"You cannot go back, Juan. The old life is over."

"And my wife and son?"

"Why should you not have them with you in the new life? There are many places in this country where the sun shines, just like in Cartagena. There are hundreds of thousands of Colombians here, legal immigrants, now settled and happy."

"But how could they . . . ?"

"We would bring them. You could raise Pedro here. In Cartagena, what would he be? A welder like you? Going every day to sweat in the dockyards? Here he could be anything in twenty years. Doctor, lawyer, even a senator?"

The Colombian welder stared at him openmouthed.

"Pedro, my son, a senator?"

"Why not? Any boy can grow up to become anything here. We call it the American dream. But for this favor, we would need your help."

"But I have nothing to offer."

"Oh yes you do, Juan my friend. Here in my country, that white powder is destroying the lives of young people just like your Pedro. And it comes in ships, hidden in places we can never find it. But remember those ships, Juan, the ones you worked on . . .

"Look, I have to go." Cal Dexter stood and patted Cortez on the shoulder. "Think things over. Play the tape. Irina grieves for you. Pedro cries for his dead papá. It could all be so good for you if we bring them out to join you. Just for a few names. I'll be back in twenty-four hours.

"I'm afraid you cannot leave. For your

own sake. In case anyone saw you. Unlikely but possible. So stay here and think. My people will look after you."

The tramp steamer *Sidi Abbas* was never going to win any beauty prizes, and her entire value as a small merchantman was a pittance compared to the eight bales in her hold.

She came out of the Gulf of Sidra, on the coast of Libya, and she was heading for the Italian province of Calabria. Contrary to the hopes of tourists, the Mediterranean can be a wild sea. The huge waves of a storm lashed the rusty tramp as she plodded and wheezed her way east of Malta toward the toe of the Italian peninsula.

The eight bales were a cargo that had been unloaded a month earlier with the complete agreement of the port authorities at Conakry, capital of the other Guinea, out of a bigger freighter from Venezuela. From tropical Africa the cargo had been trucked north, out of the rain forest, across the savannah and over the blazing sands of the Sahara. It was a journey to daunt any driver, but the hard men who drove the land trains were accustomed to the rigors.

They drove the huge rigs and trailers hour after hour and day after day over pitted roads and tracks of sand. At each border and customs post, there were palms to be greased and barriers to be lifted, as the purchased officials turned away with fat rolls of high-denomination euros in their back pockets.

It took a month, but with every yard nearer to Europe the value of each kilo in the eight bales increased toward the astronomical European price. At last the landtrains ground to a halt at a dusty shack stop just outside the major city that was the true destination.

Smaller trucks, or more likely rugged pickups, took the bales from the roadside around the city to some noisome fishing village, a huddle of adobe huts, by an almostfishless sea where a tramp like the *Sidi Abbas* would be waiting at a crumbling dock.

That April, the tramp was heading on the last stage of the journey, to the Calabrian port of Gioia, which was wholly under the control of the Ndrangheta mafia. At that point, ownership would change. Alfredo Suárez in faraway Bogotá would have done his job; the self-styled "Honorable Society" would take over. The fifty percent debt would be settled, the enormous fortune laundered through the Italian version of Banco Guzman.

From Gioia, a few miles from the office of the state prosecutor in the capital of Reggio di Calabria, the eight bales in much smaller packets would be driven north to Italy's cocaine capital, Milan.

But the master of the *Sidi Abbas* neither knew nor cared. He was just glad when the harbor mole at Gioia slid past and the wild water was behind him. Four more tons of cocaine had reached Europe, and many miles away the Don would be pleased.

In his comfortable but lonely jail, Juan Cortez had played the DVD of the funeral many times, and each time he saw the devastated faces of his wife and son he was brought to tears. He longed to see them again, to hold his son, to sleep with Irina. But he knew the *Yanqui* was right; he could never go back. Even to refuse to cooperate and send a message would be to sentence them to death or worse.

When Cal Dexter came back, the welder nodded his agreement.

"But I also have my terms," he said. "When I hold my son, when I kiss my wife, then I will remember the ships. Until then, not one word."

Dexter smiled.

"I asked for nothing else," he said. "But

now we have work to do."

A recording engineer came and a tape was made. Though the technology was not new, neither was Cal Dexter, as he occasionally joked. He preferred the old Pearlcorder, small, reliable and with a tap so tiny it could be hidden in many places. And pictures were taken. Of Cortez facing the camera, holding a copy of that day's *Miami Herald* with the date clearly visible, and of the welder's strawberry birthmark, like a bright pink lizard, on the right thigh. When he had his evidence, Dexter left.

Jonathan Silver was becoming impatient. He had demanded progress reports, but Devereaux was infuriatingly noncommittal. The White House chief of staff bombarded him constantly.

Elsewhere, the official forces of law and order continued as before. Huge sums from the public purse were allocated, and still the problem seemed to worsen.

Captures were made and loudly acclaimed; interceptions happened, the tonnages and prices — always the street price, rather than the at-sea price, because it was higher.

But in the Third World, confiscated ships miraculously slipped their moorings and vanished out to sea; accused crews were bailed and disappeared; worse, impounded shipments of cocaine simply went missing while in custody, and the trade went on. It seemed to the frustrated myrmidons of the DEA that everyone was on the payroll. This was the burden of Silver's complaint.

The man taking the call in his Alexandria town house as the nation packed up for the Easter break remained icily courteous but refused any concession.

"I was given the task last October," he said. "I said I needed nine months to prepare. At the right moment, things will change. Have a happy Easter." And he put the phone down. Silver was enraged. No one did that to him. Except, it seemed, the Cobra.

Cal Dexter flew back into Colombia via the Malambo air base again. This time, with Devereaux's assistance, he had borrowed the CIA Grumman executive jet. It was not for his comfort but for a fast getaway. He rented a car in the nearby town and drove to Cartagena. He had brought no backup. There are times and places where stealth and speed alone bring success. If he heeded muscle and firepower, he would have failed anyway.

Though he had seen her in the doorway, kissing her husband farewell as he left for work, Señora Cortez had never seen him. It was Semana Santa, and the district of Las Flores was a-bustle with preparations for Easter Sunday. Except Number 17.

He cruised the zone several times, waiting for dark. He did not want to park by the curb for fear of being spotted and challenged by a nosy neighbor. But he wanted to see the lights go on just before the curtains were drawn. There was no car on the hard pad, indicating no visitors. When the lights went on, he could see inside. Señora Cortez and the boy; no visitors. They were alone. He approached the door and rang the bell. It was the son who answered, a dark, intense lad whom he recognized from the funeral film. The face was sad. It did not smile.

Dexter produced a police badge, flashed it briefly and put it away.

"Teniente Delgado, Policía Municipal," he told the boy. The badge was actually a duplicate of a Miami PD badge, but the child did not know that. "Could I speak to your mama?"

He settled the issue by sliding quietly past the boy into the hallway.

Pedro ran back into the house called,

"Mamá, está un oficial de la policía."

Señora Cortez appeared from the kitchen, wiping her hands. Her face was blotched from crying. Dexter smiled gently and gestured toward the living room. He was so obviously in charge, she just did as he suggested. When she was seated with her son protectively beside her, Dexter crouched and showed her a passport. An American one.

He pointed out the eagle on the cover, the insignia of the USA.

"I am not a Colombian police officer, señora. I am, as you see, American. Now, I want you to take a real grip on yourself. And you, son. Your husband, Juan. He is not dead, he is with us in Florida."

The woman stared uncomprehending for several seconds. Then her hands flew to her mouth in shock.

"No se puede," It cannot be, she gasped. "I saw the body . . ."

"No, señora, you saw the body of another man under a sheet, burned beyond recognition. And you saw Juan's watch, his wallet, his medallion, his signet ring. All these he gave us. But the body was not his. A poor tramp. Juan is with us in Florida. He has sent me to fetch you. Both. Now, please . . ."

He produced three photos from an inside

213

pocket. Juan Cortez, very much alive, stared back. A second showed the recent *Miami Herald* in his hands with the date visible. The third showed his birthmark. It was the clincher. No one else could know.

She began to cry again. *"No comprendo, no comprendo,"* she repeated. The boy recovered first. He began to laugh.

"Papá está en vida," Daddy is alive, he crowed.

Dexter produced his recorder and pressed the Play button. The voice of the "dead" welder filled the small room.

"Dearest Irina, my darling. Pedro, my son. It is truly me . . ."

He ended with a personal plea that Irina and Pedro pack one suitcase each of their dearest possessions, say adieu to Number 17 and follow the American.

It took an hour of rushing about, between tears and laughter, packing, discarding, packing again, choosing, rejecting, packing a third time. It is hard to pack an entire life into one suitcase.

When they were ready, Dexter insisted they leave the lights on and the drapes closed to extend the period until their departure was discovered. The señora wrote a letter, dictation, leaving it for the neighbors under a vase on the main table. It said she and Pedro had decided to emigrate and start a new life.

In the Grumman back to Florida, Dexter explained her nearest neighbors would receive letters from her, sent from Florida, saying she had secured a cleaning job and was safe and well. If anyone investigated, they would be shown the letters. They would have the correct postmark but no return address. She would never be traced because she would never be there. Then they landed at Homestead.

It was a long reunion, again with a combination of tears and laughter, in the VIP suite. Prayers were said for the resurrection. Then, according to his word, Juan Cortez sat down with a pen and paper and started to write. He may have been a man of limited formal education, but he had a phenomenal memory. He closed his eyes, thought back over the years and wrote a name. And another. And another.

When he had finished, and assured Dexter there was not a single one more that he had worked on, his list comprised seventy-eight ships. And by the fact he had been summoned to create ultra-secret compartments in them, every one a coke smuggler.

CHAPTER 7

It was fortunate for Cal Dexter that Jeremy Bishop's social life was as busy as a bomb site. He had spent Easter feigning jollity in a country hotel, so when Dexter apologetically mentioned he had urgent work that would need the computer genius at his data banks, it was like a ray of sunshine.

"I have the names of some ships," said Dexter. "Seventy-eight in all. I need to know all about them. How big, type of cargo, owner, if possible, but probably a shell company. Handling agent, present charter and, above all, location. Where are they now?

"You had better become a trading company, or a virtual one, with cargoes that need transporting. Inquire of the handling agents. When you have traced one of the seventy-eight, drop the charter inquiry. Wrong tonnage, wrong place, wrong availability. Whatever. Just tell me where they are and what they look like."

"I can do better," said the happy Bishop. "I can probably get you pictures of them."

"From above?"

"From above? Looking down?" Bishop asked.

"Yep."

"That is not the angle ships are usually pictured."

"Just try. And concentrate on those plying routes between the western/southern Caribbean and ports in the U.S. and Europe."

Within two days, Jeremy Bishop, sitting contentedly at his array of keyboards and screens, had located twelve of the ships named by Juan Cortez. He passed Dexter the details so far. All were in the Caribbean Basin, either proceeding from it or heading to it.

Dexter knew some of those named by the welder would never show up on commercial shipping lists. They were scabby old fishing boats or tramps below the tonnage that the commercial world would bother about. Finding the last two categories would be the hard part but vital.

The big freighters could be denounced to the local customs at port of destination. They would probably have taken on a shipment of cocaine out at sea and possibly been relieved of it in the same manner. But they could still be impounded if the sniffer dogs detected residual traces in the secret hiding places on board, which they probably would.

The vessels that so frustrated Tim Manhire and his analysts in Lisbon were the smaller smugglers emerging from the mangroves and docking at timber jetties along West African creeks. It turned out that twenty-five of the "Cortez list" were logged by Lloyd's; the rest were below the radar. Still, twenty-five taken out of use would blow a huge hole in the cartel's shipping reserve. But not yet. The Cobra was not ready yet. But the TR-1s were.

Major João Mendoza, Brazilian Air Force, retired, flew into Heathrow at the beginning of May. Cal Dexter met him outside the doors of the customs hall of Terminal 3. Recognition was not a problem; he had memorized the face of the former fast-jet pilot.

Six months earlier, Major Mendoza had been the result of a long and painstaking search. At one point, Dexter had found himself at lunch in London with a former chief of Air Staff, Royal Air Force. The air chief marshal had considered his main question long and hard.

"I don't think so," he said finally. "Out of a clear blue sky, eh? No warning? I think our chaps might have a bit of a problem with that. A conscience issue. I don't think I could recommend anyone to you."

It was the same response Dexter had gotten from a two-star general, USAF, also retired, who had flown F-15 Eagles in the first Gulf War.

"Mind you," said the Englishman as they parted, "there is one Air Force that will blow a cocaine smuggler out of the sky without compunction. The Brazilians."

Dexter had trawled the São Paulo community of retired Air Force pilots and finally found João Mendoza. He was in his mid-forties and had flown Northrop Grumman F5E Tigers before retiring to help run his father's business as the old man became frailer with age. But his efforts had not availed. In the economic collapse of 2009, the company had gone into receivership.

Without easily marketable skills, João Mendoza had gravitated to any office job and regretted ever leaving flying. And he still grieved for the kid brother whom he had almost raised after their mother died and their father worked fifteen hours a day. While the pilot had been at his fighter base in the north, the youth had fallen into the company of the gutter and died of an overdose. João never forgot and he never forgave. And the offered fee was huge.

Dexter had a hired car, and he drove the Brazilian north to that flat county by the North Sea whose lack of hills and position on the east coast had made it, during World War II, such a natural for bomber bases. Scampton had been one of them. Through the Cold War, it had been the home of part of the V-bomber force, carrying the UK's atomic bombs.

By 2011 it was host to a number of non-military enterprises, among them a group of enthusiasts who were slowly restoring two Blackburn Buccaneers. They had the pair up to fast-taxiing level but not yet airborne. Then they had been diverted, for a fee that solved many of their problems, to the converting of a South African Bucc that Guy Dawson had flown up from Thunder City four months earlier.

Most of the Buccaneer enthusiasts' group were not and never had been fast-jet fliers. They were the riggers and fitters, the electricians and engineers, who had maintained the Buccs when they flew either for the Navy or the RAF. They lived locally, giving up their weekends and evenings to toil away, bringing the two salvaged veterans back to the air again.

Dexter and Mendoza spent the night at a local hostelry, an old coaching inn, with dark low beams and roaring logs, with glinting horse brasses and hunting prints that fascinated the Brazilian. In the morning, they motored over to Scampton to meet the team. There were fourteen of them, all engaged by Dexter with the Cobra's money. Proudly they showed the Bucc's new pilot what they had done.

The main change was the fitting of the guns. In its Cold War days, the Buccaneer had carried a range of ordnance suitable for a light bomber and especially a ship killer. While a warplane, her internal and underwing payload had been a frightening variety of bombs and rockets, up to and including tactical atom bombs.

In the version Major Mendoza examined that spring day in a drafty hangar in Lincolnshire, all this payload had been converted to fuel tanks, giving her an impressive range or hours of "loiter" time. With one exception.

Although the Bucc had never been an interceptor fighter, the ground crew's instructions had been clear. She had now been fitted with guns.

Under each wing, on the pylons that once

supported her rocket pods, were bolt-on gun packs. Each wing was armed with a pair of 30mm Aden cannons with enough fire-power to blow apart anything they hit.

The rear cockpit had not yet been converted. Soon it would have yet another reserve fuel tank and an ultra-modern communications set. The flier of this Bucc would never have a radio operator behind him; instead he would have a voice in his ear, thousands of miles away, telling him exactly where to head to find his target. But first it had to take the instructor.

"She's beautiful," murmured Mendoza.

"Glad you like her," said a voice behind him. He turned to find a slim woman of about forty. She held out a hand.

"I'm Colleen. I'll be your flying instructor for the conversion."

Cdr. Colleen Keck had never flown Buccs when she flew for the Navy. In the Buccaneer's day, the Fleet Air Arm had no female pilots. She had perforce joined the regular Navy and transferred to the Air Arm. After qualifying as a helicopter pilot, she had finally achieved her ambition — to fly jets. After her twenty years, she had retired and, living nearby and on a whim, joined the enthusiasts. A former Bucc pilot had "converted" her to Bucc qualification before he became too old to fly.

"I look forward to it," said Mendoza in his slow and careful English.

The whole group returned to the inn for a party on Dexter's tab. The next day, he left them to recover and start the training. He needed Major Mendoza and the six-strong maintenance team that would be coming with him installed on the island of Fogo by the last day in June. He flew back to Washington in time for another group of identifications from Jeremy Bishop.

The TR-1 is seldom mentioned and even more rarely seen. It is the invisible successor to the famous U-2 spy plane in which Gary Powers was once famously shot down over Siberia in 1960, and it went on to discover the Soviet missile bases being built in Cuba in 1962.

By the Gulf War of 1990/1991, the TR-1 was America's principal spy plane, higher and faster, with cameras that could transmit real-time images with no need to labor home with rolls of film. Dexter had asked to borrow one to operate out of USAF base Pensacola, and it had just arrived. It began work in the first week of May.

Dexter, with help from the tireless Bishop, had located a marine designer and architect whose talent was to identify almost any ship from almost any angle. He worked with Bishop on the top floor of the warehouse in Anacostia while the Third World relief blankets piled up below them.

The TR-1 ranged the Caribbean Basin, refueling at Malambo in Colombia or the U.S. bases in Puerto Rico whenever needed. The spy plane sent back high-definition pictures of harbors and ports cluttered with merchant vessels or ships at sea.

The shipping ace, with a powerful magnifying glass, pored over the pictures as Bishop downloaded them, comparing them with the details discovered earlier by Bishop from the names given by the welder.

"That one," he would say eventually, pointing out one of three dozen in a Caribbean port, "that must be the *Selene*," or, "There she is, unmistakable, handy size, almost gearless."

"She's what?" asked the perplexed Bishop.

"Medium tonnage, only one derrick, mounted forward. She's the *Virgen de Valme*. Sitting in Maracaibo."

Each was an expert and, as in the manner of experts, each found the specialty of the other impossible to understand. But between them they were identifying half the cartel's oceangoing fleet.

■ ■ ■ ■

No one goes to the Chagos Islands. It is forbidden. They are just a small group of coral atolls in the lost center of the Indian Ocean a thousand miles south of the southern tip of India.

Were they allowed, they might, like the Maldives, have resort hotels to take advantage of the limpid lagoons, all-year sun and untouched coral reefs. Instead they have bombers. Specifically, the American B-52.

The largest atoll of the group is Diego Garcia. Like the rest, it is British owned but long leased to the USA and a major air base and naval fueling station. It is so covert even the original islanders, pretty harmless fishermen, have been removed to other islands and forbidden to return.

What happened during that winter and spring of 2011 on Eagle Island was a British operation although part paid for by contributions out of Cobra's budget. Four Royal Fleet auxiliaries in succession, anchored offshore with tons of tools and equipment and Navy engineers, built a small colony.

It was never going to be a resort hotel, but it was habitable. There were rows of assemble-in-a-day flat-pack housing units. Outdoor latrines were dug. A food hall was assembled and equipped with kitchens, refrigerators and a fresh-water-producing desalination plant, all powered by a generator.

By the time it was finished and ready for occupation, it could accommodate over two hundred men, provided they had among them enough engineers, chefs and handymen to maintain all the facilities in running order. Kind to a fault, the Navy even left behind a sports shed with masks, snorkels and flippers. Whoever was going to be sequestered there could even snorkel the reefs. And there was a library of paperback books in English and Spanish.

For the sailors and engineers, it was not an arduous mission. On the horizon was Diego Garcia, a mini-America in the tropics equipped with every facility the U.S. serviceman far from home expects — which is the lot. And the British tars were welcome to visit, which they did. The only disturbance in this tropical paradise was the constant thunder of the bombers coming and going on their training missions.

Eagle Island had one other characteristic. It was almost a thousand miles from the nearest mainland, over a sea teeming with sharks, and virtually escape-proof. That was the point.

The Cape Verde Islands are another zone blessed with year-round sunshine. In mid-May, the new flying school on Fogo Island was officially opened. Once again, there was a ceremony. The Defence Minister flew in from Santiago Island to preside. Happily for them all, Portuguese was the only language spoken.

The government had, after rigorous testing, selected twenty-four young Verdeans to become air cadets. Not all might achieve their wings, but there had to be a margin for those who did not make it. The dozen Tucano twin-seat trainers had arrived from Brazil and were lined up in a neat row. Also at attention were the dozen instructors on loan from the Brazilian Air Force. The only person missing was the commanding officer, identified as a certain Major João Mendoza. He was detained on flying duties elsewhere and would join his command within a month.

It mattered little. The first thirty days would be spent on classroom work and aircraft familiarization. Informed of all this, the minister nodded his grave assent and approval. There was no need to tell him that

Major Mendoza would be arriving in his personal airplane, which he could afford to fly for recreation.

Had the minister known about the aircraft, which he did not, he might have understood why the storage tank of JP-8 fuel for the trainers was separate from the much more volatile JP-5 fuel needed by high-performance Navy jets. And he never penetrated the extra hangar dug into the rock face with steel doors. Told it was a storage facility, he lost interest.

The eager cadets settled into their dormitories, the official party left for the capital and classes started the next day.

In fact, the missing CO was at 20,000 feet over the gray North Sea east of the English coasts on a routine navigational exercise with his instructor. Cdr. Keck was in the rear cockpit. There had never been controls in the rear cockpit, so the instructor was in a "total trust" situation. But she could still monitor the accuracy of intercepts of imaginary targets. And she was content with what she saw.

The following day was free time because the vital night flying would commence the night after. And then finally RATO and gunnery practice, for which the targets would be brightly painted barrels floating in the sea, dropped at agreed locations by one of their group who had a fishing boat. She had no doubt her pupil would pass with flying colors. She had quickly noted that he was a natural flier and had taken to the old Bucc as a grebe to water.

"Have you ever flown with rocket-assisted takeoff?" she asked him a week later in the crew hut.

"No, Brazil is very large," he joked. "We always had enough land to build long runways."

"Your S2 Bucc never had RATO because our aircraft carriers were long enough," she told him. "But sometimes in the tropics the air is too hot. One loses power. And this plane was in South Africa. It needs help. So we have no choice but to fit RATO. It will take your breath away."

And it did. Pretending the huge Scampton runway was really too short for unassisted takeoff, the riggers had fitted the small rockets behind the tail skid. Colleen Keck briefed him carefully on the takeoff sequence.

Park right at the end of the tarmac. Hand brakes on hard. Run up the Spey engines against the brakes. At the moment they can hold no more, release brakes, power to maximum, flick the rocket switch. João Mendoza thought a train had hit him in the back. The Buccaneer almost reared and threw herself down the tarmac line. There was a blur of runway, and she was airborne.

Unbeknownst to Cdr. Keck, Major Mendoza had spent his evenings studying a pack of photos sent to him at the inn by Cal Dexter. They showed him the Fogo runway, the approach lights pattern, the touchdown threshold coming in from the sea. The Brazilian had no doubts left. It would be, as his English friends liked to call it, a piece of cake.

Cal Dexter had examined the three pilotless drones, the Unmanned Aerial Vehicle, or UAVs, manufactured by the USA with enormous care. Their role was going to be vital in the Cobra's coming war. He finally discarded the Reaper and the Predator and chose the "unweaponized" Global Hawk. Its job was surveillance and only surveillance.

Using Paul Devereaux's presidential authority, he had lengthy negotiations with Northrop Grumman, the manufacturers of the RQ-4. He already knew that a version dedicated to "broad area maritime surveillance" had been developed in 2006 and that the U.S. Navy had placed a very large order.

He wanted two extra capabilities, and he was told there need not be a problem. The technology existed.

One was for the onboard memory bank to memorize the images brought back by the TR-1 spy planes of almost two score ships as seen directly from above. The pictures would be broken down into pixels that would represent a distance no more than two inches on the deck of the real ship. It would then have to compare what it was looking down at with what was in its data bank and inform its handlers, miles away at their base, when it found a match.

Second, he needed communications-jamming technology, enabling the Hawk to surround the vessel beneath it with a ten-mile-diameter circle in which no communication of any electronic kind would work.

Though it packed no rocket, the RQ-4 Hawk had all the details Dexter needed. It could fly at 65,000 feet, far out of sight or sound of what it was watching. Through sun, rain, cloud or night, it could survey forty thousand square miles a day and, sipping its fuel, could stay up there for thirty-five hours. Unlike the other two, it could cruise at 340 knots, far faster than its targets.

By the end of May, two of these marvels had been installed and were dedicated to Project Cobra. One was set up to operate out of the Colombian coastal base of Malambo, northeast of Cartagena.

The other was on the island of Fernando de Noronha, off the northeastern coast of Brazil. Each unit was lodged in a facility set away from all prying eyes on the other side of the air base. On the Cobra's instruction, they began to prowl as soon as installed.

Although operated on the air bases, the actual scanning was accomplished many miles away in the Nevada desert at U.S. Air Force Base Creech. Here, men sat at consoles staring at the screens. Each had a control column like that of a pilot in his cockpit.

What each operator saw on his screen was exactly what the Hawk could see staring down from the stratosphere. Some of the men and women in that quiet, air-conditioned control room at Creech had Predators hunting over Afghanistan and the border mountains leading to Pakistan. Others had Reapers over the Persian Gulf.

Each had earphones and a throat mike to receive instructions and inform higher authority if a target hove into view. The concentration was total and therefore the shifts short. The Creech control room was the face of wars to come.

With his dark humor, Cal Dexter gave each patrolling Hawk a nickname to tell them apart. The eastern one he called "Michelle," after the First Lady; the other one was "Sam," after the wife of the British Prime Minister.

And each had a separate task. Michelle was to gaze down, identify and track all merchant marine vessels identified by Juan Cortez and found and photographed by the TR-1. Sam was to find and report on everything flying or sailing out of the Brazilian coast between Natal and Belém, or heading eastward across the Atlantic passing longitude 40°, direction Africa.

Both the control decks at Creech in charge of the two Cobra Hawks were in direct touch with the dowdy warehouse in the Washington suburb, twenty-four hours a day, seven days a week.

Letizia Arenal knew what she was doing was wrong, against the strict instructions of her papá, but she could not help herself. He had told her never to leave Spain, but she was in love, and love trumped even his instructions.

Domingo de Vega had proposed to her and she had accepted. She wore his ring on her hand. But he had to return to his post in New York or lose it, and his birthday was in the last week of May. He had sent her an open ticket with Iberia to Kennedy and begged her to come and join him.

The formalities at the American Embassy had been accomplished as if on oiled wheels; she had her visa waiver and was cleared by Homeland Security.

Her ticket was in business class, and she checked in at Terminal 4 with hardly any wait. Her single valise was tagged for "New York Kennedy" and slid away down the conveyor belt to baggage handling. She took no notice of the man behind her hefting a large grip as his personal and only carry-on luggage.

She could not know it was full of newspapers or that he would turn away as soon as she disappeared toward security and passport control. She had never seen Inspector Paco Ortega before and she never would again. But he had memorized every detail of her single valise and of the clothes she was wearing. Her photo had been taken from long distance as she stepped from her cab at the curb. All would be in New York before she even set off.

But just to be on the safe side, he stood at an observation window, looking out at the airfield, and watched as, far away, the Iberia jet turned into the breeze, paused, then roared toward the still-snowcapped peaks of the Sierra de Guadarrama and the Atlantic. Then he called New York and had a few words with Cal Dexter.

The airliner was on time. There was a man in ground-staff uniform in the jetway as the passengers streamed off. He murmured two words into a cell phone, but no one took any notice. People do that all the time.

Letizia Arenal passed through passport control with no more than the usual formality of pressing one thumb after another onto a small glass panel and staring into a camera lens for iris recognition.

As she went through, the immigration official turned and nodded silently at a man who stood in the corridor the passengers were now taking toward the customs hall. The man nodded back and wandered after the young woman.

It was a heavy day for traffic, and the luggage was delayed by an extra twenty minutes. Eventually, the carousel gurgled, thumped into life, and suitcases began to spew onto the moving band. Her own case was neither first nor last but somewhere in the middle. She saw it tumble from the open mouth of the tunnel and recognized the bright yellow tag that she had affixed to help her pick it out.

It was a hard frame with wheels, so she slung her tote bag over her left shoulder and towed the valise toward the green channel. She was halfway through when one of the customs officers, as if standing idly by, beckoned to her. A spot check. Nothing to worry about. Domingo would be waiting for her in the concourse beyond the doors. He would have to wait a few minutes longer.

She pulled her case toward the table the officer indicated and lifted it. The latches were facing toward her.

"Would you please open your case, ma'am?" Scrupulously polite. They were always scrupulously polite, and they never smiled or joked. She unflicked the two catches. The officer turned the case around toward himself and lifted the lid. He saw the clothes ranged on top, and, with gloved hands, lifted off the top layer. Then he stopped. She realized he was staring at her over the top of the lid. She presumed he would now close it and nod that she could leave.

He closed it, and said very coldly, "Would

you come with me, if you please, ma'am."

It was not a question. She became aware that a big man and a burly woman, also in the same uniforms, were standing close behind her. It was embarrassing; other passengers were staring sideways as they scuttled through.

The first officer snapped the catches closed, hefted the case and went ahead. The others, without a word spoken, came up behind. The first officer led them through a door in the corner. It was quite a bare room, with a table at the center, a few plain chairs against the walls. No pictures, two cameras in different corners. The valise went flat on the table.

"Would you please open your valise again, ma'am?"

It was the first inkling Letizia Arenal had that something might be wrong, but she had not a clue what it might be. She opened her case, saw her own neatly folded clothes.

"Would you take them out, please, ma'am?"

It was underneath the linen jacket, the two cotton skirts and the several folded blouses. Not large, about the size of a one-kilo bag of grocery-store sugar. Filled with what looked like talc. Then it hit her; like a wave of fainting nausea, a punch in the solar plexus, a silent voice in the head screaming:

No, it is not me, I did not do this, it is not mine, someone must have placed it there . . .

It was the burly woman who sustained her, but not out of any spirit of sympathy. For the cameras. So obsessional are the New York courts with the rights of the accused, and so keen are defense attorneys to pounce upon the tiniest infraction of the rules of procedure to procure a dismissal of a charge, that, from officialdom's point of view, not even the smallest formality may be ignored.

After the opening of the suitcase and the discovery of what at that point was simply unidentified white powder, Letizia Arenal went, in the official phrase, "into the system." Later it all seemed a single nightmarish blur.

She was taken to another, better-appointed room in the terminal complex. There was a bank of digital recorders. Other men came. She did not know, but they were from the DEA and the ICE, the U.S. Immigration and Customs Enforcement. With U.S. customs, that made three authorities detaining her under different jurisdictions.

Although her English was good, a Spanish-speaking interpreter arrived. She was read her rights, the Miranda rights, of which she had never heard. At every sentence, she was asked, "Do you understand, ma'am?" Always the polite "ma'am," although their expressions told her they despised her.

Somewhere, her passport was being minutely examined. Elsewhere, her suitcase and shoulder bag received the same attention. The bag of white powder was sent for analysis, which would happen outside the building at another facility, a chemical lab. Not surprisingly, it turned out to be pure cocaine.

The fact that it was pure was important. A small quantity of "cut" powder might be explained as "personal use." Not a kilo of pure.

In the presence of two women, she was required to remove every stitch of clothing, which was taken away. She was given a sort of paper coverall to wear. A qualified doctor, female, carried out an invasive body search into orifices, ears included. By now, she was sobbing uncontrollably. But the "system" would have its way. And all on camera, for the record. No smart-ass lawyer was going to get the bitch off this one.

Finally, a senior DEA officer informed her she had the right to ask for a lawyer. She had not been formally interrogated, not yet. Her Miranda rights had not been infringed.

She said she knew no New York lawyer. She was told a defense attorney would be appointed, but by the court, not by him.

She repeatedly said her fiancé would be waiting for her outside. This was not ignored, not at all. Whoever was waiting for her might be her accomplice in crime. The crowds in the concourse beyond the doors of the customs hall were thoroughly vetted. No Domingo de Vega was found. Either he was a fiction or, if her accomplice, he had fled the scene. In the morning they would check for a Puerto Rican diplomat of that name at the UN.

She insisted on explaining all, waiving her right to an attorney being present. She told them everything she knew, which was nothing. They did not believe her. Then she had an idea.

"I am a Colombian. I want to see someone from the Colombian Embassy."

"It will be the consulate, ma'am. It is now ten at night. We will try to raise someone in the morning."

This was from the FBI man, though she did not know it. Drug smuggling into the USA is a federal, not state, offense. The Feds had taken over.

JFK Airport comes under the East District of New York, the EDNY, and is in the borough of Brooklyn. Finally, close to midnight, Letizia Arenal was lodged in that borough's federal correctional institution, pending a magistrate's hearing in the morning.

And of course a file was opened, which rapidly became thicker and thicker. The system needs a lot of paperwork. In her single, stiffling cell, odorous of sweat and fear, Letizia Arenal cried the night away.

In the morning, the Feds contacted someone at the Colombian Consulate, who agreed to come. If the prisoner expected some sympathy there, she was to be disappointed. The consular assistant could hardly have been more hatchet-faced. This was exactly the sort of thing the diplomats loathed.

The assistant was a woman in a severe black business suit. She listened without a flicker of expression to the explanation and believed not a word of it. But she had no choice but to agree to contact Bogotá and ask the Foreign Ministry there to trace a private lawyer called Julio Luz. It was the only name Ms. Arenal could think of to turn to for help.

There was a first hearing at the magistrate's court, but only to arrange a further remand. Learning that the defendant had

241

no representation, the magistrate ordered that a public defender be found. A young man barely out of law school was traced, and they had a few moments together in a holding cell before returning to the court-room.

The defender made a hopeless plea for bail. It was hopeless because the accused was foreign, without funds or family, the alleged crime was immensely serious and the prosecutor made plain that further investigations were afoot into the suspicion that a much larger chain of cocaine smugglers could be involved with the defendant.

The defender tried to plead that there was a fiancé in the form of a diplomat at the United Nations. One of the Feds slipped a note to the prosecutor, who rose again, this time to reveal there was no Domingo de Vega in the Puerto Rican mission at the UN nor ever had been.

"Save it for your memoirs, Mr. Jenkins," drawled the magistrate. "Defendant is remanded. Next."

The gavel came down. Letizia Arenal was led away in a flood of fresh tears. Her so-called fiancé, the man she had loved, had cynically betrayed her.

Before she was taken back to the cor-rectional institute she had a last meeting with her lawyer, Mr. Jenkins. He offered her his card.

"You may call me anytime, señorita. You have that right. There is no charge. The public defender is free for those with no funds."

"You do not understand, Mr. Jenkins. Soon will come from Bogotá Señor Luz. He will rescue me."

As he returned by public transport to his shabby law office, Jenkins thought there has to be one born every minute. No Domingo de Vega, and probably no Julio Luz.

He was wrong on the second point. That morning, Señor Luz had taken a call from the Colombian Foreign Ministry that almost caused him to have a cardiac arrest.

CHAPTER 8

Julio Luz, the advocate from the city of Bogotá, flew into New York clothed in outward calm, but internally a thoroughly frightened man. Since the arrest of Letizia Arenal at Kennedy three days earlier, he had had two long and terrifying interviews with one of the most violent men he had ever met.

Though he had sat with Roberto Cárdenas in the meetings of the cartel, that had always been under the chairmanship of Don Diego, whose word was law and who demanded a level of dignity to match his own.

In a room in a farmhouse miles off the beaten track, Cárdenas had no such limitations. He had raged and threatened. Like Luz, he had no doubt his daughter's luggage had been interfered with and had convinced himself the insertion of cocaine had been accomplished by some opportunist lowlife in the baggage hall at Barajas

244

Airport, Madrid.

He described what he would do to this baggage handler when he caught up with him, until Julio Luz felt nauseated. Finally, they concocted the story they would present to the New York authorities. Neither man had ever heard of any Domingo de Vega and could not surmise why she had been flying there.

Prisoners' mail out of U.S. correctional institutions is censored, and Letizia had not written any such letter. All Julio Luz knew was what he had been told by the Foreign Ministry.

The lawyer's story would be that the young woman was an orphan, and he was her guardian. Papers were concocted to that effect. Money traceable back to Cárdenas was impossible to use. Luz would draw monies from his own practice, and Cárdenas would reimburse him later. Luz, arriving in New York, would be in funds, entitled to see his ward in jail and seeking to engage the best criminal attorney money could buy.

And this he did, in that order. Faced with her fellow countryman, even with a Spanish-speaking woman from the DEA sitting in the corner of the room, Letizia Arenal poured out her story to a man she had met only for dinner and breakfast at the Villa

Real Hotel.

Luz was aghast, not just at the story of the devilishly handsome pseudo-diplomat from Puerto Rico, nor at the incredibly stupid decision to disobey her father by flying the Atlantic, but at the prospect of the volcanic rage of that father when he heard, as hear he must.

The lawyer could add two and two and come up with four. The phony art-fan Vega was clearly part of a Madrid-based smuggling gang using his gigolo talents to recruit unsuspecting young women to act as "mules" by carrying cocaine into the U.S. He had little doubt that soon after his return to Colombia, there would be an army of Spanish and Colombian thugs coming to Madrid and New York to find the missing Vega.

The fool would be snatched, taken to Colombia, handed over to Cárdenas and then God help him. Letizia told him there had been a photo of her fiancé in her purse and a larger one in her flat in Moncloa. He made a mental note to demand the first back and have the larger one removed from the Madrid apartment. They would help in the search for the rogue behind this disaster. Luz calculated the young smuggler would not be hiding deep because he would not know who was coming for him, only that he had lost one of his cargoes.

He would, under torture, give up the name of the baggage handler who had inserted the bag of coke at Madrid. A full confession from him, and New York would have to drop the charge. So he reasoned.

Later, there was total denial of there being any photo of any young man in the purse confiscated at Kennedy, and the one in Madrid had already gone. Paco Ortega had seen to that. But first things first. Luz engaged the services of Mr. Boseman Barrow, of Manson Barrow, considered the finest advocate at the criminal bar of Manhattan. The sum involved for Mr. Barrow to drop everything and cross the river into Brooklyn was deeply impressive.

But as the two men returned from the federal correctional institution to Manhattan the following day, the New Yorker's face was grave. Internally, he was not so grave. He saw months and months of work at astronomical fees.

"Señor Luz, I must be brutally frank. Things are not good. Personally, I have no doubt your ward was lured into a disastrous situation by the cocaine smuggler who called himself Domingo de Vega and that she was unaware of what she was doing. She

247

was duped. It happens all the time."

"So that is good," interjected the Colombian.

"It is good that I believe it. But if I am to represent her, I must. The problem is, I am neither the jury nor the judge, and I am certainly not the DEA, the FBI or the District Attorney. And a much bigger problem is that this Vega man has not only vanished, but there is not a shred of evidence that he existed."

The law firm's limousine crossed the East River and Luz stared down glumly at the gray water.

"But Vega was not the baggage handler," he protested. "There must be another man, the one in Madrid who opened her case and put in the package."

"We do not know that," sighed the Manhattan counselor. "He may have been the baggage handler as well. Or have had access to the baggage hall. He may have passed for an Iberia staffer or customs officer with right of access. He may even have been either of these things. How energetic will the Madrid authorities be to divert their precious resources to the task of trying to liberate one they probably see as a dope smuggler, and a non-Spanish to boot?"

They turned onto the East River Drive

toward Boseman Barrow's comfort zone, downtown Manhattan.

"I have funds," protested Julio Luz. "I can engage private investigators on both sides of the Atlantic. How you say, 'the sky is the limit.' "

Mr. Barrow beamed down at his companion. He could almost smell the odor of the new wing on his mansion in the Hamptons. This was going to take many months.

"We have one powerful argument, Señor Luz. It is clear that the security apparatus at Madrid Airport screwed up badly."

"Screwed up?"

"Failed. In these paranoid days, all airline baggage heading to the U.S. should be X-ray screened at the airport of departure. Especially in Europe. There are bilateral compacts. The outline of the bag should have shown up at Madrid. And they have sniffer dogs. Why no sniffer dogs? It all points to an insertion *after* the usual checks . . ."

"Then we can ask they drop the charges?"

"On an administrative foul-up? I'm afraid dropping the charges is out of the question. As for our chances in court, without some blistering new evidence in her favor, not good. A New York jury simply will not believe a screwup in Madrid Airport is possible.

"They will look at the known evidence, not the protestations of the accused. One passenger from, of all places, Colombia; slipping through the Green Channel; one kilogram of Colombian pure; floods of tears. I am afraid it is very, very common. And the city of New York is getting very, very sick of it."

Mr. Barrow forebore to say that his own engagement would not look good either. Olympian quantities of money were associated by low-budget New Yorkers, the sort who end up on juries, with the cocaine trade. A real, innocent mule would be abandoned to the Legal Aid Office. But no need to secure his own departure from the case.

"What happens now?" asked Luz. His entrails were starting to melt again at the idea of confronting the volcanic temper of Roberto Cárdenas with this.

"Well, she will soon appear before the Federal District Court for Brooklyn. The judge will not grant bail. That is a given. She will be transferred to an upstate federal jail on remand, pending trial. These are not nice places. She is not street hardened. Convent educated, you said? Oh dear. There are aggressive lesbians in these places. I am deeply sorry to say that. I doubt it is different in Colombia."

Luz put his face in his hands.

"Dios mío," he murmured. "How long there?"

"Well, not less than six months, I fear. Time for the Prosecutor's Office to prepare its case, somewhere in its vast workload. And for us, of course. For your private eyes to see what they can turn up."

Julio Luz also declined to be frank. He had no doubt a few private eyes would be Cub Scouts compared to the army of hard men Roberto Cárdenas would unleash to find the destroyer of his daughter. But he was wrong in that. Cárdenas would do no such thing, because Don Diego would find out. The Don did not know about the secret daughter, and the Don insisted on knowing everything. Even Julio Luz had thought she was the gangster's girlfriend and the envelopes he carried were her allowance. He had one last timid question. The limousine hissed through the slush to a halt outside the luxury office block whose penthouse floor housed the small but gold-plated law firm of Manson Barrow.

"If she is found guilty, Señor Barrow, what would be the sentence?"

251

"Hard to say, of course. Depends on mitigating evidence, if any; my own advocacy; the judge on the day. But I fear in the present mood it might be felt necessary to create an example. A deterrent. In the area of twenty years in a federal penitentiary. Thank heavens her parents are not around to see it."

Julio Luz moaned. Barrow took pity.

"Of course, the picture could be transformed if she became an informant. We call it 'plea bargaining.' The DEA does trade deals for insider information to catch the much bigger fish. Now, if . . ."

"She cannot," moaned Luz. "She knows nothing. She is truly innocent."

"Ah well, then . . . such a pity."

Luz was being quite truthful. He alone knew what the jailed young woman's father did, and he certainly did not dare to tell her.

May slipped into June, and Global Hawk Michelle silently glided and turned over the eastern and southern Caribbean, seeming like a real hawk to ride the thermals on an endless quest for prey. This was not the first time.

In the spring of 2006, a joint Air Force/DEA program had put a Global Hawk over the Caribbean from a base in Florida. It was a Maritime Demonstration Program, and short-term. In its brief time aloft, the Hawk managed to monitor hundreds of sea and air targets. It was enough to convince the Navy that BAMS, or Broad Aspect Maritime Surveillance, was the future, and it placed a huge order.

But the Navy was thinking Russian fleet, Iranian gunboats, North Korean spy ships. The DEA was thinking cocaine smugglers. The trouble was, in 2006 the Hawk could show what it could show, but no one knew which was which, the innocent and the guilty. Thanks to Juan Cortez the wonder-welder, the authorities now had Lloyd's-listed cargo ships by name and tonnage. Close to forty of them.

At AFB Creech, Nevada, shifts of men and women watched Michelle's screen, and every two or three days her tiny onboard computers would make a match — pitting the "Identi-Kit" deck layout provided by Jeremy Bishop against the deck of something moving far below.

When Michelle made a match, Creech would call the shabby warehouse in Anacostia to say:

"Team Cobra. We have the MV *Mariposa.* She is coming out of the Panama Canal into the Caribbean."

Bishop would acknowledge, and punch up details of the *Mariposa* on her present voyage. Cargo heading for Baltimore. She might have taken on a consignment of cocaine in Guatemala or at sea. Or maybe not yet. She might be taking her cocaine right into Baltimore itself or dropping it to a speedboat by dead of night somewhere in the vast blackness of Chesapeake Bay. Or she might not be carrying at all.

"Shall we alert Baltimore customs? Or the Maryland Coast Guard?" asked Bishop.

"Not yet" was the answer.

It was not Paul Devereaux's habit to explain to underlings. He kept his logic to himself. If searchers went straight to the secret place, or even made a pretense of finding it with dogs, after two or three successful discoveries the coincidences would be too neat for the cartel to ignore.

He did not want to make intercepts or hand them gift-wrapped to others once the cargo had landed. He was prepared to leave the American and European importing gangs to the local authorities. His target was the Brotherhood, and they took the "hit" directly only if the intercept was at sea, before handover and change of ownership.

As was his habit from the old days when

the opponent was the KGB and its satellite goons, he studied his enemy with extreme care. He pored over the wisdom of Sun-tzu as expressed in the *Ping-fa,* the *Art of War.* He revered the old Chinese sage whose repeated advice was "Study your enemy."

Devereaux knew who headed the Brotherhood, and he had studied Don Diego Esteban, landowner, gentleman, Catholic scholar, philanthropist, cocaine lord and killer. He knew he had one advantage that would not last forever. He knew about the Don, but the Don knew nothing of the waiting Cobra.

On the other side of South America, right out over the Brazilian coast, Global Hawk Sam had also been patrolling the stratosphere. Everything it saw was sent to a screen in Nevada and then patched to the computers at Anacostia. The merchant vessels were much fewer. Trade by big carriers from South America due east to West Africa was slimmer. What there was was photographed, and though the vessels' names were usually out of sight from 60,000 feet, their images were compared to the files of the MOAC in Lisbon, the UN's ODC in Vienna and the British SOCA in Accra, Ghana.

Five matches could be given names that

were on the Cortez list. The Cobra stared at Bishop's screens and promised himself their time would come.

And there was something else Sam noticed and recorded. Airplanes left the Brazilian coast heading due east or northeast for Africa. The commercials were not many and not a problem. But every profile was sent to Creech and then Anacostia. Jeremy Bishop quickly identified them all by type, and a pattern emerged.

Many of them had not the range. They would not make the distance. Unless they had been internally modified. Global Hawk Sam was given fresh instructions. Refueled at the air base on Fernando de Noronha, it went back up and concentrated on the smaller aircraft.

Working backward, as from the rim of a bicycle wheel down the spokes to the hub, Sam established they almost all came from a huge estancia deep inland from the city of Fortaleza. Maps of Brazil from space, the images sent back by Sam and discreet checks within the office of land management at Belém identified the ranch. It was called Boa Vista.

The Americans got there first, as they had the longest cruise ahead of them. Twelve of them flew into Goa International Airport masquerading as tourists in mid-June. Had anyone delved deep into their baggage, which no one did, the searcher would have found that, by a remarkable coincidence, all twelve were fully qualified as merchant seamen. In truth, they were the same U.S. Navy crew that had originally brought the grain vessel now converted into the MV *Chesapeake*. A coach hired by McGregor brought them down the coast to the Kapoor shipyard.

The *Chesapeake* was waiting, and as there was no accommodation inside the yard they went straight on board for a long sleep. The next morning they began two days of intensive familiarization.

The senior officer, the new captain, was a Navy commander, and his first officer one rank down. There were two lieutenants and the other eight ran from chief petty officer down to rating. Each specialist concentrated on his individual kingdom: bridge, engine room, galley, radio shack, deck and hatch covers.

It was when they penetrated the five huge grain holds that they stopped in amazement. There was a complete Special Forces barracks down there, all without portholes or natural daylight and therefore all invisible from the outside. At sea, they were told, they would have no call to come forward from their own quarters. The SEALs would fix their own chow and generally look after themselves.

The crew would confine themselves to the ship's normal crew quarters, which were more spacious and more comfortable than they would have had, for example, on a destroyer.

There was a double-bunked guest cabin, purpose unknown. If the SEAL officers wished to confer with the bridge, they would walk belowdecks through four water-tight doors connecting the holds and then upward into the daylight.

They were not told, because they did not need to know, or not yet, why the hold nearest the bow was a sort of jail to take prisoners. But they were definitely shown how to remove the hatch covers over two of the five holds to bring their contents up into action. This exercise they would practice repeatedly on their long cruise; partly to while away the hours, partly until they could do it in double time and in their sleep.

On the third day, the parchment-skinned McGregor saw them off to sea. He stood on the end of the seamost groyne, as the *Chesapeake* came under way and slid past him, and raised an amber glass. He was prepared to live in conditions of heat, malaria, sweat and stench, but never to be without a bottle or two of the distillation of his native islands, the Hebrides.

The shorter route to her destination would have been across the Arabian Sea and through the Suez Canal. Because of the long shot of Somali pirates proving troublesome off the Horn of Africa, and because she had the time, it had been decided she would turn southwest for the Cape of Good Hope, then northwest to her sea rendezvous off Puerto Rico.

Three days later, the British arrived to pick up the MV *Balmoral*. There were fourteen, all Royal Navy, and under the guidance of McGregor they, too, went through a two-day familiarization process. Because the U.S. Navy is "dry" in alcohol terms, the Americans had brought no duty-free spirits from the airport. The inheritors of Nelson's navy have no such rigors to endure, and they made their mark with Mr. McGregor by bringing several bottles of single malt brew from Islay, his favorite distillery.

When she was ready, the *Balmoral* also put to sea. Her sea rendezvous was closer; around the Cape of Good Hope and northwest to Ascension Island, where she would meet, out of sight and land, a Royal Fleet Auxiliary carrying her complement of Special Boat Service Marines and the equipment they, too, would need.

When the *Balmoral* was over the horizon, McGregor packed up what was left. The converter crews and internal outfitters were long gone and their motor homes taken back by the hire company. The old Scot was living in the last of them on his diet of whisky and quinine. The brothers Kapoor had been paid off from bank accounts no one would ever trace and lost all interest in two grain ships they had converted to dive centers. The yard went back to its habitual regime of dismembering ships full of toxic chemicals and asbestos.

Colleen Keck crouched on the wing of the Buccaneer and puckered her face against the wind. The exposed flat plains of Lincolnshire are not balmy ever in June. She had come to say good-bye to the Brazilian of whom she had become fond.

Beside her, in the forward cockpit of the fighter bomber, sat Major João Mendoza, making last and final checks. In the rear cockpit, where she had sat to train him, the seat was gone. Instead was yet another extra fuel tank, and a radio set that fed straight into the flier's headphones. Behind them both, the two Spey engines rumbled at the idling pitch.

When there was no point in waiting anymore, she leaned in and gave him a peck on the cheek.

"Safe journey, João," she shouted. He saw her lips move and realized what she had said. He smiled back and raised his right hand, thumb erect. With the arctic wind, the jets behind him and the voice from the tower in his ears, he could not hear her.

Cdr. Keck slid off the wing and jumped to the ground. The Perspex canopy rolled forward and closed, locking the pilot into his own world; a world of control column, throttles, instruments, gunsight, fuel gauges and tactical air navigator, the TACAN.

He asked for and got final clearance, turned onto the runway, paused again, checked brakes, released and rolled. Seconds later, the ground crew in the van by the tarmac, who had come to see him off, watched as 22,000 pounds of thrust from twin Speys powered the Buccaneer into the skies and saw it bank toward the south.

Because of the changes made, it had been decided Major Mendoza would fly back to the mid-Atlantic by a different route. In the Portuguese islands of the Azores is the U.S.

Air Force base of Lajes, home of the 64th Wing, and the Pentagon, operating to unseen strings, had agreed to refuel the "museum piece" ostensibly heading back to South Africa. At 1,395 nautical miles, it was no problem.

Nevertheless, he overnighted in the officers' club at Lajes in order to leave at dawn for Fogo. He had no wish to make his first landing at his new home in the dark. He took off at dawn for the second leg, 1,439 miles to Fogo, well under his 2,200-mile limit.

The skies over the Cape Verde Islands were clear. As he dropped down from his cruise altitude of 35,000 feet, he could see them all with total clarity. At 10,000 feet, the wakes of a few speedboats out at sea were like little white feathers against the blue water. At the south end of the group, west of Santiago, he could make out the jutting caldera of Fogo's extinct volcano and, tucked into the southwestern flank of the rock, the sliver of airport runway.

He dropped farther in a long, curving sweep over the Atlantic, keeping the volcano just off port wing. He knew that he had a designated call sign and frequency, and that the language would not be Portuguese but English. He would be "Pilgrim," and Fogo

Central was "Progress." He pressed the Transmit button and called.

"Pilgrim, Pilgrim . . . Progress Tower, do you read me?"

The voice that came back he recognized. One of the six from Scampton who would be his technical and support team. An English voice, North Country accent. His friend was sitting in the Fogo Airport control tower beside the Verdean traffic controller of commercial flights.

"Read you fine, Pilgrim."

The Scampton enthusiast, another retiree recruited by Cal Dexter with Cobra money, stared out of the plate-glass window of the stumpy little control box and could clearly see the Bucc curving over the sea. He delivered landing instructions: direction of runway, wind strength and direction.

At 1,000 feet, João Mendoza lowered undercarriage and flaps to landing setting, watched the airspeed and altitude drop. In such brilliant visibility, there was not much need for technology; this was flying as it used to be. Two miles out, he lined up. The froth of foaming surf swept under him, the wheels thumped the tarmac at the very threshold marker, and he was braking gently down a runway half the length of the Scampton strip. He was fuel light and unweaponed. It was not a problem.

As he came to a halt with two hundred yards to spare, a small pickup swerved in front, and a figure in the back beckoned him to follow. He taxied away from the terminal to the flight-school complex and finally shut down.

The five who had preceded him from Scampton surrounded him. There were cheery greetings as he climbed down. The sixth was approaching from the tower on his rented scooter. All six had arrived by a British C-130 Hercules two days earlier. With them came rockets for RATO departures, every tool needed to maintain the Bucc in her new role and the all-important Aden cannon ammunition. Among the six, all now assured of much more comfortable pensions than they had faced six months earlier, were rigger, fitter, armorer (the "plumber"), avionics expert, air comms (radio) technician and the air traffic controller who had just talked him down.

Most missions yet to come would be in darkness, both takeoff and landing, which would be trickier, but they had another fortnight to practice. For the moment, they took him off to his quarters, where his kit was already laid out. Then he went to the main mess hall to meet his fellow Brazilian instructors and the Portuguese-speaking cadets. The new CO and his personal museum piece had arrived. The youngsters were eagerly looking forward, after four weeks of classwork and aircraft familiarization, to their first dual-controls flights in the morning.

Compared to their basic simple little Tucano trainers, the former Navy ship killer looked formidable. But it was soon towed to the steel-doored hangar and out of sight. That afternoon, she was refueled, her rockets fitted and her canno packs armed. Night familiarization was two evenings away. A few passengers trooping off the Santiago shuttle into the civilian terminal saw nothing.

That evening, speaking out of Washington, Cal Dexter had a short conversation with Major Mendoza, and, in answer to the obvious question, told him to be patient. He would not have long to wait.

Julio Luz was trying to act normally. He had been sworn to secrecy by Roberto Cárdenas, and yet the thought of deceiving the Don, even by nondisclosure, terrified him. They both terrified him.

He resumed his fortnightly visits to Madrid as if nothing had happened. On this particular trip, his first since his visit to New York and yet another utterly miserable hour reporting to Cárdenas, he was again invisibly followed. He was quite unaware, as was the excellent management of the Villa Real Hotel, that his habitual room had been bugged by a team of two from the FBI, directed by Cal Dexter. Every sound he made was listened to by another hotel client, who had taken a room two floors above him.

The man sat patiently with "cans" over his ears and blessed the wiry ex–Tunnel Rat who had installed him in a comfortable room instead of his usual billet on stakeouts: a cramped van in a parking lot with rotten coffee and "no facilities." When the target was out at the bank, dining or taking breakfast, he could relax with the TV or the funnies of the *International Herald Tribune* from the lobby newsstand. But on this particular morning, the day of the target's departure back to the airport, he was listening hard with his cell in his left hand.

The lawyer's personal physician would have been completely understanding of the middle-aged patient's abiding problem. The constant cross-Atlantic journeys played havoc with his constipation. He carried his own supply of syrup of figs at all times. This had been discovered during a raid on his room while he was at the bank.

After ordering a pot of Earl Grey tea in bed, he retired to the marble bathroom and thence to the lavatory cubicle as always. There he patiently waited for nature to take its course, a sojourn that took up to ten minutes. During that time, with the door closed, he could not hear his own bedroom. That was when the eavesdropper made his call.

On the morning in question, the room was silently entered. The key code was different with every visit, of course, indeed changed for every occupant of the room, but it posed no barrier to the lockpicker Cal Dexter had brought with him again. The deep pile of the carpet reduced footfalls to utter silence. Dexter crossed the room to the chest where the attaché case rested. He hoped the roller sequence had not been altered, and he was right. It was still the Bar Association membership number. He had the lid up, the job done and the lid replaced in seconds. He rolled the numbers back to where they had been before. Then he left. Behind the bathroom door, Señor Julio Luz sat and strained.

He might have made it to the first-class departure lounge at Barajas without opening his briefcase, if only he had had his airline ticket in his breast pocket. But he had put it in his travel wallet in the interior lid of the case. So as his hotel checkout record was being printed, he opened his case to get it.

If the shock call from the Colombian Foreign Ministry ten days earlier had been bad, this was calamitous. He felt so weak, he thought he might be having a heart attack. Disregarding the proffered printout, he retired to sit on a lobby chair, case on lap, staring haggard at the floor. A bellhop had to tell him three times that his limo was at the door. Finally, he staggered down the steps and into the car. As it drew away, he glanced behind. Was he being followed? Would he be intercepted, dragged away to a cell for the third degree?

In fact, he could not have been safer. Invisibly tailed on arrival and during his stay, he was now being invisibly escorted to the airport. As the limo left the suburbs behind, he checked again, just in case of an optical illusion. No illusion. It was there, right on top. A cream manila envelope. It was addressed simply to "Papá."

The British-crewed MV *Balmoral* was fifty miles off Ascension when she met her Royal

Fleet Auxiliary. As with most of the older RFAs, she was named after one of the Knights of the Round Table, in this case Sir Gawain. She was at the tail end of a long career at her specialty, resupply at sea, known as RAS, or "razzing." Or "coopering."

Out of sight of any prying eyes, the two ships made the transfer, and the SBS men came aboard.

The Special Boat Service, based very discreetly on the coast of Dorset, England, is far smaller than the U.S. Navy SEAL unit. There are seldom more than two hundred "badged" personnel. Though ninety percent drawn from the Royal Marines, they operate like their American cousins on land, sea or in the air. They operate in mountains, deserts, jungles, rivers and the open ocean. And there were just sixteen of them.

The CO was Major Ben Pickering, a veteran of over twenty years. He had been one of the small team who witnessed the massacre of Talib prisoners by the Northern Alliance at the fort of Qala-i-Jangi, northern Afghanistan, in the winter of 1991. He was still a teenager back then. They lay on top of the wall of the fortress looking down on the bloodbath as the Uzbeks of General

Dostum slaughtered their prisoners following the Taliban revolt.

One of two CIA special operatives also present, Johnny "Mike" Spann, had already been killed by the Taliban prisoners, and his colleague Dave Tyson had been snatched. Ben Pickering and two others went down into the hellhole, "slotted" the three Taliban holding the American and dragged Tyson out of there.

Major Pickering had done time in Iraq, Afghanistan (again) and Sierra Leone. He also had extensive experience in interception of illegal cargoes at sea, but he had never before commanded a detachment on board a covert Q-ship, because since the Second World War it had never been done.

When Cal Dexter, ostensibly a servant of the Pentagon, had explained the mission at the SBS base, Major Pickering had gone into a huddle with his CO and the armorers to work out what they needed.

For at-sea interceptions, he had chosen two 8.5-meter rigid inflatables, called RIBs, and had picked the "arctic" version. It would take eight men sitting upright in pairs behind the CO and the coxswain, who would actually drive it. But he could also take on board a captured cocaine smuggler, two experts from the "rummage crews" of

HM customs and two sniffer dogs. They would follow the attack RIB at a more sedate pace so as not to upset the dogs.

The rummage men were the experts in finding secret compartments, slithering through the lowest holds, detecting cunning deceptions aimed at hiding illegal cargoes. The dogs were cocker spaniels, trained not only to detect the odor of cocaine hydrochloride through several layers of covering but to detect changes in air odor. A bilge that has been opened recently smells different from one not opened for months.

Major Pickering stood beside the captain on the open wing of the bridge of the *Balmoral* and saw his RIBs swung gently onto the deck of the freighter. Thence, the *Balmoral*'s own derrick took over the cradles and lowered the inflatables into their hold.

Of the SBS's four Sabre Squadrons, the major had a unit from M Squadron, specializing in Marine Counter-Terrorism, or MCT. These were the men who swung aboard after the RIBs, and after them their "kit."

It was voluminous, involving assault carbines, sniper versions, handguns, diving equipment, weather- and sea-proof clothing, grapnel hooks, scaling ladders and a ton of ammunition. Plus two American communications men to liaise with Washington.

Support personnel consisted of armorers and technicians, to maintain the RIBs in perfect working order, and two helicopter pilots from the Army Air Corps, plus their own maintenance engineers. Their concern was the small "chopper" that came aboard last. It was an American Little Bird.

The Royal Navy might have preferred a Sea King or even a Lynx, but the problem was the size of the hold. With rotors spread, the larger helicopters would not fit through the hatch cover to emerge from its below-decks hangar into the open air. But the Boeing Little Bird could. With a main rotor span of just under twenty-seven feet, it would pass through the main hatch, which was forty feet wide.

The helo was the one piece that could not be winched across the gap of choppy sea separating the two vessels. Freed of its swathes of protective canvas under which it had ridden down to Ascension Island, it took off from the foredeck of the *Sir Gawain,* circled twice and settled on the closed forward hatch of the *Balmoral.* When the two rotors, main and tail, ceased to turn, the nimble little helicopter was hefted by the on-deck derrick and lowered carefully into the enlarged hold, where she was cleated to the deck beneath her.

When there was finally nothing left to transfer and the *Balmoral*'s fuel tanks were full again, the vessels parted. The RFA would go back north to Europe, the now very dangerous Q-ship would head for her first patrol station, north of the Cape Verdes, in the mid-Atlantic between Brazil and the curve of failed states running along the West African seaboard.

The Cobra had divided the Atlantic into two, with a line running north-northeast from Tobago, easternmost of the Antilles, to Iceland. West of that line he designated, in terms of cocaine destination, "Target Zone USA." East of the line was "Target Zone Europe." The *Balmoral* would take the Atlantic. The *Chesapeake*, about to meet her supply ship off Puerto Rico, would take the Caribbean.

Roberto Cárdenas stared at the letter long and hard. He had read it a dozen times. In the corner, Julio Luz was trembling.

"It is from the rogue, Vega?" he queried nervously. He was seriously wondering whether he was going to get out of the room alive.

"It has nothing to do with Vega."

273

At least the letter explained, without saying so, what had happened to his daughter. There would be no revenge on Vega. There was no Vega. Never had been. There was no freelance baggage handler at Barajas Airport who had picked the wrong suitcase in which to plant his cocaine. There never had been. The only reality was twenty years in an American jail for his Letizia. The message in the replica envelope to the ones in which he used to send his own was simple. It said:

"I think we should talk about your daughter Letizia. Next Sunday, at 4 p.m., I will be in my suite under the name of Smith at the Santa Clara Hotel, Cartagena. I shall be alone and unarmed. I shall wait one hour. Please come."

CHAPTER 9

The U.S. Navy SEALs boarded their Q-ship one hundred miles north of Puerto Rico, where the supply vessel had herself been loaded at Roosevelt Roads, the U.S. base on that island.

The SEALs are at least four times larger than the British SBS. Their parent group, the Naval Special Welfare Command, contains twenty-five hundred personnel, of which just under a thousand are "badged" operatives and the rest support units.

The ones who wear the coveted trident emblem of a SEAL are divided into eight teams, each with three forty-man troops. It was a platoon of half that number that had been assigned to live on the MV *Chesapeake,* and they came from SEAL Team 2 based on the East Coast at Little Creek, Virginia Beach.

Their CO was Lt. Cdr. Casey Dixon, and, like his British opposite number out in the

Atlantic, he, too, was a veteran. As a young ensign, he had taken part in Operation Anaconda. While the SBS man was in northern Afghanistan watching the slaughter at Qala-i-Jangi, Ensign Dixon had been Al Qaeda hunting in the Tora Bora White Range when things went badly wrong.

Dixon had been one of a troop coming into land on a flat area high in the mountains when his Chinook was raked by machine-gun fire from a hidden nest in the rocks. The huge helicopter was mortally hit and lurched wildly as the pilot fought for control. One of the helicopter crew skidded on the hydraulic fluid washing around on the floor and went over the tail ramp into the freezing darkness outside. He was saved from falling by his tether.

But a SEAL near the falling man, Boatswain's Mate Neil Roberts, tried to catch him and also slipped out. He had no tether and fell to the rocks a few feet below. Casey Dixon reached wildly for Roberts's webbing, missed by inches and watched him fall.

The pilot recovered, not enough to save the ship but enough to limp three miles and dump the Chinook out of machine-gun range. But Roberts was left alone in the rocks surrounded by twenty Al Qaeda killers. It is the pride of the SEALs that they have never left a mate behind, alive or dead. Transferring to another Chinook, Dixon and the rest went back for him, picking up a squad of Green Berets and a British SAS team on the way. What followed is hallowed in SEAL legend.

Neil Roberts activated his beacon to let his mates know he was alive. He also realized the machine-gun nest was still active and ready to blast any rescue effort out of the sky. With his hand grenades, he wiped out the machine-gun crew but gave away his position. The Al Qaeda came for him. He sold himself very dear, fighting and killing down to the last bullet and dying with his combat knife in his hand.

When the rescuers came back, they were too late for Roberts, but the Al Qaeda were still there. There was an eight-hour, close-quarter firefight among the rocks, as hundreds more jihadis poured in to join the sixty who had ambushed the Chinook. Six Americans died, two SEALs were badly injured. But in the morning light, they counted three hundred Al Qaeda corpses. The U.S. dead were all brought home, including the body of Neil Roberts.

Casey Dixon carried the body to the evacuation chopper, and, because he had taken a flesh wound to the thigh, was also flown to the States, and attended the memorial service a week later at the base chapel at Little Creek. After that, whenever he glanced at the jagged scar on his right thigh, he remembered the wild night among the rocks of Tora Bora.

But nine years later, he stood in the warm evening east of the Turks and Caicos and watched his men and their kit transfer from the mother ship to their new home, the former grain carrier, now the *Chesapeake.* High above, a patrolling EP-3 out of Roosevelt Roads told them the sea was empty. There were no watchers.

For attack off the sea, he had brought one large, eleven-meter Rigid Hull Inflatable Boat, or RHIB. This could take his entire platoon and pound along over calm water at forty knots. He also had two of the smaller Zodiacs, known as Combat Rubber Raiding Craft, or CRRC. Each was only fifteen feet long, just as fast and would take four armed men comfortably.

Also transferring were two ship-search experts from the U.S. Coast Guard, two dog handlers from customs, two communications men from Command HQ and, waiting on their helicopter pad over the stern of the mother ship, the two pilots from the

Navy. They sat inside their Little Bird, something the SEALs had rarely seen and never used before.

If they were ever deployed in helicopters, it would be in the new Boeing Knight Hawk. But the little spotter was the only helo whose rotors would descend into the hold of the *Chesapeake* when its hatch covers were open.

Also in the transferring equipment were the usual German-made Heckler & Koch MP5a submachine guns, the SEALs' weapon of choice for anything close-quarter; diving gear, the standard Dräger units; rifles for the four snipers and a mass of ammunition.

As the light faded, the EP-3 above told them the sea was still clear. The Little Bird lifted off, circled like an angry bee and settled on the *Chesapeake.* As both rotors stopped, the onboard derrick lifted the small helicopter and lowered her into the hold. The deck covers, moving smoothly on their rails, closed over the holds, and the coatings sealed them against rain and spray.

The two ships parted company, and the mother ship edged away into the gloom. On her bridge, some jokester flashed a message in code from an Aldis lamp, the technology of a hundred years ago. On the bridge of the *Chesapeake,* it was the Navy captain who worked it out. It said "G-O-D-S-P-E-E-D."

During the night, the *Chesapeake* slipped through the islands into her patrol areas; the Caribbean Basin and the Gulf of Mexico. Any inquirer on the Internet would have been told she was a perfectly lawful grain ship taking wheat from the Gulf of St. Lawrence to the hungry mouths of South America.

Belowdecks, the SEALs were cleaning and checking weapons yet again; the engineers were bringing the outboards and the helicopter to combat readiness; the cooks were rustling up some dinner, as they stocked their lockers and fridges; and the comms men were setting up their gear for a twenty-four-hour listening watch on a covert and encrypted channel coming out of a shabby warehouse in Anacostia, Washington, D.C.

The call they had been told to wait for might come in ten weeks, ten days or ten minutes. When it came, they intended to be combat ready.

The Hotel Santa Clara is a luxury lodging in the heart of the historic center of Cartagena, a conversion from a nunnery hundreds of years old. Its complete details had been forwarded to Cal Dexter by the SOCA agent who lived undercover as a teacher at the naval cadet school. Dexter had studied the plans and insisted on one certain suite.

He checked in as "Mr. Smith" just after noon on the appointed Sunday. Perfectly aware that five muscled hoodlums were rather visibly sitting without drinks in the inner courtyard or studying notices pinned to the walls of the lobby, he took a light lunch in an atrium under the trees. As he ate, a toucan fluttered out of the leaves, settled on the chair opposite and stared at him.

"Pal, I suspect you are a damn lot safer in this place than I am," murmured Mr. Smith. When he was done, he signed the check to his room and took the elevator to the top floor. He had let it be seen that he was there and alone.

Devereaux, in a rare display of even a flicker of concern, had suggested he take "backup" in the form of his by-now-adopted Green Berets from Fort Clark. He declined.

"Good though they are," he said, "they are not invisible. If Cárdenas sees a thing, he will not show. He will assume they're there for his own assassination or snatch."

As he stepped out of the lift at the fifth, top floor and headed down the open-sided walkway to his suite, he knew he had complied with the advice of Sun-tzu. Always let them underestimate you.

There was a man with a mop and bucket farther down the open passage as he reached his room. Not very subtle. In Cartagena, women do the swabbing. He let himself in. He knew what he would find. He had seen pictures of it: a large, airy room cooled by air-conditioning; a tiled floor, dark oak furniture and wide patio doors that gave onto the terrace. It was half past three.

He killed the air-conditioning, drew the curtains back, opened the glass doors and stepped onto the balcony. Above was the clear blue of a Colombian summer day. Behind his head and just three feet up, the gutter and the ocher tiled roof. Ahead and five floors down, the swimming pool glittered below him. A swallow dive might almost have dropped him in the shallow end, but more likely have left a mess on the flagstones. That was not what he had in mind anyway.

He walked back into the room, pulled a wing chair to a position where the open patio doors were to his side, and he had a clear view of the door. Finally, he crossed the room, opened the door, which, like all hotel room doors, was spring loaded and self-locking, wedged it a quarter inch open and returned to his seat. He waited, staring at the door. At four o'clock, it was pushed open. Roberto Cárdenas, career gangster and many times killer, stood framed against the blue sky outside.

"Señor Cárdenas. Please, enter, take a seat."

The father of the young woman in a detention center in New York took a pace forward. The door swung closed and the bronze locking bar clicked. It would need the right plastic card or a battering ram to open it from outside.

Cárdenas reminded Dexter of a main battle tank on legs. He was burly, solid, seeming immovable if he did not want to move. He might have been fifty, but he was muscle packed, with the face of an Aztec blood god.

Cárdenas had been told that the man who had intercepted his Madrid messenger and sent him a personal letter would be alone and unarmed, but of course he did not believe it. His own men had been vetting the hotel and its surrounds since dawn. He had a Glock 9mm in his waistband at the back and a razor-edged knife against the calf inside his right trouser leg. His eyes flickered around the room for a hidden trap, the waiting squad of Americans.

Dexter had left the bathroom door open, but Cárdenas still had a quick look inside. It was empty. He glared at Dexter, as a bull in a Spanish ring who can see his enemy is small and weak but cannot quite understand why he is there without protection. Dexter gestured to the other wing chair. He spoke in Spanish.

"As we both know, there are times when violence works. This is not one of those times. Let us talk. Please, sit."

Without taking his eyes off the American, Cárdenas lowered himself into the padded chair. The gun in the small of his back caused him to sit forward slightly. Dexter did not fail to notice.

"You have my daughter." He was not a great man for small talk.

"The New York law authorities have your daughter."

"It would be better for you if she is well."

A Julio Luz almost urinating with fear had told him what Boseman Barrow had said about some of the upstate women's penitentiaries.

"She is well, señor. Distressed, of course, but not maltreated. She is retained in Brooklyn, where conditions are comfortable. In fact, she is on suicide watch . . ."

He held up his hand as Cárdenas threatened to come roaring out of his chair.

"But only as a ruse. It means she has her own room in the hospital annex. She does not need to mix with other prisoners, the riffraff, so to speak."

The man who had risen from the gutters of the barrio to key member of the Brotherhood, the controlling cartel of the world's cocaine industry, stared at Dexter, still unable to make him out.

"You are a fool, gringo. This is my city. I could take you here. With ease. A few hours with me, and you would be begging to make the call. My daughter for you."

"Very true. You could, and I would. The trouble is, the people at the other end would not agree. They have their orders. You of all people understand the rules of absolute obedience. I am too small a pawn. There would be no swap. All that would happen is that Letizia would go north."

The black-eyed, hate-filled stare did not flicker, but the message went home.

The idea that the slim, gray-haired American was not a pawn but a main player, he discounted. He himself would never have gone into enemy territory alone and unarmed, so why should the *Yanqui?* A snatch would not work — either way. He would not be snatched, and there was no point in taking the American.

Cárdenas thought back to the report from Luz on the advice of Barrow. Twenty years, an exemplary sentence. No viable defense, an open-and-shut case, no Domingo de Vega to say it was all his idea.

While Cárdenas was thinking, Cal Dexter reached with his right hand to scratch his chest. For a second, his fingers went behind his jacket lapel. Cárdenas came forward, ready to draw his hidden Glock. Mr. Smith smiled apologetically.

"Mosquitoes," he said. "They will not leave me alone."

Cárdenas was not interested. He relaxed as the right hand came out. He would have been less relaxed had he known the fingertips had touched a sensitive Go button on a wafer-thin transmitter clipped to the inside pocket.

"What do you want, gringo?"

"Well," said Dexter, impervious to the rudeness of the address. "Unless there is an intervention, the people behind me cannot stop the justice machine. Not in New York. It cannot be bought and it cannot be diverted. Soon, even the mercy of keeping Letizia out of harm's way in Brooklyn will have to be terminated."

"She is innocent. You know that, I know that. You want money? I will make you rich for life. Get her out of there. I want her back."

"Of course. But, as I say, I am but a pawn. Perhaps there is a way."

"Tell me."

"If the UDYCO in Madrid were to discover a corrupt baggage handler and he were to give a full and witnessed confession that he chose a suitcase at random after the usual security checks and inserted the cocaine to be retrieved by a colleague in New York, then your lawyer could ask for an emergency hearing. It would be hard for a New York judge not to drop the case. To go on would be to refuse to believe our Spanish friends across the Atlantic. I honestly believe that is the only way."

There was a low rumble, as if storm clouds were gathering out of a blue sky.

"This . . . baggage handler. He could be discovered and forced to confess?"

"He might. It depends on you, Señor Cárdenas."

The rumble grew louder. It separated into a rhythmic *whump-whump.* Cárdenas repeated his demand.

"What do you want, gringo?"

"I think we both know that. You want a

swap? That is it. What you have in return for Letizia."

He rose, tossed a small pasteboard card to the carpet, walked through the patio doors and turned left. The snaking steel-cord ladder came around the corner of the hotel roof, flailing in the downdraft.

He jumped to the balustrade, thought, I'm too goddamn old for this, and leapt at the rungs. He could sense above the roar of the rotors that Cárdenas was coming out onto the terrace behind him. He waited for the bullet in the back, but it never came. At any rate, not in time. If Cárdenas fired, Dexter would not have heard it. He felt the rungs bite into his palms, and the man above leaned back hard and the Black Hawk went up like a rocket.

Seconds later, he was lowered to the sandy beach just beyond the walls of the Santa Clara. The Black Hawk settled as two or three dog walkers gawped; he ducked into the crew door, and the helicopter rose again. Twenty minutes later, he was back inside the base.

Don Diego Esteban prided himself on running the Hermandad, the supreme *cocaine* cartel, like one of the most successful corporations on the planet. He even indulged in the conceit that the governing authority was the board of directors rather than himself alone, even though that was palpably not true. Despite the huge inconvenience to his colleagues of spending two days dodging the tailing agents of Colonel Dos Santos, he insisted on quarterly meetings.

It was his custom to name, by personal emissary only, the hacienda, one of fifteen he owned, where the conclave would take place, and he expected his colleagues to arrive un-followed. The days of Pablo Escobar, when half the police were in the cartel'spocket, were long gone. Colonel Dos Santos was an unbribable attack dog, and the Don both respected and loathed him for it.

His summer meeting he always held at the end of June. He convened his six colleagues, omitting only the Enforcer, Paco Valdez, El Animal, who was summoned only when there were matters of internal discipline to be attended to. That time, there were none.

The Don listened with approval to reports on increased production from the peasants but without any rise in price. The production chief, Emilio Sánchez, assured him enough *pasta* base could be grown and bought in to meet any needs from other branches of the cartel.

Rodrigo Pérez was able to assure him that internal thievery of the product prior to export was down to a reduced percentage, thanks to several hideous examples that had been made of those who thought they could cheat the cartel. The private army, mainly recruited from the jungle-living former terrorist groups known as FARC, was in good order.

Don Diego, playing the benign host, personally refilled Pérez's wineglass, a signal honor.

Julio Luz, the lawyer/banker who had been completely unable to make eye contact with Roberto Cárdenas, reported that the ten banks around the world who helped him launder billions of euros and dollars were content to continue and had not been penetrated or even suspected by the forces of banking regulation.

José-María Largo had even better news on the merchandising front. Appetite in the two target zones, the USA and Europe, was now climbing to unprecedented levels. The forty gangs and sub-mafias who were the clients of the cartel had placed even larger orders.

Two big gangs, in Spain and Britain, had been rounded up en masse, tried, sentenced and were out of the field. They had been smoothly replaced by eager newcomers. Demand would be at record levels for the coming year. Heads leaned forward as he produced his figures. He would need a minimum of three hundred tons of pure delivered intact to the handover points on each continent.

That put the focus on the two men whose job it was to guarantee those arrivals. It was probably a mistake to snub Roberto Cárdenas, whose international network of on-the-payroll officials in airports, docks and customs sheds across both continents was crucial. The Don simply did not like the man. He gave the star role to Alfredo Suárez, the maestro of transportation from Colombian source to northern buyer. Suárez preened like a peacock, and made his servility to the Don plain.

"Given what we have all heard, I have no doubt that the six-hundred-ton delivery figure can be met. If our friend Emilio can produce eight hundred tons, we have a twenty-five percent margin for loss by interception, confiscation, theft or loss at sea. I have never lost anything like that percentage.

"We have over one hundred ships served by more than a thousand small boats. Some of our dedicated ships are big freighters, taking on our cargoes at sea and being relieved of them before arrival. Others take the cargo from dockside to dockside, assisted at both ends by officials on the payroll of our friend here, Roberto.

"Some of these carry sea containers, now used worldwide for freight of every kind and description, including ours. Others in the same group use secret compartments created by the clever little welder of Cartagena who died a few months ago. His name escapes me."

"Cortez," growled Cárdenas, who came from that city. "His name was Cortez."

"Precisely. Well, whatever. Then there are the smaller craft, tramp steamers, fishing boats, private yachts. Between them, they carry and land almost a hundred tons a year. And finally we have our fifty-plus freelance pilots who fly and land or fly and drop.

"Some fly into Mexico to hand over to our Mexican friends, who bring the cargoes over the U.S. border in the north. Others go direct to one of the million creeks and bays along the southern coast of the U.S. The third category flies across to West Africa."

"Are there any innovations since last year?" asked Don Diego. "We were not amused by the fate of our fleet of submarines. A massive expenditure, all lost."

Suárez swallowed. He recalled what had happened to his predecessor who had backed a policy of submersibles and an army of one-journey mules. The Colombian Navy had traced and destroyed the subs; the new X-ray machines being deployed across both target continents were reducing successful in-stomach shipments to under fifty percent.

"Don Diego, those tactics are virtually extinct. As you know, one submersible that was at sea at the time of the naval strike was later intercepted, forced to surface and arrested in the Pacific off Guatemala. We lost twelve tons. For the rest, I am downgrading the use of mules with a single kilo each.

"I am concentrating on one hundred shipments per target continent at an average of three tons per cargo. I guarantee, my Don, I can deliver safely three hundred tons per continent after notional losses of ten percent to interception and confiscation and five percent to loss at sea. That is nothing like the twenty-five percent margin that Emilio suggests between his eight hundred tons of product and six hundred tons of safe delivery."

"You can guarantee that?" asked the Don.

"Yes, Don Diego. I believe I can . . ."

"Then let us hold you to that," murmured the Don. The room chilled. Through his own bombast, the cringing Alfredo Suárez was on life support. The Don did not tolerate failure. He rose and beamed.

"Please, my friends, lunch awaits us."

The tiny padded envelope did not look like much. It arrived by recorded delivery at the one-use safe house on the card Cal Dexter had dropped on the hotel-room floor. It contained a memory stick. He took it to Jeremy Bishop.

"What's on it?" asked the computer wizard.

"I wouldn't have brought it to you if I knew."

Bishop's brow furrowed.

"You mean you can't insert it into your own laptop?"

Dexter was slightly embarrassed. He could do many things that would leave Bishop in intensive care, but his grasp of cybertechnology was lower than basic. He watched as Bishop performed, for him, a kindergarten task.

"Names," he said. "Columns of names, mostly foreign. And cities — airports, harbors, docks. And titles — they look like officials of some kind or another. And bank accounts. Account numbers and lodgments. Who are these people?"

"Just print them out for me. Yes, black-and-white. On paper. Indulge an old man."

He went to a phone that he knew to be ultra-secure and called a number in Alexandria's Old Town. The Cobra answered.

"I have the Rat List," he said.

Jonathan Silver called Paul Devereaux that evening. The chief of staff was not in his best humor, but he was not known for it anyway.

"You've had your nine months," he snapped. "When can we expect some action?"

"So kind of you to call," said the voice from Alexandria, cultured, with a hint of Boston drawl. "And so fortuitous. Starting next Monday, actually."

"And what will we see happening?"

"At first, nothing at all," said the Cobra.

"And later?"

"My dear colleague, I wouldn't dream of spoiling your surprise." And he replaced the receiver.

In the West Wing, the chief of staff found himself staring at a buzzing handset.

"He's hung up on me," he said in disbelief. "Again."

■ ■ ■ ■

Part Three
Strike

■ ■ ■ ■

CHAPTER 10

By chance it was the British Special Boat Service that secured the first prey; a question of the right place at the right time.

Shortly after the Cobra issued his "open season" edict, Global Hawk Sam picked up a mystery vessel on the ocean far below, which was tagged "Rogue One." Sam's wide-spectrum television scanner was narrowed as she dropped to 20,000 feet, still completely out of sound and sight. The images concentrated.

Rogue One was clearly not big enough to be a liner or Lloyd's-listed freighter. She might be a very small merchantman or coaster, but she was miles away from any coast. Or she might be a private yacht or fisherman. Whatever she was, Rogue One had passed longitude 55° heading east for Africa. And she behaved oddly.

She cruised through the night and then disappeared. That could only mean that at sunrise she closed down, her crew spread a sea blue tarpaulin and bobbed the day away on the water almost impossible to spot from above. That maneuver could only mean one thing. Then at sundown she rolled up the tarp and began to cruise east again. Unfortunately for Rogue One, Sam could see in the dark.

Three hundred miles off Dakar, the MV *Balmoral* turned south and went to flank speed to intercept. One of the two American comms men stood beside the captain on the bridge to read out the compass headings.

Sam, drifting high above the rogue, passed her progress details to Nevada, and AFB Creech told Washington. At dawn the rogue closed down and went under her drape. Sam returned to Fernando de Noronha Island to refuel and was back before dawn. The *Balmoral* steamed through the night. The rogue was caught at dawn of the third day, well south of the Cape Verdes, and still five hundred miles from Guinea-Bissau.

She was about to cover herself for her penultimate day at sea. When her captain saw the danger, it was too late to spread the canopy or roll it up and pretend to be normal.

High above, Sam switched on her jammers, and the rogue was enveloped at the base of a cone of "no transmit, no receive" electronic dead space. At first the captain did not try to transmit a message because he did not believe his eyes. Speeding toward him was a small helicopter barely 100 feet above the calm sea.

The reason he could not believe it was the matter of range. Such a chopper could not be that far from land, and there was no other vessel in sight. He did not know that the *Balmoral* was twenty-five miles due ahead of him and invisible just over the horizon. When he realized he was about to be intercepted, it was too late.

His drill was memorized. *First you will be pursued by the unmistakable gray shape of a warship, which will be faster. It will overhaul you and order you to stop. When the warship is still far away, use the hull of your boat to shield you and deep-six the cocaine bales over the side. These we can replace. Before you are boarded, inform us by computer with the prerecorded message to Bogotá.*

So the captain, even though he could see no warship, did as he was told. He pressed Send, but no message went out. He tried to use his sat phone, but it, too, was dead. Leaving one of his men repeatedly calling on the radio, he went up the ladder behind the bridge and stared ahead at the approaching Little Bird. Fifteen miles back, still not visible but racing at forty knots, were two ten-man RIBs.

The small helicopter circled him once and then hovered at 100 feet forward of the bridge. He could see that a rigid wasp aerial jutted downward, with a stiff flag spread behind it. He recognized the design. On the boom of the helicopter were the two words, "Royal Navy."

"Los Ingléses," he muttered. He still could not work out where the warship was, but the Cobra had given strict instructions; the two Q-ships must never be seen.

Peering up at the helicopter, he saw the pilot, black-visored against the rising sun, and beside him, leaning out but harnessed in, a sniper. He did not recognize a G3 scoped rifle, but he knew when a gun was pointing right at his head. His instructions were clear: *Never try to outshoot any national navy.* So he raised his hands in the international gesture. Despite the lack of "Transmission accomplished" signal on his laptop, he hoped his warning had gone out anyway. It had not.

From his vantage point, the flier of the Little Bird could see the name on the prow of the rogue vessel. It was *Belleza del Mar — Beauty of the Sea —* the most optimistic title on the ocean. She was in fact a fishing boat, rusted, stained, a hundred feet long and stinking of fish. That was the point. The ton of cocaine in roped bales was under the rotting fish.

The captain tried to take the initiative by starting his engines. The helicopter swerved and dropped until it was abeam, 10 feet off the water and thirty yards from the side of the *Belleza del Mar*. At that range the sniper could have whisked off either ear according to choice.

"Paré los motores," boomed a voice from Little Bird's loudspeaker. "Cut your motors." The captain did so. He could not hear them over the roar from the helicopter, but he had seen the spray plume of two approaching attack boats.

That, too, was incomprehensible. They were many miles from land. Where the hell was the warship? There was nothing hard to understand about the men who poured out of the two RIBs that roared up to his side, hurled grapnels over the edge, made fast and leapt aboard. They were young, black-clothed, masked, armed and fit.

The captain had himself and seven crew. The "Don't resist" instruction was shrewd. They would have lasted seconds. Two of the masked men approached him; the rest covered his crew, all of whom had their hands well above their heads. One of the masked men seemed in charge, but he spoke only English. The other man interpreted. Neither removed their black masks.

"Captain, we believe you are carrying illegal substances. Drugs, specifically cocaine. We intend to search your vessel."

"It is not true, I carry only fish. And you have no right to search my vessel. It is against the laws of the sea. It is piracy."

He had been told to say this. Unfortunately, his advice on law was less shrewd than that of staying alive. He had never heard of CRIJICA and would not have understood it if he had.

But Major Ben Pickering was perfectly within his rights. The Criminal Justice (International Cooperation) Act of 1990, known as CRIJICA, contains several clauses covering interception at sea of vessels believed to carry drugs. It also contains the rights of the accused. What the captain of the *Belleza del Mar* did not know was that he and his vessel had been quietly recategorized as a threat to the British nation like any other terrorist. That meant that, unfortunately for the skipper, the rule book, civil rights included, had just gone where the cocaine would have gone if he had had the time — over the edge.

The SBS men had been rehearsing for two weeks and had the drill cut to a few minutes. All seven of the crew and the captain were expertly frisked for weapons or devices of transmission. Cell phones were confiscated for later analysis. The radio shack was smashed. The eight Colombians were shackled with hands in front of waists and hooded. When they could neither see nor resist, they were herded to the stern and made to sit.

Major Pickering nodded, and one of his men produced a rocket tube. The maroon rocket went up five hundred feet and exploded in a ball of flame. High above, the heat sensors of the Global Hawk took in the signal, and the man over the screen in Nevada shut off the jammers. The major told the *Balmoral* she was clear to steam, and the Q-ship came over the horizon to berth alongside.

One of the commandos was in full scuba gear. He went over the edge to search the hull below the water. A common ruse was to carry illegal cargo in a blister welded on the bottom of the hull or even to dangle bales on a nylon cord a hundred feet down, out of sight during any search.

The swimmer hardly needed his full wet

suit, for the water was bathtub warm. And the sun, now well over the eastern horizon, illuminated the water as by searchlight. He spent twenty minutes down there among the weeds and barnacles of the neglected hull. There were no blisters, no secret underwater doors, no dangling cords. In fact, Major Pickering knew where the cocaine was.

As soon as the jammers were removed, he could give the *Balmoral* the name of the intercepted fisherman. She was after all on the Cortez list, one of the smaller vessels not on any international shipping list, just a dirty fisher from an obscure village. Obscure or not, she was on her seventh voyage to West Africa, carrying ten thousand times her own value. He was told where to look.

Major Pickering muttered instructions to the rummage crew from the Coast Guard. The man from customs cradled his cocker spaniel. The hold covers came off to reveal tons of fish no longer fresh but still netted. The *Belleza*'s own derrick hoisted the fish out and dumped them. A mile down, the crabs would be grateful.

When the floor of the fish hold was exposed, the rummage men looked for the panel Cortez had described. It was brilliantly hidden, and the stench of fish would have confused the dog. The hooded crew could not know what they were doing nor see the approaching *Balmoral.*

It took a jimmy and twenty minutes to get the plate off. Left alone, the crew would have done this at leisure ten miles off the mangroves of the Bijagós Islands, ready to hand the cargo over the side to waiting canoes in the creeks. Then they would have taken on fuel barrels in exchange, tanked up and headed for home.

The exposing of the bilges beneath the fish hold gave rise to an even fouler stench. The rummage men had their masks and breathers on. Everyone else stood back.

One of the rummagers went in, torso first, with a flashlight. The other held his legs. The first man wriggled back and held up a thumb. Bingo! He went in with grapnel and cord. One by one, the men on deck pulled out twenty bales, just over a hundred pounds' weight each. The *Balmoral* came alongside, towering above them.

It took another hour. The *Belleza's* crew, still hooded, were helped up the Jacob's ladder into the *Balmoral* and guided below. When they were released from shackles and hoods, they were in the forward brig, prisoners below the waterline.

Two weeks later, transferred to the Fleet

Auxiliary in a second razzing, they would be taken to the British outpost of Gibraltar, rehooded, transferred by night to an American Starlifter and flown to the Indian Ocean. The hoods would come off again to reveal a tropical paradise and the instruction:

"Have fun, don't communicate with anyone and don't try to escape."

The first of these were optional, the rest impossible.

The ton of cocaine also went aboard the *Balmoral.* It, too, would be guarded until off-loaded to American custody at sea. The last task on the *Belleza del Mar* was left to the squad's explosives man. He went below for fifteen minutes, came up and leapt over the side into the second RIB.

Most of his companions were back on board. The Little Bird was already stowed again in her hold. So was the first RIB. The *Balmoral* went to "Slow ahead," and a lazy wake appeared behind her stern. The second RIB followed her. When there was two hundred yards of clear sea between them and the scummy old fishing boat, the explosive man pressed a button on his detonator.

The shaped charges of PETN plastic explosive he had left behind uttered only a low crack but cut a hole the size of a barn door in the hull. Within thirty seconds, she was gone forever, on a long, lonely, mile-long dive to the seabed.

The RIB reboarded and was stowed. No one else in the central Atlantic had seen a thing. The *Beauty of the Sea,* her captain, crew and cargo had simply vaporized.

It was a week before the loss of the *Belleza del Mar* was wholly believed in the heart of the cartel, and even then the reaction was only perplexity.

Vessels, crews and cargoes had been lost before, but, other than the total disappearance of the death-trap submersibles heading up the Pacific Coast to Mexico, there were always traces or reasons. Some small vessel had gone down in oceanic storms. The Pacific, so named by Vasco Nuñez de Balboa, the first European to see it, because on that day it looked so calm, could sometimes go crazy. The balmy Caribbean of the tourist brochures could play host to insane hurricane winds. But it was rare.

Cargoes lost at sea were almost always hurled overboard by the crew when capture was impossible to avoid.

For the rest, losses at sea were from interceptions by law enforcement agencies or navies. The ship was impounded, the crew arrested, charged, tried and jailed, but they were dispensable and their families bought off with a gracious donation. Everyone knew the rules.

The victors held press conferences, showed the baled cocaine to gleeful media. But the only time product completely disappeared was when it was stolen.

The successive cartels that have dominated the cocaine industry have always been riven by one psychiatric defect: raging paranoia. The capacity for suspicion is instant and uncontrollable. There are two crimes that are unforgivable within their code: to steal the product and to inform the authorities. The thief and the snitch will always be hunted down and revenge exacted. There can be no exceptions.

It took a week for the first lots to sink in because, first, the receiving party in Guinea-Bissau, the chief of operation, Ignacio Romero, complained that a preannounced shipment had simply not arrived. He had waited all night at the appointed time and in the appointed place, but the *Belleza del Mar,* which he knew well, had never made landfall.

He was asked twice to reconfirm that and did. Then the question of a possible misunderstanding had to be investigated. Had the

Belleza gone to the wrong place? And even if so, why had her captain not communicated? He had carefully meaningless two-word messages to send if in trouble.

Then the dispatcher, Alfredo Suárez, had to check the weather. It had been flat calm right across the Atlantic. Fire on board? But the captain had his radio. Even if he had taken to the lifeboat, he had his laptop and cell phone. Finally, he had to report the loss to the Don.

Don Diego thought it over, examined all the evidence that Suárez brought him. It certainly looked like theft, and at the head of the queue of suspects was the captain himself. Either he had stolen the entire cargo to cut a deal with a renegade importer or he had himself been intercepted farther out at sea than the mangroves and murdered, along with his crew. Either was possible, but first things first.

If it was the captain, he would have told his family before the deed or been in contact since his treachery. His family was a wife and three children living in the same muddy village where he kept his old fishing boat, up a creek east of Barranquilla. He sent the Animal to talk to her.

The children were not a problem. They were buried. Alive, of course. In front of the mother. Still, she refused to confess. It took her several hours to die, but she clung to her story that her husband had said nothing and done nothing wrong. Finally, Paco Valdez had no choice but to believe her. He could not continue anyway. She was dead.

The Don was regretful. So unpleasant. And, as it turned out, fruitless. But unavoidable. And it posed an even bigger problem. If not the captain, then who? But there was someone else in Colombia even more distressed than Don Diego Esteban.

The Enforcer had practiced his trade after driving the family deep into the jungle. But the jungle is never quite empty. A peasant farmer of Indio descent had heard the screams and peered out through the foliage. When the Enforcer and his crew of two had gone, the peon went into the village and told what he had seen.

The villagers came with an ox wagon and took the four bodies back to the settlement by the creek. There was a Christian burial for them all. The officiating priest was Fr. Eusebio, S.J. He was disgusted by what he had seen before the crude plank coffin was closed.

Back in his mission rooms, he opened the drawer in his dark oak desk and looked down at the gizmo the local Provincial had distributed months before. Normally, he would never have dreamed of using it, but now he was angry. Perhaps one day he would see something outside the seal of confession; and then maybe he would use the American gizmo.

The second strike went to the SEALs. Again, it was a question of the right time and the right place. Global Hawk Michelle was patrolling the great swathe of the southern Caribbean that extends in an arc from Colombia to the Yucatán. The MV *Chesapeake* was in the passage between Jamaica and Nicaragua.

Two go-fasts slipped out of the mangrove swamps of the Gulf of Urabá on the Colombian coast and headed not southwest to Colón and the Panama Canal but northwest. Their journey was long, the extremity of their range, and both were packed with fuel drums apart from one ton each of baled cocaine amidships.

Michelle spotted them twenty miles out. Although not racing along at their feasible sixty knots, they were cruising at forty, and that was enough to tell Michelle's radars from 50,000 feet that they could not be anything but speedboats. She began to plot course and speed, and warn the *Chesapeake* that the go-fasts were heading in her direction. The Q-ship altered course to intercept.

It was on the second day that the two crews of the go-fasts experienced the same bewilderment as the captain of the *Belleza del Mar*. A helicopter appeared out of nowhere and was ahead of them, hovering above an empty blue sea. There was not a warship in sight. This was simply not possible.

The booming challenge from the loudspeaker to cut engines and heave to was simply ignored. Both racers, long, slim aluminum tubes packing four Yamaha 200 hps at the stern, thought they might outrun the Little Bird. Their speed increased to sixty knots, noses up, only the engines immersed in water, a huge white wake behind each of them. As the Brits had secured Rogue One, these two became Rogues Two and Three.

The Colombians were mistaken about outrunning a helicopter. As they swept under the Little Bird, she tilted her rotors into a violent turn and came after them. At 120 knots, double their speed.

Sitting beside the Navy pilot, clutching his M14 sniper rifle, was Petty Officer Sorenson, the platoon's ace sharpshooter. With a steady platform and a range of a hundred yards, he was confident he was not going to miss very much.

The pilot used his loudspeaker system again, and he spoke in Spanish.

"Close down your engines and heave to or we fire."

The go-fasts kept racing toward the north, unaware that there were three inflatables packed with sixteen SEALs powering toward them. Lt. Cdr. Casey Dixon had put his big RHIB and both his smaller Zodiacs into the water, but, fast though they were, the aluminum darts of the smugglers were even faster. It was the Little Bird's job to slow them down.

PO Sorenson had been raised on a farm in Wisconsin, about as far away from the sea as you can get. This may have been why he joined the Navy — to see the sea. The talent he brought from the boondocks was a lifelong expertise with a hunting rifle.

The Colombians knew the drill. They had not been intercepted by helicopters before, but they had been instructed what to do and that was primarily to protect their engines. Without these roaring monsters behind them, they would become helpless.

As they saw the M14 surmounted by its scope sight staring at their engines, two of the crew hurled themselves over the housings to prevent them being hit by rifle fire. The forces of law and order would never fire straight through a man's torso.

Mistake. Those were the old rules. Back on the farm, PO Sorenson had slotted rabbits at two hundred paces. This target was bigger and closer, and his rules of engagement were clear. His first shot went straight through the brave smuggler, penetrated the cowling and shattered the Yamaha's engine block.

The other smuggler, with a yelp of alarm, threw himself backward just in time. The second armor-piercing round shattered the next engine. The go-fast continued on two. But slower. She was very heavily laden.

One of the remaining three men below produced a Kalashnikov AK-47, and the Little Bird pilot veered away. From his 100 feet up, he could see the black dots of the inflatables closing the gap, creating a closing speed of a hundred knots.

The undamaged go-fast saw them, too. The helmsman could no longer bother with the enigma of where they had come from. They were there, and he was trying to save his cargo and his freedom. He decided to streak right through them and use his superior speed to get away.

He nearly succeeded. The damaged go-

316

fast closed down its other two engines and surrendered. The lead boat continued at sixty knots. The SEAL formation split and spread, swerved into shuddering turns and gave chase. Without the helicopter, the smuggler might have been able to race to freedom.

The Little Bird skimmed the flat sea ahead of the go-fast, turned at ninety degrees and spewed out a hundred yards of invisible blue nylon cord. A small cotton drogue at the end dragged the flex out into the air, and it fell to the ocean where it floated. The go-fast swerved and almost made it. The last twenty yards of the floating cord slid under the hull and wrapped itself around all four propellers. The four Yamahas coughed, choked and stopped.

After that, resistance was useless. Facing a firing squad of MP5 submachine guns, they allowed themselves to be transferred to the big RHIB, were shackled and hooded. That was the last daylight they saw until they stepped onto Eagle Island, Chagos Archipelago, as guests of Her Majesty.

An hour later, the *Chesapeake* was alongside. She took the seven prisoners. The brave dead man was given a blessing and a length of chain to help him sink. Also transferred were two tons of two-stroke fuel

317

(which could be used), various weapons and cell phones (for analysis of previous calls made) and two tons of baled Colombian *puro*.

Then the two go-fasts were riddled with holes, and the heavy Yamahas took them down. It was a pity to lose six good and powerful engines, but the instructions of the Cobra, invisible and unknown to the SEALs, were precise: nothing traceable to be left. Only the men and the cocaine are to be taken, and then only for temporary storage. Everything else disappears forever.

The Little Bird settled on the forward hatch, closed down and was lowered into her out-of-sight home. The three inflatables went up, over the side and into their own hold to be washed down and serviced. The men went below to shower and change. The *Chesapeake* turned away. The sea was empty again.

Far ahead, the freight ship *Stella Maris IV* waited and waited. Finally, she had to resume her voyage to Euro port Rotterdam, but without any extra cargo. Her first officer could only send a bewildered text message to his "girlfriend" in Cartagena. Something about not being able to make their date because his automobile had not been delivered.

Even that was intercepted by the National Security Agency at their enormous Army base at Fort Meade, Maryland, where it was decrypted and passed to the Cobra. He gave a thin smile of gratitude. The message had betrayed the go-fasts' destination, the *Stella Maris IV.* She was on the list. Next time.

It was a week after the Cobra declared open season that Major Mendoza received his first call to fly. Global Hawk Sam spotted a small twin-engined transport lifting off from the Boa Vista Ranch, clearing the coast over Fortaleza and heading out across the wide Atlantic on a heading of 045° which would take her to any landfall between Liberia and the Gambia.

Computer imaging identified her as a Transall, a onetime Franco-German collaboration that had been bought by South Africa and, at the end of her active service as a military transport, sold secondhand to the civilian market in South America.

She was not large, but a reliable workhouse. She also had a range that would in no way take her across the Atlantic, even at the shortest point. So she had been "doctored" with extra internal fuel tanks. For three hours, she plodded northeast through the near darkness of a tropical night, flying at 8,000 feet above a flat plain of cloud.

Major Mendoza pointed the nose of the Buccaneer straight down the runway and completed final checks. In his ears he did not hear the control tower speaking in Portuguese, for it was long closed down. He heard the warm tones of an American woman. The two American communications personnel on Fogo with him had taken her message an hour earlier and alerted the Brazilian to get ready to fly. Now she was patched through to his earphones. He did not know she was a U.S. Air Force captain sitting behind a screen in Creech, Nevada. He did not know she was watching a blip that represented a Transall freighter, and that soon he, too, would be a blip on that screen, and that she would bring the two blips together.

He glanced out at the ground crew that stood in the darkness of the Fogo airfield and saw the "Go" signal flashed at him. This was his "control tower," but it worked. He raised his right thumb in assent.

The two Speys increased their howl, and the Bucc shuddered against the brakes, wanting to be free. Mendoza flicked the RATO switch and freed the brakes. The Bucc flung herself forward, he emerged from the shadow of the volcanic mountain and saw the sea gleaming in the moonlight.

The rocket thrust took him in the small of the back. Speed shot up and through takeoff velocity, the wheel rumble ceased and she was up.

"Climb to fifteen thousand feet on heading one-nine-zero," said the warm molasses voice. He checked the compass, steadied the craft on 190° and climbed to height as instructed.

In an hour, he was three hundred miles south of the Cape Verdes, turning in a slow rate 1 circle, waiting. He saw the target at one o'clock low. Above the plateau of cloud, the gibbous moon had appeared and clothed the scene in a pale white light. Then he saw a flitting shadow below him and to his right. It was heading northeast; he was still halfway around a sweeping turn. He completed the turn and came up behind the prey.

"Your target is five miles ahead of you, six thousand feet below."

"Roger, I have it," he said. "Contact."

"Contact acknowledged. Clear engage."

He dropped until the outline of the Transall in the moonlight was quite clear. He had been given an album of likely planes used by cocaine fliers, and there was no doubt this was a Transall. There could simply be no innocent plane like that in the sky.

He flicked off the safety catch of his Aden cannon, placed his thumb over the Fire button and gazed ahead through the gunsight modified at Scampton. He knew his two gun packs were centered to concentrate their united firepower at four hundred meters.

For a moment, he hesitated. There were men in that machine. Then he thought of another man, a boy on a marble slab in the São Paolo mortuary. His kid brother. He fired.

There was a mixture of fragmentation, incendiary and tracer in his ammunition packs. The bright tracer would show him his line of fire. The other two would destroy what they hit.

He watched the two lines of red fire race away from him and unite at four hundred meters. Both impacted into the hull of the Transall just to the left of the rear loading doors. For half a second, the freighter seemed to shudder in midair. Then it imploded.

He did not even see it break up, disintegrate and fall. Its crew had evidently only just begun to draw on the inboard reserves, so those tanks inside the hull were brimful. They took the white-hot incendiary rounds, and the whole airplane turned molten. A shower of blazing fragments fell through the cloud layer beneath, and that was it. Gone. One plane, four men, two tons of cocaine.

Major Mendoza had never killed anyone before. He stared for several seconds at the hole in the sky where the Transall had been. He had wondered for days what he would feel. Now he knew. He just felt empty. Neither exultant nor remorseful. He had told himself many times; just think of Manolo on his marble slab, sixteen years old, never to have a life to lead. When he spoke, his voice was quite steady.

"Target down," he said.

"I know," said the voice out of Nevada. She had seen the two blips become one. "Maintain altitude. Steer three-five-five for base."

Seventy minutes later, he watched the runway lights of Fogo turn on for him and shut down when he was taxiing toward the rock hangar. Rogue Four had ceased to be.

Three hundred miles away in Africa, a group of men waited by a jungle airstrip. And waited and waited. At dawn they climbed into their SUVs and drove away. One of them would send a coded e-mail to Bogotá.

Alfredo Suárez, in charge of all shipments

323

from Colombia to clients, was in fear for his life. Barely four had been lost. He had guaranteed the Don to deliver three hundred tons to each target continent and had been promised a margin of up to two hundred tons as acceptable losses in transit. But that was not the point.

The Hermandad, as the Don was now putting it to him very personally and with frightening calm, had two problems. One was that four separate cargoes in three separate transport methods had apparently been either captured or destroyed; much more perplexing, and the Don hated to be perplexed, was that there was not a trace of a clue as to what had gone wrong.

The captain of the *Belleza del Mar* should have reported he was in trouble of some kind. He did not. The two go-fasts should have used their cell phones if anything went wrong. They did not. The Transall had also taken off, fully fueled and in good order, and without a Mayday call had vanished off the earth.

"Mysterious, would you not say, my very dear Alfredo?" When the Don spoke in terms of endearment, he was at his most frightening.

"Yes, my Don."

"And what explanation could you possibly

324

imagine?"

"I do not know. All carriers have ample means of communication. Computers, cell phones, ships' radios. And short coded messages to say what is wrong. They have tested their equipment, memorized the messages."

"And yet they are silent," mused Don Diego.

He had listened to the Enforcer's report and concluded that it was extremely unlikely the captain of the *Belleza del Mar* was the culprit in his own disappearance.

The captain was known to be a dedicated family man, he would have known what would happen if he betrayed the cartel and he had concluded six successful voyages to West Africa before.

There was only one common denominator for two of the three mysteries. Both the fishing boat and the Transall had been heading for Guinea-Bissau. Even though the two go-fasts out of the Gulf of Urabá were an enigma, the finger was still pointing at something going badly wrong in Guinea.

"Do you have another consignment for West Africa soon, Alfredo?"

"Yes, Don Diego. Next week. Five tons going by sea to Liberia."

"Change it to Guinea-Bissau. And you

have a very bright young deputy?"

"Álvaro, Álvaro Fuentes. His father was very big in the old Cali cartel. He was born to this work. Very loyal."

"Then he should accompany this cargo. And be in touch every three hours, night and day, all the way. Prerecorded messages on both laptop and cell phone. Nothing to do but press a button. And I want a listening watch at this end. Permanently, on shifts. Do I make myself plain?"

"Perfectly, Don Diego. It will be done."

Fr. Eusebio had never seen anything like it. His parish was large and rural, spread over many villages, but all humble, hardworking and poor. Not for him the bright lights and luxury marinas of Barranquilla and Cartagena. What had moored just off the mouth of the creek that led out of the mangroves to the sea did not belong there.

The whole village went to the frail timber jetty to stare. She was over fifty meters long, gleaming white, with luxury cabins on three decks and brightwork that the crew had polished until it gleamed. No one knew who owned it, and none of its crew had come ashore. Why should they? For one village with a single dirt street, where chickens pecked, and a single bodega?

What the good Father and Jesuit could not know was that the craft moored out of sight of the ocean around two curves in the creek was a very luxurious oceangoing yacht called a "Fead ship." It had six sumptuous staterooms, for the owner and guests, and a crew of ten. It had been built in a Dutch yard three years earlier to the personal order of its owner and would not have appeared in Edmiston's catalog for sale (which it was not) for less than $20 million.

It is an oddity that most people are born at night and many also die at night. Fr. Eusebio was wakened at three in the morning by a tapping on his door. It was a little girl from a family he knew to say that Grandpa was spitting blood, and Mama feared he might not see the morning.

Fr. Eusebio knew the man. He was sixty, looked ninety and had smoked the foulest tobacco for fifty years. The last two, he had been coughing up mucus and blood. The parish priest slipped on a cassock, gathered his shawl and rosary and hurried after the girl.

The family lived near the water, one of the last houses in the village that overlooked the creek. And indeed the old man was truly dying. Fr. Eusebio gave the last rites and sat with him until he drifted away into a sleep from which he would probably not wake. Before he slipped away, he asked for a cigarette. The parish priest shrugged, and the daughter gave him one. There was nothing more the priest could do. In a few days, he would bury his parishioner. For the moment, he needed to complete his night's rest.

As he left, he glanced toward the sea. On the water between the jetty and the moored cruiser was a large open boat chugging out to sea. There were three men on board and a small amount of bales in the thwarts. The luxury yacht was showing lights at her stern, where several crewmen waited to receive cargo. Fr. Eusebio watched and spat in the dust. He thought of the family he had buried ten days earlier.

Back in his room, he prepared to resume his interrupted sleep. But he paused, went to the drawer and pulled out the gizmo. He did not know about texting and did not own a cell phone. He never had. But he had a small piece of paper on which he had written the list of buttons he had to press if he wanted to use the little machine. He pressed them one by one. The gizmo spoke. A woman's voice said *"¿Oiga?"* He addressed the cell phone.

"Se habla español?" he asked.

"Claro, Padre," said the woman. *"¿Qué quiere?"*

He did not know quite how to phrase it.

"In my village is moored a very large boat. I think it takes on board a great quantity of the white powder."

"Does it have a name, Father?"

"Yes, I have seen it on the back. In gold letters. It is called the *Orion Lady.*"

Then he lost his nerve and put the phone down so nobody could trace him. The computerized database took five seconds to identify the cell phone, the user and his exact location. In another ten, it had identified the *Orion Lady.*

She was owned by Nelson Bianco of Nicaragua, a multimillionaire playboy, polo player and party giver. She was not listed as one worked on by Juan Cortez, the welder. But her deck plan was obtained from her builders and fed into the memory of Global Hawk Michelle, who found the boat before dawn as she slipped out of the creek and headed for the open sea.

Further investigations during the morning, including consultation with the social diaries, revealed Señor Bianco was due in Fort Lauderdale for a polo tournament.

As the *Orion Lady* cruised north northwest

to round Cuba by the Yucatán Channel, the Q-ship *Chesapeake* moved to cut her off.

CHAPTER 11

There were 117 names on the Rat List. They covered officials on the public payroll in eighteen countries. Two of those were the U.S. and Canada, the other sixteen in Europe. Before he would countenance the release of Ms. Letizia Arenal from her detention in New York, the Cobra insisted on one acid test at least, chosen at random. He picked Herr Eberhardt Milch, a senior customs inspector in the Port of Hamburg. Cal Dexter flew to the Hanseatic port to break the bad news.

It was a somewhat puzzled meeting that convened at the American's request at the headquarters of Hamburg's Customs Direction on the Rödingsmarkt.

Dexter was flanked by the senior DEA representative in Germany, who was already known to the German delegation. He in turn was rather mystified by the status of the man from Washington whom he had never heard of. But the instructions out of Army Navy Drive, the HQ of the DEA, were short and succinct. He has mojo; just cooperate.

Two had flown in from Berlin, one from the ZKA, the German federal customs, the other from the organized crime division of the Federal Criminal Police, the BKA. The fifth and sixth were local men, Hamburgers from the state customs and state police. The former of these two was their host; they met in his office. But it was Joachim Ziegler of the customs criminal division who carried the rank and faced Dexter.

Dexter kept it short. There was no need for explanations, they were all professionals, and the four Germans knew they would not have been asked to host the two Americans unless there was something wrong. Nor was there any need for interpreters.

All Dexter could say, and this was perfectly understood, was that the DEA in Colombia had acquired certain information. The word "mole" hung in the air unspoken. There was coffee, but no one drank.

Dexter slid several sheets of paper across to Herr Ziegler, who studied them carefully and passed them to his colleagues. The Hamburg ZKA man whistled softly.

"I know him," he muttered.

"And?" asked Ziegler. He was profoundly embarrassed. Germany is immensely proud of its vast, ultra-modern Hamburg. That the Americans should bring him this was appalling.

The Hamburg man shrugged.

"Personnel will have the full details, of course. So far as I can recall, an entire career in the service, a few years to retirement. Not a blemish."

Ziegler tapped the papers in front of him.

"And if you have been misinformed? Even dis-informed?"

Dexter's reply was to slide a few more papers across the table. The clincher. Joachim Ziegler studied them. Bank records. From a small private bank in Grand Cayman. About as secret as you can get. If they, too, were genuine . . . Anyone can run up bank records so long as they can never be checked out. Dexter spoke:

"Gentlemen, we all understand the rules of 'need to know.' We are not beginners at our strange trade. You will have understood that there is a source. At all costs, we have to protect that source. More, you will not wish to jump into an arrest and find you have a case based on un-confirmable allegations that not a court in Germany would accept. May I suggest a stratagem?"

What he proposed was a covert operation. Milch would be covertly and invisibly tailed until he intervened very personally to assist a specific arriving container or cargo through the formalities. Then there would be a spot check, seeming haphazard, a random selection by a junior officer.

If the information from Cobra was accurate, Milch would have to intervene to overrule his junior. Their altercation would be interrupted, also coincidentally, by a passing ZKA officer. The word of the criminal division would prevail. The consignment would be opened. If there was nothing, the Americans were wrong. Profuse apologies all around. No harm done. But Milch's home phone and mobile would still be tapped for weeks.

It took a week to set up and another before the sting could be used. The sea container in question was one of hundreds disgorged by a huge freighter from Venezuela. Only one man noticed the two small circles, one inside the other, and the Maltese cross inside the inner one. Chief Inspector Milch cleared it personally for loading onto the flatbed truck waiting for it before departure into the hinterland.

The driver, who turned out to be an Albanian, was at the very last barrier when, having lifted, it came down again. A young, pink-cheeked customs man gestured the truck into a lay-by.

"Spot check," he said. *"Papiere, bitte."*

The Albanian looked bewildered. He had his clearance papers, signed and stamped. He obeyed and made a rapid cell phone call. Inaudible inside his high cab, he uttered a few sentences in Albanian.

Hamburg customs normally has two levels of spot check for trucks and their cargoes. The cursory one is X-ray only; the other is "Open up." The young officer was really a ZKA operative, which was why he looked like a newcomer on the job. He beckoned the flatbed toward the zone reserved for major checking. He was interrupted by a much more senior officer hurrying from the control house.

A very new, very young, very inexperienced *Inspektor* does not argue with a veteran *Oberinspektor.* This one did. He stuck to his decision. The older man remonstrated. He had cleared this truck on the basis of his own spot check. There was no need to double-task. They were wasting their time. He did not see the small sedan slide up behind him. Two plainclothes ZKA men emerged and flashed badges.

"Was ist los da?" asked one of them quite

genially. Rank is important in German bureaucracy. The ZKA men were of equal rank to Milch, but being from the criminal division took precedence. The container was duly opened. Sniffer dogs arrived. The contents were unloaded. The dogs ignored the cargo but started sniffing and whining at the rear of the interior. Measurements were taken. The interior was shorter than the exterior. The truck was moved to a fully equipped workshop. The customs team went with it. The three ZKA men, two overt and the young undercover lad making his "bones" with his first real "sting," kept up their charade of geniality.

The oxyacetylene man cut the false back off. When the blocks behind it were weighed, they turned out to be two tons of Colombian *puro*. The Albanian was already in cuffs. The pretense was maintained that all four, Milch included, had secured a remarkable stroke of good fortune, despite Milch's earlier but understandable error. The importing company was, after all, a thoroughly respectable coffee warehouse in Düsseldorf. Over celebratory coffee, Milch excused himself, went to the gents' and made a call.

Mistake. It was on intercept. Every word was heard in a van half a kilometer away.

One of the men around the coffee table took a call on his own cell. When Milch came out of the restroom, he was arrested.

His protestations began in earnest once he was seated in the interrogation room. No mention was made of any bank accounts in Grand Cayman. By agreement with Dexter, that would have blown the informant in Colombia. But it also gave Milch a first-class defense. He could have pleaded "We all make mistakes." It would have been hard to prove he had been doing this for years. Or that he was going to retire extremely rich. A good lawyer could have got him bail by nightfall and an acquittal at trial, if it ever came to that. The words on the intercepted call were coded; a harmless reference to being home late. The number called was not his wife but a cell phone that would immediately disappear. But we all dial wrong numbers.

Chief Inspector Ziegler, who apart from a career in customs also had a law degree, knew the weakness of his hand. But he wanted to stop those two tons of cocaine entering Germany and he had succeeded.

The Albanian, hard as nails, was not saying a word, other than that he was a simple driver. Düsseldorf Police were raiding the coffee warehouse where their sniffer dogs were going hysterical over the aroma of cocaine, which they had been trained to differentiate from coffee, often used as a "masker."

Then Ziegler, who was a first-class cop, played a hunch. Milch would not speak Albanian. Hardly anyone did except Albanians. He sat Milch behind a one-way mirror but with sound from the neighboring interrogation suite turned up loud and clear. He could watch the Albanian driver being questioned.

The Albanian-speaking interpreter was putting the questions from the German officer to the driver and translating his answers. The questions were predictable. Milch could understand them; they were in his language, but he relied on the interpreter to understand the answers. Though the Albanian was really protesting his innocence, what came through the speakers was a comprehensive admission that if the driver was ever in trouble in Hamburg docks he should immediately appeal to a certain Oberinspektor Eberhardt Milch, who would sort out everything and send him on his way without cargo inspection.

That was when a shattered Milch broke. His full confession took almost two days and a team of stenographers to transcribe.

■ ■ ■ ■

The *Orion Lady* was in that sweeping expanse of the Caribbean Basin south of Jamaica and east of Nicaragua when her captain, immaculate in pressed white tropical uniform, standing beside the helmsman on the bridge, saw something that made him blink in disbelief.

He rapidly checked his sea-scanning radar. There was not a vessel in miles, horizon to horizon. But the helicopter was definitely a helicopter. And it was coming from dead ahead, low above the blue water. He knew perfectly well what he was carrying for he had helped load it thirty hours earlier, and the first eel of fear stirred deep inside. The chopper was small, not much more than a spotter craft, but when it wheeled past his port bow and turned the words "U.S. Navy" on the boom were unmistakable. He rang the main salon to alert his employer.

Nelson Bianco joined him on the bridge. The playboy was in a flowered Hawaiian shirt, baggy shorts and barefoot. His black locks were, as always, dyed and lacquer-set, and he clutched his trademark Cohiba cigar. Unusually for him, and only because of the cargo from Colombia, he did not have five or six upscale call girls on board.

The two men watched the Little Bird, just above the ocean, and then they saw that in the open circle of the passenger door, well harnessed and turned toward them, was a SEAL in black coveralls. He held an M14 sniper rifle, and it was pointed straight at them. A voice boomed out from the tiny helo.

"*Orion Lady, Orion Lady,* we are the United States Navy. Please close down your engines. We are going to come aboard."

Bianco could not figure out how they were going to achieve that. There was a helipad aft, but his own tarpaulined Sikorsky was on it. Then his captain nudged him and gestured ahead. There were three black dots on the water, one large, two small; they were nose up, racing fast and coming toward him.

"Full speed," snapped Bianco. "Full speed ahead."

It was a foolish reaction, as the captain spotted immediately.

"Boss, we will never outrun them. If we try, we just give ourselves away."

Bianco glanced at the hovering Little Bird, the racing RHIBs and the rifle pointed at his head from fifty yards. There was nothing for it but to brazen it out. He nodded.

"Cut engines," he said, and stepped out-side. The wind ruffled his hair, then died away. He spread a big, expansive smile and waved, as one delighted to cooperate. The SEALs were aboard in five minutes.

Lt. Cdr. Casey Dixon was scrupulously polite. He had been told his target was car-rying, and that was good enough. Declining offers of champagne for him and his men, he had the owner and crew shepherded aft and held at gunpoint. There was still no sign of the *Chesapeake* on the horizon. His diver donned his Dräger unit and went over the edge. He was down there half an hour. When he came up, he reported no trapdoors in the hull, no blimps or blisters and no dangling nylon cords.

The two rummage men began to search. They did not know that the short and frightened cell phone call from a parish priest had mentioned only "a great quan-tity." But how much was that?

It was the spaniel that got the scent, and it turned out to be a ton. The *Orion Lady* was not one of those vessels into which Juan Cortez had built a virtually undiscoverable hideaway. Bianco had thought to get away with it through sheer arrogance. He pre-sumed such a luxurious yacht, well known in the most expensive and famous watering holes of the world, from Monte Carlo to Fort Lauderdale, would be above suspicion, and he with it. But for an old Jesuit who had buried four tortured bodies in a jungle grave, he might have been right.

Once again, as with the British SBS, it was the spaniel's ultra-sensitivity to the aroma of air texture that caused it to worry a certain panel in the floor of the engine room. The air was too fresh; it had been lifted recently. It led to the bilges.

As with the British in the Atlantic, the rummage men donned breathing masks and slithered into the bilges. Even on a luxury yacht, bilges still stink. One by one, the bales came out, and the SEALs not on prisoner guard duty hauled them topside and stacked them between the main salon and the helipad. Bianco protested noisily that he had no idea what they were . . . It was all a trick . . . a misunderstanding . . . He knew the governor of Florida. The shouting sank to a mumble when the black hood went on. Cdr. Dixon fired his maroon rocket upward, and the circling Global Hawk Michelle switched off her jammers. In fact, the *Orion Lady* had not even tried to transmit. When he had comms again, Dixon summoned the *Chesapeake* to approach.

Two hours later, Nelson Bianco, his captain and crew, were in the forward brig with the seven surviving men from the two go-fasts. The millionaire playboy did not usually mix with such company and he did not like it. But these were to be his companions and dining partners for a long time, and his taste for the tropics was to be fully indulged but in the middle of the Indian Ocean. And party girls were off the menu.

Even the explosives man was regretful.

"We really have to waste her, sir? She is such a beauty."

"Orders," said the CO. "No exceptions."

The SEALs stood on the *Chesapeake* and watched the *Orion Lady* erupt and sink. "Hooyah!" said one of them, but the word, normally the SEALs' sign of jubilation, was said somewhat regretfully. When the sea was empty again, the *Chesapeake* steamed away. An hour later, another freighter went past her, and the merchant skipper, looking through his binoculars, saw just a grain ship going about her business and took no notice.

Right across Germany, the FLO were having a field day. In his copious confession, Eberhardt Milch, now buried under layers of official secrecy to keep him alive, had named a dozen major importers whose cargoes he had eased through the container port of Hamburg. They were all being raided and closed down.

Federal and state police were hitting warehouses, pizza parlors (the favorite front of the Calabrian Ndrangheta), food stores and craft shops specializing in ethnic carvings from South America. They were cutting open shipments of tinned tropical fruit for the pouch of white powder in each can and shattering Mayan idols from Guatemala. Thanks to one man, the Don's German operation was in ruins.

But the Cobra was very aware that if the cocaine imports had passed the point of handover, the loss was sustained by the European gangs. Only before that point was the loss down to the cartel. That included the false-backed sea container in Hamburg that had never left the docks and the cargo of the *Orion Lady* that was destined for the Cuban gang of South Florida and which was supposed to be still at sea. The nonarrival in Fort Lauderdale had not been noticed. Yet.

But the Rat List had proved itself. The Cobra had selected the Hamburg Rat at random, one of the 117 names, the odds were too long that it had all been invented.

"Shall we set the girl free?" asked Dexter.

Devereaux nodded. Personally, he could not have cared. His capacity for compassion was virtually nonexistent. But she had served her purpose.

Dexter set the wheels in motion. Due to quiet intervention, Inspector Paco Ortega of the UDYCO in Madrid had been promoted to chief inspector. He had been promised Julio Luz and the Guzman bank anytime soon.

Across the Atlantic, he listened to Cal Dexter and planned his deception. A young undercover officer played the part of the baggage handler. He was noisily and publicly arrested in a bar, and the media were tipped off. Reporters interviewed the barman and two regulars, who concurred.

Acting on further nonattributable information, *El País* ran a big feature on the breaking of a gang attempting to use baggage handlers to smuggle drugs in the luggage of unsuspecting travelers from Barajas to Kennedy, New York. Most of the gang had fled, but one such baggage handler had been taken and was naming flights on which he had opened suitcases after the usual screening in order to insert cocaine. In some cases, he even recalled the suitcases by description.

Mr. Boseman Barrow was not a betting

man. He had no taste for casinos, dice, cards or horses as a way of throwing money away. But if he was, he had to admit, he would surely have placed a large wager on Señorita Letizia Arenal going to jail for many years. And he would have lost.

The Madrid file reached the DEA in Washington, and some unknown authority ordered that a copy of those sections concerning Mr. Barrow's client go to the District Attorney's Office in Brooklyn. Once there, it had to be acted upon. Lawyers are not all bad, unfashionable though that view may be. The DA's Office apprised Boseman Barrow of the news from Madrid. He at once entered a motion to dismiss charges. Even if innocence had not been conclusively proved, there was now a doubt the size of a barn door.

There was an in-chambers hearing with a judge who had been at law school with Boseman Barrow, and the motion was granted. The fate of Letizia Arenal passed from the Prosecutor's Office to the ICE, the Immigration and Customs Enforcement. They decreed that even though she was no longer to be prosecuted, the Colombian was not to stay in the USA either. She was asked where she wished to be deported to, and she chose Spain. Two ICE marshals took her to Kennedy.

Paul Devereaux knew that his first cover was running out. That cover had been his nonexistence. He had studied with every scrap of information he could glean the figure and character of a certain Don Diego Esteban, believed to be but never proved to be the supreme head of the cartel.

That this ruthless hidalgo, this postimperial, Spanish-descended aristocrat, had remained untouchable for so long derived from many factors.

One was the absolute refusal of anyone to testify against him. Another was the convenient disappearance of anyone who opposed him. But even that would not have been enough without enormous political clout. He had influence in high places, and a lot of it.

He was a relentless donor to good causes, all publicized. He endowed schools, hospitals, bursaries, scholarships; and always for the poor of the barrios.

He donated, but much more quietly, not to one political party but to all of them, including that of President Álvaro Uribe, who had sworn to crush the cocaine industry. In each case, he allowed these gifts to become known to those who mattered. He even paid for the raising of the orphans of murdered police and customs officers, even though their colleagues suspected who had ordered the killing.

And above all he ingratiated himself with the Catholic Church. Not a monastery or priest's house fell on hard times but he would not donate toward the restoration. This he made highly visible, as also his regular worship right among the peasant and estate workers in the parish church adjoining his country mansion, meaning his official rural residence, not the many and varied farms owned in false names where he met other members of the Brotherhood he had created to manufacture and market up to eight hundred tons of cocaine each year.

"He is," mused Devereaux admiringly, "a maestro." He hoped the Don had not also read the *Ping-fa*, the *Art of War*.

The Cobra knew that the litany of missing cargoes, arrested agents and ruined buyer networks would not be written off as coincidence for much longer. There are just so many coincidences that a clever man will accept, and the higher the level of paranoia, the fewer the number. The first cover, of nonexistence, would soon be disbelieved, and the Don would realize he had a new and much more dangerous enemy who did not play by the rules.

After that would come cover number two: invisibility. Sun-tzu had declared that a man cannot defeat an invisible enemy. The wise old Chinese man had lived long before the ultra–high technology of the Cobra's world. But there were new weapons that could keep the Cobra invisible long after the Don had realized that there was a new enemy out there.

A primary factor in the exposure of his existence was going to be the Rat List. To blow away 117 corrupt officials in a series of strikes across two continents in a single campaign would be too much. He would feed the Rats into the FLO mincer very slowly until the peso dropped somewhere in Colombia. And, anyway, sooner or later, there would be a leak.

But that week in August, he sent Cal Dexter to break the sad news to three governmental authorities under conditions, he hoped, of massive discretion.

In a hard week of traveling and conferring, Cal Dexter apprised the USA there was a bad one in the docks of San Francisco; the Italians learned they had a corrupt senior customs official in Ostia; and the Spanish should start to tail a dock master at

Santander.

In each case, he begged for the arrangement of an accidental stumbling-upon of a cocaine consignment that could lead to the necessary arrest. He received his pledges.

The Cobra did not give a fig about the American and European street gangs. These scum were not his problem. But every time one of the cartel's little helpers left the stage, the interception rate would rise exponentially. And before handover at the dock gates, the loss would be taken by the cartel. And the orders would have to be replaced. And refilled. And that would not be possible.

Álvaro Fuentes was certainly not going to cross the Atlantic to Africa in a smelly fishing boat like the *Belleza del Mar*. As first deputy to Alfredo Suárez, he went on a 6,000-ton general freighter, the *Arco Soledad*.

She was big enough to have a master's cabin, not large but private, and this was taken over by Fuentes. The unhappy captain had to bunk with the first mate, but he knew his place and made no demur.

As demanded by the Don, the *Arco Soledad* had been redirected from Monrovia, Liberia, to Guinea-Bissau, where the problem seemed to lie. But she still carried a full five tons of pure cocaine.

She was one of those merchant ships on which Juan Cortez had worked his skills. Below the waterline, she carried two stabilizers welded to her hull. But they had a dual purpose. Apart from stabilizing the vessel to make her more sea-friendly and give her crew a gentler ride in wild water, they were hollow, and each contained two and half tons of carefully packed bales.

The main problem with underwater panniers was that they could be loaded and emptied only if the boat was brought out of the water. This meant either the great complexity of a dry dock, with all its chances of witnesses, or beaching until the tide went out, which meant hours of waiting.

Cortez had fitted virtually invisible snap-release catches with which a scuba diver could quickly remove large panels in each stabilizer. With these gone, the bales, thoroughly waterproofed and roped together, could be drawn out until they floated to the surface for collection by the offshore "greeter" vessel.

And finally the *Arco Soledad* had a perfectly legitimate cargo of coffee in her holds and paperwork to prove it was paid for and expected by a trading company in Bissau city. That was where the good news ran out.

The bad news was that the *Arco Soledad* had long been spotted with Juan Cortez's description and photographed from above. As she crossed the 35th longitude, the cruising Global Hawk Sam picked up her image, made the comparison, clinched the identification and informed AFB Creech, Nevada.

Nevada told Washington, and the shabby warehouse in Anacostia told the MV *Balmoral,* which moved to intercept. Before Major Pickering and his divers even got onto the water, they would know exactly what they were looking for, where it was and how to operate the hidden catches.

For the first three days at sea, Álvaro Fuentes abided strictly by his instructions. Every three hours, night and day, he sent dutiful e-mails to his waiting "wife" in Barranquilla. They were so banal and so common at sea, that normally the NSA at Fort Meade, Maryland, would not have bothered with them. But, forewarned, each one was plucked out of cyberspace and patched through to Anacostia.

When Sam, circling at 40,000 feet, could see the *Arco Soledad* and the *Balmoral* forty miles apart, she put on her jammers over the freighter, and Fuentes went into a blank zone. When he saw the helicopter fluttering above the horizon and then turning toward him, he made an emergency, out-of-sequence report. It went nowhere.

There was no point in the *Arco Soledad* attempting to resist the black-clad commandos when they came over the rail. The captain, with a fine show of indignation, brandished his ship's papers, cargo manifest and copies of the coffee order from Bissau. The men in black took no notice.

Still yelling "Piracy," the captain, crew and Álvaro Fuentes were shackled, hooded and herded to the stern. As soon as they could see nothing, the jamming ceased, and Major Pickering summoned the *Balmoral.* While she steamed toward the stationary freighter, the two divers went to work. It took just under an hour. The spaniels were not needed; they stayed on the mother ship.

Before the *Balmoral* was alongside, there were two skeins of roped bales floating in the water. They were so heavy, it took the derrick of the *Arco Soledad* to bring them on board. From the deck of the tramp, the *Balmoral* hoisted them into her guardianship.

Fuentes, the captain and five crew had gone very quiet. Even under their masks they could hear the derrick grinding and heavy thumps as a long series of objects sloshing water came aboard. They knew what they must be. Complaints of piracy ended.

The Colombians followed their cargo onto the *Balmoral.* They realized they were on a much bigger ship but could never name or describe it. From the deck, they were led to the forward brig and, with hoods removed, moved into quarters formerly occupied by the crew of the *Belleza del Mar.*

The SBS men came last, the divers streaming water. Ordinarily the sub-aqua men meeting the *Arco Soledad* would have replaced the removed panels underwater, but, bearing in mind where they were all going, they were allowed to take on water.

The explosives man was last off. When there was half a mile between the ships, he pressed his detonator.

"Smell the coffee," he joked as the *Arco Soledad* shuddered, flooded and foundered. And indeed there really was a slight odor of roasted coffee on the sea breeze as the PETN for one nanosecond reached 5,000 degrees centigrade. Then she was gone.

One RIB, still in the water, returned to the spot and gathered in the few floating pieces of detritus that a sharp observer might have spotted. These were netted, weighted and sent to the bottom. The ocean, blue and calm in early September, was as she had always been — empty.

Far away across the Atlantic, Alfredo Suárez could not believe the news reaching him or work out a way of telling Don Diego and staying alive. His bright young assistant had ceased transmitting twelve hours earlier. This was disobedience, i.e., madness, or it was disaster.

He had a message from his clients, the Cubans, who controlled most of the cocaine trade in South Florida, that the *Orion Lady* had not docked in Fort Lauderdale. She was also expected by the harbormaster, who was holding a precious-as-rubies berth for her. Discreet inquiries revealed he had also tried to raise her and failed. She was three days overdue and not answering.

There had been some successful deliveries of cocaine, but the sequence of failed arrivals by sea and air and a big customs coup in Hamburg had reduced his "safe arrival" percentage set against tonnage dispatched to fifty. He had promised the Don a minimum safe arrival percentage of seventy-five. For the first time, he began to fear that his policy of large cargoes but fewer of them, the opposite of the scattergun approach of his departed predecessor, might not be working. Though not a praying man, he prayed there was not worse to come, proof positive that prayer does not always work. There was much worse to come.

Far away in the genteel historic township of Alexandria, by the banks of the Potomac, the man who intended to create that "worse" was considering his campaign to date.

He had created three lines of thrust. One was to use the knowledge of all the merchantmen worked on by Juan Cortez to empower the regular forces of law and order — navies, customs, coast guards — to intercept the giants at sea, "accidentally" discover the secret hiding places and thus both confiscate the cocaine and impound the vessel.

This was because most of the Lloyd's-listed carriers were too big to sink unnoticed without causing a furor in the shipping world, leading to powerful interventions at governmental level. Insurers and owners would dispense with corrupt crews, and pay fines, while declaring complete innocence at board level, but losing the entire ship was a loss too far.

Intercepting at sea at a very official level also frustrated the common tactic of taking the cocaine on board at sea from one fishing vessel and off-loading it before docking in another offshore transfer. This could not last forever, or even for very long. Even though Juan Cortez was seemingly an incinerated corpse in a grave in Cartagena, it must soon become plain that someone knew far too much about all the invisible hiding holes he had created. Any subtlety in seeming to find these places by accident every time would one day run out.

In any case, these triumphs by the official authorities were never hidden. They quickly became public and leaked back to the cartel.

His second thrust was a series of irregular and apparently patternless accidents in various harbors and airports around two continents in which a terrible mischance revealed an incoming cocaine shipment and even led to the arrest of the bribed official who acted as "enabler." These also could not remain accidents forever.

As a lifelong counter-spy, he doffed his hat, a rare phenomenon, to Cal Dexter for acquiring the Rat List. He never asked who the mole inside the cartel could be, though clearly the saga of the Colombian girl framed in New York was linked.

But he hoped that mole could dig a very deep hole indeed, because he could not keep the cocaine enablers unarrested for long. As the number of crippled operations in U.S. and European ports increased, it would become clear someone had leaked names and functions.

The good news, for one who knew a bit about interrogations and who had broken Aldrich Ames, was that these officials, though greedy and venal, were not "hard men" accustomed to the laws of the criminal underworld. The German exposed so far was confessing like a mountain spring. So would most of the others. These tearful spillages would trigger a chain reaction of arrests and closedowns. And future interceptions would, without official help, skyrocket. That was part of his planning.

But his ace was the third thrust on which he had spent so much time and trouble and so much of his budget over the permitted preparation period.

He called it the "bewilderment factor," and he had used it for years in that espionage world that James Jesus Angleton, his predecessor at the CIA, once referred to as "smoke and mirrors." It was the explanationless disappearance, one after the other, of cargo after cargo.

Meanwhile, he would quietly release the names and details of four more of the Rats. In the middle week of September, Cal Dexter traveled to Athens, Lisbon, Paris and

Amsterdam. In each case, his revelations caused shock and horror, but in each case he received assurances that each arrest would be preceded by a carefully arranged accident involving an incoming cargo of cocaine. He described the Hamburg sting and proposed it as a role model.

What he was able to tell the Europeans was that there was a corrupt customs officer in Piraeus, the port of Athens; the Portuguese had a bribe taker in the quite small but busy Algarve Harbor of Faro; France was sheltering a rather large rodent in Marseilles; and the Dutch had a problem in the largest cargo destination in Europe, Euro port Rotterdam.

Francisco Pons was retiring and he was damnably glad of it. He had made his peace with his plump and homely wife, Victoria, and even found a buyer for his Beech King Air. He had explained matters to the man for whom he flew the Atlantic, a certain Señor Suárez, who had accepted his explanation of age and stiffness, and it had been agreed that this September would be his last trip for the cartel. It was not so bad, he reasoned with Señor Suárez; his eager young copilot was aching to become a full captain and earn a captain's fee. As for a newer and better plane, that was now necessary anyway. So he lined up on the runway at Fortaleza and took off. Far above, the tiny moving dot was registered by the wide-aspect radar scanner of Global Hawk Sam and logged in the database.

The memory bank did the rest. It identified the moving dot as a King Air, that it was coming out of Rancho Boa Vista, that a Beech King Air cannot cross the Atlantic without large extra in-built fuel tanks and that it was heading northeast toward the 35th longitude. Beyond that, there was only Africa. Someone in Nevada instructed Major João Mendoza and his ground crew to prepare to fly.

The oncoming Beech was two hours into its flight, almost on the last of its main wing tanks, and the copilot had the controls. Far below and somewhere ahead, the Buccaneer felt the hammer blow of the RATO rockets, plunged down the runway and roared away over the dark sea. It was a moonless night.

Sixty minutes later, the Brazilian was at his intercept station, circling at a lazy three hundred knots. Somewhere to his southwest, invisible in the blackness, the King Air plodded along, now running on reserve tanks, with the two pumpers working away behind the flight deck.

"Climb to twelve thousand, continue in rate one turn," said the warm voice from Nevada. Like the Lorelei, it was a pretty voice to lure men to die. The reason for the instruction was that Sam had reported the King Air had climbed to ride over a cloud bank.

Even without a moon, the stars over Africa are fiercely bright, and a cloudscape is like a white bedsheet, reflecting light, showing up shadows against the pale surface. The Buccaneer was vectored to a position five miles behind the King Air and a thousand feet above. Mendoza scanned the pale plateau ahead of him. It was not entirely flat; there were knobs of altocumulus jutting out of it. He eased back his speed for fear of overtaking too quickly.

Then he saw it. Just a shadow between two hills of cumulus disfiguring the line of the stratus. Then it was gone, then back again.

"I have it," he said. "No mistake?"

"Negative," said the voice in his ears. "There is nothing else in the sky."

"Roger that. Contact."

"Contact acknowledged. Stop, clear, engage."

He eased on some throttle, the distance closed. Safety catch off. Target swimming into the gunsight, range closing. Four hundred meters.

The two streams of cannon shells streamed out and coalesced at the tail of the Beech. The tail fragmented, but the shells went on into the fuselage, racing up the line through the extra fuel tanks and into the flight deck. Both pumpers died in a tenth of a second, blown apart; the two pilots would have followed, but the exploding fuel did it faster. As with the Transall, the Beech imploded, fragmented and fell blazing through the cloud sheet.

"Target down," said Mendoza. Another ton of cocaine was not going to reach Europe.

"Turn for home," said the voice. "Your course is . . ."

Alfredo Suárez had no choice about telling the Don the litany of bad news because he was sent for. The master of the cartel had not survived so long in one of the most vicious milieus on earth without a sixth sense for danger.

Item by item, he forced the director of dispatch to tell him all. The two ships and now two airplanes lost before reaching Guinea-Bissau; the two go-fasts in the Caribbean that never made their rendezvous and had not been seen since, including eight crewmen; the playboy who disappeared with a ton of *puro* destined for the valuable Cuban clients in South Florida. And the disaster in Hamburg.

He had expected Don Diego to explode in rage. The reverse happened. The Don had been taught as a boy that gentility required that even if one is irritable over small things, big disasters require a gentlemanly calm. He bade Suárez remain at the table. He lit one of his slim black cheroots and went for a stroll in his garden.

Internally, he was in a homicidal rage. There would be blood, he vowed. There would be screams. There would be death. But first, analysis.

Against Roberto Cárdenas, there could be nothing proved. One exposure of one of his on-the-payroll agents in Hamburg was probably bad luck. A coincidence. But not the rest. Not five vessels at sea and two planes in the air. Not the forces of law and order — they would have held press conferences, flaunted confiscated bales. He was used to that. Let them gloat over fragments. The entire cocaine industry was worth $300 billion a year. More than the national budget of most of the nations outside the G30 of the richest.

The profits were so vast that no amount of arrests could stop the army of volunteers screaming to take the places of the dead and imprisoned; profits big enough to make Gates and Buffett look like street vendors. The equal of their entire wealth was generated each year by cocaine.

But nonarrival, that was dangerous. The purchasing monster had to be fed. If the cartel was violent and vengeful, so also were the Mexicans, Italians, Cubans, Turks, Albanians, Spaniards and the rest whose organized gangs would slaughter over an ill-advised word.

So if not coincidence, and that was now no longer to be entertained as a reason, who was stealing his product, killing his crews, causing his shipments to vanish into thin air?

For the Don, this was treachery or theft, which was another form of treachery. And treachery had only one response. Identify and punish with insensate violence. Whoever they were, they had to learn. Nothing personal, but you cannot treat the Don like that.

He went back to his trembling guest.

"Send the Enforcer to me," he said.

CHAPTER 12

Paco Valdez, the Enforcer, and his two companions flew into Guinea-Bissau. The Don was not prepared to risk any more high-seas disappearances. Nor was he going to indulge the American DEA by having his creatures travel by scheduled commercial airline.

By the end of the first decade of the third millennium, the surveillance and control of all intercontinental airline passengers had become so total that it was unlikely that Valdez, with his unusual appearance, would not be spotted and followed. So they flew in the Don's private Grumman G4.

Don Diego was absolutely right . . . up to a point. But the twin-jet executive luxury aircraft still needed to fly a virtually straight line from Bogotá to Guinea-Bissau, and this brought her under the wide patrol circle of Global Hawk Sam. So the Grumman was spotted, identified and logged. When he heard the news, the Cobra smiled with satisfaction.

The Enforcer was met at Bissau Airport by the head of operations for the cartel in Guinea-Bissau, Ignacio Romero. Despite his seniority, Romero was very deferential. For one thing, Valdez was the Don's personal emissary; for another, his reputation was fear inspiring throughout the cocaine trade; and, for a third, Romero had been forced to report the nonarrival of four major cargoes, two by sea and two by air.

That cargoes should be lost was part of the permanent risk factor involved in the trade. In many parts of that trade, especially the direct routes into North America and Europe, those losses might hover around fifteen percent, which could be absorbed by the Don so long as the explanations were logical and convincing. But losses on the West Africa run had for Romero's entire tenure in Guinea been close to zero, which was why the Europe-bound percentage using the African dogleg had risen over five years from twenty to seventy percent of the total.

Romero was very proud of his safe-arrival figures. He had a flotilla of Bijagós canoes and several fast pseudo–fishing boats at his disposal, all equipped with GPS locators to

ensure pinpoint rendezvous at sea for cocaine transfers.

Added to this, he had the military estab-
lishment in his pocket. General Diallo's
soldiers actually did the heavy-lifting work
during unloading; the general took his
ample cut in the form of cocaine and ran
his own shipments north to Europe in
cahoots with the Nigerians. Paid off via West
Africa's army of Lebanese money brokers,
the general was already a rich man in world
terms, and, in local terms, an African Croe-
sus.

And then this. Not simply four lost cargoes
but total disappearances without a clue of
explanation. His cooperation with the Don's
emissary was a given; he was relieved that
the one called the Animal was genial and
good-humored toward him. He should have
known.

As always when a Colombian passport appeared at the airport, formalities vanished.
The crew of three was ordered to live on
the G4, use the facilities of the VIP suite,
such as it was, and never to leave the jet
without at least one onboard. Then Romero
drove his guests in his luxury SUV through
the war-gutted city and on to his mansion
by the beach ten miles out of town.

Valdez had brought two assistants with

him. One was short but immensely broad and beefy, the other tall, skinny and pock-marked. They each carried a grip that went uninspected. All experts need their tools.

The Enforcer appeared an easy guest. He demanded a vehicle of his own and a suggestion for a good lunch restaurant out of town. Romero proposed the Mar Azul, out on the banks of the Mansôa behind Quin-hámel, for its fresh lobster. He offered to drive his guests there personally, but Valdez waved away the proposal, took a map and left, with the beefy one at the wheel. They were away most of the day.

Romero was bemused. They did not seem interested in his foolproof procedures for cargo-reception and onward-transmission routes to North Africa and Europe.

On the second day, Valdez declared that as lunch by the river had been so splendid, they should all four repeat the outing. He mounted the SUV beside the beefy one, who replaced Romero's regular driver. Romero and Skinny took the rear seats.

The newcomers seemed to know the route well. They hardly referred to the map and drove unerringly through Quinhámel, the unofficial capital of the Papel tribe. The Papels had been bereft of influence since President Vieira, who was one of them, had been chopped to bits with machetes by the Army a year earlier. Since then, General Diallo, a Balanta, had been the dictator.

After the town, the signposted road to the restaurant left the main highway and went down a sandy track for another six miles. Halfway down, Valdez nodded to the side, and the beefy one swerved into an even smaller track toward an abandoned cashew farm. At this point, Romero began to plead.

"Be quiet, señor," said the Enforcer quietly. When he would not stop protesting his innocence, the skinny one drew a slim boning knife and held it under his jaw. He began to weep.

The farmhouse was little more than a shack, but it had a chair of sorts. Romero was too distressed to notice that someone had screwed its legs to the floor to stop it from rocking.

The zone chief's interrogators were quite matter-of-fact and businesslike. Valdez did nothing but stare from his cherubic little face at the surrounding cashew trees, overgrown and unharvested. His assistants hauled Romero out of the SUV, into the farmhouse, stripped him to the waist and tied him to the chair. What followed took an hour.

The Animal started, because he enjoyed

it, until the questioned one lost consciousness, then he handed over. His acolytes used
smelling salts to restore consciousness, and
after that Valdez simply asked the question.
There was only one. What had Romero
done with the stolen cargoes?

An hour later, it was almost over. The man
in the chair had ceased to scream. His
pulped lips uttered only a low moan in the
form of a "No-o-o-o-o-o" when, after a brief
pause, the two tormentors started again.
The beefy one did the hitting, the skinny
one the cutting. It was what they were best
at.

Toward the end, Romero was unrecognizable. He had no ears, eyes or nose. All the
knuckles were crushed and the nails removed. The chair sat in a pool of blood.

Valdez noticed something at his feet,
stooped and threw it out through the open
door into the eye-searing sunlight outside.
In seconds, a mangy dog approached it.
There was a dribble of white saliva around
its jaws. It was rabid.

The Enforcer pulled an automatic, cocked
it, drew a bead and fired once. The slug
went through both hips. The foxlike creature
uttered a shrill yelp and collapsed, its
forepaws scratching for traction, the two
rear legs useless. Valdez turned, holstering

the gun.

"Finish him," he said mildly. "He did not do it." What was left of Romero died with a thrust from the boning knife through the heart.

The three men from Bogotá did not try to hide what they had done. That task could be left to Romero's deputy, Carlos Sonora, who could now take over. The experience of clearing up would be salutary and a guarantee of future loyalty.

The three took off their splashed plastic raincoats and rolled them up. All were soaked in sweat. As they left, they were careful to step clear of the foaming muzzle of the dying dog. It lay snapping at thin air, still a yard short of the tidbit that had brought it from its lair. It was a human nose.

Escorted by Sonora, Paco Valdez paid a courtesy call on General Jalo Diallo, who received them in his office at Army HQ. Explaining that this was the custom of his people, Valdez brought a personal gift from Don Diego Esteban to his esteemed African colleague. It was an elaborate flower vase of finely turned native pottery and delicately hand-painted.

"For flowers," said Valdez, "so that when you look at them you can think of our profitable and comradely relationship."

371

Sonora translated into Portuguese. The skinny one fetched water from the en suite bathroom. The beefy one had brought a bunch of flowers. They made an attractive display. The general beamed. No one noticed that the vase accommodated remarkably little water, and the stalks of the flowers were rather short. Valdez noted the number of the desk telephone, one of the few in town that actually worked.

The next day was Sunday. The party from Bogotá was about to leave. Sonora would drive them to the airport. Half a mile past Army HQ, Valdez ordered a halt. On his cell phone, operated by MTN, the one local service provider, used only by the elite, the whites and the Chinese, he called the desk phone in General Diallo's office.

It took a few minutes for the general to walk through from his adjacent residential suite to his office. When he answered, he was a yard from the vase. Valdez pressed the detonator in his hand.

The explosion brought down most of the building and reduced the office to brick rubble. Of the dictator, a few fragments were found and later taken back to Balanta territory for tribal burial among the spirits of the ancestors.

"You will need a new business partner,"

Valdez told Sonora on the road to the airport. "An honest one. The Don does not like thieves. See to it."

The Grumman was ready for takeoff, fully fueled. It passed north of the Brazilian island of Fernando de Noronha, where Sam noticed and reported it. The coup in West Africa made the BBC World Service TV news, but it was a reported item without video so it did not last long.

A few days earlier, there was another newscast that raised no eyebrows, but it was on CNN out of New York. Ordinarily the deportation from Kennedy of a young Colombian student back to her studies in Madrid after the dropping of charges against her in Brooklyn might not have rated coverage. But someone pulled strings somewhere, and a crew was sent.

There was a two-minute report on the evening news. By nine p.m. it had been discontinued on editorial grounds. But while it lasted, it showed the ICE car drawing up at international departures, and two marshals escorting a very pretty young woman with a subdued manner across the concourse until they disappeared through the security barrier, where the group was not stopped.

The soundtrack narrated simply that Ms. Arenal had been the victim of an attempt by a criminal baggage handler in Madrid to use her suitcase on a trip to New York as a vehicle for a kilogram of cocaine that had been discovered in a spot check at Kennedy several weeks earlier. The arrest and confession in Spain had exonerated the Colombian student, who had been freed to return to her fine arts course in Madrid.

It made no waves, but it was spotted and recorded in Colombia. After that, Roberto Cárdenas replayed the segment frequently. It enabled him to see the daughter he had not set eyes on in years, and it reminded him of her mother, Conchita, who had been truly beautiful.

Unlike many of the top echelon of the cocaine trade, Cárdenas had never developed the taste for ostentation and luxury. He had come from the gutters and fought his way up through the old cartels. He was one of the first to spot the rising star of Don Diego and realize the benefits of centralization and concentration. This is why the Don, convinced of his loyalty, had taken him into the newly formed Hermandad at an early stage.

Cárdenas had the animal instincts of shy game; he knew his forest, he could sense danger, he never failed to settle a score. He had only one weak point, and a lawyer whose too-regular visits to Madrid had been spotted by a computer surfer far away in Washington had exposed it. When Conchita, who had raised Letizia alone after they parted, died of cancer, Cárdenas had got his daughter out of the nest of pit vipers, which was the world in which he was condemned to live because he knew no other.

He should have made a run for safety after the destruction of Eberhardt Milch in Hamburg. He knew it; his antennae did not let him down. He just refused. He hated a place called "abroad," and could run his division of bribed foreign officials only through a team of youngsters who moved like fish among the foreign coral. He could not do that and he knew it.

Like a jungle creature, he moved constantly from refuge to refuge, even in his own forest. He had fifty bolt-holes, mainly within the zone around Cartagena, and he bought use-and-throw prepaid cell phones like candies, never making more than one call before heaving the communicator into a river. He was so elusive that sometimes the cartel took a day or so to find him. And that was something the highly effective Colonel Dos Santos, head of intelligence in the anti-drug division of the Policía Judicial, could not do.

His bolt-holes tended to be working cottages, obscure, plainly furnished, even spartan. But there was one indulgence he cherished; he loved his TV. He had the best and newest model of plasma screen, the sharpest aerial dish, and they traveled with him.

He liked to sit with a six-pack of beer flicking through the satellite channels or screening movies on the DVD player below the screen. He loved the cartoons because Wile E. Coyote made him laugh, and he was not by nature a laughing man. He liked the cop dramas because he could deride the incompetence of the criminals, who were always caught, and the uselessness of the detectives, who would never have caught Roberto Cárdenas.

And he loved one taped newscast that he played over and over again. It showed a lovely but haggard young woman on a pavement at Kennedy Airport. Sometimes he would freeze-frame and stare at it for half an hour. After what he had done to enable that clip of film, he knew that sooner or later someone would make a mistake.

The mistake, when it came, was in Rotterdam, of all places. This very ancient Dutch city would hardly be recognized by any merchant who had lived there a hundred years ago or even a British Tommy who had marched through it in a welter of flowers and kisses in early 1945. Only the small Old Town still retained the elegant mansions of the eighteenth century, while the gigantic Euro port was modern, a second city of steel, glass, concrete, chrome, water and ships.

While most of the unloading of enormous quantities of oil to keep Europe functioning is accomplished at sea islands of pipes and pumps far out of reach of the city, Rotterdam's second specialty is its container port; not quite as large as Hamburg but just as modern and mechanized.

Dutch customs, working with the police and, in the time-honored phrase "acting upon information received," had exposed and arrested a senior customs officer by the name of Peter Hoogstraten.

He was clever, devious and intended to beat the charge. He knew what he had done and where he had banked the payoff money, or, more precisely, where the cartel had banked it for him. He intended to retire, and he intended to enjoy every penny of it. He had not the slightest intention of confessing or admitting a single thing. He intended to play his "civil rights" and his "human rights" down to the last card on the table. The only thing that worried him was how the authorities knew so much. Someone, somewhere, had blown him away; of that, he was certain.

Ultra-liberal though the Netherlands prides itself on being, it plays host to an enormous criminal underworld, and, perhaps because of the extreme permissiveness, a very large part of that underworld is in the hands of European foreigners and non-Europeans.

Hoogstraten worked primarily for one such gang, and they were Turks. He knew the rules of the cocaine trade. The product belonged to the cartel until it rolled out of the sea-container port onto the highways of the European Union. Then it belonged to the Turkish mafia, who had paid fifty percent up front, with fifty percent on delivery. A consignment intercepted by Dutch customs was going to hurt both parties.

The Turks would have to re-place their order, while refusing to pay any further money. But the Turks had customers who had also placed orders and demanded delivery. Hoogstraten's skill at clearing sea containers and other cargoes was invaluable and paid extremely well. He was only one asset in a procedure that, between Colombian jungle and Dutch dinner party, could easily have twenty layers of different participants, all needing to be paid a cut, but he was a crucial one.

The mistake occurred because of Chief Inspector Van der Merwe's private problem. He had been in the Royal Dutch Customs all his working life. He had joined the criminal investigation division within three years of entering the profession and had intercepted a mountain of contraband over the years. But the years had taken their toll. He had an enlarged prostate and drank far too much coffee, which exacerbated his weak bladder. It was the source of smothered grins among his younger colleagues, but, as a sufferer, he could not see the joke. Halfway through the sixth interrogation of Peter Hoogstraten, he simply had to go.

It should not have been a problem. He nodded to the colleague beside him that they would all take a break. The colleague intoned, "Interview suspended at . . . ," and switched off the digital recording machine. Hoogstraten insisted he wanted a cigarette and that meant he had to go to the "Smoking Permitted" area.

Political correctness forbade it, but civil rights allowed it. Van der Merwe longed for his retirement to the country house outside Groningen, with his beloved vegetable garden and orchard, where he could do what he damn well liked for the rest of his life. All three men rose.

Van der Merwe turned, and the tail of his jacket disturbed the file that lay in front of him on the table. The buff file turned ninety degrees, and a paper inside peeked out. It had a column of figures on it. In a second it was back inside the folder, but Hoogstraten had seen it. He recognized the figures. They were from his bank account in the Turks and Caicos Islands.

Nothing crossed his face, but a light came on inside his head. The swine had penetrated banking secrecy details. Apart from him, only two sources could know those figures and which bank, half of whose name had been showing for a fraction of a second. One source was the bank itself; the other was the cartel who filled that account. He doubted it was the bank, unless the American DEA had broken through the computer firewalls protecting the accounts.

That was always possible. Nothing was truly impregnable anymore, not even the firewalls of NASA and the Pentagon, as had been proved. Either way, the cartel should be alerted that there was a leak, and a bad one. He had no idea how to contact the Colombian cartel, whose existence he had read about in a long cocaine article in *De Telegraaf.* But the Turks would know.

Two days later at a bail hearing, Dutch customs had their second piece of bad luck. The judge was a notorious civil rights fanatic who privately favored the legalization of cocaine, which he used himself. He granted bail; Hoogstraten walked out and made his call.

In Madrid, Chief Inspector Paco Ortega finally pounced, and with the full blessing of Cal Dexter. The money-laundering lawyer Julio Luz was of no further use to him. A check on reservations at Bogotá Airport indicated he was flying to Madrid on his regular run.

Ortega waited until he was emerging from the bank while behind him two members of staff handed over a pair of heavy Samsonite hard-framed suitcases. Suddenly it rained armed Guardia Civil, led by plainclothes UDYCO men.

In the alley behind the bank, directed by UDYCO's man on a rooftop five hundred meters away, two men later shown to be hired muscle working for the Galician gangs were snatched along with the bank staff and the suitcases. These contained the fort-nightly "settlement of accounts" between the combined underworld of Spain and the Colombian cartel.

The total haul was over €10 million, packed in bricks of five-hundred-euro notes. In the Euro zone, this bill is hardly ever seen, the denomination being so high it is almost impossible to use on the street. It can realistically be used only for huge settlements in cash, and there is only one business that needs this on a constant basis.

At the front of the bank, Julio Luz was arrested, and, inside, the brothers Guzman and their senior accountant. With a court order, UDYCO seized all the books and records. To prove collusion in transcontinental money laundering was going to take a team of the best accountants months of research, but the two suitcases supplied the "holding" charge. They simply could not be lawfully explained being handed over to known gangsters. But it would be much simpler if someone confessed.

Being led to the cells, the Galicians were walked past an open door. Inside was a distraught Julio Luz being offered coffee and sweet biscuits by Paco Ortega, who was beaming down at him as he did.

One of the uniformed Guardia grinned

gleefully at his prisoner.

"That's the guy who is going to get you life in Toledo Penal," he crowed.

Inside the room, the Colombian lawyer turned toward the door and for one second made eye contact with the scowling gangster. He had no time to protest. The man outside was dragged away along the corridor. Two days later, being transferred from central Madrid to a holding jail in the suburbs, he managed to escape.

It appeared to be an awful breach of basic security, and Ortega apologized profusely to his superiors. The man's handcuffs had been badly locked, and in the van he had worked one hand free. The van did not drive into the courtyard of the jail but stopped at the curb. The two prisoners were being led across the pavement when one tore himself free and raced off down the street. Pursuit was lamentably slow, and he got away.

Two days later, Paco Ortega walked into the cell of Julio Luz and announced that he had failed to secure an extension of the arrest warrant against the lawyer. He was free to go. More, he would be escorted to the morning's departure of the Iberia flight for Bogotá and put on it.

Julio Luz lay awake all night in his cell and thought things over. He had no wife and children, and for this he was now grateful. His parents were dead. Nothing bound him to Bogotá, and he was terrified of Don Diego.

The grapevine inside the jail had been abuzz with news of the escape of the Galician thug and the inability of the authorities to find him. Certainly his fellow northwesterners in Madrid, of whom some were part of the underworld, would give him sanctuary and smuggle him home.

Julio Luz thought of the snatch of lies from the Guardia in the corridor. In the morning, he refused to leave. His defending counselor was bewildered. Luz continued to refuse.

"You have no choice, señor," said Chief Inspector Ortega. "It seems we have no case against you. Your lawyer here has been too clever for me. You have to go back to Bogotá."

"But if I confess?"

There was silence in the cell. The defending lawyer threw up his hands and left in a huff. He had done his best. He had succeeded. But even he could not defend a fool. Paco Ortega led Luz to an interview room.

"Now," he said, "let's talk. Let's really talk. About lots of things. That is, if you really want sanctuary here."

And Luz talked. On and on. He knew so much, not just about Banco Guzman but about others. Like Eberhardt Milch in Hamburg, he was just not cut out for this sort of thing.

João Mendoza's third strike was a former French Noratlas, quite unmistakable in the moonlight because of its twin-boomed tail and rear-opening cargo doors. It was not even heading for Guinea-Bissau.

The seas off Dakar, capital of Senegal to the north of Guinea, teem with big-game fish and attract sportsmen to the area. Waiting out at sea, fifty miles into the Atlantic off Dakar, was a big Hatteras game fisherman. It made a perfect cover because the sight of a fast white vessel sporting tall waving outriggers and a row of rods at the stern tends to disarm suspicion.

The *Blue Marlin* sat rocking gently on the nocturnal swell as if waiting for the fish to start biting at sunup. Thanks to the modern convenience of GPS, her position was where it was supposed to be, accurate to a square one hundred meters by one hundred. And her crew was waiting with the powerful Maglite to shine the agreed code upward when they heard the engines approaching.

But no engines came.

They had ceased to turn five hundred miles to the southwest and were lying with the remaining fragments of the Noratlas on the seabed. At dawn, the crew of the Hatteras, who had no interest in fishing, headed back to Dakar to report in coded e-mail that no rendezvous had taken place and there was no ton of cocaine in the hold beneath the engine bay.

As September moved into October, Don Diego Esteban convened an emergency council. It was not so much for analysis as postmortem.

Of the governing board, two were not present. The news of the arrest in Madrid of Julio Luz had been absorbed, though nothing was known of the fact that he had turned traitor.

Roberto Cárdenas could not be contacted. The Don intended to lose patience with the habit of the Cartagenan to disappear into the jungle and not stay in touch by cell phone. But the main point of the meeting was the figures, and the man effectively in the dock was Alfredo Suárez.

The news was bad and getting worse. Placed orders required that a minimum of three hundred tons of pure cocaine had to reach both the U.S. and Europe every year. By this time of the year, two hundred should have got through safely. That figure was under one hundred.

The disasters were happening on three fronts. In ports across the U.S. and Europe, sea containers were being stopped and subjected to spot checks on an increased basis, and far too often the choice for the spot check was accurate. It had long been blazingly obvious to the Don that he was under attack. The black cloud of suspicion fell on the dispatcher, Suárez. He alone knew exactly which sea containers were carrying a secondary cargo of cocaine.

His defense was that of over a hundred ports in two continents that received sea containers, only four had sustained successful interceptions by customs. What Suárez could not know was that there were seven more in the pipeline, as the Cobra dribbled out the names of the corrupt public servants.

The second front concerned merchantmen at sea. There had been a ferocious spike in the number of large freighters stopped and boarded in mid-ocean. These were all large ships. In some cases, the cocaine was secreted onboard in the harbor of departure and retained by the ship until it docked in the port of arrival.

But Suárez had substantially increased the practice of permitting the freighter to leave harbor "clean" and take on board several tons of cocaine from a fishing boat or go-fast at sea. This cargo would be off-loaded in the same manner before the long-distance ship arrived, while it was still up to a hundred miles from its destination. It could then arrive clean, like the *Virgen de Valme* in Seattle.

The disadvantage was that this way the entire crew could not be prevented from witnessing the transfers at both ends. Sometimes the freighters were genuinely empty of cocaine, and the boarding party had to leave with apologies and nothing else. But the proportion of discoveries in hiding places that should never have been detected was far too high.

In the western sector, three navies, those of Canada, the U.S. and Mexico were at it, along with customs and Coast Guard patrols ranging far out to sea. In the east, four European navies were increasingly active.

According to official Western propaganda, the discoveries were due to the arrival of a new piece of technology, developed from the device that could detect buried bodies under concrete and used by homicide divisions worldwide. The development, so ran the official explanations, could penetrate steel like an X-ray through soft tissue and show up packages and bales in cavities created by the late Juan Cortez.

But an impounded ship is a nonearning ship, and even the tiny proportion of merchant shipping world that had been prepared to run the risk carrying contraband was now turning against the cartel despite the cash rewards.

But it was the third front that worried the Don. Even failures had reason; even disasters had explanations. It was the litany of complete disappearances that ate at his core.

He did not know about the two Global Hawks that were operating BAMS — Broad Aspect Maritime Surveillance — over the Caribbean and Atlantic. He did not know about the deck-plan identification that Michelle and Sam could pass in seconds to AFB Creech in Nevada or the master list created by Juan Cortez and now lodged in a warehouse in Washington, D.C. He did not know about the ability of the Hawks to wipe out all radio and e-mail and cell phone communication emanating from a sea area of a circular mile. And he did not know about two Q-ships masquerading as grain merchants in the Caribbean and the Atlantic.

And, most of all, he did not know that the rules had changed and that his vessels and crews were being wiped out, sunk, imprisoned and confiscated without publicity or due process. All he knew was that vessel after vessel and plane after plane were just disappearing. He did not know that he and his cartel were now being treated like foreign-based terrorists under the law.

And it was having an effect. Not only was it harder to find big merchantmen prepared to take the risk, the drivers of the go-fasts were highly skilled mariners, not just dockside muscle, and they were becoming unavailable. Freelance pilots had taken to discovering their aircraft were out-of-order and not fit to fly.

Don Diego was a man of both logic and developed paranoia. The two kept him alive and rich. He was by now totally convinced he had a traitor, and the man was in the midst of his cartel, the Brotherhood, his Hermandad. What he would do to the wretch when he found him was something his thoughts toyed with during the night.

There was a discreet cough to his left. It was José-María Largo, the director of merchandising.

"Don Diego, I much regret to say it but I must. Our clients across two continents are becoming restive, especially the Mexicans, and in Italy, the Ndrangheta, who dominate so much of Europe. You were the one who clinched the two concordats; with La Familia in Mexico and the Calabrians, who have the lion's share of our product in Europe.

"Now they complain of a shortage of product, of orders unmet, of prices rising due to deficits of delivery."

Don Diego had to restrain himself from hitting the man. Instead he nodded somberly.

"José-María, dear colleague, I think you should make a tour. Take in our ten biggest clients. Tell them there was a localized and temporary problem which is being coped with."

And he turned smoothly toward Suárez.

"And coped with, it must surely be, would you not agree, Alfredo?"

The threat was in the air, and it applied to them all. Production would be increased to cope with shortfall. Fishing vessels and small freighters that had never been used before would have to be acquired or recruited for the Atlantic crossing. New pilots would have to be paid with irresistible fees to risk flying to Africa and Mexico.

Privately, he promised himself, the hunt

for the traitor would be stepped up until the renegade was found. Then he would be dealt with, and his passing would not be pleasant.

In mid-October, Michelle spotted a speck coming out of the jungles of Colombia and heading north over the sea. Enlargement revealed a twin-engined Cessna 441. It attracted attention because it came out of a tiny airstrip in the middle of nowhere that would normally not dispatch passenger planes to international destinations; it was not an executive jet full of business executives; and, on a course of 325°, it was heading for Mexico.

Michelle turned in pursuit and tracked the oddity past the coasts of Nicaragua and Honduras, where, had it not had extra fuel tanks, it should have been forced to land and refuel. It did not; it went on past Belize and over the Yucatán. That was when AFB Creech offered the intercept to the Mexican Air Force, which was delighted. Whoever the fool was, he was flying in daylight, unaware that he was being watched or that his watcher had realized he should have been out of fuel.

The Cessna was intercepted by two Mexican jets, who tried to contact it by radio. It failed to respond. They waved to the pilot to divert and land at Mérida. Up ahead was a large cloud formation. The Cessna suddenly made a diving break for the cloud and tried to escape. He must have been one of the Don's newcomers, not very experienced. The fighter pilots had radar but a limited sense of humor.

The Cessna went down in flames and hit the sea just off Campeche. It had been trying to make a delivery to a strip on a cattle ranch outside Nuevo Laredo on the Texan border. No one survived. Enough bales to weigh in at 500 kgs were hauled out of the shallows by local fishing boats. Some was handed over to the authorities, but not much.

By mid-October, both Q-ships needed replenishing. The *Chesapeake* met her fleet auxiliary for open-ocean razzing south of Jamaica. She took on board a full load of fuel and food, and a replacement platoon of SEALs, this time Team 3 from Coronado, California. Also leaving her were all her prisoners.

The prisoners, hooded outside their unwindowed prison, were aware from the voices that they were in the hands of the Americans, but not where they were or what vessel they were on. They would eventually be taken ashore, hooded and in a black-windowed bus, transported to Eglin Air Force Base to be led aboard a C-5 freight plane for the long flight to the Chagos Islands, where at last they would see daylight and could sit out the war.

The *Balmoral* also refueled at sea. Her SBS men remained aboard because the unit was stretched with two entire squadrons deployed in Afghanistan. Her prisoners were taken to Gibraltar, where the same American C-5 did a stopover to pick them up. The British capture of eighteen tons of cocaine was also handed to the Americans at Gibraltar.

But the captures of cocaine, twenty-three tons by the *Chesapeake* and eighteen tons by the *Balmoral,* were transferred to another vessel. This was a small freighter operated by the Cobra.

The cocaine captured in different ports in the U.S. and Europe was destroyed by the various national police authorities. Consignments seized at sea were taken in hand by the navies or coast guards responsible and destroyed by them back onshore. The cargoes shot down over the sea were lost forever. But the captures by Cobra, Paul Devereaux ordered to be stored under guard on a tiny leased islet in the Bahamas.

The low mountains of bales were in rows under camouflage netting between the palms, and a small detail of U.S. Marines lived in a series of motor homes parked in the shade just off the beach by the jetty. The only visitor they received was a small freighter bringing fresh deliveries. After the first captures, it was the little freighter that made rendezvous with the Q-ships to relieve them of their bales of drugs.

At the end of October, the message from Hoogstraten reached the Don. He did not believe that the banks had revealed their innermost secrets to the authorities. One, maybe, never two. So there was only one man who knew the numbers of the bank accounts into which the bribes were paid that assured safe clearance of cocaine cargoes in ports across the U.S. and Europe. The Don had his traitor.

Roberto Cárdenas was watching the clip of his daughter crossing the sidewalk at Kennedy Airport when the door came down. As ever, his mini-Uzi was within arm's reach, and he knew how to use it.

He took out six of the Enforcer's crew before they got him down, and he put a bullet through the hand of El Animal. But numbers will always tell eventually, and

Paco Valdez, knowing what he was up against, had brought a dozen.

In life, Roberto Cárdenas was a rough, hard, bad man. In death, he was just another corpse. In five pieces, when the chain saw had finished.

He had ever had only one daughter. And he had loved her very much.

CHAPTER 13

Throughout November, the Cobra's assault on Don Diego's cocaine empire continued remorselessly, and finally the fault lines began to show. The standing of the cartel with its numerous and ultra-violent customers across both continents became serious and deteriorating, if not yet fatal.

Don Diego had long realized that even if Roberto Cárdenas had betrayed him, the man who had controlled the Rat List could not have been his only enemy.

Cárdenas could not have known about the hiding places so skillfully constructed by Juan Cortez. He could not have known about ship identities, departure sailings and from which ports. He could not have known about night flights to West Africa and the aircraft used. But there was one man who did.

The Don's paranoia began to swerve toward the man who knew all that — Alfredo Suárez. Suárez knew perfectly well what had happened to Cárdenas and began to fear for his life.

But the first problem was production. With interceptions, destructions, losses at sea and disappearances running at fifty percent of tonnage dispatched, the Don ordered Emilio Sánchez to increase jungle production to levels never hitherto needed. And the increased costs began to bite into even the cartel's staggering wealth. Then the Cobra learned about Cárdenas.

It was the peasants who found the mutilated body. The head was missing, never to be found, but to Colonel Dos Santos the use of the chain saw said "cartel," and he asked the morgue at Cartagena for a DNA swab. It was the DNA that identified the old gangster.

Dos Santos told the DEA chief resident in Bogotá, and the American told Army Navy Drive in Arlington. The Cobra saw it on his patch-through of all communications reaching the Drug Enforcement Administration HQ.

By that point, in an attempt to save the life of the source, only twelve corrupt officials had been caught, and each by supposed coincidence. With Cárdenas dead, there was no need to protect him anymore.

Cal Dexter, accompanied by the DEA's top drug hunter, Bob Berrigan, toured Europe, eventually briefing delighted customs chiefs in twelve countries. The director of the DEA did the same for North America — Mexico, USA and Canada. In each case, the customs chiefs were urged to use the Hamburg ruse. Instead of going for an immediate snatch and arrest, they were asked to use the new information to grab both the corrupt official and an incoming cargo that he was trying to protect.

Some complied, some could not wait. But before the last of the Rat List went into custody, over forty tons of incoming cocaine had been discovered and confiscated. And it did not stop there.

Cárdenas had used banks in six secret havens for the payoffs, and these banks, under intolerable pressure, reluctantly began to disgorge the nest eggs. Half a billion U.S. dollars were eventually recovered, and most went to swell the coffers of the anti-drug campaigning agencies.

Even that was not the end of it. The great majority of the civil servants sitting in their remand cells were not tough nuts. Faced with guaranteed ruin and a possible life sentence, most sought to improve their situation by cooperating. Though mafiosi in each country put "hit" contracts on their heads, the threat was often counterproductive. It made the opposite threat of immediate release on the street even more frightening. With a top secret jail and round-the-clock guards the only way to stay alive, cooperating became the only option.

The arrested men — and they were all men — recalled the front companies that owned and ran the flatbed trucks on which the sea containers had been collected after clearance. Customs and police raided warehouse after warehouse as the gangs tried hastily to relocate their stocks. More tonnages were confiscated.

Most of these seizures did not hurt the cartel directly because ownership had already passed, but it meant the national gangs lost fortunes, were forced to re-place fresh orders and placate their own clamoring subagents and secondary purchasers. They were allowed to know the leak that was costing them fortunes had come from Colombia, and they were not pleased.

The Cobra had long presumed that there would be a breach of his security sooner or later, and he was right. It came in late August. A Colombian soldier based at Malambo was on leave when he bragged in a bar that while on base he was part of the guard detail of the U.S. compound. He detailed to an impressed girlfriend, and an even more appreciative eavesdropper farther down the bar, that the *Yanquis* flew a strange airplane out of their heavily guarded zone. High walls prevented anyone seeing it being fueled and serviced, but it was visible when it took off and flew away. Even though these landings and departures were by night, the soldier had seen it in the moon-light.

It looked like a model from a toy shop, he said; propeller-driven, with its power unit on the back. More strange still, it had no pilot, but rumors in the canteen insisted the creature had amazing cameras that could see for miles and penetrate night, cloud and fog.

Relayed to the cartel, the ramblings of the corporal could mean only one thing; the Americans were flying UAVs out of Malambo to spy on all seacraft leaving the Caribbean coast of Colombia.

A week later, there was an attack on Malambo base. For his assault troops, the Don did not employ his Enforcer, still nursing his bullet-shattered left hand. He used his private army of former guerrillas of the FARC terrorist group, still commanded by jungle veteran Rodrigo Pérez.

The attack was at night, and the assault group swept through the main gate and headed straight for the U.S. compound at the center of the base. Five Colombian soldiers died around the gate, but the shots alerted the U.S. Marine unit guarding the inner sanctum just in time.

In a suicidal wave, the attackers breached the high wall but were cut down trying to get to the hangar where the UAV was stored. The two FARC men who got inside just before they died were disappointed. Michelle was two hundred miles out to sea, turning lazily as she jammed two go-fasts while they were being intercepted by SEALs from the *Chesapeake.*

Apart from some pockmarks in the concrete, no damage was done to the hangar or the workshops. No U.S. Marines died, and just five Colombian soldiers. There were over seventy FARC bodies found in the morning. Out at sea, two more go-fasts vanished without a trace, their crews were lodged in the forward brig below the waterline and four tons of cocaine impounded.

But twenty-four hours later, the Cobra learned the cartel knew about Michelle. What Don Diego did not know was the existence of the second UAV flying out of an obscure Brazilian island.

With its guidance, Major Mendoza shot down four more cocaine traffickers in midair. This was despite the switch by the cartel from Rancho Boa Vista to another refueling hacienda even deeper in the bush. Four of the staff at Boa Vista had been lengthily tortured by El Animal and his crew when it was suspected they must be the source of the flight-plan leaks.

At the end of the month, a Brazilian financier, holidaying on Fernando de Noronha, spoke on the phone to his brother in Rio about a strange toy airplane the Americans were flying out of the far side of the airport. Two days later, there was an excited article in *O Globo,* the morning daily, and the second story was out in the open.

But the offshore island was beyond the reach even of the Don's FARC troopers; the Malambo base was strengthened, and the two UAVs went on flying. In neighboring Venezuela, hard-left president Hugo Chavez, who, despite his high moral tone, had allowed his country and its northern coast to become a major departure point for cocaine, fulminated his rage but could do little else.

Believing there might be some kind of a curse on Guinea-Bissau, pilots prepared to run the Atlantic gauntlet had insisted on flying to other destinations. The four shot down in December had been heading for Guinea-Conakry, Liberia and Sierra Leone, where they were supposed to drop their cargoes from midair, but low, over waiting fishing boats. It availed nothing because none arrived.

When the changing of the refueling stop from Boa Vista to a new ranch, and the switching of the destinations failed to work, the supply of volunteer pilots simply dried up no matter the money offered. The Atlantic run became known in crew rooms across Colombia and Venezuela as *"los vuelos de la muerte"* — the flights of death.

Detective work in Europe, with the help of Eberhardt Milch, had revealed the small stenciled code of the double circles and Maltese cross on certain steel sea containers. These had been traced back to the Suriname capital and port of Paramaribo and thence upcountry to the banana plantation from which they had all come. With American funding and help, that was raided and closed down.

A frantic Alfredo Suárez, desperately seeking to please Don Diego, realized that no freight ship had been intercepted in the Pacific, and, as Colombia has a coast on both oceans, he switched a large proportion of his dispatches away from the Caribbean side to the western rim.

Michelle spotted the change when a tramp steamer in her memory bank, one of those on the fast-diminishing Cortez list, was seen heading north past the western coast of Panama. It was too late to intercept it, but it was traced back to the Colombian Pacific port of Tumaco.

In mid-December, Don Diego Esteban agreed to receive an emissary from one of the cartel's biggest and therefore most reliable European clients. He rarely if ever received anyone personally from outside his small coterie of fellow Colombians, but his head of merchandising, José-María Largo, responsible for client relationships worldwide, had entreated him.

Immense precautions were taken to ensure that the two Europeans, important though they were, had no idea in which hacienda the reception took place. There was no language problem; the two men were Spanish and both from Galicia.

This storm-lashed northwestern province of Spain has long been the smuggling star performer of the old European kingdom. It has an ancient tradition of producing seafarers who can take on any ocean, no matter how wild. They say seawater flows in the blood along that wild coast from Ferrol to Vigo, indented by a thousand creeks and inlets, home to a hundred fishing villages.

Another tradition is a cavalier attitude to the unwanted attentions of customs and excise men. Smugglers have often been seen in a romantic light, but there is nothing lighthearted in the ruthlessness with which smugglers fight the authorities and punish squealers. With the rise of the drug culture in Europe, Galicia emerged as one of the main centers.

For years, two gangs have dominated the cocaine industry of Galicia — the Charlins and the Los Caneos. Formerly allies, they had a major falling-out and blood feud in the nineties but had recently resolved their differences and unified again into an alliance. It was a deputy from each wing that had flown to Colombia to protest to Don Diego. He had agreed to receive them because of the long and strong links between Latin America and Galicia, a heritage of many Galician sailors who settled in the New World long ago, and the size of the Galicians' habitual orders for cocaine.

The visitors were not happy. It had been two of their own whom Chief Inspector Paco Ortega had seized with two suitcases containing €10 million of laundered five-hundred-euro notes. This disaster, the Galicians maintained, had stemmed from a security failure by the lawyer Julio Luz, now looking at twenty years in a Spanish jail and reportedly singing like a canary in a plea-bargaining deal.

Don Diego listened in icy silence. More than anything else on earth, he hated to be humiliated, and now he had to sit and be lectured to, he fumed, by these two peons from Coruña. Worse, they were right. The fault was with Luz. If the fool had had family, they would have paid in pain for the absent betrayer. But the Galicians had more.

Their principal clients were the British gangs who imported cocaine into the UK. Forty percent of British cocaine came via Galicia, and these supplies came up from West Africa and entirely by sea. Those portions of the trade from West Africa that came overland to the coast between Morocco and Libya before crossing to Southern Europe went to other gangs. The Galicians depended on the marine traffic, and it had dried up.

The strongly implied question was: what are you going to do about it? He graciously bade his visitors to take wine in the sun while he went inside to confer.

How much, he inquired of José-María

Largo, are the Galicians worth to us? Too much, admitted Largo. Of the estimated three hundred tons that had to reach Europe every year, the Spanish, which was to say the Galicians, took twenty percent, or sixty tons. The only ones bigger were the Italian Ndrangheta, bigger even than the camorra of Naples and the Cosa Nostra of Sicily.

"We need them, Don Diego. Suárez needs to take special measures to keep them satisfied."

Before his amalgamation of the mini-cartels into the giant Brotherhood, the Galicians had mainly secured their supplies from the Norte del Valle cartel run by Montoya, now in an American jail. Norte del Valle had been the last of the independents to succumb to amalgamation, but they still produced their own supplies. If the powerful Galicians went back to their original provider, others might follow, provoking the steady breakup of his empire. Don Diego returned to the terrace.

"Señores," he told them. "You have the word of Don Diego Esteban. Your supplies will resume."

It was easier said than done. Suárez's switch of method from thousands of human mules swallowing up to a kilogram each, or carrying two or three kilos in a suitcase and hoping to get through airports intact, had seemed sensible at the time. The new invisible X-ray machines that penetrated clothing and body fat had certainly made stomach carrying a lost cause. Furthermore, the intensive security in baggage-handling halls, which he put down to the Islamic fundamentalists whom he cursed every day of his life, had sent suitcase interception through the roof. Big and few, had seemed a sensible new direction. But since July, there had been a welter of interceptions and disappearances, and each loss had been between one and twelve tons.

He had lost his money launderer, his controller of the Rat List had betrayed him and a hundred-plus officials who had been working covertly for him were under lock and key. At-sea interceptions of big freighters carrying cocaine were over fifty; eight pairs of go-fasts had disappeared without trace, plus fifteen smaller tramps, and the air bridge to West Africa was history.

He knew he had an enemy, and a very, very bad one. The revelation of the two UAVs constantly patrolling the skies and spotting surface craft and perhaps his airplanes would explain part of his losses.

But where were the U.S. and British warships that must be doing the interceptions?

Where were his captured ships? Where were the crews? Why were they not paraded before the cameras as usual? Why were the customs officials not gloating over bales of captured cocaine as they always did?

Whoever "they" were, they could not be keeping his crews secretly prisoner. That was against their human rights. They could not be sinking his ships. That was against the laws of the sea, the rules of CRIJICA. And they could not be shooting down his planes. Even his worst enemies, the American DEA and the British SOCA, had to abide by their own laws. And, finally, why had not one of the smugglers sent a single distress call from programmed senders?

The Don suspected there was one brain behind all this, and he was right. As he ushered his Galician guests to the SUV to take them to the airstrip, the Cobra was in his elegant house in Alexandria on the Potomac enjoying a Mozart concerto on his sound system.

In the first week of 2012, a harmless-looking grain ship, the MV *Chesapeake,* slipped south through the Panama Canal and into the Pacific. Had anyone asked, or, even more unlikely, had the authority to examine paperwork, she could have proved she was proceeding south to Chile with wheat from Canada.

In fact, she did turn south on emerging into the Pacific, but only to comply with the order that she hold position fifty miles off the Colombian coast and await a passenger.

That passenger flew south from the U.S. in a CIA-owned executive jet and landed at Malambo, the Colombian base on the Caribbean coast. There were no customs formalities, and even if there had been the American had a diplomatic passport preventing his luggage being examined.

That luggage was one heavy haversack, from which he politely declined to be parted even though hefty U.S. Marines offered to carry it for him. Not that he was on base long. A Black Hawk had been ordered to stand by for him.

Cal Dexter knew the pilot, who greeted him with a grin.

"In or out this time, sir?" he asked. He was the flier who had plucked Dexter off the balcony of the Santa Clara Hotel after the hazardous meeting with Cárdenas. He checked his route plan as the Black Hawk lifted off the pad, rose and turned southwest over the Gulf of Darien.

From 5,000 feet, the pilot and his front-seat passenger could see the rolling jungle

411

beneath, and, beyond it, the gleam of the Pacific. Dexter had seen his first jungle when, as a teenage grunt, he had been flown into the Iron Triangle in Vietnam. He soon lost all illusions about rain forests back then, and had never gained any.

From the air they always looked lush and spongy, comfortable, even welcoming; but in reality they were lethal to land in. The Gulf of Darien dropped behind them, and they crossed the isthmus just south of the Panamanian border.

Over the sea, the pilot made contact, checked his course and altered it by a few points. Then minutes later the speck of the waiting *Chesapeake* came over the horizon. Apart from several fisherman close inshore, the sea was empty, and the trawlermen below them would not see the transfer.

As the Black Hawk dropped, those on board could see several figures standing on the hatch covers to receive their guest. Behind Dexter, the loadmaster eased back the door, and the warm wind, lashed by the rotors above, washed into the cabin. Due to the single derrick jutting up from the *Chesapeake* and the wide sweep of those rotors, it was agreed Dexter would go down by harness.

First his haversack was lowered on a thin

steel cable. Down below, the haversack swung in the downdraft until strong hands caught and unhooked it. The cable came back up. The loadmaster nodded to Dexter, who rose and stepped to the door. The two double cleats were hooked to his harness, and he stepped out into space.

The pilot was holding the Black Hawk rock steady at 50 feet above the deck; the sea was a millpond; the reaching hands grabbed him and brought him down the last few feet. When his boots touched the deck, the cleats came off and the cable was whisked back up. He turned, gave the thumbs-up to the faces staring down and the Black Hawk turned for base.

There were four to greet him: the captain of the vessel, the U.S. Navy commander pretending to be a merchant seaman; one of the two comms men who kept the *Chesapeake* in contact at all times with Project Cobra; Lt. Cdr. Bull Chadwick, commanding the Team 3 SEALs; and a burly young SEAL to carry the haversack. It was the first time Dexter had let go of it.

When they were off the deck, the *Chesapeake* came under power, and they headed farther out to sea.

The waiting took twenty-four hours. The two comms men spelled each other in their radio shack until, the following afternoon, AFB Creech in Nevada saw something on the screen that Global Hawk Michelle was transmitting.

When the Cobra team in Washington had noticed the cartel switching their traffic from Caribbean to Pacific two weeks earlier, Michelle's patrol pattern had also changed. She was now at 60,000 feet, sipping gasoline, staring down at the coast from Tumaco in the deep south of Colombia up to Costa Rica, and as far as two hundred miles out into the ocean. And she had spotted something.

Creech passed the image to Anacostia, Washington, D.C., where Jeremy Bishop, who never seemed to sleep and lived on lethal fast food at his computer banks, ran it through the database. The vessel that would have been an invisible speck from 60,000 feet was magnified to fill his screen.

It was one of the last vessels on which Juan Cortez had worked his magic with the welding torch. It had last been seen, and photographed, at berth in a Venezuelan port months earlier, and its presence in the Pacific confirmed the switch of tactics.

The vessel was too small to be Lloyd's listed; a 6,000-ton rust-bucket tramp steamer more accustomed to working along

414

the Caribbean coast or making sorties to the many islands supplied only by such coasters. She had just come of out of Buenaventura, and her name was the *Maria Linda.* Michelle was ordered to keep tracking her northward, and the waiting *Chesapeake* moved into position.

The SEALs were now highly practiced at their routine, with several interceptions already behind them. The *Chesapeake* positioned herself twenty-five miles farther out to sea than the freighter, and just after dawn of the third day the Little Bird was hoisted to the deck.

Clear of the derrick, her rotors whirled, and she lifted off. Cdr. Chadwick's big RHIB and his two lighter CRRC raiders were already in the water, and as the Little Bird rose they raced toward the freighter over the horizon. Sitting in the rear of the RHIB, with the two-man rummage crew, the dog handler and his spaniel, was Cal Dexter, clutching his haversack. The sea was flat, and the deadly little flotilla piled on the power to skim the surface at forty knots.

Of course the helicopter got there first, swerving past the bridge of the *Maria Linda* to let her captain see "U.S. Navy" on the boom, then hovering forward of the bridge with a sniper rifle pointing straight at his face while the loudspeaker ordered him to heave to. He obeyed.

The captain knew his orders. He muttered a short command to his mate, out of sight down the companionway to the cabins, and the mate tried to send out the warning message to the listening cartel operator. Nothing worked. He tried the cell phone, a text on the same machine, the laptop and, in desperation, an old-fashioned radio call. Overhead, out of sight and sound, Michelle just turned and jammed. Then the captain saw the RIBs racing toward him.

Boarding was not a problem. The SEALs, clad in black, masked, H&K MP5s on each hip, just swarmed over each side, and the crew threw up their hands. The captain protested, of course; Cdr. Chadwick kept it formal and very courteous, of course.

The crew had time to see the rummage crew and the spaniel come aboard, then the black hoods went on and they were herded to the stern. The captain knew exactly what he was carrying and prayed the raiders would not find it. What awaited, he thought, would be years in a *Yanqui* jail. He was in international waters; the rules were on the side of the Americans; the nearest coast was Panama, which would cooperate with Washington and extradite them all north of that dreadful border. All servants of the cartel, from the highest to the lowest, have a horror of extradition to the U.S. It means a long sentence and no chance of a quick release in return for a bribe.

What the captain did not see was the older figure, a bit stiffer in the joints, being helped on board with his haversack. When the hoods went on, not only was sight blotted out but also sound; the hoods were internally padded to muffle external noise.

Thanks to the confession of Juan Cortez, which he had overseen, Dexter knew exactly what he was looking for and where it was. While the rest of the raiders pretended to scour the *Maria Linda* from top to bottom and stem to stern, Dexter went quietly to the captain's cabin.

The bunk was mounted to the wall with four strong brass screws. The heads were grimed with dirt, showing they had not been unscrewed in years. Dexter wiped away the muck and unscrewed them. The bunk assembly could then be moved away to expose the hull. The crew, about an hour away from handover point, would have done that themselves.

The steel of the hull looked untouched. Dexter felt down for the unlocking catch, found it and turned. There was a low click, and the steel panel loosened. But it was not the sea that rushed in. The hull was double at that point. As he gently lifted away the steel plate, he saw the bales.

He knew the cavity extended well to the left and right of the aperture, as well as upward and downward. The bales were all shaped like cinder blocks, no more than eight inches deep, for that was the depth of the space. Piled one on top of the other, they created a wall. Each block contained twenty briquettes, sealed in layers of industrial-strength polyethylene, and the blocks were in jute sacking, crisscrossed with knotted cord for easy handling. He calculated two tons of Colombian *puro,* over a hundred million dollars' worth when bashed, or cut, to six times the volume and inflated to street prices inside the USA.

Carefully, he began to unknot some of the blocks. As he expected, each polyethylene-wrapped block had a design and number on its wrapper, the batch code.

When he had finished, he replaced the blocks, enveloped them in jute and reknotted the jute exactly as it had been. The steel panel slid back and clicked into place the way Juan Cortez had designed it to.

His final task was to push the bunk assembly back where it had been and screw it in place. Even the smear of dust and grease that had covered the screwheads was thumbed back over the brass. When he was finally done, he mussed up the cabin, as if it had been searched in vain, and climbed back topside.

As the Colombian crew were hooded, the SEALs had taken their own masks off. Cdr. Chadwick looked at Dexter and raised an eyebrow. Dexter nodded and climbed back over the edge into the RHIB, pulling his mask back on. The SEALs did the same. The hoods and shackles were taken off the crew.

Cdr. Chadwick spoke no Spanish, but SEAL Fontana did. Through his officer, the SEAL leader apologized profusely to the *Maria Linda*'s captain.

"We have obviously been misinformed, *Capitán.* Please accept the apologies of the United States Navy. You are free to proceed. Good journey!"

When he heard the *"¡Buen viaje!,"* the Colombian smuggler could hardly believe his luck. He did not even pretend outrage at what had been done to him. After all, the *Yanquis* might start again and find something at the second attempt. He was still beaming hospitably when the sixteen masked men and their dog went back into their inflatables and roared away.

He waited until they were well over the horizon and the *Maria Linda* was chugging north again before he handed the helm to his mate and went below. The screws seemed intact, but, to be on the safe side, he undid them and pulled his bunk to one side.

The steel hull seemed untouched, but to make sure he opened the trap and checked the bales inside. They, too, had not been touched. He quietly thanked the craftsman, whoever he was, who had made a cache of such amazing ingenuity. It had probably saved his life, and certainly his freedom. Three nights later, the *Maria Linda* made landfall.

There are three giant cocaine cartels in Mexico and a few smaller ones. The giants are La Familia, the Gulf cartel operating mainly in the east on the Gulf of Mexico, and the Sinaloa, which works the Pacific Coast. The *Maria Linda*'s offshore rendez-vous with a smelly old shrimper was off Mazatlán in the heart of Sinaloa country.

The captain and his crew received their enormous (by their standards) fee and a bonus for their success, as one of the extra lures the Don had instituted to refresh the supply of volunteers. The captain saw no point in mentioning the interlude off the coast of Panama. Why make trouble over a lucky escape? His crew agreed with him.

A week later, something very similar happened in the Atlantic. The CIA jet flew quietly into the airport on Sal Island, the most northeasterly of the Cape Verdes. Its only passenger had diplomatic status, so he was waved through passport and customs formalities. His heavy haversack was not examined.

Leaving the airport concourse, he did not take the regular bus south to the island's only tourist resort at Santa María but took a cab, and asked where he might hire a car.

The driver did not seem to know, so they proceeded the two miles to Espargos and asked again. Finally, they ended up at the ferry port of Palmeira, and a local garage owner rented a small Renault. Dexter overpaid the man for his trouble and drove away.

Sal is called "Salt" for a reason. It is flat and featureless save for miles of salt pans, which had once been the source of its very passing prosperity. It now possesses two roads and a track. One road goes east-west from Pedra Luame via the airport to Palmeira. The other runs south to Santa

María. Dexter took the track.

It runs north over bleak, empty country to the lighthouse at Fiúra Point. Dexter abandoned the car, pinned a note to the windshield to inform any curious finder that he intended to return, hefted his haversack and walked to the beach beside the lighthouse. It was dusk, and the automatic light was starting to turn. He made a cell phone call.

It was almost dark when the Little Bird came at him across the inky sea. He flashed the recognition code, and the small craft settled gently on the sand beside him. The passenger door was just an open oval. He climbed in, tucked his haversack between his legs and buckled up. The figure in the helmet beside him offered him a duplicate with headphones.

He pulled it on, and the voice in his ears was very British.

"Good trip, sir?"

Why do they always assume you are a senior officer? thought Dexter. The insignia next to him said sublieutenant. He had once made sergeant. It must be the gray hair. He liked the young and eager anyway.

"No problems," he called back.

"Good show. Twenty minutes to base. The lads will have a nice cup of tea on the brew."

422

Good show, he thought. I could do with a nice cup of tea.

This time, he actually landed on the deck without need of ladders. The Little Bird, so much smaller than the Black Hawk, was lifted gently by the derrick and lowered into her hold, whose hatch then closed over her. The pilot went forward, through a steel door, to the Special Forces mess hall. Dexter was led the other way; into the stern-castle and up to meet the vessel's skipper and Major Pickering, the SBS team commander. At dinner that night, he also met his two fellow Americans, the comms team who kept the MV *Balmoral* in touch with Washington and Nevada, and thus the UAV Sam, somewhere above their heads in the darkness.

They had to wait three days south of the Cape Verdes until Sam spotted the target. She was another fishing boat, like the *Belleza del Mar,* and her name was *Bonita.* She did not announce it, but she was heading for an offshore rendezvous in the mangrove swamps of Guinea-Conakry, another failed state and brutal dictatorship. And, like the *Belleza,* she smelled, using the odor to mask any possible aroma of cocaine.

But she had made seven trips from South America to West Africa, and although twice

423

spotted by Tim Manhire and his MAOC-Narcotics team in Lisbon there had never been a NATO warship handy. This time there was, although she did not look the part, and even MAOC had not been told about the grain carrier *Balmoral*.

Juan Cortez had also worked on the *Bonita*, one of his first, and he had placed the hiding place at the far stern, abaft the engine room, itself reeking in the heat of engine oil and fish.

The procedure was almost exactly as it had been in the Pacific. When the commandos left the *Bonita*, a bewildered and extremely grateful captain received a full apology on behalf of Her Majesty personally for any trouble and delay. When the two arctic RIBs and the Little Bird had disappeared over the horizon, the captain unscrewed the planking behind his engine, eased away the false hull and checked the contents of the hidey-hole. They were absolutely intact. There was absolutely no trick. The gringos with all their probing and sniffing dogs had not found the secret cargo.

The *Bonita* made her rendezvous, passed on her cargo, and other fishing smacks took it up past the African coast, past the Pillars of Hercules, past Portugal, and delivered it to the Galicians. As promised by the Don.

424

Three tons of it. But slightly different.

The Little Bird took Cal Dexter to his bleak strand by the Fiúra Lighthouse, where he was pleased to see his battered Renault still untouched. He drove it back to the airport, left a message for the garage owner to come and retrieve it and a bonus and took a coffee in the restaurant. The CIA jet, alerted by the comms men on the *Balmoral*, picked him up an hour later.

At dinner that night aboard the *Balmoral*, the captain was curious.

"Are you sure," he asked Major Pickering, "that there was nothing at all on that fisherman?"

"That's what the American said. He was down in that engine room with the hatch closed for an hour. Came up covered in oil and stinking to high heaven. Said he had examined every possible hiding place, and she was clean. Must have been misinformed. Terribly sorry."

"Then why has he left us?"

"No idea."

"Do you believe him?"

"Not a chance," said the major.

"Then what is going on? I thought we were supposed to abduct the crew, sink the trash can and confiscate the coke. What was he up to?"

"No idea. We must rely again on Tennyson. 'Ours is not to reason why . . .' "

Six miles above them in the darkness, UAV Sam turned again and headed back to the Brazilian island to refuel. And a twin-engined executive jet borrowed from an increasingly irritable CIA sped back to the northwest. Its sole passenger, offered champagne, preferred a beer from the bottle. He at least knew why the Cobra insisted on keeping his confiscations from the incinerators. He wanted the wrappers.

CHAPTER 14

It fell to the British Serious and Organised Crime Agency and London's Metropolitan Police to carry out the raid. Both had been laying the groundwork for some time. The target was going to be a drug-smuggling gang called the "Essex Mob."

Scotland Yard's Special Projects Team had known for some time that the Essex Mob, headed by a notorious London-born gangster named Benny Daniels, was a major importer and distributor of cannabis, heroin and cocaine, with a reputation for extreme violence if crossed. The only reason for the gang's name was that Daniel had used crime's profits to build himself a large and very flash country mansion in Essex, east of London and north of the Thames Estuary, just outside the harmless market town of Epping.

As a younger hoodlum in the East End of London, Daniels had built both a reputation for brutality and a crime sheet. But with success came an end to successful prosecutions. He became too big to need to touch the product personally, and witnesses were hard to come by. The timid among them quickly changed their testimony; the brave disappeared, to be found very dead in the riverside marshes or never at all.

Benny Daniels was a "target" criminal and one of the Met's top ten desired arrests. The break the Yard had been waiting for resulted from the Rat List provided by the late Roberto Cárdenas.

The UK had been lucky inasmuch as only one of its officials had appeared; he was a customs officer in the east coast port of Lowestoft. That meant that top men in customs and excise were brought in at a very early stage.

Quietly, and in extreme secrecy, a multi-unit task force was assembled, equipped with state-of-the-art phone-tapping, tracking and eavesdropping technology.

The Security Service, or MI5, one of the partners of SOCA, loaned a team of trackers known simply as the "Watchers," reckoned among the best in the country.

As wholesale importing of drugs now rated as significant as terrorism, Scotland Yard's CO19 Firearms Command was also available. The task force was headed by the Yard's Cdr. Peter Reynolds, but the ones closest to the bribe taker were his own colleagues in customs. The few who were aware of his crimes now bore him a sincere but covert loathing, and it was they who were best placed to watch his every move. His name was Crowther.

One of the senior men at Lowestoft conveniently developed a serious ulcer and left on sick leave. He could then be replaced by an expert in electronic surveillance. Cdr. Spindler did not want only one bent official and one truck; he wanted to use Crowther to roll up an entire narcotics operation. For this, he was prepared to be patient, even if it meant allowing several cargoes to pass untouched.

With the port of Lowestoft being on the Suffolk coast, just north of Essex, he suspected Benny Daniels would have a finger somewhere in the pie, and he was right. Part of Lowestoft's facilities involved roll-on, roll-off juggernauts coming across the North Sea, and it was several of these that Crowther was apparently keen to assist unexamined through the customs channel. In early January, Crowther made a mistake.

A truck arrived on a ferry from Flushing, the Netherlands, with a cargo of Dutch cheese for a noted supermarket chain. A junior officer was about to request an examination of the cargo when Crowther hurried up, pulled rank and gave speedy clearance.

The junior was not in on the secret, but the replacement was watching. He managed to slip a tiny GPS tracker under the rear bumper of the Dutch truck as it rolled out of the dock gates. Then he made an urgent phone call. Three unmarked cars began to follow, switching places with one another so as not to be noticed, but the driver appeared unworried.

The lorry was tailed halfway across Suffolk until it pulled into a lay-by. There it was met by a group of men, who disgorged from a black Mercedes. A passing tracker car swept by, did not stop but took the number. Within seconds, the Benz was identified. It belonged to a shell company but had been seen weeks earlier entering the grounds of Benny Daniels's mansion.

The Dutch driver was taken in a perfectly friendly manner to the café behind the lay-by. Two of the gang stayed with him for the two hours his truck was missing. When it was returned to him, he was handed a fat wad of cash and allowed to proceed to the Midlands unloading bay of the supermarket.

The whole procedure was a replica of that used to smuggle illegal immigrants into the UK, and the task force feared they might just end up with a clutch of bewildered and dejected Iraqis.

While the Dutchman sipped his coffee in the roadside café, the other two men from the Mercedes had driven his lorry away to unload its real treasure; not Iraqis looking for a new life but a ton of high-grade Colombian cocaine.

The truck was tailed off the Suffolk lay-by and south into Essex. This time the driver and his companion were wary all the way, and it took the tailing cars all their skill to switch and pass each other to remain unsuspicious. As it crossed the county line, Essex police provided two more unmarked surveillance vehicles to help out.

Finally, the destination was reached, an old and seemingly abandoned aircraft hangar in the salt marches flanking the estuary of the Blackwater. The landscape was so flat and bleak that the watchers dared not follow, but a helicopter from the Essex traffic division spotted the doors of the hangar rolling closed. The truck remained in the hangar for forty minutes before it emerged and drove back to the waiting Dutch driver in the café.

By the time it left, the lorry had ceased to be of much interest, but there was a team of four rural surveillance experts hidden deep in the reedbeds with powerful binoculars. Then a call was made from the warehouse; it was recorded by SOCA and Government Communications HQ at Cheltenham. It was answered by someone inside Benny Daniels's mansion twenty miles away. It referred to the removal of "goods" the following morning, and Cdr. Reynolds had little choice but to mount the raid for that night.

In agreement with previous requests from Washington, it was decided that the raid should have a serious public relations angle, and a TV team from the program *Crimewatch* should be allowed to attend.

Don Diego Esteban also had a public relations problem, and a bad one. But his public was confined to his twenty major clients: ten in the U.S. and ten in Europe. He ordered José-María Largo to tour North America, reassuring the ten biggest buyers of the cartel's product that the problems that had dogged all their operations since the spring would be overcome and delivery resumed. But the clients were genuinely angry.

Being the big ten, they were among the privileged of whom only a fifty percent down payment was demanded. But that still ran into tens of millions of dollars per gang. They would be required to produce only the fifty percent balance on safe arrival of the consignment.

Every interception, loss or disappearance in transit between Colombia and the handover point was a loss to the cartel. But that was not the point. Thanks to the disaster of the Rat List, U.S. customs and state or city police had made scores of successful raids on inland depots, and the losses were hurting badly.

And there was more. Each giant importing gang had a huge grid of smaller clients whose needs had to be satisfied. There is no loyalty in this business. If a habitual supplier cannot supply and a different one can, the smaller dealer will simply switch his custom.

Finally, with safe arrivals running at fifty percent of expectations, a national shortage was developing. Prices were rising in accordance with market forces. Importers were cutting the *puro* not six or seven to one but up to ten to one, trying to spin out supplies and keep customers. Some users were snorting only a seven percent mix. The bulking-up materials were becoming more and more just junk, with the chemists throwing in insane quantities of substitute drugs like ketamine to try to fool the user that he was getting a high-quality sensation instead of a large dose of horse tranquilizer, which just happened to look and smell the same.

There was another dangerous spin-off from the shortage. The paranoia that is never really absent from professional criminality was moving to the surface. Suspicions arose between the big gangs that others might be getting preferential treatment. The very possibility that the secret depot of one mob might be raided by a rival crew threw up the chance of an extremely violent underworld war.

It was Largo's task to try to calm the shark pool with assurances of a speedy resumption of normal service. He had to start with Mexico.

Although the USA is assailed by light aircraft, speedboats, private yachts, airline passengers and mules with a full stomach, all smuggling cocaine, the gigantic headache is the three-thousand-mile meandering border with Mexico. It runs from the Pacific south of San Diego to the Gulf of Mexico. It borders California, Arizona, New Mexico and Texas.

South of the border, northern Mexico has been virtually a war zone for years as rival gangs fight for supremacy or even a place in the scramble. Thousands of tortured and executed bodies have been thrown into the streets or tossed in the deserts as the cartel leaders and gang bosses have employed virtually insane enforcers to exterminate rivals, and thousands of innocent passersby have died in the cross fire.

Largo's task was to talk to the chiefs of the cartels known as Sinaloa, Gulf and La Familia, all in a state of rage at their nonarriving orders. He would start with the Sinaloa, covering most of the Pacific Coast. It was just his misfortune that, although the *Maria Linda* had got through, the day he flew north the successor to that freighter had simply disappeared without trace.

The task of Europe was given to Largo's deputy, the clever, college-educated Jorge Calzado, who spoke fluent English, apart from his native Spanish, and had a working knowledge of Italian. He arrived in Madrid the night the SOCA raided the old hangar in the Essex marshes.

It was a good raid, and it would have been even better if the whole Essex mob had been

435

there to be arrested, or even Benny Daniels himself. But the gangster was too clever to be within miles of the drugs he imported into southern England. He used underlings for that.

The intercepted phone call had mentioned a pickup and transfer of the contents of the hangar "in the morning." The raiding party moved silently into position, lights out, black on black, just before midnight and waited. There was a complete ban on speech, flashlights, even coffee flasks in case of a tinkle of metal on metal. Just before four a.m., the lights of a vehicle came down the track to the darkened building.

The watchers heard the rumble of the doors rolling open and saw a dim light inside. As there was no second vehicle coming, they moved. The CO19 Firearms officers were first to secure the warehouse. Behind them came amplifiers booming commands, dogs straining, snipers squinting in case of armed defense, searchlights bathing the target in a harsh white blaze.

The surprise was total, considering that there had been fifty men and women crouching in the reeds with their equipment. The catch was satisfying in terms of drugs, rather less so in criminals.

There were three of the latter. Two had

come with the truck. They were, at a glance, low-level errand runners, and they belonged to a Midlands gang for whom part of the cargo was destined. The other part would have been distributed by Benny Daniels.

The night watchman was the only Essex Mob member caught in the net. He turned out to be Justin Coker, late twenties, a bit of a babe magnet, with dark good looks, and a long criminal record. But he was not a main player.

What the truck had come to collect was piled on the open concrete floor where the light aircraft of the long-departed flying club had been serviced. There was about a ton, and it was still in its jute wrapping, held together with crisscrossed cords.

The cameras were allowed to enter, one for TV and one press photographer for a major agency. They photographed the square pile of bales and watched as a senior customs man, masked to preserve his anonymity, sliced through some cords to rip the jute away and expose the polyethylene-encased blocks of cocaine inside. There was even a paper label on one of the blocks with a number on it. Everything was photographed, including the three arrested men with blankets over their heads, only handcuffed wrists visible. But more than enough to make prime-time TV and several front pages. A pink midwinter dawn eventually began to steal across the Essex marshes. For the senior police and customs officers, it was going to be a long day.

Another plane went down somewhere east of the 35th longitude. On instructions, the desperate young pilot, who had defied the advice of older men not to fly, had been uttering short and meaningless blips on his radio to indicate "sign of life." He did this every fifteen minutes after leaving the Brazilian coast. Then he stopped. He was heading for an upcountry airstrip in unpoliced Liberia, and he never arrived.

With an approximate indication of where he must have gone down, the cartel sent a spotter aircraft in broad daylight to fly the same route, but low over the water, to look for traces. It found nothing.

When an aircraft hits the sea in one piece, or even several, various bits float until finally, waterlogged, they drift down. They may be seat cushions, items of clothing, paperback books, curtains, anything lighter than water, but when an airplane becomes one huge fireball of exploding fuel at 10,000 feet all that is flammable is consumed. Only the metal falls to the sea, and metal sinks.

The spotter gave up and turned back. That was the last attempt to fly the Atlantic.

José-María Largo flew out of Mexico to the U.S. via private charter airplane; just a short hop from Monterrey to Corpus Christi, Texas. His passport was Spanish and quite genuine, obtained for him through the good offices of the now-defunct Banco Guzman. It should have served him well, but the bank had let him down.

That passport had once belonged to a genuine Spaniard with a reasonable resemblance to Largo. A mere facial comparison might have fooled the immigration officer at the Texas airport. But the former passport holder had once visited the U.S. and had thoughtlessly stared into the lens of the iris-recognition camera. Largo did the same. The iris of the human eye is like a DNA sample. It does not lie.

The face of the immigration officer did not move a muscle. He stared at the screen, noted what it told him and asked the visiting businessman if he would step into a side room. The procedures took half an hour. Then Largo was profusely apologized to and allowed to go. His inner terror turned to relief. He was through, undetected after all. He was wrong.

Such is the speed of IT communication that his details had gone through to the ICE, the FBI, the CIA and, bearing in mind where he was coming from, the DEA. He had been covertly photographed and flashed onto a screen at Army Navy Drive, Arlington, Virginia.

The ever-helpful Colonel Dos Santos of Bogotá had provided facial pictures of all the high members of the cartel of which he could be certain, and José-María Largo was one of them. Even though the man in the archive at Arlington was younger and slimmer than the visitor kicking his heels in southern Texas, feature-recognition technology identified him in half a second.

Southern Texas, by far the biggest campaign zone for the USA's anti-cocaine struggle, teems with DEA men. As Largo left the concourse, picked up his rental car and rolled out of the parking lot an unmarked coupe with two DEA men in it slid in behind him. He would never spot them, but trailing escorts would follow him to all his client meetings.

He had been instructed to contact and reassure the three biggest all-white biker gangs importing cocaine into the U.S.: the Hell's Angels, the Outlaws and the Bandidos. He knew that while all three could be psychopathically violent and loathed one another, none would be stupid enough to harm an emissary of the Colombian cartel if they ever wanted to see another gram of the Don's cocaine.

He also had to contact the two main all-black gangs; the Bloods and the Crips. The other five on his list were fellow Hispanics: the Latin Kings, the Cubans, his fellow Colombians, the Puerto Ricans and, by far the most dangerous of all, the Salvadoreans, known simply as MS-13 and headquartered mainly in California.

He spent two weeks talking, arguing, re-assuring and sweating profusely before he was finally allowed to escape back from San Diego to the sanctuary of his native Colombia. There were some extremely violent men there also, but at least, he comforted himself, they were on his side. The message he had received from the cartel's clients in the U.S. was clear: profits were plunging and the Colombians were responsible.

His private judgment, which he relayed to Don Diego, was that unless the wolves were satisfied with successfully arriving consignments, there would be an intergang war to make northern Mexico look like a barn dance. He was glad he was not Alfredo Suárez.

The Don's conclusion was slightly different. He might have to dispense with Suárez, but that was not the solution. The point was that someone was stealing vast quantities of his product, an unforgivable sin. He had to find the thieves and destroy them or be himself destroyed.

The charging of Justin Coker at Chelmsford Magistrates Court did not take long. The charge was being in possession with intent to supply a Class A drug, contrary to etc., etc.

The legal adviser to the magistrates read out the charge and asked for remand in custody on the grounds, as Your Worships will well understand, that police investigations were continuing etc., etc. Everyone knew it was all a formality, but the Legal Aid lawyer rose to ask for bail.

A nonprofessional justice of the peace, the magistrate flicked through the terms of the Bail Act of 1976 as she listened. Before agreeing to become a magistrate, she had been headmistress of a large girls' school for years and had heard just about every excuse known to the human race.

Coker, like his employer, had come from the East End of London, starting in petty crime as a teenager and graduating to "a likely lad" until he had caught the attention of Benny Daniels. The gang leader had taken him on as a general dogsbody. He had no talent as muscle — Daniels had several truck-built thugs in his entourage for that sort of thing — but he was streetwise and a good runner of errands. That was why he had been left overnight in charge of a ton of cocaine.

The defense lawyer — the "dock brief" — finished his hopeless application for bail, and the magistrate offered a quick smile of encouragement.

"Remand in custody for seven days," she said. Coker was removed from the dock and down the steps to the cells beneath. From there he was led to a closed white van, accompanied by four outriders from the Special Escort Group just in case the Essex Mob had any clever ideas of getting him out of there.

It seemed that Daniels and his crew were satisfied that Justin Coker would keep his mouth shut for they were nowhere to be found. They had all gone on the run.

In earlier years it was the custom of British mobsters to take refuge in southern Spain, buying villas on the Costa del Sol. With a rapid-extradition treaty between Spain and the UK, the Costa was no longer a safe haven. Benny Daniels had built himself a chalet in the enclave of northern Cyprus, an unrecognized mini-state that had no treaty with the UK. It was suspected he had fled there after the raid on the hangar to let things cool down.

Nevertheless, Scotland Yard wanted Coker under their eye in London; Essex had no objection, and from Chelmsford he was driven to Belmarsh Prison in London.

The story of a ton of cocaine in a marshland warehouse was a good one for the national press and even bigger one for the local media. The *Essex Chronicle* had a large front-page picture of the haul. Standing beside the pile of cocaine briquettes was Justin Coker, face blurred to protect his anonymity according to the law. But the stripped-down jute packaging was clearly visible, as were the pale bricks beneath it and the wrapping paper with the batch number.

Jorge Calzado's tour of Europe was no more agreeable than José-María Largo's experience in North America. On every side he was met with angry reproaches and demands for a restoration of their regular supply. Stocks were low, prices were rising, customers were switching to other narcotics, and what the European gangs did have left were being cut ten to one, almost as weak as it could get.

Calzado had no need to visit the Galician gangs who had already been reassured by the Don himself, but the other main clients and importers were vital.

Though over a hundred gangs supply and trade cocaine between Ireland and the Russian border, most acquire their stocks from the dozen giants who deal directly with Colombia and sub-franchise once the product has safely arrived on European land.

Calzado made contact with the Russians, Serbians and Lithuanians from the east; the Nigerians and Jamaican "Yardies"; the Turks, who, although originally from the southeast, predominated in Germany; the Albanians, who terrified him; and the three oldest gang groups in Europe — the mafia of Sicily, the camorra of Naples and the biggest and most feared of them all, the Ndrangheta.

If the map of the Republic of Italy looks like a riding boot, Calabria is the toe, south of Naples, facing Sicily across the Strait of Messina. There were once Greek and Phoenician colonies in that harsh and sun-scorched land, and the local language, hardly intelligible to other Italians, derives from Greek. The name Ndrangheta simply means "the Honorable Society." Unlike the highly publicized mafia of Sicily or the more recently famous camorra of Naples, the Calabrese pride themselves on an almost invisible profile.

Yet it is the biggest in number of members and the most internationally far-flung of them all. As the Italian state has discovered, it is also the hardest to penetrate, and the only one in which the oath of utter silence, the *omertà,* is still unbroken.

Unlike Sicily's mafia, the Ndrangheta has no "Don of All Dons"; it is not pyramid shaped. It is not hierarchic, and membership is almost entirely based on family and blood. Infiltration by a stranger is absolutely impossible, a renegade from inside virtually unheard of and successful prosecutions rare. It is the abiding nightmare of Rome's Anti-Mafia Commission.

In its traditional homeland, inland of the provincial capital of Reggio de Calabria and the main coast highway, is a shuttered land of villages and small towns running into the Aspromonte Range. In its caves, hostages were until recently kept pending ransom or death, and here is the unofficial capital of Platí. Any stranger proceeding here, any car not recognized at once, is detected miles away and made very unwelcome. It is not a tourist magnet.

But it was not here that Calzado had to come to meet the chiefs, for the Honorable Society has taken over the entire underworld of Italy's biggest city, its industrial powerhouse and financial motor, Milan. The real Ndrangheta had migrated north and created in Milan the country's, and perhaps the continent's, cocaine hub.

No Ndrangheta chieftain would dream of bringing even the most important emissary to his home. That is what restaurants and bars are for. Three southern suburbs of Milan are dominated by the Calabrese, and it was at the Lion's Bar in Buccinasco that the meeting took place with the man from Colombia.

Facing Calzado to listen to his excuses and assurances were the *capo locale* and two officeholders, including the *contabile,* the accountant, whose profit figures were bleak.

It was because of the Honorable Society's special qualities, its secrecy and unforgiving ruthlessness in imposing order, that Don Diego Esteban had accorded it the honor of being his primary European colleague. Through this relationship, it had become the single biggest importer and distributor continentwide.

Apart from its own wholly run port of Gioia, it acquired a large part of its supplies from the land trains coming up from West Africa to the North African coast opposite Europe's southern shore and from the seafaring Galicians of Spain. Both supplies, it was made plain to Calzado, had been badly disrupted, and the Calabrese expected the Colombians to do something about that.

Jorge Calzado had met the only dons in Europe who dared speak to the head of the Hermandad of Colombia as an equal. He retired to his hotel — like his superior, Largo, looking forward to a return to his native Bogotá.

Colonel Dos Santos did not often take journalists, even senior editors, out for lunch. It ought to have been the other way around. Editors were the ones with the fat expense accounts. But the lunch bill usually arrives in the lap of the one who wants the favor. This time it was the head of the intelligence division, Policía Judicial. And even he was doing it for a friend.

Colonel Dos Santos had good working relationships with the senior men of both the American DEA and the British SOCA posted in his city. Cooperation, so much easier under President Álvaro Uribe, bought mutual dividends. Even though the Cobra had kept the handover of the Rat List to himself, since it did not concern Colombia, other gems discovered by the cameras of the ever-circling Michelle had proved extremely useful. But this favor was for the British SOCA.

"It's a good story," insisted the policeman, as if the editor of *El Espectador* could not recognize a story when he saw one. The editor sipped his wine and glanced down at the new item he was being offered. As a journalist, he had his doubts; as an editor, he could foresee a return favor coming his way if he was helpful.

The item concerned a police raid in England on an old warehouse where a newly arrived shipment of cocaine had been discovered. All right, it was a large one, a full ton; but discoveries were being made all the time and were becoming too ordinary to make real news. They were so much the same. The piled-up bales, the beaming customs officers, the glum prisoners paraded in handcuffs. Why was the story from Essex, of which he had never heard, so newsworthy? Colonel Dos Santos knew, but he dared not say.

"There is a certain senator in this city," murmured the politician, "who frequents a very discreet house of pleasure."

The editor had been hoping for something in exchange, but this was ridiculous.

"A senator likes girls?" he protested. "Tell me the sun rises in the east."

"Who mentioned girls?" asked Dos Santos. The editor sniffed the air appreciatively. At last he smelled payback.

"All right, your gringo story goes on page two tomorrow."

"Front page," said the policeman.

"Thanks for lunch. A rare pleasure not to pick up the tab."

Privately, the editor knew his friend was up to something but he could not fathom what. The picture and caption came from a big agency, but based in London. It showed a young hoodlum called Coker standing beside a pile of cocaine bales with one of them ripped open and the paper wrapper visible. So what? But he put it on the front page the next day.

Emilio Sánchez did not take *El Espectador,* and, anyway, he spent much of his time supervising production in the jungle, refinement in his various laboratories and packing ready for shipment. But two days after publication, he was passing a newsstand on his drive back from Venezuela. The cartel had established major laboratories just inside Venezuela where the poisonous relations between Colombia and the fiefdom of Hugo Chavez protected them from the attentions of Colonel Dos Santos and his police raids.

He had ordered his driver to stop at a small hotel in the border town of Cúcuta so that he could use the lavatory and take a coffee. In the lobby was a rack with the two-day-old copy of *El Espectador.* There was something about the picture that jolted him. He bought the only copy on the stand and worried all the way back to his anonymous house in his native Medellín.

Few men can retain everything in his head, but Emilio Sánchez lived his work and prided himself on this methodical approach and his obsession with keeping good records. Only he knew where he kept them, and for security reasons they took an extra day to visit and consult. He took with him a magnifying glass, and, having pored over the picture in the paper and his own dispatch records, he went white as a sheet.

Once again the Don's passion for security slowed the meeting down. It took three days shaking off surveillance before the two men could meet. When Sánchez had finished, Don Diego was extremely quiet. He took the magnifying glass and studied the records

Sánchez had brought him and the picture in the paper.

"There can be no doubt about this?" he asked with deadly calm.

"None, Don Diego. That dispatch note refers only to a consignment of product that went to the Galicians on a Venezuelan fishing boat called the *Belleza del Mar* months ago. It never arrived. It vanished in the Atlantic without trace. But it *did* arrive. That is its cargo. No mistake."

Don Diego Esteban was silent for a long time. If Emilio Sánchez tried to say something, he was waved to silence. The head of the Colombian cartel now knew at last that someone had been stealing his cocaine in transit and lying to him about its nonarrival. He needed to know many things before he could act decisively.

He needed to know how long it had been going on; who exactly among his clients had been intercepting his vessels and pretending they had never arrived. He had no doubt his ships had been sunk, his crews slaughtered and his cocaine stolen. He needed to know how wide the conspiracy had spread.

"What I want you to do," he told Sánchez, "is prepare me two lists. One contains the dispatch numbers of every bale that was on a vessel that went missing and was never seen again. Tramps, go-fasts, fishing boats, yachts, everything that never arrived. And another list of every vessel that got through safely and every bale, by batch number, that they were carrying."

After that it was almost as if the gods were at last smiling on him. He had two lucky breaks. On the Mexican-U.S. border, U.S. customs, working in Arizona near the town of Nogales, intercepted a truck that had penetrated the border in the dark of a moonless night. There was a large seizure, and it was lodged locally pending destruction. There was publicity. There was also slack security.

It cost Don Diego a huge bribe, but a renegade official secured the batch numbers on the cargo. Some had been on the *Maria Linda* that had arrived safely and discharged her bales into the possession of the Sinaloa cartel. Other bales had been in two go-fasts that had disappeared in the Caribbean months earlier. They, too, had been heading for the Sinaloa Canal. And now they had shown up in the Nogales intercept.

Another stroke of luck for the Don came out of Italy. This time it was a juggernaut-load of Italian men's suits of a very fashionable Milan-made brand seeking to cross the Alps into France, destination London.

It was just bad luck, but the truck took a puncture in the Alpine pass and caused a ferocious tailback. The carabinieri insisted the rig be lifted out of the way, but that meant lightening the vehicle by off-loading part of the cargo. A crate split and disgorged jute-wrapped cargo that was definitely not going to adorn the backs of trendy young bond traders in Lombard Street.

The contraband was immediately impounded, and as the source of the cargo had been Milan the carabinieri did not need the services of Albert Einstein to work out the name Ndrangheta. The local warehouse was visited in the night; nothing was taken, but batch numbers were noted and e-mailed to Bogotá. Some of the cargo had been on the *Bonita,* which had safely been delivered to the Galician coast. Other bales had been in the hull of the *Arco Soledad,* which had apparently gone down with all hands including Álvaro Fuentes on its way to Guinea-Bissau. Both cargoes had been due to go north to the Galicians and the Ndrangheta.

Don Diego Esteban had his thieves, and he prepared to make them pay.

Neither the U.S. customs at Nogales nor the carabinieri at the Alpine crossing had paid much attention to a soft-spoken American official whose papers said he was with the DEA and who had appeared with commendable lack of delay at both situations. He spoke fluent Spanish and halting Italian. He was slim, wiry, fit and gray-haired. He carried himself like an ex-soldier and took notes of all the batch numbers on the captured bales. What he did with them, no one asked. His DEA card said he was called Cal Dexter. A curious DEA man also attending at Nogales rang Arlington HQ, but no one had heard of any Dexter. It was not particularly suspicious. Undercover men are never called what their cards say.

The DEA man at Nogales took it no further, and in the Alps the carabinieri were happy to accept a generous token of friendship in the form of a box of hard-to-get Cuban Cohibas and let an ally and colleague enter the warehouse containing their impounded triumph.

In Washington, Paul Devereaux listened to his report attentively.

"Both ruses went down well?"

"It would appear so. The three so-called Mexicans at Nogales will have to spend a little time in an Arizona jail, then I think we can spring them. The Italian-American truck driver in the Alps will be acquitted because there will be nothing to link him to his cargo. I think I can have them back with their families, and a bonus, in a couple of weeks."

"Did you ever read about Julius Caesar?" asked the Cobra.

"Not a lot. My schooling was part in a trailer, part on a series of construction sites. Why?"

"He was once fighting the barbarian tribes in Germany. He surrounded his camp with large pits covered with light brushwood. The bases and sides of the pits were studded with sharpened stakes pointing up. When the *Germani* charged, many of them took a very sharp stake right between the cheeks."

"Painful and effective," observed Dexter, who had seen such traps prepared by the Vietcong in 'Nam.

"Indeed. Do you know what he called his stakes?"

"No idea."

"He called them *'stimuli.'* It seems he had a rather dark humor, did old Julius."

"So?"

"So let us hope our stimuli reach Don Diego Esteban, wherever he may be."

Don Diego was at his hacienda in the ranch country east of the Cordillera, and, despite its remoteness, the disinformation had indeed reached him.

A cell door in Belmarsh Prison opened, and Justin Coker looked up from his trashy novel. As he was in solitary, he and the visitor were not to be overheard.

"Time to go," said Cdr. Peter Reynolds. "Charges dropped. Don't ask. But you'll have to come in from the cold. You'll be blown when this gets out. And well done, Danny, well done indeed. That comes from me and from the very top."

So Detective Sergeant Danny Lomax, after six years undercover infiltration of a London drug gang, came out of the shadows and to a promotion to detective inspector.

■ ■ ■ ■ ■

PART FOUR
VENOM

■ ■ ■ ■ ■

CHAPTER 15

Don Diego Esteban believed in three things. His God, his right to extreme wealth and dire retribution for anyone who impugned the first two.

After the impounding at Nogales of bales of cocaine that were supposed to have disappeared from his go-fasts in the Caribbean, he was convinced he had been comprehensively cheated by one of his principal clients. The motive was easy — greed.

The identity could be deduced from the place and nature of the interception. Nogales is a minor town right on the border and the center of a small zone whose Mexican side is exclusively the territory of the Sinaloa cartel. Across the border, it is the home of the Arizonan street gang who call themselves the "Wonderboys."

Don Diego had become convinced, as the Cobra had intended, that the Sinaloa cartel had hijacked his cocaine at sea and were thus doubling their profits at his expense. His first reaction was to instruct Alfredo Suárez that all Sinaloa orders were now canceled and not a further gram should be sent to them. This caused a crisis in Mexico, as if that unhappy land did not have enough already.

The chiefs of the Sinaloa knew they had stolen nothing from the Don. In others, this might have provoked a sense of bewilderment, but cocaine gangs have only one mood other than satisfaction and that is rage.

Finally, the Cobra, through DEA contacts in northern Mexico, put it about among the Mexican police that it was the Gulf cartel and their allies La Familia who had betrayed the Nogales border crossing to the American authorities; the opposite of the truth — that the Cobra had invented the entire episode. Half the police worked for the gangs and passed on the lie.

It was, for Sinaloa, a declaration of war, and they duly declared it. The Gulf people and their friends in La Familia did not know why, since they had shopped nobody, but had no choice other than to fight back. And for executioners they brought in the Zetas, a mob that hired itself out for the business of the most gruesome murders.

By January, the Sinaloa hoodlums were being slaughtered by the score. The Mexican authorities, Army and police simply stood back and tried to pick up the hundreds of bodies.

"What exactly are you doing?" Cal Dexter asked the Cobra.

"I am demonstrating," said Paul Devereaux, "the power of deliberate disinformation, which some of us learned the hard way over forty years of the Cold War."

All intelligence agencies during those years realized that the most devastating weapon against an enemy agency, short of a real mole inside the fabric, was the enemy's belief that he had one. For years the obsession of the Cobra's predecessor, James Angleton, that the Soviets had a mole inside the CIA nearly tore that agency apart.

Across the Atlantic, the British spent years fruitlessly trying to identity the "Fifth Man" (after Burgess, Philby, Maclean and Blunt). Careers were broken when suspicion fell on the wrong man.

Devereaux, working his way up from new college boy to CIA mandarin over those years, had watched and learned. And what he had learned over the previous year, and the only reason he had thought the task of destroying the cocaine industry might be feasible where others had quickly given up, was that there were marked similarities between the cartels and gangs on one side and spy agencies on the other.

"They are both closed brotherhoods," he told Dexter. "They have complex and secret rituals of initiation. Their only diet is suspicion amounting to paranoia. They are loyal to the loyal but ferocious to the traitor. All outsiders are suspect by the simple fact of being outside.

"They may not confide even in their own wives and children, let alone social friends, so they tend to socialize only with one another. As a result, rumors move like wildfire. Good information is vital, accidental misinformation regrettable, but skillful disinformation deadly."

From his first day of study, the Cobra had realized that the situations of the USA and Europe were different in one vital regard. Europe's points of entry for the drug were numerous, but ninety percent of the American supply came via Mexico, a country that actually created not one gram of it.

As the three giants of Mexico and the various smaller cartels fell upon one another, competing for the diminished quantities and avenging scores constantly repeated by fresh onslaughts on one another, what had been a product shortage north of the border became a drought. Until that winter, it had been an abiding relief to the American authorities that the insanity south of the border stayed there. That January, the violence crossed the border.

To disinform the gangs of Mexico, all the Cobra had to do was feed the lie to the Mexican police. They would do the rest. North of the border, that was not so easy. But in the USA, there are two other vehicles for spreading disinformation. One is the network of thousands of radio stations; some are so shady they actually serve the underworld, others feature young and fiercely ambitious "shock jocks" desperate to become rich and famous. These have scant regard for accuracy but an insatiable appetite for sensational "exclusives."

The other vehicle is the Internet and its bizarre offspring, the blog. With the genius-level technology of Jeremy Bishop, the Cobra created a blog whose source could never be traced. The blogger portrayed himself as a veteran of the complex array of gangs that infest the USA. He purported to have contacts in most of them and sources even inside the forces of law and order.

Using the patched-through information lines from the DEA, CIA, FBI and another dozen agencies that the Presidential Order had given him, the blogger was able to reveal genuine tidbits of information that were enough to stun the main gangs of the continent. Some of these gems were about themselves, others about their rivals and enemies. In and among the true material went the lies that provoked the second civil war — among the prison gangs, the street gangs and the biker gangs who, among them, controlled cocaine from the Rio Grande to Canada.

By the end of the month, young shock jocks were perusing the gang blog on a daily basis, elevating the items found to gospel truth and broadcasting them state by state.

In a rare flicker of humor, Paul Devereaux called the blogger "Cobra." And he started with the biggest and most violent of the street gangs, the Salvadorean MS-13.

This giant gang had started as a residue of El Salvador's vicious civil war. Young terrorists, immune to pity or remorse, found themselves unemployed, and unemployable, and named their gang "La Mara" after a street in the capital San Salvador. As their crimes became too much for such a small country, they spread to neighboring Honduras, recruiting over thirty thousand members.

When Honduras passed draconian laws and imprisoned thousands, the leaders left for Mexico, and, finding even that country too crowded, moved to Los Angeles, adding the "13" of 13th Street to their name.

The Cobra had studied them intensively — their all-over tattooing; the pale blue-and-white clothing, after the colors of the Salvadorean flag; their taste for hacking up their victims with machetes; and their reputation. This was such that even in the patchwork quilt of American gangs, they had no friends or allies. Everyone feared and hated them, so the Cobra began with MS-13.

He went back to the Nogales confiscation, telling the Salvadoreans that the cargo had been intended for them until it was stopped by the authorities. Then he inserted two pieces of information that were true and one that was not.

The first was that the crew in the truck had been allowed to escape; the second was that the confiscated cocaine had vanished between Nogales and the capital, Flagstaff, where it was due for incineration. The lie was that it had been "liberated" by the Latin Kings, who had thus stolen it from MS-13.

With the MS-13 having branches, known as "cliques," in a hundred cities in twenty states, it was impossible that they did not hear this, even though it was only broadcast in Arizona. Within a week, MS-13 had declared war on the other giant Latino gang in the USA.

By the beginning of February the biker gangs had ended a long truce: the Hell's Angels had turned on the Bandidos and their allies, the Outlaws.

A week later, the bloodletting and chaos had enveloped Atlanta, the new cocaine hub of the U.S. Atlanta is Mexican controlled, with the Cubans and Puerto Ricans working alongside but under them.

A network of great interstate highways lead from the U.S.-Mexican border northeast to Atlanta and another grid runs south to Florida, where access from the sea had been virtually ended by the DEA operation out of Key West, and north to Baltimore, Washington, D.C., New York and Detroit.

Fed by disinformation, the Cubans turned on the Mexicans, whom they were convinced were cheating them out of the diminished consignments arriving from the border zone.

The Hell's Angels, taking terrible casualties from the Outlaws and Bandidos, called for help from their friends, the all-white Aryan Brotherhood, and triggered a rash of slayings in jails across the country where the Aryans hold sway. This brought in the Crips and Bloods.

Cal Dexter had seen bloodshed before, and he was not squeamish. But as the death toll rose, he again queried what the Cobra was doing. Because he respected his executive officer, Paul Devereaux, who habitually confided in no one, invited him to dinner in Alexandria.

"Calvin, there are about four hundred cities, large and small, in our country. And at least three hundred of them have a major narcotics problem. Part of this concerns marijuana, cannabis resin, heroin, methamphetamine, or crystal meth, and cocaine. I was asked to destroy the cocaine trade because it was the vice growing completely out of control. Most of that problem derives from the fact that, in our country alone, cocaine has a profit value of forty billion dollars a year, almost double that worldwide."

"I have read the figures," muttered Dexter.

"Excellent, but you asked for an explanation."

Paul Devereaux ate as he did most things, sparingly, and his favorite cuisine was Italian. The dinner was wafer-thin piccata al limone, oil-drizzled salad and a dish of olives, helped down by a cool Frascati. Dexter thought he might have to pause on the way home for something out of Kansas, broiled or fried.

"So these staggering funds attract the sharks of every stripe. We have around a thousand gangs purveying this drug and a total national gang membership of around seven hundred fifty thousand, half of them active in narcotics. So your original question: what am I doing and how?"

He refilled both glasses with the pale yellow wine and sipped as he chose his words.

"There is only one force in the country that can destroy the twin tyranny of the gangs and the drugs. Not you, not me, not the DEA or the FBI or any other of our numerous and staggeringly expensive agencies. Not even the President himself. And certainly not the local police, who are like that Dutch boy with his finger in the dike trying to hold back the tide."

"So the single force is?"

"Themselves. Each other. Calvin, what do you think we have been doing for the past year? First we created, at considerable expense, a cocaine drought. That was deliberate, but it could never be sustained. That fighter pilot in the Cape Verdes. Those

Q-ships out at sea. They cannot go on forever, or indeed much longer.

"The instant they let up, the trade flow will resume. Nothing can impede that level of profit for more than a heartbeat. All we were able to do was cut the supply in half, creating a raging hunger among the clients. And when ferals are starved, they turn on each other.

"Second, we established a supply of bait, which we are now using to provoke the ferals into turning their violence not against lawful citizens but against each other."

"But the bloodletting is disfiguring the country. We are becoming like northern Mexico. How long will the gang wars have to last?"

"Calvin, the violence was never absent. It was only hidden. We kidded ourselves it was all on TV or on the movie screen. Well, it is out in the open now. For a while. If they let me provoke the gangs into destroying each other, their power can be shattered for a generation."

"But in the short term?"

"Alas, many terrible things will have to happen. We have visited these things upon Iraq and Afghanistan. Do our rulers and our people have the fortitude to accept it here?"

Cal Dexter thought back to what he had seen inflicted on Vietnam forty years earlier.

"I doubt it," he said. "Abroad is such a convenient place for violence."

Across the USA, members of the Latin Kings were being slaughtered as the local clique of MS-13 fell upon them, convinced they were themselves being attacked and seeking to acquire both the stocks and clientele of the Kings for their own. The Kings, recovering from the initial shock, retaliated the only way they knew how.

The slaughter between the Bandidos and Outlaws on one side and the Hell's Angels with the racist Aryan Brotherhood on the other scattered corpses from coast to coast in the USA.

Bewildered passersby saw the word "ADIOS" daubed on walls and bridges. It stands for "Angels Die in Outlaw States." All four gangs have enormous chapters in the USA's hardest jails, and the killing spread to these as flame to kindling. In Europe, the revenge of the Don was just beginning.

The Colombians sent forty picked assassins across the Atlantic. Ostensibly, they were to pay a goodwill visit to the Galicians and asked to be supplied from Los Caneos stocks with a variety of automatic weapons. The request was complied with.

The Colombians arrived by air on different flights over three days, and a small advance party provided them with a fleet of camper vans and mobile homes. With these, the avengers motored northwest to Galicia, ravaged in the February custom with rain and gales.

It was not far off Valentine's Day, but the meeting between the Don's emissaries and their unsuspecting hosts took place in a warehouse in the pretty and historic town of Ferrol. The newcomers approvingly inspected the arsenal provided for them, smacked in the magazines, turned and opened fire.

When the last thunder of automatic fire ceased to echo off the warehouse walls, most of the Galician mob had been wiped out. A small, baby-faced man known in his own country as El Animal, the Colombian leader stood over a Galician still alive and looked down at him.

"It is nothing personal," he remarked quietly, "but you just cannot treat the Don that way." Then he blew the dying man's brains out.

There was no need to remain. The killer

party embarked in their vehicles and motored thorough the border into France at Hendaye. Both Spain and France are members of the Schengen Agreement that provides for open, no-control borders.

Spelling each other at the wheel, the Colombians motored east across the foothills of the Pyrenees, over the plains of the Languedoc, through the French Riviera and into Italy. The Spanish-registered vehicles were not stopped. It took thirty-six hours of hard driving to reach Milan.

Seeing the unmistakable batch numbers of the cocaine sent across the Atlantic on the *Belleza del Mar* turning up in the Essex marshes, Don Diego had quickly learned that the whole consignment had reached Essex not via the Netherlands but from the Ndrangheta, who were supplying the Essex mob. Thus the Calabrians, to whom he had given the overlordship franchise for Europe, had also turned on him. Retribution could simply not be avoided.

The party sent to visit that retribution upon the guilty had spent hours en route studying the geography of Milan and the briefing notes sent by the small resident liaison team from Bogotá that lived there.

They knew exactly how to find the three southern suburbs of Buccinasco, Corsico and Assago that the Calabrese had colonized. These suburbs are to the southerners from the deep south of Italy as New York's Brighton Beach is to the Russians: home away from home. Even the language is different.

And the immigrants have brought Calabria with them. Shop signs, bars, restaurants, cafés — almost all bear names and serve meals from the south. The state's Anti-Mafia Commission estimates that eighty percent of Colombian cocaine entering Europe arrives at Calabria, but the distribution hub is Milan and the cockpit these three boroughs. The assassins came by night.

They had no illusions about the ferocity of the Calabrese. No one had ever attacked them. When they fought, it was among one another. The so-called second Ndrangheta war between 1985 and 1999 left seven hundred bodies on the streets of Calabria and Milan.

Italy's history is a litany of wars and bloodshed, and behind the cuisine and the culture the old cobbles have run red many times. Italians consider the Black Hand of Naples and the mafia of Sicily fearsome, but no one argues with the Calabrese. Until that night when the Colombians came.

They had seventeen residential addresses. Their orders were to destroy the head of the serpent and leave before the hundreds of foot soldiers could be mobilized.

By morning, the Naviglio Canal was red. Fifteen of the seventeen chiefs were caught at home and died there. Six Colombians took the Ortomercato, site of the King, the young generation's favorite nightclub. Walking calmly past the Ferraris and Lamborghinis parked by the entrance, the Colombians took down the four minders on the door, entered and opened fire in a series of long, raking fusillades that wiped away all those drinking at the bar and four tables of diners.

The Colombians took one casualty. The barman, in a gesture of self-sacrifice, pulled a gun from beneath his bar top and fired back before he died. He fired at a small man who seemed to be directing the fire and put a bullet through his rosebud mouth. Then he himself choked on three slugs from a MAC-10 machine pistol.

Before dawn, the Special Ops group of the carabinieri in Via Lamarmora was on crisis alert, and the citizens of Italy's commercial and fashion capital were wakened to the screams of ambulances and the wailing of police sirens.

It is the law of the jungle and of the underworld that when the king is dead, long live the next king. The Honorable Society was not dead, and in due course the war with the cartel would visit terrible revenge on the Colombians, the guilty and the innocent. But the cartel of Bogotá had one incomparable ace: reduced though cocaine availability may have been to a trickle, that trickle was still in the hands of Don Diego Esteban.

American, Mexican and European strongarms might seek to establish fresh sources in Peru or Bolivia, but west of Venezuela the Don was still the only man to deal with. After resumption, whoever he designated as the one to receive his product would receive it. Every gang in Europe, as in the U.S., wanted to be that someone. And the only way to prove worthiness to be the new monarch was to wipe out the other princes.

The six other giants were the Russians, Serbs, Turks, Albanians, Neapolitans and Sicilians. The Latvians, Lithuanians, Jamaicans and Nigerians were ready and willing and violent but smaller. They would have to wait for an alliance with the new monarch. The native German, French, Dutch and British gangs were clients, not giants.

Even after the Milanese slaughter, the

remaining European cocaine traffickers might have held their fire save that the Internet is completely international and studied worldwide. The unidentified and untraceable source of seemingly infallible information about the cocaine world, which the Cobra had established, published a supposed leak out of Colombia.

It purported to be an inside tip from within the intelligence division of the Policía Judicial. The insider claimed Don Diego Esteban had admitted in a private meeting that his future favor would fall upon the eventual clear winner of any settlement of accounts in the European underworld. It was pure disinformation. He had said no such thing. But it triggered the gang war that swept the continent.

The Slavs, in the form of the three main Russian gangs and the Serbs, formed an alliance. But they are hated by the Balts of Latvia and Lithuania, who allied to be available to help the Russians' enemies.

The Albanians are notionally Muslims and ally with the Obshina (the Chechens) and the Turks. The Jamaican Yardbirds and the Nigerians are both black and can work together. In Italy, the Sicilians and Neapolitans, habitually antagonists, formed a very temporary partnership against the outsiders, and the bloodletting began.

It swept Europe as it was sweeping the U.S. No country in the European Union was exempt, even though the biggest, and thus the richest, markets took the brunt.

The media struggled to explain to their readers, listeners and viewers what was going on. There were gang killings from Dublin to Warsaw. Tourists hurled themselves screaming to the floor in bars and restaurants as submachine carbines executed settlements of accounts across dining tables and office parties.

In London, the nanny of the Home Secretary, taking her toddler charges for a walk on Primrose Hill, found a body in the shrubbery. It had no head. In Hamburg, Frankfurt and Darmstadt, cadavers appeared on the street every night for a week. Fourteen corpses were pulled out of French rivers in a single morning. Two were black, and dental work established the rest were not French but from the East.

Not everyone in the gunfights died. The ambulance and emergency surgeries were overwhelmed. All talk of Afghanistan, Somali pirates, greenhouse gases and bloated bankers was banished from the front pages as the headlines screamed impotent outrage.

Police chiefs were called in, shouted at

and dismissed to go and shout at their subordinates. Politicians from twenty-seven parliaments in Europe and the Congress in Washington and the fifty states of the Union tried to strike an impressive pose but failed as their complete impotence became ever clearer to their constituents.

The political backlash started in the United States but Europe was not far behind. The phone lines of every mayor, representative and senator in the U.S. were jammed with callers, either outraged or fearful. The media sprouted solemn-faced experts twenty times a day, and they all disagreed with one another.

Iron-faced police chiefs were subjected to press conferences that caused them to flee back behind the curtains. Police forces were overwhelmed, and that applied also to ambulance facilities, morgue space and coroners. In three cities, meatpacking halls had to be commandeered to take the cadavers being pulled off streets, out of riddled cars and from freezing rivers.

No one seemed to have realized the power of the underworld to shock, frighten and disgust the peoples of two indulged and risk-averse continents when that underworld went insane with violence fueled by greed.

The aggregate body count rose past the

five hundred mark, and that was on each continent. Gangsters were hardly mourned save by their kith and kin, but harmless civilians were caught in the cross fire. That included children, causing the tabloid newspapers to root through the dictionaries for fresh superlatives of outrage.

It was a quiet-spoken academic and criminologist on television who explained the causal origin of the civil war that seemed to have scarred thirty nations. There is, he said gently, a total dearth of cocaine out there, and it is over the remaining miserable supplies that the wolves of society are fighting.

The alternatives — skunk, crystal meth and heroin — cannot fill the gap. Cocaine had been too easy, too long, the old man said. It has become not a pleasure but a necessity for great swathes of society. It has made too many vast fortunes, and promised many more. A $50 billion-a-year industry on each major Western continent is dying, and we are witnessing the ultra-violent death throes of a monster that has lived among us unrebuked for too long. A thunderstruck newscaster thanked the professor as he left the studio.

After that, the message surging up from the populace to the rulers changed. It became less confused. It said: Sort this out

481

or resign.

Crises may occur in societies at various levels, but there is no level more catastrophic than that politicians may have to forgo their plump employments. At the beginning of March, the phone in an elegant antebellum town house in Alexandria rang.

"Don't hang up," shouted the chief of staff at the White House.

"I wouldn't dream of it, Mr. Silver," said Paul Devereaux.

Each man had retained the habit of using the formal "Mr." address toward the other, almost unheard of in modern Washington. Neither had any talent for bonhomie, so why pretend?

"Would you please get your" — to any other subordinate Jonathan Silver would said "sad ass," but he changed it to — "presence up to the White House at six this evening? I speak on behalf of you know who."

"My pleasure, Mr. Silver," said the Cobra. And hung up. It would not be a pleasure. He knew that. But he also supposed it had always been inevitable.

CHAPTER 16

Jonathan Silver had the reputation of possessing the most abrasive temper in the West Wing. He made it plain as Paul Devereaux entered his office that he did not intend to restrain it.

He held a copy of the *Los Angeles Times* and waved it in the face of the older man.

"Are you responsible for this?"

Devereaux examined the broadsheet with the detachment of an entomologist surveying a mildly interesting larva. The front page was largely occupied by a picture and the banner headline "Hell on Rodeo." The photo was of a restaurant that had been reduced to carnage by streams of bullets from two machine pistols.

Among the seven dead, said the text, were four now identified as major underworld figures, one passerby who had been leaving as the gunmen entered and two waiters.

"Personally, no," said Devereaux.

"Well, there are a lot of people in this town who think otherwise."

"Your point, Mr. Silver?"

"My point, Mr. Devereaux, is that your goddamn Project Cobra seems to have achieved a form of underworld civil war that is turning this country into the kind of charnel house that we have seen in northern Mexico for the past decade. And it has got to stop."

"May we cut to the chase?"

"Please do."

"Almost two years ago, our mutual commander in chief asked me, quite specifically, whether it would be possible to destroy the cocaine industry and trade, both of which were clearly out of control and had become a nationwide scourge. I replied, after intensive study, that it would be possible if certain conditions were fulfilled and at certain cost — hopefully short-term."

"But you never mentioned the streets of three hundred cities running with blood. You asked for two billion dollars and you got that."

"Which was the financial cost only."

"You never mentioned the civil-outrage cost."

"Because you never asked. Look, this country spends fourteen billion dollars a year via a dozen official agencies and gets nowhere. Why? Because the cocaine industry in the U.S. alone, never mind Europe, is worth four times that. Did you really think the creators of cocaine would switch to jelly beans if we asked them? Did you really think the American gangs, among the most vicious in the world, would move into candy bars without a fight?"

"That is no reason for our country being turned into a war zone."

"Yes, it is. Ninety percent of those dying are psychos to the point of being almost clinically insane. The few tragic casualties caught in the cross fire are less than the traffic dead during the Fourth of July weekend."

"But look what the hell you've done. We always kept our psychos and sickos down in the sewers, down in the gutters. You have put them on Main Street. That is where John Q. Citizen lives, and John has a vote. This is an election year. In eight months the man down this hall is going to ask the people to trust him with their country for another four years. And I do not intend, Mr. Goddamn Devereaux, that they will refuse him that request because they dare not leave their homes."

As usual, his voice had risen to a shout. Beyond the door, more-junior ears strained to hear. Inside the room, only one of the two men retained an icy and contemptuous calm.

"They won't," he said. "We are within one month of witnessing the virtual self-destruction of American gangland, or, at any rate, its shattering for a generation. When that becomes clear, I believe the people will recognize what a burden has been lifted from them."

Paul Devereaux was not a politician. Jonathan Silver was. He knew that, in politics, what is real is not important. The important is what appears to be real to the gullible. And what appears to be real is purveyed by the media and purchased by the gullible. He shook his head and jabbed at the front page.

"This cannot go on. No matter what may be the eventual benefits. This has to stop, no matter what the price."

He took a single sheet of paper that had been facedown on his desk and thrust it at the retired spy.

"Do you know what this is?"

"You will doubtless be delighted to tell me."

"It is a Presidential Executive Order. Are you going to disobey it?"

"Unlike you, Mr. Silver, I have served

several commanders in chief and never disobeyed one yet."

The snub caused the chief of staff to turn a mottled red.

"Well, good. That is very good. Because this PEO orders you to stand down. Project Cobra is over. Terminated. Discontinued. Effective this hour. You will return to your headquarters and dismantle it. Is that plain?"

"As rock crystal."

Paul Devereaux, the Cobra, folded the paper and slipped it into his jacket pocket, turned on his heel and left. He ordered his driver to take him to the drab warehouse in Anacostia, where, on the top floor, he showed the PEO to a stunned Cal Dexter.

"But we were so close."

"Not close enough. And you were right. Our great nation can kill up to a million abroad, but not one percent of that figure of its own gangsters without sustaining a fainting fit.

"I have to leave the details, as ever, to you. Call in the two Q-ships. Donate the *Balmoral* to the British Navy and the *Chesapeake* to our own SEALs. Maybe they can use it for training. Call back the two Global Hawks; return them to the USAF. With my thanks. I have no doubt their amazing technology is the way of the future. But not ours. We are paid off. Can I leave all this in your hands? Even down to the cast-off clothes on the lower floors that can now go to the homeless?"

"And you? Can I reach you at home?"

The Cobra thought for a while.

"For a week, maybe. Then I may have to travel. Just loose ends. Nothing important."

It was a personal conceit of Don Diego Esteban's that, although he had a private chapel on this estate in the ranch country of the Cordillera, he enjoyed receiving communion at the church in the nearest small town.

It enabled him to acknowledge with grave courtesy the deferential salutations of the peons and their shawl-shrouded wives. It enabled him to beam at the awestruck, barefoot children. It allowed him to drop a donation into the collection plate that would keep the parish priest for months.

When he agreed to talk with the man from America who wished to see him, he chose the church but arrived massively protected. It was the suggestion of the American that they meet in the house of the God whom they both worshipped and under the Catholic Rite to which they both subscribed. It was the strangest request he had ever received, but its simple ingenuity intrigued him.

The Colombian hidalgo was there first. The building had been swept by his security team, and the priest sent packing. Diego Esteban dipped two fingers in the font, crossed himself and approached the altar. He chose the front row of pews, knelt, bowed his head and prayed.

When he straightened, he heard the old sun-bleached door behind him creak, felt a gust of hot air from outside, then noted the thud of the closing. He knew he had men in the shadows, guns drawn. It was a sacrilege, but he could confess and be forgiven. A dead man cannot confess.

The visitor approached from behind and took a place also in the front pew, six feet away. He also crossed himself. The Don glanced sideways. An American, lean, of similar age, calm-faced, ascetic in an impeccable cream suit.

"Señor?"

"Don Diego Esteban?"

"It is I."

"Paul Devereaux, of Washington. Thank you for receiving me."

"I have heard rumors. Vague talk, nothing more. But insistent. Rumors of a man they call the 'Cobra.' "

"A foolish nickname. But I must own to it."

"Your Spanish is excellent. Permit me a question."

"Of course."

"Why should I not have you killed? I have a hundred men outside."

"Ah, and I only my helicopter pilot. But I believe I have something that was once yours and which I may be able to return. If we can reach a concordat. Which I cannot do if I am dead."

"I know what you have done to me, Señor Cobra. You have done me extreme damage. But I have done nothing to harm you. Why did you do what you did?"

"Because my country asked me."

"And now?"

"All my life, I have served two masters. My God and my country. My God has never betrayed me."

"But your country has?"

"Yes."

"Why?"

"Because it is no longer the country to which I swore loyalty as a young man. It has become corrupt and venal, weak and yet arrogant, dedicated to the obese and the stupid. It is not my country anymore. The bond is broken, the fealty gone."

"I never gave such loyalty to any country, even this one. Because countries are governed by men, and often the least deserving of them. I also have two masters. My God and my wealth."

"And for the second, Don Diego, you have killed many times."

Devereaux had no doubt that the man a few feet away from him, beneath the veneer and the grace, was a psychopath and supremely dangerous.

"And you, Señor Cobra, you have killed for your country? Many times?"

"Of course. So perhaps we are similar after all."

Psychopaths must be flattered. Devereaux knew the comparison would flatter the cocaine lord. Comparing greed for money with patriotism would not offend.

"Perhaps we are, señor. How much of my property do you retain?"

"One hundred fifty tons."

"The amount missing is three times that."

"Most is taken by either customs, coast guards or navies and now incinerated. Some is at the bottom of the sea. The last quarter is with me."

"In safekeeping?"

"Very safe. And the war against you is over."

"Ah. That was the betrayal."

"You are very perceptive, Don Diego."

The Don considered the tonnage. With jungle production at full flow, maritime interceptions cut back to a trickle, air shipments able to resume, he could start again. He would need an immediate tonnage to bridge the gap, to appease the wolves, to end the war. One hundred and fifty tons would be just enough.

"And your price, señor?"

"I shall have to retire at last. But far away. A villa by the sea. In the sun. With my books. And officially dead. That does not come cheaply. One billion U.S. dollars, if you please."

"My property is in a ship?"

"Yes."

"And you can give me the numbers of the bank accounts?"

"Yes. Can you give me the port of destination?"

"Of course."

"And your response, Don Diego?"

"I think, señor, we have our concordat. You will leave here safely. Exchange the details with my secretary outside. And now I wish to pray alone. *¡Vaya con Dios, señor!*"

Paul Devereaux rose, crossed himself and left the church. An hour later, he was back at the Malambo air base, where his Grumman returned him to Washington. In a walled compound a hundred yards from where the executive jet turned onto the runway for takeoff, the operating crew of the Global Hawk code-named Michelle had been told they would be stood down in a week and be returned in a pair of C-5 heavy-lift freighters to Nevada.

Cal Dexter did not know where his chief had gone nor did he ask. He got on with the assigned job, dismantling the Cobra structure stone by stone.

The two Q-ships began to steam for home, the British-manned *Balmoral* to Lyme Bay, Dorset, the *Chesapeake* for Newport News. The British expressed their gratitude for the gift of the *Balmoral,* which they thought might be useful against Somali pirates.

The two UAV-operating bases recalled their Global Hawks for transfer back to the States but kept the enormous amount of data they had acquired on Broad Area Marine Surveillance, which would certainly play a role in the future, replacing far more expensive and manpower-intensive spy planes.

The prisoners, all 117 of them, were

brought back from Eagle Island, Chagos Archipelago, in a long-range C-130 of the USAF. Each was allowed to send a brief message to his ecstatic family who thought he was lost at sea.

The bank accounts, almost exhausted, were reduced to a single one to cover any last-minute payments, and the communications network run out of the Anacostia warehouse was scaled down and brought in-house to be operated along with his computers by Jeremy Bishop. Then Paul Devereaux reappeared. He expressed himself well satisfied, and drew Cal Dexter to one side.

"Have you ever heard of Spindrift Cay?" he asked. "Well, it is a tiny island, barely more than a coral atoll, in the Bahamas. One of the so-called out islands. Uninhabited except for a small detachment of U.S. Marines ostensibly camping there on some form of survival exercise.

"The center of the cay has a small forest of palm trees under which there are rows and rows of bales. You can guess what they contain. It has to be destroyed, all one hundred fifty tons of it. I am entrusting the job to you. Have you any idea of the value of those bales?"

"I think I can guess. Several billion dollars."

"You're right. I need someone I can trust absolutely to do it. The cans of gasoline have been on-site for many weeks. Your best way in is by floatplane out of Nassau. Please go and do what has to be done."

Cal Dexter had seen many things but never a billion-dollar hill, let alone destroyed it. Even one single bale, stashed in a large suitcase, meant rich for life. He flew commercial, Washington to Nassau, and checked into the Paradise Island Hotel. An inquiry at reception and a quick phone call secured him a floatplane for the dawn of the next day.

It was over a hundred miles, and the flight took an hour. In March the weather was warm, and the sea its usual impossible aquamarine between the islands, limpid pale over the sandbars. The destination was so remote, his pilot had to check the GPS system twice to confirm he had the right atoll.

An hour after dawn, he banked and pointed.

"That's it, mister," he shouted. Dexter looked down. It ought to have been in a tourist postcard rather than what it was. Less than one square kilometer inside, with a reef that enclosed a lagoon accessed by a single cut in the coral. A dark clump of palms at the center gave no hint of the deadly treasure stored beneath the fronds.

Jutting out of one shining white beach was a ramshackle jetty where presumably the supply boat docked. As he watched, two figures emerged from a camouflage-tented camp beneath the palms along the shore and stared upward. The floatplane wheeled, lost power and drifted down to the water.

"Drop me off at the jetty," said Dexter.

"Not even going to get your feet wet?" grinned the pilot.

"Maybe later."

Dexter got out, stepped onto the float and thence to the jetty. He ducked under the wing and found himself facing a ramrod-straight master sergeant. The guardian of the island had a Marine behind him, and both men wore sidearms.

"Your business here, sir?"

The courtesy was impeccable, the meaning unmistakable. You had better have a good reason for being here or go not one foot farther down this dock. For reply, Dexter took a folded letter from his jacket's inside pocket.

"Please read this very carefully, Master Sergeant, and note the signature."

The veteran Marine stiffened as he read, and only years of self-discipline kept him from expressing his amazement. He had seen the portrait of his commander in chief many times, but never thought to see the handwritten signature of the President of the United States. Dexter held out his hand for the letter.

"So, Master Sergeant, we both serve the same c in c. My name is Dexter, I am from the Pentagon. No matter. That letter trumps me, you, even the Secretary of Defense. And it requires your cooperation. Do I have it, mister?"

The Marine was at attention, staring over Dexter's head at the horizon.

"Yes, sir," he barked.

The pilot had been chartered for the day. He found a shady place under the wing over the jetty and settled down to wait. Dexter and the Marine walked back down the jetty to the beach. There were twelve tough, sun-darkened young men who for weeks had fished, swum, listened to radios, read paperbacks and kept themselves in shape with ferocious daily exercise.

Dexter noted the jerrycans of gasoline stored in the shade and headed toward the trees. The clump covered no more than two acres, and there was a walkway cut through the center. On either side were the bales, shaded by palms. They were stacked in low, cube-shaped blocks, about one hundred of them, about one and half tons each, the yield of nine months at sea by two covert raiders.

"Do you know what these are?" asked Dexter.

"No, sir," said the master sergeant. Don't ask, don't tell; though in a slightly different context.

"Documents. Old records. But ultra-sensitive. That is why the President does not want them ever to fall into the hands of our country's enemies. The Oval Office has decided they have to be destroyed. Hence, the gasoline. Please ask the men to haul up the cans and soak every pile."

The mention of his country's enemies was more than enough for the master sergeant. He shouted, "Yes, sir," and strode back to the beach.

Dexter strolled slowly up the alley between the palms. He had seen a few bales since the previous March but never anything like this. Behind him the Marines had appeared, each toting a large can, and began dousing each pile of bales. Dexter had never seen cocaine burn, but he was told it was quite flammable if given a starter blaze with accelerant.

He had for many years carried a small Swiss Army–type penknife on his key chain, and as he was traveling on an official government passport it had not been confiscated at Dulles International. Out of curiosity, he opened the short blade and jabbed it into the nearest bale. Might as well, he thought. He had never tasted it before and probably never would again.

The short blade went through the buckram wrapping, through the tough polyethylene and into the powder. It came out with a knob of white dust on the end. He had his back to the Marines down the alley. They could not see what the "documents" contained.

He sucked the white blob off the point of his knife. Ran it around his mouth until the powder, dissolving in saliva, reached the taste buds. He was surprised. He knew the taste after all.

He approached another bale and did the same. But a bigger cut and a bigger sample. And another, and another. As a young man out of the Army, back from Vietnam, studying law at Fordham, New York, he had paid for his tuition with a series of menial jobs. One was in a pastry shop. He knew baking soda very well.

He made ten other incisions in different bales before they were doused and the powerful stench of gasoline took over. Then he walked thoughtfully back to the beach. He drew up an empty canister, sat on it and stared out to sea. Thirty minutes later, the master sergeant was at his side, towering over him.

"Job done, sir."

"Torch it," said Dexter.

He heard the barked orders of "Stand clear" and the dull *whump* as the vaporizing fuel took flame and smoke rose from the palm grove. January is the time of winds in the Bahamas, and a stiff breeze turned the first flames into a blowtorch.

He turned to see the palms and their hidden contents consumed by flames. On the dock the floatplane pilot was on his feet, watching openmouthed. The dozen Marines were also staring at their handiwork.

"Tell me, Master Sergeant . . ."

"Sir?"

"How did the bales of documents reach you here?"

"By boat, sir."

"All in one cargo, one at a time?"

"No, sir. At least a dozen visits. Over the weeks we've been here."

"Same vessel each time?"

"Yes, sir. Same one."

Of course. There had to be another vessel. The fleet auxiliaries that had replenished the SEALs and the British SBS at sea had removed trash and prisoners. They had delivered food and fuel. But the confiscated cargoes did not go back to Gibraltar or Virginia. The Cobra needed the labels, batch numbers and identification codes to fool the cartel. So these trophies he had kept. Apparently here.

"What kind of ship?"

"A small one, sir. Tramp steamer."

"Nationality?"

"Don't know, sir. She had a flag at the stern. Like two commas. One red, one blue. And her crew were Asian."

"Name?"

The master sergeant's brow furrowed as he tried to recall. Then he turned.

"Angelo!"

He had to shout over the noise of the flames. One of the Marines turned and trotted over.

"What was the name of the tramp steamer that brought the bales here?"

"*Sea Spirit,* sir. Saw it on her stern. New white paint."

"And under her name?"

"Under it, sir?"

"The port of registration is usually under the name at the stern."

"Oh, yes. Poo-something."

"Pusan?"

"That was it, yes, sir. Pusan. That all, sir?"

Dexter nodded. Marine Angelo trotted off. Dexter rose and went down to the end of the jetty where he could be alone and maybe pick up reception on his cell phone. He was glad it had been on charge all night. To his gratitude and relief, the ever-faithful Jeremy Bishop was at his bank of computers, almost the last facility Project Cobra had left.

"Can that motorized sardine can of yours translate into Korean?" asked Dexter. The reply was a clear as a bell.

"Any language in the world, if I put in the right program. Where are you?"

"Never mind. The only communication I have is this cell. What is the Korean for *Sea Spirit* or *Spirit of the Sea?* And don't waste my battery."

"I'll call you back."

It was two minutes later that the phone rang.

"Got a pen and paper?"

"Never mind. Just say it."

"Okay. The words are *Hae Shin.* That's aitch-aay . . ."

"I know how it is spelled. Can you look up a tramp steamer? Small. Named either *Hae Shin* or *Sea Spirit.* South Korean, registered Port of Pusan."

"Back in two minutes." The phone went dead. He was as good as his word. Two minutes later, Bishop was back.

"Got her. Five thousand tons, general-cargo freighter. Name: *Sea Spirit.* Name registered this year. What about her?"

"Where is she right now?"

"Hold on."

High over Anacostia district, Jeremy Bishop tapped furiously. Then he spoke.

"She does not seem to have a managing agent and she does not file. Anything. She could be anywhere. Hold on. The captain has an e-mail listing."

"Raise him and ask him where he is. Map reference. Course and speed."

More delays. The cell was running down.

"I raised him by e-mail. Put the questions. He declines to say. Asks who you are."

"Say, this is the Cobra."

Pause.

"He is very polite, but insists he needs what he called 'authority word.'"

"He means 'password.' Tell him 'HAE-SHIN.'"

Bishop came back, impressed.

"How did you know that? I have what you wanted. Care to note it?"

"I have no goddamn maps here. Just tell me where the hell he is."

"Keep your hair on. One hundred miles east of Barbados, steaming 270 degrees, ten knots. Shall I thank the captain of the *Sea Spirit?*"

"Yes. Then ask if we have a Navy warship between Barbados and Colombia."

"I'll call you back."

East of Barbados, steaming due west. Through the Windward chain, past the Dutch Antilles and straight into Colombian waters. So far south, there was no way the Korean trafficker was coming back to the Bahamas. She had taken her last cargo off the *Balmoral* where she had been told. Three hundred miles; thirty hours. Tomorrow afternoon. Jeremy Bishop came back.

"Nope. There is nothing in the Caribbean."

"Is that Brazilian major still in the Cape Verde Islands?"

"As it happens, yes. His pupils are due for graduation in two days, so it was agreed that he could see that through, then retire and bring the airplane with him. But the two American comms people have been withdrawn. They're back stateside."

"Can you raise him for me? Any which way?"

"I can e-mail him or text on his cell."

"Then do both. I want his phone number, and I want him to be on it to take my call in two hours exactly. I have to go. I'll call you from my hotel room in a hundred minutes. Just have the number I need. *Ciao*."

He walked back to the floatplane. On the island the flames were flickering and dying. Most of the palms were scorched stumps. Ecologically, it was a crime. He waved a salutation to the Marines onshore and climbed into his seat.

"Nassau Harbor, please. As fast as we can."

He was seated in his hotel room within ninety minutes and called Bishop ten after that.

"I have it," said the cheerful voice from Washington, and dictated a number. Without waiting for the time rendezvous, Dexter called. A voice answered at once.

"Major João Mendoza?"

"Yes."

"We met at Scampton, and I have been the one controlling your missions these past several months. First, I want to offer my sincere thanks and congratulations. Second,

505

may I ask a question?"

"Yes."

"Do you remember what the bastards did to your kid brother?"

There was a long pause. If he took offense, he could just hang up. The deep voice came back.

"I remember very well. Why?"

"Do you know how many grams it took to kill your brother?"

"Just a few. Maybe ten. Again, why?"

"There is a target out there which I cannot reach. But you can. It is carrying one hundred fifty tons of pure. Enough to kill your brother one hundred million times. It is a ship. Will you sink it for me?"

"Place and range from Fogo?"

"We have no overhead drone left. No Americans on your base. No guiding voice from Nevada. You would have to navigate yourself."

"When I flew for Brazil, we had single-seat fighters. That was what we did. Give me the location of the target."

Midday in Nassau. Midday in Barbados. Flying west with the sun. Takeoff, and 2,100 miles, four hours. Close to the speed of sound. Still daylight at 4 p.m. Six hours at ten knots for the *Hae Shin*.

"Forty nautical miles east of Barbados."

"I will not be able to get back."

"Land locally. Bridgetown, Barbados. St. Lucia. Trinidad. I will fix the formalities."

"Give me the exact map reference. Degree minute, second, north of the equator, west of Greenwich."

Dexter gave him the name of the ship, description, flag she would be flying and the map reference, adjusted for six hours' cruising due west.

"Can you do it?" insisted Dexter. "No navigator, no radio guidance, no direction finder. Maximum range. Can you do it?"

For the first time, he seemed to have affronted the Brazilian.

"Senhor, I have my plane, I have my GPS, I have my eyes, I have the sun. I am a flier. It is what I do."

And the phone went down.

CHAPTER 17

It took half an hour from the moment Major João Mendoza clicked off his cell phone until he felt the surge of power from the last two RATO rockets in the stores, and the old Buccaneer hurled herself into the sky for her last mission.

Mendoza had no intention of skimping his preparations so that his target could cover a few less miles of sea. He had watched as his British ground crew tanked the Bucc to her full 23,000 pounds of fuel, giving him around 2,200 nautical miles airborne.

The cannon had been loaded with one hundred percent armor-piercing shells. There would be no need of a tracer in the daylight or incendiary to start a fire. The target was steel.

The major worked on his maps, plotting height and speed, track and time to target the old-fashioned way, with map and Dalton computer. The map, folded into oblong sheets, he would strap to his right thigh.

By chance, Fogo Island lies almost exactly on the 15th parallel of latitude, and so does Barbados. The course would be due west, then down the degree heading 270. He had an exact map reference for the position of his target when it was given to the American two hours earlier. In four hours' time, his GPS display would give his own position with the same exactitude. What he had to do was adjust that to account for six hours' cruising by the target, descend to low level and go hunting with his last few pounds of fuel. And then make Bridgetown, Barbados, on little more than vapor. Easy.

He packed his few valuables, with a passport and some dollars, into a small tote bag and stuffed it between his feet. He bade farewell to the ground team, embracing each embarrassed Englishman in turn.

When the "assist" rockets cut in, he felt the usual mule-kick surge, held the control steady until the blue, foam-fringed waves were almost under him, then eased back and flew.

Within minutes he was on the 15th parallel, nose due west, climbing to operational 35,000 feet and setting power to maximum range with lowest consumption. Once at altitude, he set his speed at .8 Mach and watched the GPA ticking away the disappearing miles.

There are no landmarks between Fogo and Barbados. The Brazilian ace looked down at fluffy white altocumulus far below, and between the puffs of cloud, the deep blue of the Atlantic.

After three hours, he calculated he was slightly behind where he had hoped to be and realized he had a stronger-than-foreseen headwind. When his GPS told him he was two hundred miles behind the target and gave its presumed position, he eased off some of the power and began to drop toward the ocean. He wanted to be at 500 feet ten miles behind the *Hae Shin.*

At 1,000 feet, he leveled, and dropped his speed and power setting to maximum endurance. Speed was no longer the option; he needed time to search because the sea was empty, and, because of the headwind, he had used more fuel than he had hoped. Then he saw a small tramp steamer. She was off to his port, sixty sea miles short of Barbados. He dropped his wing, lowered the nose and began a sweep past her stern to see her name and flag.

At 100 feet, running at three hundred knots, he saw the flag first. He did not recognize it. Had he known, it was the convenience flag of Bonaire in the Dutch Antilles. There were faces staring up at the black apparition howling past the stern. He noted a deck cargo of timber, then the name. *Prins Willem.* She was a Dutchman with deal planks for Curaçao. He pulled back up to 1,000 feet and checked fuel. Not good.

His position, revealed by his Garmin GPS system, almost exactly blended onto the map reference of the *Hae Shin* as she had been six hours earlier. Other than the Dutchman off to one side, he could see no tramp steamer. She could have diverted from track. He could not raise the American sitting chewing his nails in Nassau to ask. He gambled the cocaine carrier was still ahead of him and powered along compass heading 270°. And he was right.

Unlike the jet at 35,000 feet with a headwind, the *Hae Shin* had had a following sea and was making twelve knots, not ten. He found her thirty miles short of the Caribbean holiday resort. A sweep past her stern showed him the two teardrops, red and blue, of the South Korean flag, and her new name, *Sea Spirit.* Again, small figures ran onto the hatch covers to stare up.

Major Mendoza had no desire to kill the

crew. He elected to rip apart her prow and her stern. Pulling away, he took the Buccaneer up and out in a wide circle to approach the target from the side. He flicked his cannon from Safe to Fire, turned and dropped the nose into the bombing run. He had no bombs, but his cannon would have to do.

Back in the late 1950s, the Royal Navy had wanted a new, jet-powered low-level naval bomber to take on the menace of the USSR's Sverdlov-class cruisers. The job went out to tender, depending on acceptance of the submitted design. The Blackburn Aircraft Company offered the Buccaneer, and a limited order was placed. She first flew in 1962, almost as a stopgap warplane. She was still combat flying against Saddam Hussein in 1991, but over land for the Royal Air Force.

At the time of her birth, the Blackburn Company was on short commons, reduced to making metal bread bins. With hindsight, the Bucc was a product of near genius. She was never pretty; but she was tough and adaptable. And reliable, with two Rolls-Royce Spey engines that never failed.

For months, Major Mendoza had used her as a midair interceptor, knocking seventeen cocaine carriers out of the sky and sending twenty tons of the white powder to the ocean floor. But when Mendoza turned onto his low, sea-skimming attack run, the veteran Bucc reverted to what she had always been. She was a ship killer.

At eight hundred yards, he jammed his thumb on the Fire button and watched a raking line of 30mm AP cannon shells stream toward the bow of the *Hae Shin.* Before he lifted his thumb, hauled back and howled over the tramp steamer, he had seen the shells tear out her bow.

The tramp stopped dead in the water as she ran into a wall of ocean thundering into her forward holds. Then small figures were running for the lifeboat, ripping off the canvas cover. The Buccaneer rose and turned in another long arc as the pilot gazed out through the top of his canopy at the victim below.

The second strike was from the stern. Major Mendoza hoped the engineer had got out of the engine room; it was right in his sights. The second stream of cannon shells tore open the stern, taking rudder, propellers, two prop shafts and the engine and turning them into scrap.

The figures on deck had the lifeboat in the sea and were tumbling into it. Circling at 3,000 feet, the flier could see the *Hae*

Shin was sinking by both stem and stern. Certain that she was gone and that the *Prins Willem* would pick up the crew, Major Mendoza turned for Barbados. Then the first of his Speys, having flown on vapor for the second run, flamed out.

A glance at the fuel gauges revealed the second engine was also running on vapor. He used his last few pounds of gas to climb, and when the second Spey died he had clawed the Bucc up to 8,000 feet. The silence, as always after a flameout, was eerie. He could see the island ahead of him, but out of reach. No glide was ever going to be stretched that far.

Below his nose was a small white feather on the water, the V wake of a tiny fisherman. He dived toward it, converting height to speed, raced across the staring faces at 1,000 feet, then hauled back, converting speed to height, pulled the ejector seat handle and blew out straight through the canopy.

Messrs. Martin and Baker knew their stuff. The seat took him up and away from the dying bomber. A pressure-operated trigger tumbled him out of the steel seat, which fell harmlessly to the water, and left him dangling in the warm sunshine under his parachute. Minutes later he was being hauled, coughing and spluttering, onto the aft deck of a Bertram Moppie.

Two miles away, a geyser of white foam erupted from the sea as the Buccaneer plunged nose first into the Atlantic. The pilot lay between three dead wahoos and a sailfish, as the two American charter fishermen leaned over him.

"You okay, buddy?" asked one.

"Yes, thank you. Fine. I need to call a man in the Bahamas."

"No problem," said the elderly sportsman, as if naval bomber pilots were always dropping out of the sky on him. "Use my cell."

Major Mendoza was arrested in Bridgetown. An official from the American Embassy secured his release by sundown and brought a change of clothes. The Barbadian authorities accepted a tale to the effect that a training flight from a U.S. carrier far out at sea had suffered a catastrophic engine failure, and the flier, although a Brazilian, was on secondment to the U.S. Navy. The diplomat, himself puzzled by his order, knew it was nonsense, but they are trained to lie convincingly. Barbados was content to let the Brazilian fly home the next day.

EPILOGUE

The modest compact trundled into the small town of Pennington, New Jersey, and its driver stared around at the landmarks of his home, which he had not seen for so long.

South of the junction marking the center of town, he passed the Civil War–vintage white clapboard house with the shingle of "Mr. Calvin Dexter, Attorney-at-Law." It looked neglected, but he knew he would enjoy fixing it back up and seeing if he still had a practice left.

At the junction of Main Street and West Delaware Avenue, the heart of Pennington, he toyed between a strong black coffee at the Cup of Joe café, or something more at Vito's Pizza. Then he noticed the new food mart and recalled he would need provisions for his home on Chesapeake Drive. He parked the car, bought from a lot close to where he had landed at Newark Airport, and entered the mart.

He filled a whole shopping cart and ended up at the checkout. There was a lad there, probably a student working his way through college as he had once done.

"Anything else, sir?"

"That reminds me," said Dexter. "I could do with some sodas."

"Right across there in the cold case. We have a special offer on Coke."

Dexter thought it over.

"Maybe some other time."

It was the parish priest at St. Mary's on South Royal Street who raised the alarm. He was sure his parishioner was in Alexandria because he had seen the man's housekeeper Maisie with a cartful of shopping. Yet he had missed two Masses, which he never did. So after morning service the priest walked the few hundred yards to the elegant old house at the junction of South Lee and South Fairfax streets.

To his surprise, the gate to the walled garden, although seemingly closed as ever, opened with a light push. That was odd. Mr. Devereaux always answered on the intercom and pressed a buzzer inside to release the catch.

The priest walked up the pink brick path to find the front door also open. He went pale and crossed himself when he saw poor Maisie, who had never harmed anyone, sprawled on the hallway tiles, a neat bullet hole drilled through her heart.

He was about to use his cell phone to call 911 for help when he saw the study door was also open. He approached in fear and trembling to peer around the jamb.

Paul Devereaux sat at his desk, still in his wing chair, which supported his torso and head. The head was tilted back, sightless eyes gazing with mild surprise at the ceiling. The medical examiner would later establish he had taken two close-bracketed shots to the chest and one to the forehead, the professional assassin's pattern.

No one in Alexandria, Virginia, understood why. However, when he learned of it from the TV evening news at his home in New Jersey, Cal Dexter understood. There was nothing personal about it. But you just cannot treat the Don that way.

ABOUT THE AUTHOR

Frederick Forsyth is the author of fifteen novels and short story collections, from 1971's *The Day of the Jackal* to 2006's *The Afghan*. A former pilot and print and television reporter, he has had five movies made from his works, and a television miniseries.